THE BAALBECK
DECISION

THE BAALBECK DECISION

DAVID CULLEN

Culpro Books

The Baalbeck Decision
First published 2010

A catalogue record of this book is available from the British
Library

Cover design by Pauline Diegnan

ISBN: 978-0-9559911-4-1

www.lulu.com/davidcullen

Published Culpro Books
an imprint of Cullen Productions

There is probable cause to believe that the decision to assassinate former Prime Minister Rafik Hariri could not have been taken without the approval of top-ranked Syrian security officials and could not have been further organized without the collusion of their counterparts in the Lebanese security services.
- paragraph 124 of the Report of the International Independent Investigation Commission established pursuant to UN Security Council Resolution 1595 (2005)[the Mehlis Report]

Or could it...?

Clean feet leave no footprints
- Syrian proverb

For Joe Ibrahim
- both of them

Cast in order of appearance

Rafic Hariri [Abu Bahaa] – *Prime Minister of Lebanon 1992-98, 2000-2004.*

Basil Fleihan – *former Economy Minister of Lebanon.*

The Djinn – *a myth or reality?*

Marwan Mebarak – *a Captain of the Lebanese Army.*

A Corporal – *Lebanese Army.*

A Sergeant – *Lebanese Army.*

Colonel F – *Lebanese Army.*

Ghazi Kanaan [Abu Yo'roub] – *head of Syrian security in Lebanon 1982-2002, Syrian Interior Minister 2004-2005.*

An interrogator – *now dead.*

The Owner – *of many things, but not of what he wants.*

Al-Rajul [The Commander] – *a mercenary, an assassin.*

Samir Kassir - *professor, political commentator and journalist.*

George Hawi [Abu Anis] – *politician, former Secretary-General of the Lebanese Communist Party.*

Gebran Tueni – *newspaper editor and publisher, TV producer and host.*

Walid Eido [Abu Khaled] – *politician, former public prosecutor for North Lebanon.*

A member of the Syrian *mukhabarat.*

The Damascene – *a mercenary, an assassin.*

Maroun Khoury – *a Captain of the Lebanese Department of General Security.*

Yehya al-Arab [Abu Tarek] – *Head of Rafic Hariri's personal security.*

Jihad Merhi [Abu Samer] – *a Captain of the Lebanese Internal Security Force.*

Gisele Merhi – *wife of Jihad, formerly an agent of the Lebanese Department of General Security.*

Mama – *mother of Gisele.*

Deeb el-Gharib – *a Sergeant of the Lebanese Internal Security Force.*

Fadi Lattouf – *a Captain of the Civil Police of the Palestinian Security Force.*

A homosexual – *just doing business but went too far.*

Zahia Zalloum – *a Gatherer.*

Mohammed – *an earnest youth. Too earnest.*

Chadi – *friend of earnest Mohammed.*

Aboud – *an emissary, also* mukhabarat.

Karim The Butcher

Salin Namroud – *a young Palestinian.*

Kabalan Elb – *a young Palestinian.*

Elias Massoud – *a young Palestinian.*

Ahmad Adass – *a young Palestinian.*

Yazbek Nader – *a young Palestinian.*

Ibrahim - *a Lieutenant of the Civil Police of the Palestinian Security Force.*

Nada – *wife of Fadi Lattouf.*

Bassem el-Khazem - *a Sergeant of the Civil Police of the Palestinian Security Force.*

Selim Himo – *a Lieutenant of the Lebanese* Gendarmerie, *Bekaa Inquiry Brigade.*

A greasy man – *in charge of a warehouse in Beirut port.*

Major Ghanem – *Lebanese Internal Security Force.*

Mohamed Hassan – *an old refugee living in Bourj el-Barajneh.*

The young brother of Elias Massoud

FOREWORD
مقدمة واحدة

This book is a thriller, an adventure. It is not a book about 'the situation' in the Middle East, although politics play an integral part in the story. Where necessary I have included political narrative in order to assist in understanding the events.

There are many books written about the Middle East. To those wishing to understand more about the complexities of the situation in Lebanon in the late twentieth century, I can recommend Robert Fisk's *Pity The Nation* (Oxford University Press 1990/2001). For detailed insight, comment and facts on the events which form the backbone of *The Baalbeck Decision*, I recommend *Rafiq Hariri and the Fate of Lebanon* by Marwan Iskandar (Saqi Books 2006) and *Killing Mr Lebanon* by Nicholas Blanford (I.B. Tauris 2006).

Who killed Rafic Hariri? The answer to that question is unlikely ever to be known, scapegoats, tethered lambs and the suicided notwithstanding.

The Baalbeck Decision might be the answer.

Al-Haqiqa? Maybe. Murder is never what it seems.

Ma'ak,

David Cullen
ديفيد كولين

PROLOGUE
مقدمة اثنين

14 February 2005
5 Muharram 1426

Beirut, Lebanon

His socks were on fire.

Those who were first on the scene – those that were not killed or maimed, blinded or deafened in the one thousand kilogram TNT blast – said that the body of the large man lying in the road was unrecognisable. This was not true. They were simply in a state of disbelief – their minds unable to comprehend what their eyes surely saw.

Most of his blue suit had been blasted off, yet his undergarments were scorched but intact – death granting an important dignity to this Sunni Muslim. His hair – which had recently changed from his sixty year old 'salt and pepper' to pure silver, almost overnight – was gone, as were his eyebrows and moustache. His face was burnt yellow, his eyes swollen to slits.

He was lying on his back, but his arms were bent at the elbows and poking up into the air, his hands claw-like as if they were still gripping the steering wheel of his Mercedes S-600, which was ten metres back down Minet el-Hosn Street on the edge of the three metres deep crater outside the St George Hotel.

His left arm was on fire, yet the flames seemed gentle, almost reverential.

Someone started hitting the flames with an *abaya*, a cloak. With each whack, the body bounced, the last movements it would ever make. But at least the flames went out.

The area was black with smoke. Gunfire cracked rapidly, as if a manic battle was being waged. But there was no one to fire the guns. Most of those that would were dead. The gunfire was the seven hundred and fifty rounds of ammunition of the large man's bodyguards exploding in the flames.

Bodies were lying in the road. Parts of bodies were strewn over a wide area. Some pieces of human flesh were indeterminate, others – like the delicate woman's hand with carefully painted and manicured fingernails, rings still attached, one of the fingers still twitching, resting against the kerb – were obvious.

A boy, no more than a teenager, staggered out of the smoke, arms in front of him, two gaping holes where his eyes had been only seconds before.

Skeletons sat in the front of some of the cars of the shattered six vehicle convoy, their skin already burnt off by the intensity of the flames.

Other skeletons staggered out of the wrecked vehicles, hoping against hope that they could live. One, his clothes shredded to ribbons, called "Yasma, Yasma!", but his wife was in Geneva where he had left her the day before[*].

There was blood, so much blood. Some of it cooking in the flames, smelling no different from the odours coming from the nearby *Spagheterria* restaurant.

And the large man's socks were on fire.

Across in Nejmeh Square, just a kilometre away, outside the Parliament building, The Djinn began to cry.

---

[*]*Basil Fleihan was to survive for sixty-four days before dying of 95% burns in the Percy Military Hospital, Clamart, Paris.*

5 years earlier...

3 January 2000
26 Ramadan 1420

Dinnieh, Lebanon

It was a bright, sunny day, the sky an impressive blue for the time of year. But it was cold, so, so cold. The sun was fighting a losing battle against the snow on the ground up here in the mountains of northern Lebanon, and the forecast was for an overnight downfall of reinforcements for the crud.

Captain Marwan Mebarak sniffed at his own military analogy as he led his team of four back down the mountainside. He wished he could be pleased. No casualties and they had left five dead insurgents back in the caves. The clean-up team would remove the bodies for identification later, but it was unlikely their families would come forward to claim them for fear of retaliation.

It had started five days ago. The reports were that four members of the Syrian intelligence *mukhabarat* travelling in a car had been ambushed and killed by armed Sunni Islamists across the border up near Homs (Emesa). The Syrian security forces had begun a massive manhunt, leading – if the reports were to be believed – to a series of battles that had intensified as the days went on. In the end, eight hundred people had been arrested. It was, claimed *Al-Quds al-Arabi* (the Syrian branch of the Muslim brotherhood), a huge over-reaction to what had been a simple local skirmish. It was even suggested that the original ambush had been staged by Syria to exaggerate the Sunni Islamist threat and show the United States that Syria was the only guarantor of stability in the region (in other words, to convince the US of the need for the permanent presence of Syrian forces in Lebanon, even if the Israeli army withdrew from the south).

Almost immediately, orders had been received at the Bahjat Ghanem North Region Army Command base in Tripoli. A group of up to three hundred Sunni militants known as *Takfir wal-Hijra* (Excommunication and Exodus), originally a splinter group of the Muslim Brotherhood, had established themselves in the Dinnieh mountains. They were to be routed.

Thirteen thousand Lebanese army troops, with tanks and artillery, had saturated the area. Official figures would later claim that eleven soldiers and twenty-five rebels were killed in the fighting, with fifty-five rebels captured. The true figures, Captain Mebarak knew, were much more on both sides.

Mebarak turned to his men. They were walking down the mountainside behind him in approved anti-sniper wraggle-taggle formation, no straight lines, at least ten metres between each man, their tigerstripe commando camouflage uniform effective even in the snow. He nodded his approval.

"Is that it, *Naqeeb*?" asked the nearest man, an *'Areef Awwal* (Corporal First Class), slightly out of breath but not breaking stride. "Is that the end of them? Is it over?"

"I certainly hope so," replied Mebarak. Under his breath he said, "*Insha'Allah.*"

"I'm sorry, Captain? Did you say something?" The Corporal came level with him.

"No. *Maalesh.* It should be all over now. Time for a rest."

Only when he reached the temporary area command at the town of Aassoun thirty minutes later did he find out that he was wrong.

"*Naqeeb!* Captain!" A *Raqeeb* (Sergeant) stuck his head out of the communications truck as Mebarak approached.

"What?" Mebarak's boots crunched in the snow.

"The Colonel, sir. He has been trying to reach you!"

"Radio reception is never good up there, he knows that. What did he want?"

"He's on now, sir."

"Tell him mission completed. We did a good job. Needs to send the cleaners in now."

"Sir." The Sergeant disappeared back inside the truck.

As his team began to arrive back one by one, Mebarak went over to the nearest tree and unzipped his trousers.

"Sir?" It was the Sergeant again.

"For God's sake, man!" The Captain shouted over his shoulder. "Can't I have a piss in peace?"

"The Colonel wants you, sir. Urgent."

"One second. My old man takes precedence over that old man." Mebarak finished what he was doing, put himself away and zipped up his trousers.

There were two *Jundi 'Awwal* (Soldier First Class) in the truck, their green/brown US Woodland camouflage uniforms distinctly different from Mebarak's grey-green tigerstripe.

Mebarak took the proffered headphones and put them on. "*'Aqeed?*" he said into the microphone

"You on speaker?" asked Colonel F.

"No."

"Good. Just between us. There's some left in Kfar Habou."

"What?" Mebarak's mind flashed back to that morning's activities. About twenty gunmen had taken over the town of Kfar Habou, seven kilometres back down the mountainside on the road to Tripoli. Mebarak and his team, aided by army regulars, had been sent in. It had been bloody. Five gunmen were arrested and they had presumed the other fifteen were dead. Obviously they were not (sometimes you could not tell the gunmen from the locals – which was the rebels' intention).

"Lahoud* wants these Sunnis finished, and finished now," said the Colonel.

Until his election as President in 1998, Emile Lahoud was Chief of Staff of the Lebanese Army. Under the 1943 National Pact, and ratified by the 1990 Taef Accord, the President of Lebanon is always a Maronite Christian.

"Yes, sir."
"Do it."

5 January 2000
28 Ramadan 1420

Lebanese Broadcasting Corporation (LBC), Beirut

"The fighting in the al-Dinnieh region is over, the Guidance Department of the Army confirmed today. The fighting had been going on for nearly a week, with many rebels killed or captured. The army also sustained casualties. In the last major battle, in the town of Kfar Habou, four soldiers were killed and their commanding officer is reported missing."

10 January 2000
3 Shawal 1420

Aanjar, Bekaa Valley

The place on the western edge of the Bekaa Valley, just off the main Beirut to Damascus road and under five kilometres from the Syrian border, had been associated with power before.

It was founded as Haouch Moussa in the eighth century by Caliph al-Walid Ibn Abdel Malik who built himself a magnificent palace full of arches and colonnades, a mosque, Roman-style *hammam* (baths), a residential quarter and a souk with over sixty shops. The ruins can still be seen to this day.

Caliph al-Walid was the ruler of the Levant, and was based in Damascus prior to taking residence here in the Bekaa. He was of the Omayyads, the first great dynasty of the Arab Muslim empire. A warrior dynasty.

Haouch Moussa was chosen for its strategic importance, being near enough halfway between Damascus to the south-east, Beirut to the north-west and Sidon to the south-west.

Over twelve hundred years later, France built the town of Aanjar on malarial marshland immediately to the south of the ruins of the palace. It was built to house Armenian refugees from Alexandretta, a Syrian province which France had ceded to Turkey in 1939. The houses were built in an unaesthetic eastern European style, small and squat - but in compensation the French included the wide, tree-lined avenues they so love.

But even the warrior Caliph al-Walid would have been surprised, and possibly even a little intimidated, by the power that was to be wielded from Aanjar in the late twentieth century. Because for nearly thirty years it was the base of the Syrian *mukhabarat* in Lebanon. And for twenty of those years it was the headquarters of the man who was dubbed the 'King of Lebanon', the man who effectively ruled the country as Syria's pro-consul. No political decisions were made in Lebanon without his agreement, even the election of the President. During the civil war, all militia leaders of whatever confession (sectarian persuasion) came under his influence. Through his web of agents and bureaucrats and politicians 'loyal to Syria', and backed by the Syrian military presence, and using his notorious charm and flattery, coupled with bribery and force, he gradually subdued the warring Lebanese militias. He manipulated the many-headed beast that is Lebanese politics, playing one side against the other, to ensure that Syria's interests always dominated. It was rumoured that he was as involved as anybody with the corruption that was rife in Lebanon after the civil war, receiving 'taxes' from the hashish growers in the Bekaa Valley and from the heroin and cocaine refiners in the remote reaches of Baalbeck and Hermel, not to mention the nightly plundering of fifty per cent of the takings from the Casino du Liban.

He was the head of Syrian intelligence in Lebanon: Abu

Yo'roub, Brigadier General Ghazi Kanaan.

One and a half kilometres to the south of Aanjar, on an area of flat arable land, were several single-storey buildings, looking as they were meant to look: like a farm. But what was farmed there was not crops or animals: it was human blood.

The place was known as The Onion Factory, and it was Syria's main detention and interrogation centre in Lebanon. Local residents, working on their own farms, had long since learned to ignore the screams which could often be heard coming from the buildings. Hear nothing, see nothing, say nothing. For if they did not, the next screams they heard might be their own.

It was a cold Lebanese winter's night, but up above the sky was clear and riddled with an impossible number of stars. Light could be seen coming from behind one of the small shuttered windows of one of the buildings, but there was no sound. No screams.

For the man who now sat bound and naked on the metal chair in the centre of the large shed would never scream. Never. No matter what the provocation. No matter what was done to him.

His hands were taped behind him. His legs were taped to the chair legs, so that they were apart and his genitals were exposed. His feet were in a trough filled with rank, filthy liquid which might at one time have been water. His eyes were bound with an old rag. His tanned body was streaked with dirt and sweat. He stank of body odour, blood, piss and shit.

There were six other men in the room. Four were normal foot soldiers of the *mukhabarat*, dressed in their ubiquitous 'uniform' of black leather jackets, light cotton trousers and sandals. Another, the interrogator, had replaced his sandals with farm boots, and instead of his jacket he wore a long, rubber apron, streaked with the dried blood of hundreds of souls. He wore a face mask over his nose and mouth, and gardening goggles. In his hand he held the thirty centimetre long soldering iron which he had just removed from the subject's anus.

The sixth man was Ghazi Kanaan.

"I am a reasonable man," Kanaan gently removed the rag from the subject's eyes with his fingertips and dropped it on the floor. "Why will you not co-operate? All I want to know is your name."

The prisoner blinked his one good eye. The other was swollen shut.

"Is that too much to ask?" continued Kanaan. "Just your name. Then we can be friends. I can be a good friend, you know."

Still nothing. The one good eye stared at Kanaan.

"What were you doing there?"

Nothing.

"Were you seeking refuge? Or were you looking for someone? Who? You can talk to me, you know. I will not harm you. I just want to know. Then I can help you. Were you looking for someone? Perhaps I know where they are."

Nothing.

Then Kanaan said, "What would someone like you be doing at Ein Hilweh?"

This time there was a reaction. Slight, but a reaction nevertheless. The one good eye flickered. The swollen lips moved. A sound came out.

Kanaan smiled. "What was that, my friend? What did you say?"

The lips moved again. The mouth opened. And a bloody stump of tooth fell out onto the prisoner's chest.

"What did you say?" Kanaan ignored the red drool rolling down the prisoner's chin. He came closer, pretending concern, cocking his left ear. "Talk to me."

"Nahr."

"What?"

"Al-Bared."

"Did you say Nahr al-Bared?"

"Nahr."

Kanaan smiled. His ruse at naming the wrong Palestinian refugee camp where the prisoner had been arrested had worked, getting a reaction. "What were you doing there?"

"Don't know."

"What is your name?"

"Don't know."

"Please tell me then we can move on."

Suddenly the prisoner shook his head, nostrils flaring, snot spraying. His one good eye was wild. He started to shout. "Don't know, don't know, don't know! Sunni! Don't know! Kill! Kill!"

Kanaan stepped back. He looked at the interrogator. "Is he a lunatic?"

The interrogator pulled down his face mask. "Could be, sir. He has said nothing of sense." He bent down and put the soldering iron on the floor, picking up a welding torch.

Kanaan looked at the prisoner, who had now quietened down again. "Who are you?"

Nothing.

Kanaan nodded to the interrogator, who took a cigarette lighter from his pocket.

"I have lost interest," said Kanaan. "Disappear him." Then he turned and walked away, back outside to the black limousine that was waiting for him.

In the shed, there was a whoosh as the interrogator lit the end of the welding torch. The flame was instantly orange.

Outside, the car pulled away.

The interrogator walked forward, the noise and heat of the torch increasing as he came closer.

Suddenly the prisoner began to laugh. Not madly, not wildly, just humour-filled laughter, as if he had just shared a joke.

"You'll be laughing out of your arse in a minute, scumbag,"

sneered the interrogator. "It's wide enough."

The prisoner's good eye looked directly at his torturer. His cheeks moved, almost in a smile. He spoke, clearly and distinctly, with just a gentle hiss through the missing teeth. "Smokeless fire."

"What? What did you say?" Was that just a hint of worry in the interrogator's eyes?

"Smokeless fire," repeated the prisoner. "Born out of smokeless fire. You shouldn't have taped my hands, you should have knotted them. I would have been powerless then."

The interrogator's eyes widened, this time in genuine fear.

Moments later he was screaming.

PART ONE
الجزء الأول

FOUNDATION
الأساس

26 August 2004
8 Rajab 1425

Mediterranean Sea
15 miles off the southern coast of Cyprus 0:00

The yacht could not been seen at midnight.

The *Heliopolis* was a two hundred foot tri-deck, with a tonnage in excess of five hundred. Built by Oceanco Holland and registered in the Cayman Islands, amongst other things it had six state rooms, an integral swimming pool and games area, a skylounge taking up the complete upper deck, the expected 'mod cons' for an indulged and indulgent class of person, and superior quarters for a crew of five. And a helicopter pad aft. Discreetly hidden behind bulwarks on the top of the vessel were a range of aerials, antennae and satellite dishes for broadcasting, receiving – and listening.

It could have been a rich man's toy, which was the impression it wanted to give. In fact it was the home of the owner who, although he had seven passports which showed he was American, British, French, Israeli, Lebanese, Saudi and Syrian, lived on the yacht permanently. The last time his feet had touched 'dry land' was eight years ago.

The man in the wheelchair grimaced as he waited alone in the dark on the balcony of the upper deck. Eight years ago was the last time his feet would touch anything – because he no longer had any. Not since the incident. Eight years ago. When he had been blown up in his car.

Lucky to be alive, they said. The bomb had been attached too far forward underneath the Audi Sports Coupé. He had 'only' lost both legs at the knee, and his manhood had been irreversibly damaged. He had nearly bled out before someone had realised that one of the blackened bodies in the wreck of the car was still alive. But they had saved him.

And the irony of it all was that he was not the intended victim. He was collateral damage. He had owned the car for less than thirty minutes – a gift from the intended victim, the man he had gone to see, to challenge, to criticise, to ask why, *why*, he had agreed the 1996 April Accord with Israel ('The Grapes of Wrath Understanding') just nine days after the Qana massacre when Israeli artillery had killed one hundred and six people in the UN compound. The man who had visited him in hospital a week after the blast and given him a personal cheque for twenty million US dollars 'in compensation' and promised him anything he wished for to make his life easier.

He wished for a boat. And he had been given one.

But there was one thing he could not be given, not even by his billionaire benefactor: he wanted his wife back. But even Rafic Hariri could not raise people from the dead.

Lucky to be alive, they said. Alive with no wife, no legs and no manhood.

Alive to spend the rest of his days in mourning – and in a wheelchair.

And the yacht could not be seen at midnight.

His reverie was interrupted by the lights on the helicopter pad suddenly bursting on. They must have received word in the control room that his guest was close by.

Only then did he hear the faint rapid percussion of the rotor blades, sounding like the distant retort of a machine gun. From the south-east two faint lights appeared in the black sky, but he had to strain to make out the silhouette of the Bell 206-B3 JetRanger.

With a well-practised flick of his left hand, he turned the wheelchair around and moved quickly back into the skylounge. Small LEDs in the floor illuminated his way over to the lift. The door was already open, and as he entered he said "Office", and the lift door closed silently.

He was sitting behind his desk when the visitor was shown in, the wheelchair invisible behind the vast slab of solid oak that was the desk top and the equally solid modesty board at the front. The floors were also uncovered oak, to accommodate the wheelchair, but two-metre high uplighting around the walls gave the impression that the room was more intimate and cosy than it was.

The man who was shown into the room was himself two metres tall. Upwards, he wore expensive trainers, faded blue jeans, and a black v-neck T-shirt under a leather jacket. On his head he wore a white *gutrah* (Arabic headdress) held in place by a black *ogal*. Underneath could be seen the outline of his *thagiyah* which held his hair in place. The *gutrah* covered his nose and mouth and was swept over his left shoulder; only his dark eyes were visible.

Al-Rajul said nothing as he stood in front of the desk and looked at the man sitting behind it.

The Owner nodded at the crew member by the door, who nodded back and then went out, closing the door behind him.

For a moment neither man spoke. Then The Owner said, "*Al-salaam 'aalaykum.*" His voice was high, a little nasally, some might say effeminate.

Al-Rajul raised his black eyebrows. "*Marhaba.*" In contrast to The Owner, his voice was low.

"*Tfaddal?*" The Owner held out his hand to a table on the right which was adorned with fruit and juices.

"*Laa.*" Al-Rajul shook his head.

"Or something stronger perhaps?" The Owner pointed to a glass-fronted liquor cabinet.

"*Laa*. But thank you."

"Please sit down."

Al-Rajul sat in the plush leather armchair at one o'clock to the desk.

"It has taken me a long time to find you," said The Owner.

"As it should. I am found only when I want to be." The deep voice was not muffled by the *gutrah*.

"And you wanted to be?"

"I am found only when I want to be."

The Owner nodded thoughtfully. "*D'accord*." Their eyes touched for a few seconds. Then The Owner asked, "You know who I am?"

The eyes creased in a smile. "I have done my research. I know who you used to be."

It was The Owner's turn to smile, nodding again. "*Touché*. And how very true. For eight years I have been nobody."

"For eight years the world has thought you were as good as dead."

This time a bitter laugh burst from The Owner's lips. "As good as dead! How right the world is. Never, ever, underestimate the world, *rafee*."

"I never have. Provided the world does not underestimate me."

The Owner leant forward and opened a silver box on the desk top. He turned it towards the visitor. "Do you indulge?"

"And take this down so that the cameras - which I am sure you have hidden here - can record my face? No."

The Owner turned the box back and took out a large cheroot. He lit it from a ornamental silver lighter. His voice was almost sad. "There are cameras, yes, you are right. But they are not on. Not for this conversation."

"Why?" asked Al-Rajul.

Instead of replying directly, The Owner asked "What do you know about Rafic Hariri?"

Rafic Bahaa el deen al-Hariri, the Prime Minister of Lebanon. A Sunni Muslim, as all Prime Ministers must be under the National Pact and the Taef Accord.

Born in Sidon, Lebanon, in 1944 to a modest family, he studied business administration and obtained a degree in accounting from the Arab University, Beirut, in the late 1960s. He went to Saudi Arabia, where he became a teacher and then a professional accountant, then started investing in business on his own account.

It was the time of the oil-boom, and Saudi was the place to be. In 1976 Hariri was in partnership with a Palestinian contractor. Hariri was already known and respected as a hard worker and a deeply religious man (he never failed to pay his zakat *(paying part of his income as a religious obligation)), and the partnership was given a contract by King Khaled to construct a new hotel and conference centre in Taef, the Saudi summer capital in the mountains. But there was one snag: the contract had to be completed from scratch within ten months.*

Hariri knew that the rest of his career depended on this single contract. The project was brought in a week ahead of schedule.

And Hariri was made for life.

He achieved the good graces of King Khaled and gained the support of Crown Prince Fahd (who himself became King in 1980). Hariri bought Oger, *a French construction firm on the verge of bankruptcy. From then on, it was used by the Saudi Royal Family to undertake all of their important construction work. In the five years between 1977 and 1982, the value of this work exceeded ten billion US dollars.*

Hariri wanted to give back to his community, to make his own personal zakat. *He developed major educational facilities in Lebanon, including the Hariri Foundation (originally the Islamic Institute for Culture and Higher Education).*

In 1982, Lebanon was into its seventh year of its fifteen year 'civil war'. After Israel withdrew from its occupation of Beirut in September, Hariri was asked by President Amine Gemayel to help restore the city. He secured aid from King Fahd and contributed twelve million dollars of his own money to clear up the streets of the destroyed city, to remove the rubble, get rid of the wild animals, help the displaced people, restore the water, re-open the roads – at the very minimum.

He became the envoy of the Saudi Royal Family, and gradually achieved international recognition for his humanitarian efforts.

Hariri was, first and foremost, a businessman and a philanthropist, but the complex tendrils of Lebanese politics were enveloping him. And once they envelope you, they will not let you go.

He was the Saudi's 'strong man' in the country. The Palestine Liberation Organisation had effectively collapsed and there was no Sunni leadership in the country to oppose and counteract the rising Shi'ite Amal militia.

Hariri was the force behind the Saudi-inspired Taef Conference in 1989; it is also strongly suggested that Hariri wrote the first draft of the Taef Accord, which brought the warring Lebanese factions together and put an end to the 'civil war'.

In 1992, with the support of the Saudis and under Syria's military 'occupation', Hariri became Prime Minister. In 1993, he oversaw the birth of Solidère (Société Libanaise pour le Développement et Reconstruction), *the company that is rebuilding Beirut.*

But six years is a long time in politics – especially Lebanese politics. Hariri had gotten along well with the Syrians, he had even been their friend, but he was opposed to the Syrian 'candidate' (choice) of Head of Army Emile Lahoud as President; Hariri supported the not-popular President Elias Hrawi, whose term in office he had been instrumental in extending by three years in 1995 through an amended constitution.

Through his opposition to Lahoud, Hariri had displeased the Old Guard of the Levant, those that really pulled the strings. And so the character-assassination of Hariri had commenced: the criticisms, the allegations of corruption (that everything Hariri did was first and foremost to line his own pockets), the true fact that the Lebanese public debt had increased nearly ten-fold in the time Hariri was in office – overlooking the fact that it might have increased more without him at the helm, ignoring that he was rebuilding the shattered country and dismissing the fact that he was trying to drag the most sectarian-

divided country in the world out of civil war and into the twenty-first century.

Hariri wanted electoral reform and change in the administration of Lebanon. What he got from his vociferous opponents was constant, poisonous questioning and vilification.

In 1998, unable to extend Hrawi's term in office even more, Hariri watched as Emile Lahoud was duly elected President – and Hariri 'did not accept' the nomination to continue as Prime Minister.

But he remained active in Lebanese politics, and in 2000 – despite Lahoud being President, despite the continuing and constant smear campaign against him – he returned as Prime Minister. It would become an era of regeneration but tension, with the Prime Minister and President constantly in disagreement and often openly hostile.

"And it remains so to this day," concluded Al-Rajul.

The Owner was quiet, his round head nodding gently. Then he said, "Impressive. You are an educated man. That was almost unbiased." He finished his cheroot and spoke through the smoke. "You like Hariri?"

"I respect Hariri. I am not Sunni."

"What are you?"

The eyes stared. "I am nothing."

The Owner leant forward and stubbed the butt of the cheroot in a crystal ashtray. "We are all something, *mon ami.*"

"If you say so."

The Owner took another cheroot out of the box and lit it. He said, "Ten million US dollars."

There was no reaction in the visitor's eyes. "What about it?"

"That is what I want to give you. Half of it right here. Right now. Tonight. You can take it with you or I can have it transferred."

"For what?"

The Owner looked at the smouldering tip of his cheroot. Then he said, "For ten million dollars I want you to kill Rafic Hariri."

26 September 2004
11 Sha'ban 1425

Baalbeck, Lebanon 20:00

The four men were stiff when they climbed out of the Mitsubishi Pajero after the sixty kilometre journey from Beirut. The SUV had tinted windows with a one-way view, so they could see where they were going but they themselves could not be seen inside. Which was probably safer all round. Nobody could witness the collection of individuals being transported against their will.

Each had received a phone call that day, 'inviting' them on the trip. They were instructed where to be, at what time – and to come alone and tell no one. They had been picked up one by one from different locations in the city by two urbane, very polite but ultimately taciturn men in leather jackets, light trousers and sandals. Syrian *mukhabarat*. Each had been surprised when they saw their fellow travellers. But knowing how these things worked, they had said nothing to each other on the journey.

Three of the men knew each other well. The first to be picked up was Samir Kassir, the handsome, stubbled forty-four year old professor, political commentator and journalist. A Christian Orthodox, he was a strong and vocal advocate of the rights of Palestinians (his father was a Lebanese Palestinian) and of democracy in Lebanon and Syria.

The second to be picked up was George Hawi, the white-haired, moustached sixty-six year old politician and former secretary-general of the Lebanese Communist Party. Born into a Greek Orthodox Christian family, he was a professed atheist. That very month with Samir Kassir he had formed the Democratic Left Movement, a group of leftist intellectuals advocating social democracy for Lebanon and an end to Syrian hegemony.

The third man was Gebran Tueni, the smooth, dark-haired, moustached forty-seven year old Chief Editor and publisher of *An-Nahar* (The Day) newspaper and TV producer and host. A Greek Orthodox Christian, he was a long-time political critic of the Syrian presence in Lebanon.

The fourth man was different from the others. He was Walid Eido, the dapper, greying, balding, clean-shaven sixty-two year old former public prosecutor for north Lebanon who had been elected to parliament four years previously. A Sunni Muslim, he was a close friend of Prime Minister Rafic Hariri.

Now out of the vehicle, the men looked around, puzzled. They knew where they were, but why had they been brought here?

"This way please," said one of their escorts, indicating that they should follow him through the entrance to the temples. The other escort brought up the rear as they passed a long, black limousine that was parked as close to the gate as it could get without blocking the entrance.

Baalbeck, the Roman City of The Sun, is one of the major historical sites of Lebanon. The iconic image of the six pillars of the Temple of Jupiter, with or without the snow-capped Mount Lebanon range as a backdrop, is the country's second national symbol after the cedar tree. Little remains of the Temple of Jupiter except the six pillars, but the more intact outer courtyard and inner sacrificial courtyard hint at the majesty that was once this monument to Baal, the Phoenician warrior god of sun, thunder and lightning.

The later, smaller temples of Venus and Mercury (the latter

erroneously known today as the Temple of Bacchus) have survived their two thousand years better, with the Temple of Mercury almost completely intact. It was towards this temple that the four men were now led.

It was sunset, and the site was closing for the day. The few straggling tourists heading for the exit paid no heed to the six men walking inwards. The late summer Lebanese evening was warm and all four men were in shirtsleeves, no jackets.

They reached the temple and began to walk up the steps towards the doorway with its friezes of corn sheaves, poppies, ivy and vine leaves. On the keystone above was a carving of an eagle carrying garlands of pomegranates and cedar cones in its beak, and with the thunderbolts of Jupiter and the caduceus of Mercury in its talons.

"Please, we wait here," said the escort as they reached the top. He stayed with the four men, the other escort was positioned down at the bottom of the steps.

The 'guests' turned around, surveying the ruins. At one o'clock in front of them was the small Temple of Venus. At eight o'clock behind them was the Temple of Jupiter. And immediately to their left was the sacrificial courtyard.

"Poignant, perhaps?" George Hawi was the first of them to speak.

"What is?" asked Gebran Tueni.

Samir Kassir gave an ironic laugh. "The sacrificial courtyard! Do you think, *mes amis*? Is it our turn?"

"They would not dare," said Walid Eido.

"You? No," agreed Kassir. "They would not dare to touch you, *akh*. But the rest of us..."

"Too symbolic," said Tueni.

"And too complicated," Hawi sighed. "For them."

They became aware of some shadowy figures approaching the steps down below from the way they had just come. Had whoever it was been waiting in that limo, watching them pass?

There were three figures. Two stayed at the bottom of the

steps with the second escort, the third began to walk up on his own.

"My God..." said Hawi lowly as he saw who it was. "I don't believe it."

"Not your God," said Kassir. "You don't have one. And this is no God."

"But it is perhaps a devil," said Eido.

"A devil we have not seen for two years," said Tueni.

"No." There was anger in Hawi's voice as it grew louder. "Not *a* devil. *The* devil."

Part of the third step from the top had broken away sometime over the years to create a deeper, wider section of the fourth step. The figure stopped on this ledge and looked up at the four men.

"*Messieurs. Massah el-khair,*" said Ghazi Kanaan.

The rule of Brigadier General Ghazi Kanaan as head of Syrian intelligence in Lebanon had lasted for twenty years. In 2002 he had been summoned back to Syria to become the overall head of Syria's political intelligence. Sold as a promotion, it was regarded by many – including Kanaan himself – as a demotion. Certainly in Damascus he was closer to the seat of power, but even here the old adage of 'keep your enemies closer still' applied. He was a powerful Alawite, and the powerful Alawite rulers of Syria did not want another powerful Alawite – who was regarded on a 'better the devil you know' basis by the US and its allies – potentially being groomed to take over should something sudden and unexpected happen to their new, young and still relatively fresh President.

And now here he was, in the penumbra of evening, in Baalbeck.

Kanaan climbed up the last three steps and nodded for the escort to leave them.

"Thank you for coming," he said to all four men.

Eyebrows were raised. As if they had any choice! The men

said nothing, letting what they saw sink in. Kanaan was dressed in denim jeans and a loose white shirt, not the suave suit and tie that he had worn constantly when he ruled the country. He looked older, much older than the addition of the two years since he had last been seen in Lebanon. Something had taken its toll on him.

He began to walk around the men like a potential buyer at a slave auction. "Four thorns," he spoke as he walked. "Four out of the many, many thorns in my side, in the side of Syria. But the most vociferous."

"What are you doing here?" asked Eido, his body turning to face Kanaan.

"Come to that, what are *we* doing here?" asked Kassir.

Kanaan had done a complete circle around them. He stopped and after a moment sat down with a sigh on one of the fallen columns. "But even thorns have thorns. You are thorns in my side, I am a thorn in other people's sides."

"What the hell are you talking about?" snapped Hawi.

"Are you well?" asked Tueni. "You look... haggard."

"Haggard!" mocked Kanaan. "Haggard! In the name of Allah the most merciful, you would be haggard too! I nearly had to call off our meeting. Do you know what happened today? Today. In my own backyard." He raised his hands and ran them down either side of his face.

"No, we haven't seen the news," sneered Kassir. "We have been otherwise engaged during the last two and a half hours as guests of Syria."

"Today," said Kanaan, "in al-Zahera, Damascus, the Jews detonated a car bomb. They murdered Izz el-Deen Khalil, the Hamas Commander."

Hawi shrugged. "So? What is that to do with us?"

"To do with you, Abu Anis? Nothing. It is nothing to do with you. But," Kanaan began to shout, "it explains why I am looking fucking haggard!" He stopped, breathing hard. Then he said in a normal but still edgy voice, "Do you know what they want me to do, what Assad wants me to do?" He looked up at the four men, as if they had any idea of the answer. "He wants me to become Interior Minister. To counter and eradicate this threat in our own country. And we all know what happens if I cannot do that."

"And you have brought us here for what?" said Hawi. "Our sympathy?"

Kanaan narrowed his eyes. "Time was I would have sent you to The Onion Factory for a remark like that."

"Yes? And? What?" Now it was Hawi who was shouting. "Time was if I was a much younger man I would strangle you with my bare hands. You bring us here against our will - "

"You were asked to come."

"Bullshit. What for? A meeting of the Abu Yo'roub Appreciation Society? And why here, why Baalbeck? Such a beautiful place. But this is Hizbullah land. The Ain Bourdai training base is just down the road, and over there is the Sheik Abdallah barracks*. Is this supposed to intimidate us?"

"George, George," Kassir took Hawi by the arm, gripping and ungripping his elbow in warning. There were four armed *mukhabarat* at the bottom of the steps.

"I – I - ..." With a huge sigh Hawi said, "This man makes me so angry. Why can they not just leave us alone?"

"I know... I know." Kassir nodded in sympathy.

Suddenly Kanaan said, "I want your help. I have a decision to make."

In the hastening darkness, four sets of brows furrowed. The men were stunned for a moment. Then Eido said, "*You* want *our* help?"

"To decide, yes."

"What on earth is going on here?" asked Tueni. "What are you up to, Kanaan?"

Kanaan got up and again started the menacing walk around

The storage facility for kidnapped hostages, including Westerners, during the civil war.

the men. Then he stopped, as if he had made up his mind about something. "Sit, sit," he invited calmly, indicating two other fallen columns at angles to the one he had been sitting on. Reluctantly, the men sat down, two on each. Kanaan resumed sitting on his column. "'eeh!" he called to the guards down below. One came quickly up the steps, hand inside his leather jacket.

All four of the guests tensed. Which one would be shot first?

The guard's hand came out of his jacket - with a candle. A lighter was produced from his trousers. He ran the flame over the bottom of the candle and then stuck it on the column between Kanaan and the men. He lit the wick, stayed to make sure it was alight, and then walked away back down the steps.

The light from the candle made it easier to see, but it also cast small sinister shadows over Kanaan's face.

"One month ago," explained Kanaan. "One month ago to this very day. There was a meeting in Damascus."

"Don't I know it!" snorted Eido.

He was interrupted by Kanaan's raised hand. "I was not present, but I have a transcript of it. So you know what happened, Abu Khaled?"

"I have been told," nodded Eido.

"By Abu Bahaa?"

"By his Head of Security."

"And what have you been told?"

Eido looked from one man to the other. "We all know that Hariri and Lahoud hate each other and that Lahoud wants an extension of his presidency, just like Hrawi got in ninety-five. Hariri opposes this, he wants a new President he can work with. You – Syria – want Lahoud to stay in office, for so-called continuity in the region now that the US has imposed sanctions on you. President Assad called the Prime Minister to Damascus to inform him of Syria's decision and to ask him to - " he made air quotes with his fingers, " – clarify his position. He said to Hariri, 'This extension is going to happen or I will break

Lebanon over your head.' And he threatened to 'get' him and his family. The next day, the Prime Minister agreed to the amendment of the constitution to allow the extension of Lahoud's presidency."

Kanaan leant forward with his elbows on his knees, resting his chin on his steepled fingers. "And do you think that really happened? That the President of Syria, a very honourable man, would use such threatening language?"

Eido did not reply.

"What about the rest of you?" Kanaan looked from one to the other. They remained silent also.

Kanaan sat upright, causing a draft which made the candle flicker. "There are plots hatching. Wheels within wheels, thorns in the side of thorns. Hariri is the lynch-pin in all of this. His fate is the future of the entire region, perhaps beyond. I have an involvement in the matter, and there is something I must decide."

"What are you saying?" asked Kassir.

"The people of Lebanon. Where are they?" Kanaan looked around theatrically and gave a huge shrug. Then he looked back at the men. "Why here they are." He held his arms wide, almost in an embrace. "There are four of them. The biggest thorns in Syria's side along with Rafic Hariri."

The men were staring in disbelief. Had the great dictator of Lebanon gone mad?

"There are two options," continued Kanaan. "There are people, not only from the West, that want Bashar al-Assad removed as President of Syria. But what is the alternative? The Alawites are a minority in the country yet they rule – because there is, no longer, any opposition, no viable alternative. There cannot be an alternative to the Alawites. But there can be an Alawite alternative to Assad."

"You," Hawi nodded as if it had all become clear.

"I did not say that. Syria cannot be invaded at this time, not by anyone, especially with what is happening in Iraq. Regime change must be more subtle. It must be seen to come from within, even if it doesn't. One idea is to destabilise Greater Syria." (Walid Eido flinched at the all-inclusive term for the area which included the land-mass of a non-existent Lebanon.) "To commit an act so outrageous, so unexpected, that the finger of blame will be pointed directly at Assad. That he will have to go or be got rid of by any means. With the reports of Assad's animosity towards him being exaggerated, even fabricated from scratch, one idea is to kill Hariri - "

"What!" Eido jumped up.

"Sit down, sit down." Kanaan flapped his hand. "To kill Hariri spectacularly, in public, in broad daylight and have the mark of Syria all over the atrocity."

"This is outrageous." Eido was attracting attention from the guards below. Hawi tugged his arm to make him sit down.

"After which other enemies of Syria will be removed one by one."

"Other enemies...?" Hawi let the question hang. They all knew who Kanaan was talking about.

"We are not Syria's enemies," said Kassir.

"But it is seen that way." Kanaan paused. Then he went on. "Assad will go, with direct evidence pointing at him and with certain video and audio tapes they have of him plotting Hariri's murder and authorising the removal of the other enemies."

"Who are *they*?" asked Tueni. He was not answered.

"It is wonderful what they can do with impersonators, body doubles and this new thing, CGI," said Kanaan. "Assad doesn't even know he is being set up." Before he could be interrupted yet again, he went on "But there is an alternative. Let the thorn linger, let it grow, turn septic. Now there is Resolution 1559[*], and the world wants to interfere again in Lebanese affairs. If we allow Hariri to go on unhindered, if we encourage it, his very

---

[*] *Adopted earlier that month, the UN Security Council Resolution demanded a withdrawal of Syrian troops from Lebanon, the disarming of Hizbullah and a free and fair Lebanese presidential election. Even in Lebanon, many thought it was an unwarranted intrusion in Lebanese affairs.*

presence, his plans for Lebanon, together with UN interference, will quickly push Syria out of the country, Lahoud or no Lahoud. And Assad will still have to go, the UN will make sure of it. Either way Syria has a new president."

"And Kanaan is the winner," sneered Kassir.

"It is not to do with Kanaan. I have not said I will take over from Assad."

"But you have not said you will not," observed Hawi.

"That is up to others."

"Who's backing you, Kanaan?" persisted Tueni.

Kanaan's famous temper flashed. "That is not for you to ask!" He leant back away from the flame. His face was now completely in shadow. "But I have a decision to make. So, why have I brought you here?" Although the question was rhetoric, he still paused. "I want to warn you. I want to *ask* you. To lower your profile. Stop your attacks on Syria, mute them, tone them down. Let whatever is going to happen, happen. It will benefit Lebanon."

"Let you kill Hariri!" Eido was beside himself.

"I have not said Hariri will be killed. I have told you that is a decision to be made." He was quiet, his hard eyes on the men. He continued. "Stop making yourselves targets. Take the attention away from yourselves. Distance yourself. Then there will be no need for... final measures. Hariri has a lot of enemies, I know that there are others who are after him." He moved forward once more so that the flickering candlelight again painted his face. "To kill Hariri, to let Hariri be killed by somebody else, or to protect him...?" Kanaan licked his fingers and rubbed out the flame of the candle. In the darkness he said, "And that decision I have just made."

27 September 2004
12 Sha'ban 1425

Old City, Damascus, Syria 19:00 - 22:30

The Damascene sat alone in an alcove in the steam room in the bathhouse, the *Hammam al-Selesa* near the Umayyad Mosque. He wore nothing but a towel around his waist and old flip-flops on his feet, so the scars and long-healed burns and gouges on his muscular body were visible, had anybody been around and had they cared to look. Which they weren't and they didn't.

His long hair was wet and stuck to his shoulders and down his back. His tanned face wore a day's stubble.

The room was dim. Grubby white tiles stretched halfway up the wall and then gave way to light blue paint, with damp patches here and there as if it was fresh plaster waiting to go off. Equally grubby light blue tiles formed the seating ledge in the alcove and spread out across the floor. He was glad the soles of his feet were covered.

The steam was more subtle than might have been expected, gradually creating cleansing heat and sweat from within the body rather than assailing the skin from outside. The place stank of the odours of men, even though he was the only one there.

He folded his arms and waited.

On cue five minutes later, the door opened and another towelled figure walked in. This body was older, the skin lax, showing the greyness of age.

"Peace be upon you," said the new arrival as he came over

and sat down in the alcove.

The Damascene inclined his head, not saying what he wanted to say, not doing what he wanted to do – which was to reach out and rip this man's head from his body. But that would serve no purpose, not right now. Four years ago, maybe. But the time would come again.

"You are well?" asked Ghazi Kanaan.

"You are interested?" asked The Damascene.

"I like my prized weapons to remain in top condition," Kanaan patted The Damascene's right thigh, impressed at its solidity. "Good. You still train."

"You wanted something?"

Kanaan removed his hand. "I have been trying to contact you for the last month. You have been elusive."

"I have been around, here and there, back and forth. I do have a life outside of the jobs I do for you."

Kanaan sniffed condescendingly. "You have a life because I say you have a life, remember? Ah but you don't, do you? Remember? Not all of it."

The Damascene said nothing.

"As it transpires," Kanaan went on, "the timing now is perfect. I have been trying to contact you to prepare you for an assignment, but I did not know quite what that assignment was going to be. I do now." He rubbed his hands over his face as he began to sweat. "You like these places, these bathhouses?"

"Yes. They serve a purpose. They cleanse the body. And the soul."

"Is your soul clean?"

"As clean as yours, Abu Yo'roub."

Kanaan gave a gentle laugh. Then he said, "The usual terms? One hundred thousand US dollars?"

And I allow you to live, thought The Damascene. He said, "It all depends what for."

"Oh, does it now?" Kanaan did not notice the other man's fingers flex. "Perhaps this time I should ask you for a discount."

"Why should you ask for that?"

"This time it is different. A decision has been made."

The Damascene sat on his hands. "Abu Yo'roub, what are you talking about?"

The famed Kanaan anger and derision flashed in the older man's eyes. But he bit off his trenchant response as The Damascene turned full on to him and he could see the raw hole where the younger man's left ear had once been.

"It – it is of no concern," said Kanaan. "But this time it is not the usual request."

"So you don't want me to kill the President? So what is it? Do you want me to rob a bank?"

"Facetiousness does not suit you. There are plots afoot. Plots within plots, wheels within wheels, thorns in the side of thorns."

The Damascene frowned. Was Kanaan going mad?

"These are not your concern," continued Kanaan. "You must be your usual invisible self. You cannot be seen to do what I am about to ask, and certainly the request can never, ever be known to have come from me. No one would believe it anyway."

"You are speaking in riddles." A waft of garlic blew into Kanaan's face as The Damascene spoke lowly, mockingly. "Riddles within riddles." He turned away in disdain and stood up. As he did so, the towel fell away from his waist and he stood there stark naked. From the neck down, there was not a hair on his body.

It was not the first time Kanaan had seen him naked. He was impressed by, and very envious of, the physique - despite the scars. He stared as The Damascene bent and picked up his towel, putting it back around his waist.

"There are plots to kill Rafic Hariri," said Kanaan. "I have reliable intelligence to that effect. There is one in particular, from an unusual but unclarified source."

The Damascene swept his hair forward across the left side of his face. "I think Hariri's death would suit the purposes of Syria just fine."

"No, it would not."

"But it would suit your purposes."

Kanaan sighed. "In some respects, possibly. But that is not the road I am travelling. It suits my purpose that he stays alive. For now. Your job, my dear *Naqeeb*, is to prevent the assassination of Rafic Hariri."

It was dusk as The Damascene walked back through the Old City, but in the narrow, twisting lanes it was so dark it could have been midnight. The upper stories of the mainly two-storey buildings overhung the alleyways and forbade entry to the moonlight. Now and then there would be a group of illuminated shops, huddled together as if for safety from the darkness, or the mysterious entrance to a bazaar or souk.

But he did not mind the darkness, it did not bother him. He was dressed in a grey *burnus*, an all-in-one full-body cloak with hood, below which at the ankles showed the hem of his white cotton *dishdasha*. The hood was pulled up over his head and hid the top half of his face. His feet were sandaled. His footsteps were heavy on the cobbles. Perhaps the darkness was afraid of *him*.

His meetings with Ghazi Kanaan only happened two or three times a year, but he always left feeling angry. Kanaan was an arrogant, haughty, nasty individual who looked down on most people, not only the Lebanese. But what irritated The Damascene more than the machinations of the scheming Alawite was the fact that he owed Kanaan his life.

And he did remember, more than Kanaan realised. In fact, he remembered it all. Back to when he was a different man, back to when he was a normal human being. Back to when he was Captain Marwan Mebarak of the Lebanese Army Commando Unit...

It was supposed to be a simple mopping-up operation in Kfar

Habou, back in January 2000 (Ramadan 1420). Even now he did not know what had gone wrong. Perhaps it was just tiredness. He and his team of four had been fighting in the town in the morning and they thought they had finished off the Sunni *Takfir wal-Hijra* rebels who had taken over the place. Then they had gone further up into the Dinnieh mountains to root out and kill five more. That should have been the end of their efforts for the day, but on returning to camp Mebarak and his team had been sent back to Kfar Habou – and that was when it had all gone wrong.

His team were killed with a frightening efficiency by a group who looked like – but obviously with hindsight were not – locals calling to them for help. They had gone over to the beckoning men who had suddenly produced pistols from their robes and despatched the soldiers to Allah for judgment.

Mebarak had been beaten, stripped to his undergarments and thrown into the back of an old van, which had sped off, presumably back down towards Tripoli.

The van exploded twenty minutes into the journey.

It was unlikely to be a roadside bomb; it could have been something they were carrying, or it could have been a rocket-propelled grenade launched by either the Lebanese or Syrian army. Whichever, Mebarak knew nothing until he woke up amongst the rats in a smelly back alley somewhere. Literally he knew nothing, not even who he was. How he had gotten there was a mystery. But, perversely, he recognised the area. He was near the Nahr al-Bared refugee camp. But that was Palestinian. Something in his shocked, addled mind said that he should be somewhere Sunni.

No sooner had he staggered out of the alley than hands were grabbing him again, a shit-smelling sack was rammed over his head, there was a thump and a little flash of light, and then he woke up in The Onion Factory. He did not know where he was at the time. He did not know who he was or even what he was. He just knew that he had a soldering iron up his anus and that the man who was defiling him was going to die.

He also knew the bastard Ghazi Kanaan the minute he saw him.

Before leaving, Kanaan had ordered that he be 'disappeared', which meant he would be taken to Syria and would never be heard of again. His restraints were not knotted, so he had broken through them easily, and he had killed the five Syrians in the building quickly, skilfully and with pleasure.

But he had not reckoned on Kanaan and his three bodyguards returning. He had heard the car drive away.

He was picking through the pockets of one of the dead *mukhabarat* – the one whose nose was now back in his brains, beyond his ears – when Kanaan had reappeared in the doorway. The car's headlights were on outside, and all that could be seen of Kanaan was an evil, malevolent silhouette.

"Well what have we here?" sneered Kanaan's voice. "Someone who refuses to go." With that, Kanaan raised the pistol in his hand and shot the captive in the head.

At that moment Captain Marwan Mebarak died.

And The Damascene was born.

Kanaan was everything everyone said about him, but he was also a pragmatist, a recogniser of talent. No one, in the twenty-plus years of Syrian 'assistance' in Lebanon, had ever overpowered and killed five armed *mukhabarat* in the same room, at the same time, with their bare hands. Kanaan was impressed. He was ecstatic when he realised he had not killed the captive but had merely blown away the flesh from the left side of his head, including his ear.

Mebarak was truly disappeared. A local man in Aanjar who bore a passing resemblance to him in stature, was taken and freshly slaughtered. His body, with its shot-away face, was taken up north and carefully positioned in the hills behind Kfar Habou where it would be found two weeks later after the wild animals had had their fill.

Captain Marwan Mebarak was given a funeral with full military honours. He had no wife or other family, which was fortunate because it saved Kanaan the expense of hiring a local gang to sort out the problem.

The Damascene knew nothing about this. He did not know who he was, his history or where he came from. But everything else he knew. The history of Lebanon and Syria, the language, the culture, politics both present and past, old songs, new songs, people who were famous or had been famous. From a guarded apartment in the new area of Damascus, he healed.

And soon he worked. Nasty jobs of elimination at Kanaan's request. He was told they were threats to the Syrian regime, but quickly he came to realise that they were threats to the Kanaan regime of plots and machinations. No one stood in Kanaan's way for long. And work was work.

When Kanaan was recalled to Damascus in 2002, The Damascene had to be moved out of the now un-guarded apartment. Now Kanaan was back in the centre of Syrian power, he could not be seen to have his own personal killer, kept like a pet to be unleashed at the will of his master. Kanaan had bought him a three-room apartment on the upper floor of a building in the Old City and he was given his freedom. He still undertook 'errands' for his old master, but now he was paid at Middle Eastern going rates.

And what Kanaan guessed at, but did not know for sure, was that he began undertaking errands for other people as well, often mediating in local disputes between the tradesmen and residents of the Old City, sometimes even regularising the affairs of politically-linked businessmen in the new area. All for little stipends. Usually his presence was enough to settle matters (he was over two metres tall), sometimes a quiet word was necessary. Only rarely a broken bone. But he only killed for Kanaan.

Then, late in 2003, he remembered.

He did not suffer any shock, any sudden emotional wrench,

any kick in the head by a mule. He just woke up one morning and remembered. Everything.

Anonymous telephone enquiries of the authorities in Beirut informed him of the fate of Captain Marwan Mebarak, a true hero of Lebanon. And it was then that he decided that, someday, he would kill Ghazi Kanaan.

The Damascene walked out of the shadows and passed Ahmad al-Nakhal's carpet shop and the next door barber's shop. He turned left, passing the antiques and souvenir shop on the right. A woman dressed in a black *jilbaab*, head covered by a black *khimar*, passed by but did not look at the tall, hooded figure.

Soon he was walking up the outside staircase to his upper level apartment.

The building was higher than its neighbours, so during daylight he could see out from his window with its rotting wooden frame over the domed rooftops, littered with satellite dishes and solar panels as if they had been haphazardly thrown down by Allah, to the ninth century magnificence of the Umayyad Mosque. Not that he ever went to the mosque. He did not believe. In anything.

Beyond the mosque was 'new' Damascus, with its already outdated high rises.

But now it was night, so all he could see (if he cared to look, which he didn't) was darkness punctuated by glows from skylights, bunched together like the lights in the alleys below. The mosque was an imposing, bulky shadow beyond which the more regular lights of new Damascus spread out like a nocturnal carpet of glitter.

A cooling, but not cool, breeze came through the wide-open window. It carried no sound. But as soon as he entered, the breeze told him he was not alone. He could smell another being in the apartment.

The Damascene left his old wooden front door open but he

did not reach for the switch on the wall. There would be light in the room soon enough. He kicked off his sandals and removed his *burnus*, throwing it in the direction of a chair. The floorboards creaked as he walked towards his heavily and exotically cushioned double floor-mattress on the far side of the room.

He was halfway across the room when he saw the shadow entering from the washing area at the rear of the apartment. It was accompanied by a glow of diffused light, spreading out in a two metre circumference. A hand was shielding the flame, the source of the light.

The Damascene stopped.

The shadow and the light came towards him. He could smell jasmine.

The light moved to the right and downwards. It became stronger as the candle was placed on a wicker table next to the mattress. The being's back was towards him.

Then came the sound. A delicate *tinging*, singular and gentle at first, becoming stronger as the being moved one hand and then the other, expertly playing the silver metal zills.

She turned around, beginning the gentle shimmies of a *raqs baladi*, country dance. She was small, almost delicate, but he knew already that her body was hard and strong. She was dressed in her own variation of the dancing costume, different shades of red with gold accessories: beaded and coined headdress, small facial veil covering her nose and mouth, sleeveless top knotted between her breasts, a coined chiffon hip scarf above a sheer skirt. Her feet and abdomen were bare.

From above the veil, her heavily made-up eyes looked at him challengingly, seductively, as her belly undulated. She turned her back towards him and bent over at ninety degrees from the hips, fingers playing the zills, snake arms flowing in the air, her long black hair falling downwards, a black and gold hair clip reflecting the candle light.

The Damascene stared as she straightened up, made a hip

circle turn, and then bent backwards again, her legs apart for balance, her delights visible beneath the diaphanous skirt. This sight he did care to look at.

Back up, with hip lifts and drops, then more shimmies as she came towards him with her musical arms open wide. He could smell her musk mixed in with the jasmine-based perfume.

She looked down and her eyes creased in pleasure as she saw that he had reacted to her beneath his *dishdasha*.

Still moving, she danced to within a centimetre of him. Then she stopped playing and her hennaed left hand came up to unclip her veil. Her breath was warm and pure as she said, "Master." Her fingers gave the lightest caress of his stubbled face then moved more firmly downwards through his still damp long black hair. Her hand stopped on his chest, the solidity of his nipple evident beneath the robe.

She looked down at her own chest. "Would you?" she asked. "You know I cannot untie knots."

He untied her top and then moved his hands to cup both of her small breasts, throwing the top to the floor. He said, "Or uncover anything that has been covered."

He bent down, crooked his right arm underneath her bottom and lifted her up. There was genuine warmth in his smile as he said, "My Djinn."

Her arms were around his neck as he carried her to the mattress and gently laid her on it. Then he laid himself on her.

Not so gently.

28 September 2004
13 Sha'ban 1425

Old City, Damascus, Syria 05:00

She was not there when he woke up. He knew she wouldn't be, she never was. That was why he had left the front door open, so she could leave. He was playing along with the little game. For real *djinni* cannot open closed doors. If she wanted to play at being a *djinn*, that was fine by him. She always gave him what he wanted, he could be tolerant.

Kanaan never mentioned her, but The Damascene knew she came from him. She turned up those two or three times a year after he met with Kanaan, a little sweetener against whatever distasteful job Kanaan had asked him to do. A reward. A payment in addition to the hundred thousand US.

And The Damascene had to admit that he enjoyed her visits. Her talents were plentiful. In his line of work, in his line of existence, there was no possibility of permanent relationships, so the assurance that she would appear before each assignment was welcome. And, of course, the wily bastard Kanaan knew that the unspoken promise of The Djinn's body would make him keener to accept whatever task he was given.

The Damascene wondered what The Djinn would do once he had killed Kanaan?

But that was for the future. Now he had the hardest job he had ever been given. Hurt, maim, kill – yes. But to *prevent* somebody being killed...

An interesting challenge. More so than Kanaan knew. For he

hated Sunnis, and now he had to keep one alive.

The muezzin's call to *fajr* (dawn prayer) booming loudly from the twelve loudspeakers atop the Umayyad Mosque's minaret had awoken him, as it did every day. *"Hayya la-l-faleah - Hayya la-l-faleah."* Hasten to real success.

He got up and strolled naked over to the window. The morning light was pushing in from the east. Morning of light, morning of joy.

Something *zizzed* past the hole that was his left ear. Morning of insects! Normally they did not bother him, he was not to their taste. But they must be able to detect the essence of The Djinn on him. He had been bitten during the night. He always was after she had been with him. He scratched the top of his right hand.

Damned *Hasharaat*.

The Jeep was waiting for him downstairs, as he knew it would be. Inside were two Syrian army conscripts, one driving, one sitting in the back. The Jeep was sideless and The Damascene threw his large holdall onto the empty back seat and climbed in next to the driver. No longer dressed in local clothing, he wore a loose white collarless shirt, blue denim jeans and desert boots. His head was unadorned, his long hair tied into a ponytail with a simple rubber band; it just about covered the hole in the side of his head.

Although the sun was rising, it was still dark in the alleys and the Jeep's full beams blasted light onto the closed and shuttered buildings as they drove away.

There was no Ghazi Kanaan, for Kanaan had given him his job, they had discussed the requirements at length, and now Kanaan would distance himself. They would not meet again until Kanaan had another job for him. The Damascene settled down in the front seat and permitted himself an inner smile. Or maybe this time they would not meet again until The Damascene had his hands around the bastard's throat...

Soon they crossed over the disused railway line and then

turned onto the highway, heading west to Lebanon...

Bekaa Valley, Lebanon 06:30

There were no formalities at the border, the army vehicle simply swept through with hardly a reduction in speed, joining the narrower road on the Lebanese side. The sun was climbing higher in the sky, and presently the natural air-conditioning of the open-sided vehicle would not be able to cool them against the heat.

Soon they were passing Aanjar on the right. The soldiers were not aware of the slight tensing in The Damascene's arms.

They took the fork to the left, and as they started the dead straight eight kilometres between Barr Elias and Chtaura across the Bekaa Valley, The Damascene thought back to his meeting in the *hammam* yesterday evening...

"Are you acting on your own in this or are you acting for Syria?" The Damascene's dark eyes looked down at Kanaan, still sitting in the alcove.

"That is none of your business," Kanaan wiped the back of his hand across his sweat-streaked brow. "I am paying you to do a job."

"Syria wants to keep Hariri alive?"

"Some parts of it."

"Or is it Kanaan that wants to keep Hariri alive?"

Kanaan said nothing.

The Damascene stretched upwards, his muscles flexing. As he brought his arms back down, he again moved his hair to cover the hole in the left side of his head. "And how am I to prevent an assassination? The Prime Minister of Lebanon? Am I to become Hariri's head of security? Chief of the army? He has many foes."

"And many friends." Kanaan pushed himself up from the alcove seat. The Damascene still towered over him. "Which do you think are the more dangerous?"

"He has enemies within?"

"We all do."

"Enemies that want him dead?"

"I did not say that."

The Damascene raised his arms against the wall and began some vertical presses. Kanaan watched the scarred muscular back and the firm buttocks beneath the towel.

"And how long am I to prevent this assassination?" The Damascene spoke into the wall. "Forever?"

"Assassinations are never long-term, they are usually decided upon and... executed. I would wish to see you back within, say, six months."

You may never see me back, thought The Damascene. He said, "And after six months?"

"They can blow him to hell for all I care."

The Damascene straightened up and turned around. "What are you plotting, Kanaan?"

The Syrian smiled. "Me? Plotting? The Syrian Interior Minister-elect plotting?" The smile fell from his face. "Just remember who you work for."

The Damascene's stare was ice cold. "Oh, I know who I work for."

"Good."

Not you. "Massage?" He pulled open the old wooden door.

"What?"

"You going for a massage?"

"With that fat sadist Abdul? I don't think so."

"Too scared?" asked The Damascene.

"Too old," said Ghazi Kanaan.

Mount Lebanon 08:30

The pace of the Jeep slowed as the road climbed into the mountains after Chtaura, but soon they were passing through

Bhamdoun and were on the downward run into Beirut. Just west of Jamhour they took a right off the main road onto a rough cinder track and pulled up in front of a new three-storey apartment block.

Without a word, The Damascene climbed out of the Jeep. He had hardly lifted his large holdall from the back before the vehicle sped off, dust and gravel flying from its back wheels.

The block had magnificent views out over Beirut, and in his pocket he had the keys to one of the two apartments on the top floor. His home for the next six months. Courtesy of Ghazi Kanaan. Or the Syrian taxpayer. Or both.

A blonde haired woman and three young children (a boy and twin girls) were coming out of the front door of the building, and the woman held the door open for him as he approached. She smiled in acknowledgement of his *"Shukran"* and then called to her children to hurry up because Mama and Buba were waiting.

The Damascene climbed the stairs. His shirt was wet against his back from the drive. He undid the buttons as he climbed. He needed a shower.

Opening the front door, he pulled his shirt off as he stepped inside the apartment. The chill of the air conditioning made him feel instantly welcome. His skin crinkled with the coolness.

The apartment was a duplex, spacious and well furnished. Tiled flooring, minimal but tasteful decoration, good quality appliances – even a flat screen Sony Bravia on the wall. He wondered what other uses the place was put to. A safe house? A luxurious holding facility? A love nest?

Throwing the holdall onto a leather couch, he walked over to the full-length sliding windows, pulled them open and stepped out onto the balcony, his naked torso once again enveloped by the heat of the day. He undid the rubber band and let his hair fall down either side of his face.

The views out over the city were indeed enviable. Far in the distance he could see the Mediterranean. He knew Beirut well and he narrowed his eyes and focused in on its heart, the downtown district, his eyes travelling from Martyr's Square (El Bourj) in the east, across the administrative hub in the Nejmeh and Serail districts. Then he looked further west, towards the Koreitem district.

Somewhere down there was the man at the centre of more than one target: Rafic Bahaa el deen al-Hariri. Rebuilder, saviour and Prime Minister of Lebanon. The man whom The Damascene's Syrian overlord had asked him to keep alive.

He threw back his head and laughed loudly.

In the name of everything he did not believe in, he had a job on his hands.

More than anyone knew.

One hour later, having showered, worked-out and showered again, The Damascene, naked and glistening with water (he preferred to dry naturally rather than to towel), lifted the holdall from the couch and put it on a nearby glass table. Inside the holdall were an assortment of clothes and various items which he might need during his assignment. He pulled out the clothes and threw them onto the couch. Then he pulled out something flat, square and metallic.

He looked at the item now in his hands: a Lebanese number plate, black numbers and lettering on a white background, with a white cedar tree on a blue background on the left. He had seen what he wanted on his way in, further back up in Jamhour, in the old repair shop near the Bejco dealership.

These false plates would fit perfectly.

29 September 2004
14 Sha'ban 1425

Koreitem, Beirut 08:00

It was known as Koreitem Palace, the term used in its colloquial sense, not regal. The man who had built it would never have regarded himself as royalty. He was Prime Minister. Lebanon did not have kings.

The mansion next to the Lebanese American University Campus in Tabbara Street was indeed palatial. It was not only the personal residence of Rafic Hariri and his family but it also served as his operational offices and housed his vast security team. It was set back behind the protective trio of high barbed-wire topped stone walls, canvas screens and hedges of dense pine trees. Security cameras, security men and security floodlights were everywhere, even in the streets outside. Men with sniffer dogs regularly patrolled the area.

The official offices of the Prime Minister of Lebanon are in the building known as the Grand Serail over on Serail Hill overlooking central Beirut, a few blocks from the Parliament Building on Nejmeh Square. Hariri had refurbished the sandstone building in Serail during his first term in office, adding the third floor to the original two and constructing luxurious and imposing offices.

Prime Minister Hariri would be at the Grand Serail during business hours, but billionaire entrepreneur Rafic Hariri operated out of Koreitem. He preferred, if he could, to keep the two elements of his life separate – but having been Prime

Minister for ten out of the last twelve years that was impossible.

Hariri's aide, Lieutenant Colonel Wissam al-Hassan, had wanted that morning's visitor to schedule an appointment at the Grand Serail, that's what other Members of Parliament (Deputies) did. But Walid Eido had played the friend card. He had already had to wait three days since the meeting at Baalbeck, and that was three days too long. Now he sat on the opposite side of the breakfast table at Koreitem, watching Rafic Hariri eat his usual morning repast of *labneh*, toast, tomatoes and cucumbers (Hariri was trying to lose weight and to watch his blood pressure – damn doctors). A coffee pot sat on the table between the two men.

"Are you sure you won't have some, my dear friend?" Hariri gestured to his own plate. "Can I not tempt you?"

"You are most gracious, Abu Bahaa, but thank you." Eido shook his head. "The coffee will suffice."

"What would we do without it?" The big man smiled. "Coffee makes the wheels of commerce and the wheels of power turn. Only money is better." He wiped his mouth and put his cloth napkin on the table, a sign that he had finished eating. He poured his own coffee and refilled his friend's cup. His lips pursed under his moustache. "So what was he thinking?"

Eido shrugged. "With Kanaan, who knows? Of himself, of his own interest, most certainly."

"But to take the four of you to Baalbeck was an act of outrageous intimidation. He threatened you. He threatened us all. And he wanted to decide whether I should live or die!" The smile in Hariri's eyes was interspersed with flashes of anger. "How dare he! Who does he think he is?"

"We know who he is."

Hariri stared at his friend. Then he sat back in his chair and said, more quietly, "Yes, we do."

"I think he wants to use you to get rid of Assad."

"And then what? Take over himself?"

"Possibly."

"Or perhaps I should take over. Wouldn't that be a turn-up! Lebanon consuming Syria! Greater Lebanon!" Hariri's voice lowered. "Perhaps then I could break Syria over Assad's head..."

Eido looked around the room, concerned. "Be careful, Abu Bahaa."

Hariri raised his thick eyebrows. "Do not worry, Abu Khaled. My security is impenetrable. They are not listening."

"Are you sure?"

For the briefest of milliseconds there was a flicker in Hariri's eyes before he said, "Yes."

Eido sipped his coffee. "Kanaan said he would kill all of us if we told you of the meeting."

"I will assign some of my men to you."

"No, no! Please. You are most gracious, but no. Just please make sure no one knows of this conversation."

Hariri frowned. "But why should he be so threatening? The decision is that I be allowed to live, thanks be to Allah. So what is the problem? I profess I do not understand. Perhaps I should ask him, bring this out in the open. Maybe we could work together against Assad - "

"Please, Abu Bahaa!"

Hariri saw the pleading in his old friend's eyes. "No, no, you are right. I have given you my promise of silence and silent I will be."

"Thank you. Please."

Hariri looked pensive. "But what is Kanaan up to?"

"He said that he would arrange for you to be under his protection."

Hariri's laugh was loud and bitter. "As a wolf protects the lambs! First they threaten me and my family. Now they want to protect me. Do the Syrians really know what they want?"

"As always, Liban is being used in their own internal power struggles. Do not trust Kanaan, Abu Bahaa. Not for one second.

He is plotting."

"Hmm..." Hariri picked up the coffee pot and looked from it to his cup. "In the name of the Prophet, peace be upon him, I am still hungry. These damn diets! Can I not tempt you to join me in a little *labneh*, my friend...? Or how about some *zaatar*...?"

Grand Serail, Beirut 11:30

The meeting in the Prime Minister's office at 11:30 that morning *had* been arranged through Lieutenant Colonel al-Hassan. It was a formal appointment, logged in the PM's diary, even though it was made in haste – and woe betide the visitor if he was late. Hariri was a stickler for punctuality. The meeting would last no longer than ten minutes.

In fact, the visitor had arrived early and for the last ten minutes had sat in the busy, bustling, noisy ante-room watching the phalanx of aides, assistants, secretaries and clerks go about their business. Busy, busy, busy, computers, telephones, faxes, personal callers. He was pleased his own office was less frenetic, he could not work in such a frantic atmosphere. Which probably explained why he was not Prime Minister, only head of a very small unit within the Department of General Security.

The appointment had been made through the offices of the General Director of General Security, Brigadier General Jamil Al Sayed. It was the Brigadier General who had ordered Maroun Khoury to report what he had discovered to the Prime Minister in person.

Khoury was slim and fit-looking for his age, mid-forties. He was bald on top, so he kept the hair at the sides and back cropped short, blending in with the trim, greying beard on his face. He wore a fawn suit and opened-necked white shirt, no tie.

At precisely 11:30, Lieutenant Colonel al-Hassan showed him into the Prime Minister's office, announced his name, and then left the room, closing the door firmly.

Rafic Hariri was looking out of one of the windows at the far side of the room, beyond his expansive desk. Khoury waited. He wondered whether to cough but then thought better of it.

After a few moments, Hariri turned. He was dressed in a grey suit, white shirt and colourful tie. It was Khoury's first meeting 'in the flesh' with the man dubbed Mister Lebanon, and he was impressed at his size. Not only his height and famed girth, but also by the size of his presence which filled the room without any words being spoken.

Hariri's frown gave way to a polite half smile as he acknowledged his visitor. "Mr Khoury."

"Prime Minister."

"Please." Hariri indicated an upright wooden chair in front of his desk. He did not offer his hand. "May I offer you some coffee?" He walked back over and sat behind the desk. "And perhaps something light to go with it?"

"*Merci.*" Khoury shook his head and noted that Hariri actually looked disappointed at his refusal.

"The Brigadier General sent you?"

"He has asked me to report to you personally, sir. Something my department has discovered."

"And what department is that exactly?"

Khoury leant forward, hands clasped together between his knees. "We could best be described as information gatherers."

"Is that not Internal Security? Captain Eid?"

"We are... external security."

"And I have never heard of you?"

"Few have."

Hariri sniffed. "Including, it seems, the Prime Minister."

"Sir."

"So, what information have you gathered that Jamil Al Sayed sends you over here?"

Khoury sat back. "We keep watchful eyes and watchful ears on areas outside Lebanon's borders. Something has come to our attention - "

"How?"

"Please."

"Okay, I will not ask."

"Something has come to our attention concerning your security."

"A threat? Tell me something I don't know. From our friends in the east or in the south?"

"The east. But not a threat exactly. In fact, quite the reverse."

Hariri frowned again, this time in amusement. "The reverse of a threat?" He shook his head. "Hariri is confused."

"No more confused or bewildered than we were, sir. Kanaan is involved - "

"Now why am I not surprised?"

"The information we have gathered is that Kanaan has sent his pet thug into Lebanon."

"His pet thug! Kanaan dares to send a pet thug after Hariri!"

"Well, no sir. That's the point. It seems he has been sent to protect you."

Inwardly, Hariri gave a nod of satisfaction. Walid Eido's information had been confirmed. Outwardly he was brash. "A thug to protect Hariri! I have the most sophisticated security team in the world, I am surrounded wherever I go, I travel in a convoy of six armour-plated vehicles - including an ambulance - with state of the art electronic jamming devices. And the Syrians dare to send one man to protect me!"

Khoury nodded in a show of sympathy. "How dare they indeed, sir. There is, however, another side to this situation. And that is why I am here, to apprise you of the whole position, so that you and your team are aware."

"What is it?"

"Is it Syria that is protecting you?" asked Khoury. "Or just Kanaan? Sending one man seems to indicate that Kanaan is acting alone. And we must ask ourselves this - "

"What?"

Khoury looked the Prime Minister in the eyes. "Who is it that he is protecting you from?"

South Beirut 11:40

At the exact moment that Maroun Khoury posed the question to the Prime Minister, the assassin known as Al-Rajul was in a very different part of the city from the plush, cosmopolitan downtown.

He was in the Hizbullah heartland of south Beirut. Here the city was palpably different. Restoration after 'the events' (the civil war) had not proceeded at the same pace as the rest of the city, and most buildings here carried the reminder of war, pockmarked with shell scars and myriad bullet holes. Some buildings still remained simply destroyed shells. He even saw a rusted old car still on its side as if it had taken root, in the same place as it was twenty years ago when people hid behind it from the sniper-fire. And died behind it.

The yellow and green Hizbullah flag was everywhere, in windows, draped between buildings, even painted onto walls, sometimes just abbreviated to the raised straight arm holding the machine gun. It was matched in quantity and locations by images of the Hizbullah leader, Sayyed Hassan Nasrallah.

Yet there was a sense of community about the area, a Shi'a people going about their business, confident in their leaders. Al-Rajul, who claimed to belong to no confession, was nodded at, even spoken to warmly, as he made his way along Annan Street.

Perhaps it was because of the white and black Palestinian *keffiyeh* he was wearing, a useful camouflage.

For he was heading into the Bourj el-Barajneh Palestinian refugee camp.

Antelias, north of Beirut 21:00

Frankly, Rafic Hariri had had enough for one day. Enough of Emile Lahoud, enough of Syria, enough of plots to kill him, enough of plots to save him, enough of running his beloved but constantly frustrating Lebanon – and enough of his damned diet. Tomorrow he had a meeting with President Jacques Chirac in Paris. Tonight he wanted to relax.

Late that evening, the Mercedes S-600 was seen driving quickly but stealthily out of the service entrance to the Koreitem Palace complex and turning into Madame Curie Street, heading west.

As always Hariri drove himself, but sitting next to him was his Head of Security Abu Tarek (Yehya al-Arab) and in the back were two more security men. The men were lucky. Tonight they would be dining with the Prime Minister.

Hariri did not like to dine alone. He usually ate with his family, or with friends, colleagues or allies, more often than not wheeling, dealing and sorting out problems. But today was different. He was drained and he was worried. He would not be his usual good company. He wanted to be alone, with just his trusted team around him.

Soon he was skirting St George's Bay and was on the coast road, the Debayeh Highway. Earlier an aide had telephoned 04 416 222 to make a reservation, and now Rafic Hariri was heading for one of his favourite places in Lebanon, if not the world.

The *Bourj al-Hamam* restaurant in Antelias.

The restaurant was busy but, as it was Wednesday, not over-crowded. Diners smiled when the big man who looked like the Prime Minister walked in with his three friends, and more than one client wondered to themselves if the likeness had ever been pointed out to the man. He had on an open-necked shirt, scruffy jacket and loafers, his hair was unkempt and he needed a shave, but smarten him up in a business suit and he could make a good living on the cabaret circuit as an impersonator of the PM.

One of the owners (a son of Fawzi, the founder), discreetly welcomed the party of four and guided them through the large main dining area, with its wood and cream-beige décor and the impressive back-lit faux-stained-glass windows with drawn scenes of old Lebanon (Hariri particularly liked the one of the ruins at Baalbeck with Mount Lebanon in the background). They were seated at a round table behind an ornate screen at the back of the restaurant.

Hariri did not need to see the menu. He ordered *kibbeh nayeh* (lamb kibbeh), *tabbouleh, hommous, plat légumes, makanek* (little sausages) and, to tease his guards, *cuisses de grenouilles* (frogs' legs). This would be followed by *farouj meshwi* (grilled chicken) with, of course, *frites,* and the meal would finish with fresh fruit. They would drink mineral water.

They chatted throughout the meal, the guards being respectful but not reverential. Sometimes laughter came from the table. They spoke of everything and anything – except Emile Lahoud, Syria, plots to kill, plots to save, the trials of running Lebanon.

And the big man's diet.

The person who had seen the Mercedes leave Koreitem Palace drew up outside the restaurant five minutes later. He had already watched the party enter from his position on the other side of the road, having followed the car from a safe distance all the way there. Now he parked the stolen Suzuki VL 1500 Intruder motorbike, studied the front of the restaurant for a moment, and then went inside. He had left it for the five minutes so as not to enter too close on Hariri's heels.

None of the other diners took any notice of the tall man in sandals, black slacks and loose white shirt, long hair tied in a loose ponytail so that his hair draped the sides of his face. He was greeted and shown to a small table set for two on the right near the front. He chose to sit facing inwards. The other place setting was removed and a menu was presented to him.

He ordered.

And waited.

Hariri and his team ate leisurely over the next two hours. But nature calls both the highest and lowliest of men, and as the fruit dessert was being eaten one of the men stood up.

The Damascene had wondered which one it would be. Had it been Hariri himself, it would have been the perfect introduction. But it was his Head of Security, Abu Tarek, who was the first to stand up behind the screen. No problem, that would do very nicely indeed.

Abu Tarek was a first class security chief, the best that money could buy (in this case, literally). But even he was unaware of the eyes watching him as he went round the back, or of the man who rose and followed him into the *toilette*.

Abu Tarek had cock in hand and was concentrating on his pissing when he heard the click of the main toilet door being locked behind him. He jerked his head to the right to see a tall man with long black hair standing with his back against the door, arms folded. Abu Tarek tried to do three things at once and succeeded in none of them: stop pissing on his shoes, put his cock away and reach for his gun in his shoulder holster.

"Careful, careful," The Damascene's hand was raised. "Don't panic, don't worry. Finish what you are doing."

Abu Tarek had popped himself back in without doing up his flies, and he had his hand inside his jacket.

"No need for your gun," continued the other man. "I just need to talk to you." The Damascene smiled as he pushed himself up from the door and walked towards the Herstal 9mm that was now pointing at him. "And no, this is not a *lootee* pick up. You are quite safe."

The gun did not move. Abu Tarek raised an eyebrow. Had he had his usual earpiece and throat-mike, his men would have been here already. But they had dressed casually for the evening which they had assessed as a low-risk situation. He had his cell phone in his breast pocket, one press on the hash key would send a signal –

Suddenly the gun was no longer in his hand. In a millisecond it had been taken, turned around and was now pointing at him.

The other man still smiled. "Now, do your flies up and you can have it back. A cold cock and a cocked gun is not a good combination."

For a moment Abu Tarek did not move. Then he reached down and zipped up his flies. He was surprised when the gun was held out to him, butt first. He nodded. He took the gun and held it loosely, pointing to the floor. "We have been expecting you."

"You have? Someone talked?"

"Of course."

"Despite the threats?"

"This is Lebanon."

"Of course." It was The Damascene's turn to nod. "We need to talk. I am sure you would not appreciate an approach through official channels."

"What makes you think I would appreciate any approach?"

"Hariri is in danger."

"Hariri has been in danger for the last fifteen years! Do you think we cannot cope?"

"Of course you can cope. The fact that Hariri is still alive proves you can cope, despite all the threats, despite all the attempts - "

"What attempts?"

"Oh come, come. Just because you deny them does not mean they never happened. Do you want me to list them? Shall I start with the most recent? That attack on the Italian embassy last week? It was nothing of the sort, was it? The target was Hariri."

"It was thwarted."

"Luck."

"Luck?" Abu Tarek's voice raised. "When you are protecting the Prime Minister of Lebanon, you do not rely on luck."

"Which is why you need me."

Abu Tarek shook his head. He turned and went over to the sinks, placing the gun on the unit top. He washed his hands, saying over his shoulder "Your arrogance is astounding. Rafic Hariri has the most skilled and sophisticated personal security team in the world. Kanaan sending his pet bitch to add to the protection is insulting."

"This time it is different."

"Different?" Abu Tarek dried his hands on a paper towel.

"This time the source of the threat is unusual and unknown."

"It is Syria. It always is Syria. It always will be Syria. You are murdering bastards." He threw the towel into a small bin on the floor and picked up his gun again.

"Not this time. And I am not Syrian."

Abu Tarek humphed in distain. "That is like saying that a dog does not assume the identity of its owner. Okay *chien*, your master is Syrian."

"And he is trying to protect *your* master. So perhaps that makes us both dogs."

The toilet door handle rattled as it was tried from outside. The Damascene thought it might be one of Abu Tarek's colleagues, but they would not leave Hariri's side – unless, of course, the big man wanted to piss. He was human, after all.

One more try of the door and then footsteps could be heard going away.

"Shoot me," said The Damascene suddenly.

Abu Tarek was taken aback. "What?"

"If I am a dog, shoot me, put me down." He held his arms away from his body, offering the target. Abu Tarek looked down at his gun on the unit top. He looked back up again to see the magazine of bullets being held in front of his face. He frowned – in frustration, annoyance, and admiration. Reluctantly he asked, "How on earth did you do that?"

"We need to talk."

Abu Tarek pursed his lips. Then he said "Maybe we do."

The handle rattled again and this time there was a knocking on the door. "Sir? Sir?" said a voice.

Abu Tarek coughed. "Yes, yes. In a moment."

"You are all right?" queried the voice.

"Of course I am. Can I not have a shit in peace!"

"Sir."

Abu Tarek looked at the other man as he reholstered his gun. "I am going to Faqra tomorrow evening. You know it?"

"Of course."

"Meet me there Friday. After sunrise prayer. You will be expected but no one will know your business."

"*Bien sûr.*" The Damascene unlocked the door. He turned the handle and pulled it open. "*Joumaa.* Oh, Abu Tarek Yahya?"

Abu Tarek turned as his bullet magazine was thrown towards him. He caught it in both hands.

"*Tusbih'ala al khayr.*"

Abu Tarek looked at the magazine in his hand. He nodded. "*Bon nuit.*"

From a safe distance outside, the Damascene watched as the Mercedes drove away. He was straddling the stolen Suzuki.

So, Abu Tarek regarded him as Kanaan's bitch, did he? Time was he would have killed over such an insult. But now he laughed. They had been in the right place for a male pissing contest!

But if they were using such metaphors, then Abu Tarek had made one mistake. Faqra was Hariri's mountain retreat, a good hour's drive from Beirut. They were to meet after sunrise prayer, which meant that The Damascene would have to travel there at night in darkness. And dogs and bitches didn't come out at night.

But wolves did.

He turned the key in the ignition and drove off.

30 September 2004
15 Sha'ban 1425

Bourj el-Barajneh, Beirut 20:00

It was Al-Rajul's second visit to the Palestinian refugee camp, and he knew he would never get used to the smell no matter how many times he visited.

It is not a 'camp' as most *anjabi* (foreigners) envisage, it is one square kilometre of basic brick constructions which pass as dwellings, packed so tight together that most paths between the buildings are less than half a metre wide (the one path in the whole of the camp that is nearly a metre wide is ironically called the Champs Elysees). There are no maps, no street signs. You have to know where you are going to find your way through the tight alleyways, over the broken water pipes, past the broken windows which might at any minute open into your face, through the sewage...

Posters or drawings of the smiling face of Yasser Arafat were everywhere, vying for space with posters of Fatah and Hamas.

The camp, and the others like it, was set up after *al-Naqba* – the catastrophe of 1948 when three hundred thousand Palestinians fled their homes in Palestine. It was built to deal with the 'temporary crisis' of the refugees. It was originally constructed to house ten thousand people, and the camp is forbidden to expand physically. By 2004, it was housing twenty thousand people in one square kilometre of hell.

And hell was the perfect recruiting ground for what Al-Rajul was planning.

1 October 2004
16 Sha'ban 1425

West Lebanon 05:30

The Damascene left well before dawn, driving down into Beirut, turning right at Hazmieh and soon reaching the coastal road. Traffic was lighter along the multi-lane highway at this hour than it was when he had followed Hariri to the restaurant two days before, but it was by no means sparse. There is always movement in Lebanon, people going places with things to do, either personally, professionally or politically.

This time he passed straight by Antelias and continued on to Nahr el Kalb (Dog River) where he took a right onto the main road which would eventually come out on the other side of Mount Lebanon at En Nabi Rchade on the western edge of the Bekaa Valley.

He turned off onto the secondary road at Faitroun and was grateful for the powerful motorbike between his legs. A normal car would have difficulty negotiating the climb into the mountains, he would have needed to have stolen a four-by-four.

It was getting light as he drove through Kfar Debiane, and by the time he reached Faqra the sun was shining into his eyes. Sunrise prayers would be well over.

Faqra, Lebanon 07:00

Hariri's eyrie was impressive, as The Damascene knew it would be. It sat at the top of the mountain, with the already snow-dusted ski slopes visible not too far away. It was a wide villa built of sand-coloured brick and stone, and with the ubiquitous orange tiled roof. It stretched over three stories, only two of which were visible from the rear as the building snuggled into the mountainside.

The Damascene turned off of the public road onto the much better private roadway leading upwards to the villa. He stopped at a metal barrier across the road and stared into the camera mounted on the barrier support. There were no buttons to push, no intercom to speak into.

Whoever was looking at him would have seen a swarthy man in jeans and black leather jacket with long dark hair tied simply at the back of his head. He wore no headgear, no crash helmet.

After ten seconds the barrier rose. He was expected.

He drove on, beginning to appreciate the size of the villa as he got nearer to it along the smooth, curving driveway quaintly populated at twenty-metre intervals by old-fashioned black urban streetlamps. The driveway stretched up the side of the villa through grassed lawns.

He pulled up in front of the small pine trees outside the covered main entranceway at the back. Because of its fit into the mountainside, it meant that the entrance to the building was on the middle floor. Several black important-yet-mysterious vehicles, mostly Mercedes, were parked nearby.

Two men came out of the villa. They were dressed in dark grey formal suits with white open-necked shirts – what passes for weekend casual in the world of security. Without saying a word, they gestured for The Damascene to raise his arms away from his body as he came towards them.

The body rub was professional. He was not carrying a gun (he would not have been so foolish – and it was not his preferred choice of weapon anyway) and his pockets revealed only money, a handkerchief and his apartment keys. They left the apartment keys in his pocket but took the motorbike keys out of his hand.

"*Yalla,*" said one, nodding for him to follow.

He was expertly sandwiched as they walked down a long corridor, one man slightly in front, one slightly behind, but with no body contact.

One or two people passed by, but they paid him no heed – they were used to visitors.

Up some opulently tiled stairs to the top floor of the building. They stopped outside a heavy wooden door and one of the men knocked. After a moment a voice from inside said, "*Shou?*"

The Damascene was motioned inside and the door was closed behind him.

Abu Tarek was standing with his back to a floor-to-ceiling window. Like the security men outside, he wore a suit and a white open-necked shirt. Behind him visibility was good, the Mediterranean a slash of blue in the distance beyond Jounieh.

"Ah, The Brigadier's henchman," he nodded. "The Interior Minister's envoy."

"Morning of light, Abu Tarek Yahya. And I think the expression you used two days ago was 'bitch'."

The Head of Security glared.

"Are we to continue our pissing contest?" asked The Damascene. "In which case, I will leave now. Or are we to talk like men? Your decision."

Abu Tarek stared for a few more seconds. Then, surprisingly, he smiled. "Of course. I apologise. You really must forgive me for the other day. I am not used to being accosted in the lavatory."

The Damascene bit off the witty retort that was on his lips.

"Please," continued Abu Tarek. "Sit down." He indicated a plush suite of furniture on one side of the room. There was a large coffee pot on a glass (possibly crystal) table, two bottles of Perrier, plates of figs and chocolates and a cigarette box.

The Damascene sat at one end of the large couch as Abu Tarek poured from the coffee pot. "You like Turkish?"

"Certainly."

"There is water also."

"No need."

Abu Tarek passed over a small, golden cup filled with the thick coffee. Taking his own, he sat at the other end of the couch. He took a sip and then said, "As you have probably seen on the news, the Prime Minister is in Paris. So, what do you think you can do that the entire security apparatus of the Prime Minister of Lebanon, both his official team and his private team, cannot?"

The Damascene also sipped from his cup. The coffee was exquisite. "There are two answers to that question. The first is: nothing."

Abu Tarek frowned and shook his head.

"You are right," continued The Damascene. "How many state security men does he have? Twenty? Thirty?"

"Forty."

"Plus his private team. So say fifty. And for the last fifteen years they have kept him safe. But think of the attempts there have been - " He raised the palm of his right hand as Abu Tarek opened his mouth to protest. "No, no, please. Do not treat me as a moron. We both know there have been many. You have foiled all of them. But his enemies have to get it right only once."

Abu Tarek's face was pensive. "Cigarette?" he asked.

"*Merci.*"

"A chocolate? Belgian."

"Perhaps. The second answer is: I can keep Hariri safe better than you can."

A laugh of scorn flew from Abu Tarek's lips along with his sip-full of coffee. "You *are* mad!" He leant forward, coughing. "I will have you thrown out."

"Why? That will look very good with your boss. Throwing out someone who only wants to protect his life."

Abu Tarek wiped his mouth on a handkerchief and straightened back up. "Your arrogance is astounding."

"I do not have arrogance," The Damascene's voice was low

and controlled. "I have experience."

Abu Tarek looked at him disdainfully, nostrils flared. "What are you saying?"

"How many assassins do you have on your staff?"

Abu Tarek frowned. "None of course."

"Exactly. Your men are highly trained, highly experienced *security* men. They think protection and prevention. They are defensive, reactive. They have never been in the mind of a killer. They have never had to arrange a death, an assassination."

"Your point is?"

"I have."

The Damascene stopped to let those simple two words sink in. He took a chocolate from the dish. A Belgian chocolate filled with Turkish delight – eaten in Lebanon. He smiled inwardly. International. Why not?

He looked back at Abu Tarek.

"Care to tell me who?" asked the security man.

"No, I would not. I am an assassin. I think like an assassin, not like a security operative. I have the mind of an assassin. My controller in Syria - "

"You are Kanaan's bitch."

"Please. That is not necessary. I work for the Brigadier, yes. He has information of a specific threat to the Prime Minister. As you know, the Brigadier and the Prime Minister are old - "

"Adversaries."

" – friends. Brigadier Kanaan is not without affection for the Prime Minister."

Abu Tarek raised his eyebrows sardonically. "And what is this specific threat? From whom?"

"That we do not know. The Syrian intelligence apparatus have eyes and ears everywhere. They have been listening and they have heard something. And this time it is not a group from the opposing confessions, or a collection of extremists or dissidents. This time it is believed to be one man. One man has been sent to assassinate the Prime Minister."

"And Kanaan has sent his – you – to prevent it?"

"Not quite. I am to keep the Prime Minister alive. A difference. I am not chasing an assassin."

Abu Tarek stood up, shaking his head. "I cannot believe this." He walked over to the window and stared out. "Syria. Syria! The one country that has made more threats to the Prime Minister than all his other enemies put together. Syria now wants to save his life?"

"It would seem so."

He looked out over the view west. "Does President Assad know?"

He turned when his question went unanswered. The man on the couch was staring at him. "I do not know. I simply do as instructed."

"Only obeying orders?"

"If you like."

Abu Tarek came back over and picked up the coffee pot, testing it for weight. He raised his eyebrows in a query and held the pot out.

"Yes," nodded The Damascene.

Abu Tarek poured and then refilled his own cup. "So, what can you offer?"

"I offer you me. An assassin with an assassin's mind. I will not interfere. Like a security programme on a computer, I will be working in the background. I will be the firewall. You will not see me. I need just one stream of information from you: I need to know the Prime Minister's plans and whereabouts at all times. Day and night. Any last minute changes must be notified to me immediately. And only you should know of my existence." He swilled back his coffee in one.

Abu Tarek thought. Then he said, "And how do I notify you of these things if I will not see you?"

The Damascene stood up and put his hand into an inside pocket of his leather jacket. Abu Tarek tensed. The hand came back out, seemingly with nothing.

The Damascene opened his palm to show a tiny, flat object no bigger than two centimetres by one. It was a mobile phone SIM card. He offered it to Abu Tarek. "No one has that number except you and me. The number you are to contact me on is already in there. Get yourself a phone to put it in and leave it on. If you wish to take advantage of my offer, I will expect to hear from you within forty-eight hours. That is the one and only voice call you will ever make on that number. After that you will communicate with me by text message only. Twice a day, at sunrise and sunset, you will send me a message with Hariri's activities for the next twelve hours. I will never reply to you."

Abu Tarek took the SIM card, looking at it as if it was a poison chalice. "How long for?"

"I understand the threat is present. I will contact you – not on the telephone – when it is time to stop."

"And what if we don't wish to take advantage of your offer?"

"I have a job to do," The Damascene flicked a piece of hair which had fallen in front of his face. For the briefest of seconds, Abu Tarek glimpsed the hole in the left side of his head. "With or without your help, Abu Tarek Yahya, I will do it."

"I don't even know your name," said Abu Tarek.

"That does not matter," said The Damascene. "I no longer have one."

As the Suzuki VL 1500 Intruder roared off back down the mountainside, Abu Tarek entered a room on the ground floor of the villa. It was a smaller room, designed as an intimate study.

"What do you think?" he asked as he closed the door behind him.

The face of Rafic Hariri looked up from the large monitor on the desk. He had been watching the meeting on a live video feed in Paris. Abu Tarek could see an empty coffee cup and the skeletal vine of a bunch of eaten grapes on the desk next to the Prime Minister. He wondered if he had breakfasted yet – it was 06:00 in Paris.

Hariri smoothed his right eyebrow pensively. "Interesting. The Syrians wish to protect me?"

"Kanaan wishes to protect you. There is a difference." Abu Tarek spoke lowly but distinctly so that the link would carry his words clearly.

"Indeed." Hariri smoothed his other eyebrow. "Hmm..." He sniffed, then said "Trust in Allah, Abu Tarek – but tie your camel! There is no danger in having extra insurance. Let us see what happens."

"Yes, sir." The Head of Security moved his hand towards the mouse.

"And Abu Tarek?" Hariri moved closer, which made his face fill the entire screen.

"Sir?"

"Keep him close," instructed Rafic Hariri. "Then closer still."

Beirut 09:05

The Damascene reached the north-eastern edge of Beirut just after 09:00 and turned left at the Saloume roundabout, heading south and east for the further twenty minute drive to his apartment.

At that exact moment Marwan Hamade, Lebanon's Economy Minister and a friend and ally of Rafic Hariri, left his apartment overlooking the seafront corniche and climbed into his black Mercedes for the short drive south to Parliament in Nejmeh Square. He was accompanied by his driver Oussama Abdel Samad and his police escort Sergeant Ghazi Bou Karoum.

One hundred metres down the road, a parked Mercedes exploded as Hamade's car passed[*].

---

* Due to driver Abdel Samad manoeuvring to avoid a speed bump, the blast hit the back of Hamade's car rather than the side. Sergeant Bou Karoum was killed and Abdel Samad was relatively unscathed. Marwan Hamade had all his ribs broken and one of his feet; his hands were burnt and he needed 450 stitches in his face and head.

Faqra, Lebanon 09:25

Up in Faqra, Abu Tarek was back on the webcam with Prime Minister Hariri immediately on hearing the news of the car bomb from security sources.

"Is he dead?" Hariri was grim-faced and looked ashen.

"We don't know," Abu Tarek was also solemn. "One person is dead, two are alive. We must pray to almighty Allah that he has been saved."

"Damn, damn, damn!" shouted Hariri. "This is it, you know. They've destroyed the new government. This is Lahoud's doing, I know it. Him and his allies."

"Be quiet, *zaim*, be quiet!" ordered Abu Tarek curtly. "These connections are not secure. You cannot say such things out loud, even on our own network."

Hariri sneered. "Damn each and every one of them."

Abu Tarek understood Hariri's anger. "You know we cannot accuse without proof. And that we will never have. Even now I am sure the streets are being cleaned, items taken away to be 'unfortunately lost' in official possession."

Hariri held his head with his right hand. "What am I to do? Why do the killings go on and on? It is like the events have never finished, except now only the generals are killed."

"I know, *zaim*, I know. Perhaps, dare I say, it might be prudent for you to remain away. Stay longer in Paris."

Hariri shook his head. "No. No, that I will not do. They will call me a coward. They will attempt to oust me from office while I am not there. I am meeting with Monsieur Chirac again in a few minutes to tell him what has happened. Then I will be on my way back. If they want Hariri out, they must do it in his presence."

"But you could be in danger."

"They dare not touch me!"

Abu Tarek did not let Hariri hear his sigh. He said, "Then we will take our usual precautions. You will travel nowhere except in the convoy. An immediate embargo will be placed on your calendar. Only you, me and al-Hassan will know exact details, Baba* to a lesser extent."

"Whatever," said Hariri. "As you wish."

"I will return to Koreitem immediately. We will issue a Press Release to say you are staying on in Paris and not announce your return until you are safely back in Koreitem. I will meet you at the airport later."

"*D'accord.*"

"And there is one other matter we now know the answer to."

"What is that?" Hariri popped a date into his mouth from an off-screen tray.

"What we spoke about earlier."

"*Naam.*"

"I will arrange it."

Mount Lebanon 09:40

The Damascene had just closed the front door of the apartment behind him when one of his two mobile phones rang, the Samsung D900 with the ringtone of the four-note opening of Shakira's *Suerte*. Only one person had this number. His brow creased in mild surprise at the speed of the response.

He put it to his ear as he went over to the window and looked out over Beirut. "*Oui?*"

"All right," said Abu Tarek. "We will accept your offer. What have we got to lose?"

---

* *Adnan Baba, Hariri's personal secretary for 28 years*

PART TWO
الجزء الثاني

CONSTRUCTION
البناء والتشييد

2 October 2004
17 Sha'ban 1425

Sin El Fil, Beirut 21:00

The Dubai Hall of the Metropolitan Palace Hotel, Habtoor's semi-circular five-star model of opulence and elegance, throbbed with the noise of the music, the cheering and the clapping. Especially the clapping.

The sixty or so guests stood either side of the dance floor clapping their hands in unison, like a modern version of a *sahjeh* dance. Some of the crowd whistled. In the centre of the floor Jacqui and Joe, the bride and groom, danced their first dance as a married couple. It was a slow love song but it was nearly drowned by the clapping.

After a minute they were joined by both sets of parents, dancing with their opposite partners. Then the clapping petered out as other couples began to wander onto the dance floor. Soon nearly everyone was dancing. The Dubai Hall was hot, heavy with the scent of food, tobacco and alcohol.

Suddenly the love song stopped and was instantly replaced by a pounding, thudding up-tempo number. The shouting and whistling started again as couples became individuals, dancing off on their own, each celebrating the wedding of this popular couple.

One man in particular was enjoying himself. He had long since removed his jacket and tie and had rolled up his shirt sleeves. Now he danced arms outstretched, stomping his feet, gyrating, occasionally dropping to his haunches and back up again (he would pay for that the next morning). He was happy to be at this gathering of family and friends, at the wedding of his brother-in-law.

But he was not as young as he was. After an admirable ten minutes of celebration he was relieved to see his wife Gisele beckoning from their table. She was standing next to Mama and one of the hotel staff. Gratefully, he made his way back through the dancing bodies.

"Jihad, look at the state of you!" scolded Mama as she looked at the saturated shirt clinging to his body. "You will kill yourself going on like that."

"Pah! How often do we have a wedding in the family?" he smiled at his mother-in-law. "I thought Joe would never get married. This is a great occasion." He looked at his wife. "And it will probably be years more before your sisters get married. We must enjoy these times when we have them." He grabbed a glass from the table and gulped down whatever it contained. Coke. "Mind you," he pulled out a chair, "I don't seem to be able to last as long as I used to," he exchanged a cheeky glance with his wife. "On the dance floor."

"Don't sit down, Jihad," Gisele touched his arm. "This gentleman has a message for you."

The smile dropped from Jihad's face and he groaned. No, not today. He looked at the smart, suited man.

"I am sorry to disturb you, sir, but there is a telephone call for you."

Jihad put his hands on his hips. He was not tall but he had stature, a presence. Many of his colleagues had come to fear that stance. "You are kidding me."

"Alas, no. The gentleman was most persistent. I explained that you were engaged, but he insisted. Short of hanging up on him there was nothing I could do but agree to inform you. Shall I tell him I have checked and that you are not available? He would not give his name."

There was no need for a name. Jihad knew who it was. That

was why he had left his mobile at home.

"*Merde alors*" he mumbled, then said "No, no. I'd best take it. Where's the phone?"

"In the manager's office, sir. If you would care to come with me?"

Mama was making grumbling noises about work. Jihad looked at Gisele apologetically. "I won't be long. You know how it is."

Gisele nodded. She had been in the same business herself, so she knew.

He nodded at the hotel man. "*Yalla.*"

They walked around the edge of the hall to avoid the dancers and left by the main door. Outside the drop in sound volume was so sudden he thought he had gone deaf, until he heard the wheels of the trolley.

The two metres high wedding cake was being pushed along the corridor towards the doors. There were fireworks on it which would be lit just before it entered the hall. The ceremonial cutting sword was on the trolley next to it.

Jihad stopped and put up his hand. "Can you wait?" he said to the three white-coated catering staff. "Just for two minutes. I will be back."

They collectively shrugged and nodded.

Nodding his thanks and looking like thunder, Captain Jihad Merhi of the Lebanese Internal Security Force continued on towards the manager's office.

Left alone in the small but well appointed office, Merhi snatched up the telephone and said without preamble "Can't I be left in peace just for one day?"

"Sorry boss, I thought you'd want to know." Sergeant Deeb el-Gharib was used to his boss's 'little ways'. He had learnt over the years simply to ignore the implied criticisms or reprimands and go straight to the point.

"What is it?"

"Lattouf called you."

For a moment Merhi was quiet. Then he said, "Shit."

"I thought you'd want to know straight away."

"How to ruin a good fucking wedding."

"Yes, boss. Sorry."

Merhi sighed. "No, no, Deeb, you did right." He half-sat on the edge of the manager's desk, wondering why his forty-five year old legs felt stiff. "Did he say what he wanted?"

"As usual, no. He wants to meet."

"Balls."

"Yes, boss. Tomorrow morning at eleven. Usual place."

Merhi rubbed his left knee as he spoke. "Tomorrow? Sunday? Christ, that means I'll miss mass again!"

"Then it's not all bad."

Merhi laughed. "Nothing a good penance won't sort out. Perhaps I should climb to the top of Harissa on my knees and kiss the Virgin's feet!"

"Even better, make Lattouf do it for you."

"Now there's an idea. But I think the gesture would be wasted on that fat Palestinian slob. Does he want me to call him?"

"I can do it."

"Okay, *merci*. Nothing else tonight, Deeb."

"I promise, boss. I had thought of leaving Lattouf but knowing how delicate these things are I thought you would want to know. I won't contact you again tonight, even if the earth opens up and swallows the whole of Mount Lebanon."

"Good. And not even then. I've got to get back, the cake is going in and the fireworks are about to go off."

Merhi put down the phone, not realising the prophetic accuracy of his last words.

3 October 2004
18 Sha'ban 1425

Verdun, Beirut 11:10

Merhi's description of Fadi Lattouf was two-thirds accurate at least. He was fat and he was Palestinian. Whether he was a slob was subjective. His wife would certainly agree that he was. His five children would say he was a cuddly Baba who always had time for them (when he was not asleep in his chair). His staff would not dare to comment publicly, although in private their opinions were split. Those miscreants he had locked up in his role as Captain of the Civil Police of the Palestinian Security Force in the Bourj el-Barajneh refugee camp would say, quite simply, that he was a bastard.

To Merhi's relief, his meetings with Lattouf were infrequent. Under laid down protocol, the Palestinian refugee camps in Lebanon are no-go areas for the Lebanese authorities. Lebanon is forbidden from interfering or intervening in the camps and from sending troops or other officials inside, including police. The camps have their own Palestinian police, colloquially called the Blue Police because of the colour of their uniforms.

Part of Jihad Merhi's duties was to be the liaison link between the Lebanese Internal Security Force and the Palestinian Police controlling the refugee camps in the Beirut area. His opposite number was Captain Fadi Lattouf.

They always met in the food court on the second floor of the Dunes Shopping Mall. It was one of the oldest shopping malls in Beirut, in the Verdun area over near the west coast and on the same block as the Holiday Inn Hotel. The location was Lattouf's choice: an easy drive from the Bourj in the south yet not too far out of his comfort zone for a quick return if necessary.

Naturally he did not wear his uniform when venturing north. This being a Sunday, to blend in with the other shoppers he was wearing rough blue denim jeans, for which he was about twenty years too old and fifty kilos too heavy, and a loose pink and blue checked shirt. But at two metres high and about the same around his waist, blend in was something Fadi Lattouf would never do, anywhere.

Merhi was ten minutes late (Sunday traffic up on Dunant Street), and Lattouf was already seated at a table in the food court, tray in front of him. The table looked like it had been hit by a litter bomb.

He saw Merhi coming towards him and raised his hand in greeting. "Morning of light, my dear Captain!" He half rose as they shook hands and then he gratefully plopped back down again, his backside consuming the chair beneath him.

"Morning of..." Merhi looked at the table. "A Big Mac and large fries, Fadi?"

The huge man looked bashful. "Well, you know how it is. A man gets hungry."

"Can I get you something else?"

"No, no."

"I'm having a coffee."

"Oh, well, in that case," Lattouf wiggled the cardboard cup which was dwarfed in his right hand. "*Merci ktir*. And perhaps a banana cupcake as well? Must have my fruit."

Merhi smiled and walked on. There was no queue at *Cup Cake* and he was back within minutes.

"Bless your hands," said Lattouf as the tray with two large coffees and three cupcakes (one banana, one chocolate, one carrot) was placed in front of him.

"The chocolate one's mine," said Merhi taking the cake and his coffee.

"Of course."

Merhi sat down. It must have been nearly a year since he had last seen the Palestinian and he looked bigger than ever. It was not helped by the fact that he was in those ridiculous clothes, and he was not wearing his captain's cap which he would do at formal meetings. He had a severe comb-over of the remaining strands of his black hair which served to emphasise rather than hide his bald dome. His beard was of the unshaven-look rather than the cultivated variety. There were flecks of grey – and flecks of Big Mac – in it.

"How is your dear Gisele?" Crumbs of banana cupcake were added to his beard as Lattouf spoke.

"Well, thank you. And Nada?"

Lattouf shrugged and nodded. "As ever."

"Number six not on the way yet?"

"Hah!" A large chunk of cake shot back out of Lattouf's mouth, landed with unerring accuracy in the half-used cartonette of tomato sauce, was retrieved and popped back in the mouth again. "I keep telling her that fertility is a blessing from Allah, but she is having none of it. She says five is enough. As far as she is concerned, in the bedroom we now have twelve months of Ramadan!"

Merhi could not help but smile. "Please wish Allah's blessings upon her." He tried to push thoughts of a naked and rampant Lattouf from his mind.

"Thank you. And blessings to Gisele too."

"Thank you."

There was a silence. Then Lattouf took a sip of coffee and said, "I have a body."

Merhi did not react. He broke his cupcake in half and then in half again and put a piece in his mouth. People died every day in the camps, of course, and it was an internal Palestinian job to bury or otherwise dispose of the bodies. The simple four-word sentence indicated something more, and he knew what it was. He blew on his coffee before tipping the cup to his lips.

"Or at least," continued Lattouf. "I have part of a body. The rodents have had the rest of it."

Merhi grimaced. Still he did not say anything.

Both men simultaneously swilled their coffees.

"Should I report it?" asked Lattouf.

"Does it need reporting?"

Lattouf shrugged.

"Male or female?" asked Merhi.

"We don't know."

"What?"

"The clothing of the young these days, even in the camps, they all dress the same!" Lattouf gave a false, almost nervous, half-laugh. "And most of it was ripped or removed."

"A sexual assault?"

"Who knows?"

Merhi was confused. "What do you mean? What are you saying?"

Lattouf gave a huge sigh. "We do not know if there was a sexual assault, we do not know for sure even what sex the body was, because... there is nothing there." He nodded downwards.

"It has been cut off? Defiled?"

"Eaten."

Merhi looked around the food court. It was beginning to fill up as it approached midday. He pushed his cake away. "That's the reason for the ripped and removed clothing. To hasten the feast. Somebody knew what he was doing."

"The entire epidermis has been gnawed. We do not know if there were any breasts, we do not know if there were any body hairs..."

"What about the head?"

"Destroyed. Caved in. Beaten to a pulp. We think that was the cause of death."

"You think? Time of death?"

Lattouf shrugged again. "Recently. There was no putrefaction. The rodents move fast but the maggots usually move faster. Within the last days."

"Could it have been an accident? A fall? Off of one of the buildings perhaps?"

Lattouf shook his head. "I do not know, my friend. I have seen such injuries before, thankfully infrequently. When I was stationed in Gaza. It has all the indications of death by trauma, by a blunt instrument to the head and face."

"With action taken to disguise, if not destroy, the identity of the victim."

Lattouf nodded.

"Anybody reported anyone missing?"

Lattouf looked almost aggrieved. "What do you think? This is the camp. Over-populated by one hundred per cent. Illegal by one hundred per cent. No one is going to report anyone missing, even to their own police force. In case of outside repercussions."

"Where is the body?"

"Somewhere cool. But not cool enough. It will be walking out by its own accord soon. Do you want to see it?"

Merhi looked at the Palestinian. "Why would I want to see it? It was obviously an accident. No need to report it to the ISF."

Lattouf nodded, grateful. "Good, I thought you would see it that way. I agree."

"Feel free to dispose of the remains."

"I will."

"Do you need any quicklime or acid?"

"No, we have our own."

"Okay then. Good."

"Just one thing, Abu Samer."

"What?"

Lattouf looked at the table. "If you are not going to eat your cupcake, may I have it?"

6 October 2004
21 Sha'ban 1425

Bourj el-Barajneh, Beirut 19:00

Al-Rajul entered the camp at dusk. On his previous visit he had worn the full white *dishdasha*, which had been a mistake. It had ended up covered in blood and gore. Thankfully he had worn his street clothes underneath, so after the elimination he had simply removed it and thrown it away in a doorway (one of the poor wretches of the camp might be grateful for it, if they could get the stains out).

Tonight he wore khaki cargo pants, a loose off-white collarless shirt and the white and black Palestinian *keffiyeh* loosely wrapped around the lower half of his face.

He knew his way around the first third of the camp now and he needed to familiarise himself with the rest of it before the recruiting exercise could begin. He had the luxury of time because his employer had specified the date on which the contract was to be effected; not a day before, not a day after.

The camp was only one square kilometre but it seemed as large and complex as a major city. Lack of street names did not help (lack of streets did not help), and there was no set pattern, no grid system, no logic. Many alleyways resulted in a dead end, some turned back on themselves and led you back out exactly where you came in, others went on for a long distance and then just seemed to peter out as if they had lost the will to live – like many of the inhabitants of this hell on earth.

And the smell. The word vile would not describe it. It clung to you, got inside you, became you. Or you became it.

What had the Palestinians done to deserve this? The answer was: nothing. And yet the people retained their dignity, retained their pride. They knew that history was timeless and that their troubles, although nearly sixty years old now, were but a speck in the timeline. And they also knew that, very soon in timeline terms, they would get back their homeland. Allah would not forsake them.

Al-Rajul had been angry about what had happened on his previous visit. But it had been necessary. What had to be done, had to be done. In his line of work you did not dwell on causes, circumstances and results. You simply learnt from them and moved on.

It had been later than this, it had been dark. Many people had been indoors, eating with their families, listening to battery-operated radios or trying to watch old televisions when the intermittent power supply would let them. But some people were still out and about, upon their own business.

He did not carry a torch, that would have marked him out. He used the diffused light from the buildings to see by, until the intervals when the power was cut. He worked out that the power failed every twenty minutes for at least five minutes a time, so when he knew a cut was coming he would pause in a quiet doorway or sheltered alley and close his eyes. This was a trick he had been taught many years ago, so his eyes were more accustomed to the dark when the darkness came.

It was just before one of the power cuts when he was leaning on a wall with his eyes closed, listening to the far-away voices in the dwellings, that he heard a voice closer to him say, "*Salaam.*"

He opened his eyes. On the other side of the alley stood a youth of about sixteen. Like Al-Rajul he was dressed in a loose *dishdasha*, but with nothing on his head. He had a large mop of curly dark hair and a smooth face which was smiling. His eyes seemed very dark.

Al-Rajul nodded.

"Can you understand what I am saying?" asked the youth. His voice was low and smooth.

"I speak farsi."

"Really? That is good. We can communicate better."

"What are you doing here? You are not Palestinian."

The smile grew in intensity. "I work here."

Al-Rajul said nothing.

"You had your eyes closed. Are you tired?" The youth took two slow steps across the alley. "Did you want to sleep?"

Al-Rajul could now see that the youth's eyes were smeared with mascara. "No."

"Did you want to sleep with me?" The full lips pouted.

"No."

"I am very good. Look what I have." The *dishdasha* was raised, rucking upwards like a curtain in a theatre. The youth's penis was flaccid, but even in this state it must have been about eighteen centimetres long.

"Go away."

"You do not like me?"

"I am not that way inclined."

"I can turn round for you." The eyes were wide, the lips slightly open as he took two more paces forward. "You might like it. You might like me. Am I not beautiful? And I bet you are beautiful too."

It was at that moment that fate decided that the youth would die. Had he left his action two seconds later, the power would have been cut and he would not have been able to see. He reached up and pulled the *keffiyeh* away from Al-Rajul's face. He smiled at the last thing he ever saw and said, "Yes, you are."

Then the lights went out.

Al-Rajul was a professional. And like others in his business, he would not return to a scene of a hit just to gawp or to check that the victim was either still there or had been discovered or removed – he left that suicidal idiocy to amateurs or fiction writers. But he needed to know the geography of the camp, therefore he started that evening from as close as possible to where his scouting had been brought to an abrupt halt the previous week.

People were still out, shops (what there were of them) were still open, youths still played soccer in the occasional open space. And Al-Rajul wasn't paid any attention whatsoever.

It took four hours of walking, backwards and forwards, up alleys and down alleys, along streets, through derelict spaces. At the end, he knew every decorative mural, every political wall-painting, every Palestinian flag hanging limply from a window or attached to a wall, and every copy of the exact same picture of President Yasser Arafat.

And he also now knew intimately the Bourj el-Barajneh refugee camp.

So the recruitment exercise could begin.

He reached Annan Street and headed north, back into Beirut.

10 October 2004
25 Sha'ban 1425

Mount Lebanon 16:00

For ten days it had worked well. A text message twice a day had advised The Damascene of the Prime Minister's movements, mostly trips between Koreitem and parliament (three different routes being taken to and from, with Abu Tarek deciding at the last moment which route to take, not even telling Hariri in advance) and one visit to Faqra.

The Damascene would risk assess the location and routes, and each time the Hariri convoy drove past, the Suzuki VL 1500 Intruder and its rider would be somewhere in the background, observing.

But already he was beginning to wonder whether this was a waste of time. The convoy was impressive. The lead vehicle was a Toyota Land Cruiser carrying members of the national Internal Security Force. Then came a Mercedes S-500 with four of Hariri's private bodyguards. This was followed by Hariri himself, driving his armour-plated Mercedes S-600, and then another S-500 carrying Abu Tarek and three others. More private security personnel were in the fifth vehicle, another S-500, and then came a black Chevrolet ambulance containing paramedics and state-of-the-art medical equipment.

They drove in strict formation. The fourth vehicle, the one containing Abu Tarek, drove slightly to the right behind Hariri's car. The fifth vehicle slightly to the left, so covering both flanks in case of an attack. The ambulance kept back from the rest of the convoy by about thirty metres, so that it would miss any direct attack and be ready to deal with any consequences.

The personal bodyguards carried Heckler and Koch MP5 machine pistols, the other personnel carried M-16 rifles.

The three S-500s contained electronic jammers powerful enough to stop remote signals being sent to any bombs or other devices within a half kilometre radius of the convoy.

So, wondered The Damascene, what was the point of him being wherever Hariri was? The convoy was attack-proof. It could not be bombed because of the high-powered (and ironically Israeli-made) jammers, and there were so many security people around Hariri that any other direct assault would be suicidal for the attacker.

The only way to get to him would be from long-range sniping or close-up, body-to-body knife, gun or suicide bomb. And nobody would be allowed to get that close. Unless, of course, Rafic Hariri decided to go on another of his incognito night time sojourns when his appetite got the better of his diet. But that was now unlikely. Two weeks ago, maybe. But now, with the extension of the mandate of President Lahoud and Hariri's power in parliament weakening by its isolation, the pressure was on. Hariri was too busy fighting for survival, for his plans for Lebanon, to go off on a jaunt.

So, by a process of elimination (The Damascene raised an eyebrow at his own words), the most successful way of killing Hariri would be by sniper fire – a most un-Middle Eastern way of doing things. But perhaps that was what was called for: the surprise element.

He would have to revise his way of working. There was no need for him to be there when the convoy drove past, that was far too late. He did not need to know routes, nothing was going to pass through the armour-plated Mercedes and its bullet-and-everything-else-proof windows. He needed to know departures and destinations. When Hariri would be out of the car.

He had seen Abu Tarek observe him in various places. Their

eyes had locked but there had been no amateurish nods of recognition. He would need to contact the security man to tell him that he needed to know Hariri's calendar earlier than twelve hours in advance. He would also want to know of any last-minute changes, although these were not as important as they may seem – they were a good deterrent against planned sniping. But he had to cover every contingency. He had to cover the eventualities that the security team could not, instead of duplicating their impressive efforts.

He had to think at a tangent. To think like the assassin he usually was. Quite simply, he had to wake up each morning, check the Prime Minister's calendar and think *How can I kill Rafic Hariri today?*

Koreitem, Beirut 21:00

Winter in Beirut is December and January, when the temperatures plunge into the teens Celsius and thunderous rain falls in enough quantities to make up for its absence the rest of the year. In October the evenings are still warm. Pedestrians can still venture out without coats. But The Damascene was on his motorbike, so he wore his black leather jacket and denim jeans.

Temperatures might hold off until winter overpowers them, but nightfall holds off for no one. It had already been dark for two hours when The Damascene set off down the main Damascus to Beirut road into the city. It was a Sunday night and the traffic was heavy, but that did not matter with a bike.

Beirut was unusual in that, at that time, there were hardly any traffic lights in the whole of the city. Power cuts were so frequent that it was considered far more dangerous to have lights that went off without notice than it was to leave the traffic to fend for itself. In certain parts of the city, at certain times, gridlock was commonplace. In a car he would have gotten nowhere.

The Koreitem district was much quieter than downtown in

the Nejmeh area. He passed Koreitem Palace and pulled up close to the mosque on Madame Curie Street.

The earlier text message from Abu Tarek had confirmed that Hariri was staying 'home' tonight. The Damascene was going to text Abu Tarek to demand an urgent meeting, so that he could explain his need for both more frequent and longer-term diary dates. Rather than give the Head of Security any pretext to delay, he would explain that he was outside and wanted to see him right now.

He turned and looked back at the palace as he took out the Samsung phone. The place was ablaze with floodlighting, as it always was at night, and there were two security men in the street with dogs. Inside there would be many more.

He was halfway through the text when he saw the main gate opening.

Two black 4x4s came through the gates, turned left onto Madame Curie Street, away from The Damascene, and then swiftly took a right into the back streets, heading south.

The Damascene's finger was poised above the keypad as he stared down the street. Had he just seen what he thought he had seen? Impossible, surely? But in his line of work he could trust no one - except himself. And he trusted what he had just seen.

Vehicles and visitors came and went at all hours at Koreitem Palace, that was the nature of it being not only a billionaire's residence but also the home of the Prime Minister. But there was only one person in the whole of the palace that would warrant a salute from one of the security men outside.

The Damascene turned around and roared the Suzuki back into life. He made a U-turn and sped off down the street in pursuit.

South Beirut 21:20 – 00:00

The two 4x4s were being driven determinedly but without excessive speed. It was easy to keep up with them, and to maintain a safe and inconspicuous distance.

The wind blew through The Damascene's long hair and made a hollow sound in the hole on the left side of his head.

As they headed further into south Beirut, banners and posters began to appear in the streets and on the houses. The green on yellow flag – the upstretched forearm with the hand holding the gun – and pictures of the bespectacled, bearded yet handsome face of Shi'a Cleric Sayyed Hassan Nasrallah, the Secretary-General of Hizbullah. Impressive and sending its message even in the shadowy illumination of the few street lights.

And The Damascene knew exactly where Rafic Hariri was going.

He found a discreet alley in which to park the Suzuki and took off his leather jacket and pulled his shirt out of his jeans. He had two days' rough stubble on his tanned face, which would help him blend in with the locals. His hair was longer than most, but that would not matter; he tied it back into the single ponytail.

To get too near the walled and gated compound would be foolish, it would be well-guarded and there would be security cameras around. But he needed to keep a watch on the place. He wandered the nearby streets, looking casual as if he knew the area well, but always with circumspect glances back towards the house. He found an old, run-down shisha café and ensconced himself inside with a Turkish coffee and a shisha of apple-flavoured tobacco. There were only two other locals inside, and after a few nods and muttered greetings they paid him no heed.

He could not see the compound directly from the café, but he could see the street and any vehicles that left through the gates.

After an hour he left the café to muttered wishes for a evening of peace, and wandered the streets in reverse formation to the way he had come, back to the bike. He put his leather jacket back on and, in case of any watchful eyes, spent twenty minutes crouched next to the bike pretending to inspect the wheels and engine.

After twenty-one minutes, he saw the gates to the compound opening and the two 4x4s drove swiftly out. A turn of the key and the Suzuki purred into life (the old repair shop up in Jamhour had done a good job). He moved off after them as it became Monday.

11 October 2004
26 Sha'ban 1425

Beirut 00:30

Why was Rafic Hariri, the Sunni Prime Minister of Lebanon, meeting with the leader of the Shi'a Hizbullah? A meeting so clandestine that the whole of Hariri's security apparatus had been stood down and replaced by two – what were they? Nissan Pathfinders? It hardly made sense. And who was the security in them? Hizbullah?

Secret meetings and changes of itinerary were anathema to an assassin. But had it not occurred to them that whilst Hariri was probably quite safe from personal threat, he could get mixed up in an attempt to take out the Israelis' number one target, Nasrallah? History would have a hard time explaining that one away.

But, reflected The Damascene as his hair blew backwards and the wind again echoed into the hole that had been his left ear, that was none of his business. What was his business was knowing Hariri's whereabouts at all times.

Abu Tarek had lied to him. Lying by omission. The text had said Hariri was home that evening. That much had been true, but it had said nothing about him going out again later.

Did the Hariri team want him to help? Or were they only co-operating to appease Ghazi Kanaan...?

The two 4x4s reached the Saeb Salam Avenue intersection, but instead of turning left onto the avenue towards Koreitem, they continued on into the centre of the city. The motorbike with dipped beam followed a quarter of a kilometre behind.

In the early hours of the morning, Beirut was now much quieter but by no means empty. They reached the intersection with General Fouad Chehab Avenue and continued on north, into the downtown area.

The two cars took a right into Emir Bechir Street and then they slowed almost to a crawl by the nearly completed Mohammed al-Amine Mosque on the south-west corner of Martyrs' Square.

The Damascene stopped outside St George's Maronite Cathedral further back and smiled. Hariri was financing the construction of the mosque. Had he made a detour to see how his project was coming along, how his money was being spent? If he had, he would be pleased. The mosque was magnificent.

After a few moments, the cars made a U-turn at the bottom of Martyrs' Square and came back down Emir Bechir Street, passing the motorcyclist on the other side of the road bending down looking at his engine.

The Damascene watched them go, on their way back to Koreitem.

Well, that had been an adventurous unplanned evening. There was an old expression: never let a day be wasted (for you never know when it will be your last). This had been a very productive day. He had found out that Rafic Hariri had a link with Sayyed Hassan Nasrallah and, perhaps more importantly for this assignment, he had learnt some of the geography of south Beirut. In his profession, knowledge of geography was paramount.

He climbed back onto the Suzuki and took the second right at Martyrs' Square into Damascus Street. It would be a direct ride back to the apartment. He had had enough for one evening, he told himself.

But in that he was wrong.

Mount Lebanon 01:30 – 08:30

The rough cinder track leading to his apartment block dipped deeply away from the Damascus road, so as he turned left onto it he was able to turn off the bike's engine so as not to wake his neighbours at this early hour. He cruised down and parked outside the front entrance. There was a parking area underneath the block but he always kept the bike outside in case he needed it quickly.

There had been no lights anywhere, in the buildings, in the street, for the last kilometre, so he knew they were having a power cut. That was why the modern apartment blocks had no elevators and were only three or so storeys high. And why they had no electronic entry systems – they relied on good old-fashioned keys.

He let himself into the block. It was pitch black inside. Using the light from one of his mobile phones, he walked silently up the stairs. There was not a sound in the building. The walls of each apartment had been built with brick and the front doors were of solid wood, so any nocturnal human noises were retained within.

He reached the top floor and turned his key in the lock. The door opened and closed soundlessly. He did not need the light from the mobile inside, night-time Beirut glistened beyond the full-length windows and cast a subtle penumbra in the apartment.

He walked over to the windows and opened them about twenty centimetres to let in some air. Then he pulled off his jacket and shirt and threw them on the leather couch, and undid the elastic band in his hair. Kicking off his trainers, he pulled down his jeans. He wore no underwear, no socks. He never had done. Not since Captain Marwan Mebarak had been stripped, tortured and murdered in Aanjar. He flicked the jeans onto the couch and enjoyed the feeling of being naked.

Cleanliness was important to him. He would shower before

he slept.

Stretching his arms in the air, he breathed in and then stopped abruptly.

Perhaps he wouldn't be showering or sleeping.

Slowly he lowered his arms as he sniffed again.

Jasmine.

This was unusual, but most welcome. He smiled, waiting for the gentle sound of the zills.

But it did not come. All was quiet, and he wondered if he had been mistaken. Wishful thinking maybe. Then he felt the gossamer touch of an angel's hand against his back and he knew he had not been wrong.

He did not turn, he did not move, except for the involuntary appearance of goose-bumps as the hand travelled slowly, softly down his spine. It reached the small of his back, made one circular motion so that the fingers were pointing downwards, and then continued on over the crest of his buttocks.

The thumb and index finger were on one cheek, the third and fourth fingers on the other. The middle finger followed the natural ravine, moving down.

A voice whispered, "Master."

He controlled his heavy breathing. "That should be my job. My Djinn."

He reached round and gently took hold of her hand as he turned. She was wearing nothing except the small veil on her face and an ornate black clip in her hair. As always, he could smell her musk.

The eyes above the veil spoke without words. He reached down and took the veil in his big right hand. He thought of slipping it up and over her head and down her long black hair, but lust was not that subtle. He yanked the veil downwards and off.

She gave a little gasp. For a moment they both stood there in the shadows without moving, each completely naked. Her body matched The Damascene's for lack of hair. Then she raised the hand that had been caressing him to her lips and stared at him challengingly as she put the middle finger into her mouth.

"That," he said, "is rude."

She pouted and her low voice asked, "Do you want to be rude with me, Master?"

She got her answer over the next two hours.

He awoke at eight in the morning to sunshine and a breeze coming in through the open bedroom window. His hand moved across the wide bed, across the crumpled and in some places still damp sheet - but of course she was not there.

Like most men, he always slept well after sex. When he was with her, even more so. A smile creased his face as he thought of what they had done a few hours previously. How many ways were there to make love? And what she had done with, and into, the hole of his left ear was frankly obscene.

The answer to how had she gotten into the apartment was easy. This was a *mukhabarat* safe-house. Kanaan had obviously given her a key. But how she had arrived and left again was less evident. She might have parked in the area underneath the block. Or maybe she had a bike like him?

Whatever. Once again, The Damascene was grateful for the interlude. He needed it. In fact, he realised with just a slight feeling of surprise, he needed *her*. Which was interesting. That was almost an emotion. Only the living had emotions – and he was a dead man.

He got out of bed and went over to the open window. The breeze blew against his body, cooling. Now he would have that shower.

He scratched his left shoulder.

And once again he had been bitten by a mosquito when her scent was on him. Obviously he wasn't the only one who liked The Djinn!

Twenty minutes later, showered and drying naturally, wet hair falling down either side of his face, he walked naked out onto the balcony. Her odour had been washed away so the bugs would no longer be interested in him.

In his hand he carried the Samsung mobile. He switched it on and looked out over Beirut as he waited to connect to the service. The sun had just come over the top of the block, illuminating the panorama in front of him. It was another fine Mediterranean day. He could hear the children in the apartment next door but because of the design of the balconies he could not see them and, importantly, they could not see him.

It was a Monday, the start of a new business week. And the start of a new political week. He could guess what Hariri's itinerary would be today.

He had decided not to berate Abu Tarek about the lack of information. If they did not wish to tell him things and Hariri died as a result – well, that was up to them. But, as he had reasoned before, Hariri was perfectly safe on impromptu movements, unless he became collateral damage in other events – in which case there was nothing The Damascene could do about it anyway. It was the norm they had to worry about, the predictable, publicised known itinerary, not the unnorm.

The mobile throbbed in his hand. The expected text message, sent an hour earlier.

KOREITEM. SERAIL. PARLIAMENT. SERAIL. KOREITEM.

The exact routes would not be known until Abu Tarek made the last-minute decision. Hariri was safe.

For today.

Ras en Nabaa, Beirut 09:00

Captain Maroun Khoury of the Department of General Security did not wear a uniform. Indeed, he had never been issued with one. He would never appear in public, never need to make a show of his authority, either internally or externally. People in his line of work never did. In fact their existence was not even admitted.

And he did not like the designation of rank either. He was a team leader, the emphasis being on Team. His team were information gatherers and listeners, operating mostly outside Lebanon's borders. Anything and everything. Just in case. Protecting Lebanon from all threats.

He now sat with one of his Gatherers, Zahia Zalloum – colloquially known as ZiZi – a dark-haired Lebanese in her late twenties, one of the most trusted field agents of the DGS. For the fifth time they listened to the voice captured on the memory stick.

It was a man's voice, low, anxious but not distressed. "Get away. Get away from me, you bastard. Leave me alone. I'm not that way. Don't touch that - " There was a gap of twenty seconds during which the breathing became heavy as if some sort of physical exhaustion had occurred. Then it calmed and the voice said normally, "I didn't want that to happen. That was your fault. Look at my clothes! Well, to hell with you, the rats can have you."

Khoury looked up from the computer. "That is all?"

"That is all," nodded Zahia. "It doesn't last long, as you know."

"No... What do you think?"

Zahia shrugged. "The rats can have you? A sewer? Somebody pushed into a sewer?"

"Maybe. Nothing else? Nobody turned up in a sewer?"

"Not that we've heard."

Khoury stroked his beard. "No bodies turned up anywhere?"

"None that we know of. Could be early days though."

"Could be." Khoury was pensive. Then he said, "Okay. Let's monitor. Eyes and ears, ZiZi."

She nodded, smiling. "Eyes and ears, Chief."

16 October 2004
2 Ramadan 1425

Bourj el-Barajneh, Beirut 16:30 – 22:30

Al-Rajul had been watching for five days. Already he had chosen three young men in their late teens or early twenties. He needed two more.

He saw the next candidate kicking an old, semi-deflated football against a wall in the north-east of the camp. A typical dark-haired, olive-skinned young man with a wispy beard, dressed in jeans and a two-seasons-out-of-date Manchester United shirt. He had the agility of the young and his stamina was impressive: it was Ramadan, the sun had been up for many hours and the young man would not have had anything to eat or drink, including water, in that time. Yet his prowess with the ball was remarkable: he was on his twenty-eighth keepy-uppy and did not look like flagging.

Al-Rajul stepped casually out of the alleyway from where he had been watching. Today his head and face were uncovered, the Palestinian *keffiyeh* tied around his neck like a scarf and falling over his chest in front of his shirt. He walked as if he was going somewhere, nodding to the youth as he passed *"Ramadan Mubarak."*

"Ramadan Mubarak," mumbled the youth. Thirty-two, thirty-three.

Al-Rajul stopped as if he had just thought of something and turned back with a smile. "You are very good."

The youth concealed his irritation as he stopped at thirty-six, capturing the ball under his right foot. "Thank you, *ustaz*."

Al-Rajul held in his laugh. Did he look that old? "Maybe you will play for Palestine one day, huh? In the World Cup."

The youth's snort was derisive but not impolite. "*Insha'Allah*."

"You must have had a good *Sahur*, to still have the energy to do that."

"I find it easy."

"Or do you cheat?"

"At football?"

"At fasting."

The youth frowned. "I am a good Muslim."

"Here," Al-Rajul rummaged in a back pocket of his cargo pants and pulled out a small, flat flask. He held it out. "Water. Even the Prophet, peace be upon him, would not mind if it meant Palestine winning the *Mondial!*"

"No, *ustaz*, no." The youth looked genuinely shocked as he shook his head.

"No?" Al-Rajul put the flask back. "Good. That is very good. How old are you?"

"What?"

"How old are you?"

"Nineteen."

"Nineteen. That is a good age. You live here?"

"Would I be here otherwise?"

Al-Rajul nodded. "A very good point. You have family?"

The youth bent down and picked up the old football. "Why all these questions?"

"I am sorry. Please excuse me." Al-Rajul turned and began to walk away.

"No, no. It is I who should be sorry. Please excuse my rudeness, *ustaz*."

Al-Rajul stopped again and turned back.

"I live with my mother and my sister," said the youth. "And two uncles."

"Your father?

"No. He is dead."

"I am sorry."

The youth shrugged.

Al-Rajul looked from side to side and then stepped nearer to the youth, close enough to smell his Ramadan breath. He spoke quietly. "I am on a mission. From Abu Ammar." He flicked his scarf. "You know him."

"*Meen*? No."

"Oh you do. He is your President."

The youth's eyebrows rose and frowned at the same time.

"Are you *Fatah*?" Al-Rajul looked from side to side again. "*Hamas*?"

Another shrug. "*Fatah*, I suppose."

"Good, good." Al-Rajul coughed and pulled away from the youth as two older men walked by. When they were out of earshot, he continued. "The President has asked me to recruit trustworthy *Fatah* men for a special mission."

"What is it?"

"I cannot tell you more at this time. The President has many reserves at his disposal to reward those he chooses. Should he chose you, I can guarantee that you, your mother and sister will be removed from this place."

"To where? Where is there to go?"

"Wherever you want to. Back to Palestine? It is only a matter of time now before the Zionists are routed. Or anywhere. Jordan, Syria, UAE? It will be your choice."

"And my uncles?"

"Of course."

The youth bounced the ball once off the ground. "What do I have to do?"

"Not here. Not now. Can you meet me tonight?"

"Maybe."

"After *Iftar*. Make an excuse to leave your family. Do not tell them or anyone of this conversation. Meet me at Annan Street at ten o'clock. Can you do that?"

From one of the dwellings, a baby began to cry.

"Can I not tell my mother?" asked the youth.

"Not at this time. But you will be the hero of the family on the day you tell them that you, and you alone, have managed to get them out of this place. That is your reward if the President chooses you. Can you meet me?"

"Yes."

"*Shoo 'es-mak?*"

"Mohammed."

"Same as me! We are both worthy of our name. Tonight. Annan Street. At ten. *Yaatik al-aafieh.*" Al-Rajul turned and walked away, disappearing into the alleys. After a moment he heard the ball bouncing again in the distance.

He turned down a passage where the tangle of electricity wires between the buildings was hanging so low that he had to duck his head. He trod in something wet on the ground, grateful that he wore trainers not sandals.

The test had been set. Would the youth pass it? The other three he had already chosen had. A simple test of trustworthiness.

He passed by an elaborate mural and nodded in gratitude at the image of Abu Ammar: Mohammed Abdel Rahman Abdel Raouf Arafat al-Qudwa al-Husseini, popularly known as Yasser Arafat. The President of the Palestinian National Authority.

And bait for the youth.

Mohammed was unaware of the man tailing him.

He lived only three alleyways and two open sewers from where he had been playing with the ball. It was getting dark when he reached home. Conveniently for Al-Rajul the rooms Mohammed inhabited with his family were on the ground floor of a three-storey block.

Al-Rajul watched him enter through an old, broken wooden doorway. There was a window to the alley and Al-Rajul moved over to it like a wraith. He could hear women's voices talking to Mohammed. No other men. He moved away from the window and into the shadows.

Minutes later, as a call to *Maghrib* prayer came from somewhere distant, two men in their late thirties came along from the opposite direction, talking animatedly. They went in through the broken door. Uncles.

Al-Rajul glided back over to the open window and stayed there for twenty minutes.

The talk was inconsequential. If Mohammed was going to say anything, he would probably have blurted it out straightaway. At one point one of the uncles, to the derision of his brother, was announcing his ideas for a new commercial venture which would get the family at least into better accommodation, if not out of the camp altogether. The conversation became quite heated. An ideal moment for Mohammed to speak up about the *ustaz* who had approached him that afternoon, who had offered the whole family a way out of here. But he did not. He was a good boy.

The smells of cooking (not all of them pleasant) reminded Al-Rajul that he was hungry. He looked at his watch. Over three hours before his meeting with the youth.

He would not eat in the camp. He would go back out to Beirut, there were plenty of places there. He might even indulge in a shisha.

He pushed away from the wall, melted into shadow and silently disappeared.

Al-Rajul had been watching the Annan Street entrance to the camp since 21:30. It was a busy area and he could loiter unnoticed. He would have liked to have worn the *keffiyeh* on his head, but he needed to look exactly as he did this afternoon so that Mohammed would recognise him. Nevertheless, the Palestinians coming and going naturally thought he was one of their own. Except for the occasional greeting, he was left alone.

He saw Mohammed coming along at 21:55. Good, he was keen.

Because of the volume of other people, he did not notice for several seconds that Mohammed had someone with him.

"*Merhaba, ustaz,*" greeted Mohammed. Al-Rajul smiled as they shook hands, his eyes pointedly travelling to the other person, a youth similar to Mohammed but plumper. "I hope you do not mind," said Mohammed in explanation. "This is my friend Chadi. I thought he might be able to help the President also."

Al-Rajul shook the outstretched hand. "*Al-salaam 'aalaykum.*"

"*'aalaykum al-salaam, ustaz,*" Chadi was respectful but perhaps just a little nervous.

"Mohammed has told you of our mission?"

"To help the President, yes."

"Good, let us walk."

The two youths came forward.

"No, no," Al-Rajul gestured behind them. "Back into the camp. It is quieter there. We can find somewhere to talk. Come. You like football, Chadi...?"

As they walked, Al-Rajul moved his *keffiyeh* up over his head and threw the end across the lower half of his face, across his shoulder.

They walked for five minutes. The lanes narrowed so that they could walk only two abreast, and Al-Rajul let them go in front of him.

Tonight it was dark in the camp, even without a power cut, but the residual light from the buildings and the growing moon gave them enough light to see by, providing they watched where they were walking.

They were chatting about the merits of the Reds versus the Blues (Chadi confessed to being a Chelsea supporter), when Al-Rajul gestured to a lane to the right. "Down here. I know it is a quiet place."

They walked down, avoiding a dripping waste outlet which

was perilously close to a frayed electricity cable. "Mohammed has explained the rewards, Chadi?"

"Oh yes, *ustaz*," said Chadi over his shoulder "I would do anything to help my mother and father get out of here. And to help the President, of course."

"The President is looking for good men." Al-Rajul put his hand into his right pants pocket, caressing the small wooden object he always carried with him. It was a Holding Cross, a ten centimetre long piece of solid olive wood carved into the shape of a cross with the cross beam uneven to fit comfortably between a person's fingers. He had bought it a while ago now, in Beit Sahour, near Bethlehem in Palestine. "Men like you. To be chosen, a man has to be strong, courageous and trustworthy." He brought the cross out of his pocket, enveloped in the palm of his hand. "Which is, of course Mohammed, where you have failed."

He twitched his right hand so that the down beam of the cross flicked upwards from its place in his palm to poke out between his first and middle finger, the cross beam held within his fist. He rammed it across and to his left, hitting Mohammed in his head above and behind his right ear. The young man's skull broke on impact.

Chadi was aware only of the sound of a crack followed by his friend falling against the wall, as if he had tripped on an uneven piece of earth. Then his own throat was seized so that he could not cry out and the last thing he saw was the hand with the bulbous, rigid sixth finger hurtling towards his left eyebrow.

Chadi's skull fractured with the first blow, but Al-Rajul kept hitting him as he caught the body, dull thuds of splintering bone. By the time he had lowered the body to the ground, with a bizarre gentleness, Chadi's skull was gaping open and pink matter was flowing out like lava from a volcano and dropping onto the dry, dusty ground. His eyes were open and staring, his tongue hanging out.

Al-Rajul went over to Mohammed and felt for a pulse. He

still had one, weak, but he was too far gone even to groan in pain. Al-Rajul thought of hitting him again but decided not to. The cosmetics would take care of him.

He stood up, looked about and listened. No change in the background sounds, faraway voices from the dwellings, the occasional shout, the intermittent static from a radio, the baby howling. There had been no noise during the killings, just the sound of fast-moving scuffling.

Chadi's gore was on Al-Rajul's shirt and pants. The pants he would have to live with, but the shirt might attract attention. It would be a snug fit, but he would take Mohammed's shirt. The youth would not be needing it now. Or ever again.

At that moment, the lights from the buildings went out. Power cut. Perfect timing.

Al-Rajul knelt down and began the cosmetics.

20 October 2004
6 Ramadan 1425

Mount Lebanon 08:00

The Damascene stood on the balcony, strong coffee in his right hand, Samsung mobile in his left. The text was as expected.

KOREITEM. SERAIL. KOREITEM.

It was 08:00. Already Hariri's security team and their dogs would have made the first sweep of the day, both inside and outside Koreitem Palace, looking for explosives or anything untoward. All the vehicles would have been searched and scanned with an explosives detector.

The six-vehicle convoy would leave for the Prime Minister's offices at the Grand Serail at 09:00. As always, Hariri would be driving himself in the armour-plated Mercedes S-600, the third car.

A similar sweep would have been made at the Grand Serail, and Hariri would not alight from his car until he was inside the complex in a secure area.

No one in this life was ever completely safe, but that was as safe as it got. There was no room for snipers.

Today The Damascene would continue with a little experiment had had been trying recently: attempting to guess which of the three routes from Koreitem to Downtown the convoy would take: the coastal route, the central route or the southern route. He had been unsuccessful so far, one correct guess out of five, just a normal average.

Abu Tarek would normally announce the route just as they were leaving. True randomness was the highest security. But if there was a pattern, even just a subconscious one, then that was a weakness.

The Damascene would study and analyse the frequency, patterns and timings of the routes chosen.

Because if he could work out a pattern, so could an assassin.

Central Beirut 09:20

That morning they took the southern route, through Sanayeh and turning left at Zoqaq el Blat. The Damascene had not expected it because it was the third time in succession that they had gone that way. Although that was good and would fool someone with ill-intent today, they needed to be careful. Too much use of one choice meant that it was unlikely to be used next time, which narrowed the guess down from three to two – or improved an assassin's choice from one in three to fifty-fifty.

But that was still too much choice for a lone sniper. Unless...

The Damascene pulled the Suzuki over to the side of the road in Syria Street, outside the Grand Theatre and looked back at the rebuilt centre of Beirut.

Unless there was a team.

Three routes. Three choices. Three strategically placed snipers.

He shook his head. No. That would still mean Hariri getting out of his car at some point along the route and within range of a sniper. That was something that just would not happen.

But then he had thought that Hariri having clandestine meetings with Sayyed Hassan Nasrallah was something that just would not happen.

It was a possibility to note, but not a concern.

A team would have to work some other way.

Mount Lebanon 18:00

In the perversely ironic way that fate operates, The Damascene was one of the last to find out about the momentous events of that day. He lunched in *l'Entrecôte* in Achrafieh, had other things to do, and then returned to the apartment in the early evening. He stripped and showered, grabbed a bottle of *Sohat* mineral water from the fridge, and then stood naked in front of the television, drying.

It was on every channel.

Rafic Hariri had resigned as Prime Minister of Lebanon.

His letter of resignation had been delivered to President Lahoud and Speaker Nabih Berri early that afternoon. Former Prime Minister Omar Karami had been asked to head a new government until the elections scheduled for mid-2005.

The Damascene did not care about politics. Any interest he had had in affairs of state had died when Captain Marwan Mebarak had been murdered. As he looked at the reports on the screen, he wondered how this affected his assignment – or if he now had an assignment at all.

Hariri was no longer Prime Minister, so the threat to his person would diminish accordingly. He was remaining as a Member of Parliament, and he would still be a thorn in the side of his opponents and his enemies, but the act of resigning had immediately downgraded his security risk from Code Black to Code Yellow.

Would there still be a threat to him?

Would he still require enhanced protection?

Those questions actually did not matter. The only question that needed answering was: was Hariri alive still of any use to Ghazi Kanaan?

He would telephone Kanaan, he had a direct line number to his office in Damascus. He would use the alternative mobile, the Motorola, but he would not call from the apartment. Calls made to the Syrian Interior Ministry were bound to be monitored, if not by the Lebanese then certainly by some other alien power, and he could be triangulated and located within just a few minutes. Not that he had done anything wrong, for the sake of Allah – he was helping to protect the Prime Minister (make that ex-Prime Minister). But he did not want any interest taken in him – and a call from the edges of Beirut to the Interior Minister's office in Damascus would at least spark curiosity.

He would travel further up the mountain, to Bhamdoun, about twenty minutes away. He might even take in a meal at the *Janna* restaurant with its magnificent views over the St Martin Valley. He would be on his own but he was sure a table for one would not be a problem.

Just for a moment he thought of The Djinn and what it would be like to have dinner with her, to get to know her – as a person, rather than his sexual reward – but then he dismissed such ideas. She might be a person. He was not. He was a dead man.

He dressed in a loose white shirt over beige cargo pants, let his still-damp hair hang loose and went out.

Maybe his thoughts were still on The Djinn, that was why he missed it. Or if it did register, maybe his subconscious dismissed it as just another resident of the building, which indeed it was.

As The Damascene walked quickly down the stairs, the front door to the apartment directly under his opened, just a crack. Just enough for somebody to look out at the man going down the stairs.

Then it closed again.

Bhamdoun, Lebanon 21:00

He telephoned from the lobby of the Sheraton Hotel. He was in the seating area near Reception, and looked no different from the others going about their business. Opposite him, a Jordanian had a laptop open on the coffee table.

It was unlikely that Kanaan would be in his office at 21:00, but this was a dedicated number and he was sure there would be a message for him.

It was answered on the sixth ring, a man's voice with a simple "'eeh?"

The Damascene identified himself by the name he was known as. He asked no other question.

After two beats, the voice said "You will be contacted" and the line went blank.

The Damascene closed his phone, stood up and left the hotel.

21 October 2004
7 Ramadan 1425

Mount Lebanon 00:30 – 15:00

He arrived back after midnight. The block was in darkness. He did not turn on the stairwell lights, preferring to use the light from his mobile phone.

The local cuisine at *Janna* had been superb and afterwards he had treated himself to a shisha while he watched the belly dancers and listened to the live music.

He had been told on the phone that he would be contacted. On his way back down the Damascus road he allowed himself to wonder if it would be his usual contact – The Djinn. Was the non-tactile entertainment in the restaurant the only form of belly dancing he would be experiencing tonight?

Immediately he opened his front door, he knew the answer. Tonight there was no subtle scent of jasmine, the apartment was awaft with the heady, full-on aroma of frankincense. Candles had been placed around the room, the walls seeming to move with the flickering. Background music was playing a distinct *raqs sharqi* beat.

She was standing in the middle of the floor, looking at him challengingly, defiantly. There was nothing on her head save for the ornate black hair clip. Her face was bare. A small, tasselled bra top covered her breasts. Below her navel was a golden, coined belt on top of black, diaphanous harem pants. Her feet were bare. In her hands she held a metre length of rope with a knot at each end.

Out through the windows, Beirut twinkled behind her.

The Damascene leant with his back against the front door, watching as her hips picked up the beat. The *raqs sharqi* dance was more defined than the *raqs baladi* country dance, and with each hip thrust she walked a step towards him. She played with the rope, first down her back, then between her breasts. Her eyes held his as she moved the rope down between her legs.

Then her hips began to shimmy then circle with the music. She came close to him. Reaching up, she placed the end of the rope that had been between her legs over his right shoulder.

She pushed his hair back and put her right hand over the hole that was his left ear, caressing it gently with her thumb.

The Damascene smiled. "Well, well. I did wonder."

She was pressed close against his body, her thighs astride his right knee. She moved against his leg. "You wondered what, Master?" Her right hand went around the back of his head and brought round the end of the rope.

"Whether it would be you that contacted me."

Her cardamom-scented breath was warm in his nostrils. "You want contact with me, Master?"

"Oh yes."

She pulled sharply on the rope, forcing his face down onto hers, tongues meeting, their lust irresistible.

The first time finished when he erupted inside her while she was bent forwards over the back of the leather couch. The second time was on the stairs. Only the third time was in the bedroom.

He awoke to light streaming in through the bedroom window, his body still sticky with the sweats of night time. His mouth and chin were crusty.

As always, she was not there. Pushing himself up onto his elbows, he looked at the bedside cabinet. The clock said 07:45. Had she left a message for him from Kanaan? A note?

There was nothing there.

Getting up, he stretched and ran his hands down his body, stopping at his balls to tug them comfortable. Walking over to the bedroom window, he stood with his hands on his butt, looking out over Beirut. Yet another sunny day. He scratched a mosquito bite on his left cheek, grateful that he usually slept on his front – otherwise the bite would have been too close for comfort!

Then he heard a sound.

Just one, a sharp *tink*.

He turned and ran silently over to the half-open bedroom door, pressing himself against the wall.

The sound came again. Another *tink*.

Silently he stepped out onto the landing and looked over.

Then he grinned. A moment later he was walking down the stairs, still completely nude.

He realised that he had never seen her in the daylight before, she had always come to him at night. She was in the kitchen preparing coffee – and she looked even more beautiful. She was wearing a white T-shirt with the English word PRINCESS in pink on the front. The shirt did not quite cover the cheeks of her bottom. Her long glossy black hair was bunched at the back and held by the black hair clip. Her face still bore the traces of last night's make-up.

"*Sabah el-khair,*" he said warmly as he walked across the room.

Her gaze first went to his groin, then up the scarred, hairless body to his face. "*Bonjour,*" she smiled.

"*Kifik?*"

"I am well, thank you. *Kifak?*"

"*Mnih.*"

He stood in front of her, and for a moment it was as if neither of them knew what to do. Then they both laughed.

"I have never seen you - " he began.

"With my clothes on?"

"In the morning. Or in daylight for that matter."

"I hope I do not disappoint you."

"Far from it."

"You want a message from me. I could not give it to you while you were asleep or... otherwise engaged. I have always been taught never to speak with my mouth full."

He nodded and just resisted the urge to lean forward and thwack her bottom.

Slowly she pressed the plunger on the cafetière, making even that act seem very sensual. He felt himself give a little reaction and, remembering his nakedness, hastily asked, "What is the message? Does he want me to carry on?"

"Yes. You are to carry on. Until you are told otherwise."

"I see. That is from Kanaan himself?"

"Who else?"

She began to pour the coffee into two mugs.

"And you?" he asked.

"Me?" She stared at him and shrugged, smiling cheekily. "My orders are the same as yours. To carry on with my mission."

He took a mug. "Good."

"So," she said, stretching out a hand and grabbing hold of his far from flaccid component. "Before I continue with my mission, can I ask you a question?"

"Of course." He felt the warm sensation as she started to rub him.

"Do you have *any* food in this place or just the packet of coffee?"

He received a text message at 08:00, while they were making love. He ignored it until he had finished at 08:05 and then studied the phone without speaking, just giving a little nod.

She left at 08:30. Her 'street clothes' were the PRINCESS T-shirt, tight blue denim jeans and black leather ankle boots. Her dancing clothes were in a brown Louis Vuitton bag which she carried on her shoulder. Her hair was down, with the clip at a jaunty angle on the right of her head. Had The Damascene been capable of expressing any feelings, he would have said she looked charming. And sexy. He thought these things, but he could not express them.

As she was leaving, he asked "Will I see you again?"

She stopped by the front door, which he was holding open. Because of her small frame, the Louis Vuitton bag looked enormous on her shoulder. "Is your mission completed?"

"No. You know I have been told to carry on."

"Well then," she said. "As I told you, I will carry on too. *A bientôt, chéri.*"

And with that she left. A little part of him, deep down inside, wanted to follow her, to see where she went, but he knew better. Those were the actions of a lovesick fool. She might even come from base in Syria, it was only an hour away by bike, which was what he suspected she used. He had to remind himself that she was the gift of the Brigadier, nothing more than Kanaan's whore. She would perform her duties whether she liked him or loathed him. Feelings were unnecessary and pointless.

He showered, dried naked on the balcony for ten minutes and then dressed, packing the things he needed for the day into his cargo pants pockets.

He went out at 09:30.

At midday, a white Opel car turned off the Damascus road and crunched down the slope, coming to a halt in front of the apartment block. The man who got out was on the tall side, slim but obviously fit, with short-cropped dark hair and the obligatory stubble. He was dressed in a black leather jacket, light shirt, light cotton trousers and sandals - the standard Syrian *mukhabarat* outfit.

He stood by the car and looked up at the building before going over to the front door. It was so quiet around here. Someone had chosen the safe house well.

The front door of the building would not open at his tug. There were six buttons on the wall in the same pattern as the apartments they serviced, with name plates next to them. Top left was 'Ibrahim', underneath that 'Ghorra', with 'Abu Jouade' on the ground floor. The three plates on the right were blank.

He pressed the top right button.

Nothing happened. He noticed that there was no remote entry system, no intercom, so the residents would have to come downstairs to let people in.

He gave it another minute and one more bell press.

Nothing.

Okay, he would wait. He was in no hurry. He leaned against the side of the car - not knowing that from above he was being watched...

Fifteen minutes later, the front door opened outwards and a boy about seven years old, dressed in the completely red kit of Liverpool Football Club, came out and walked over towards a cream Ford Galaxy parked nearby.

The man caught the front door before it closed but then had to step back as an attractive tall blonde woman and twin girls of about five came through. He did not respond to the woman's nod of thanks, he just let them pass and then went inside.

Upstairs, the door to the top right apartment was of course closed. But to this one he had a key. He would berate the idiots at base for not giving him one to the block as well.

He knocked on the door.

No answer.

He took the key from his pocket and slipped it into the lock. The door opened soundlessly. Leaving the door ajar, he went inside. He stood looking about the place. This was impressive. There was money somewhere in this business.

He noticed two unwashed mugs on the kitchen draining board next to a third-full cafetière. The jug was cold to his touch. Pity, he could do with a coffee after the journey he had

had. Was there a microwave? Where was the kettle? He might be in for a long wait.

He emptied the contents of the cafetière into the sink, turned on the tap and then frowned as the dregs had difficulty going down.

He was swirling them around with the index finger of his right hand when he felt a sharp prick like a wasp sting on the back of his neck.

"Shit!" He jumped and his left hand went upwards to his neck. There was nothing there, no sting had been left behind. "In the name of Allah!" he mumbled.

Out of the corner of his eye he saw something and turned. His hand was still holding his neck. He frowned and then smiled at the person standing there. "I'm sorry," he said. "Please excuse my language. Damn wasp!" He gave an apologetic laugh.

"Who are you?" asked the other person.

"Excuse me. I'm sorry. Yes, my name is Aboud," he rubbed his neck and took his hand down. "I am a friend of..." He gave the name The Damascene was known by.

"He has no friends."

"Well, actually, I'm a colleague – my goodness, what a view!" Aboud nodded towards the window.

The other person did not turn. "He has no colleagues."

"Well, we're in the same line of business - "

"You are an assassin?"

"No. Well - "

"You don't even know him, do you?"

"Of course I do."

"And you broke into his apartment?"

"I have a key. I need to see him."

"Why?"

"Why? Well..." Aboud frowned. Suddenly he did not feel well at all. His head was heavy. The room was moving like a wave. Was he having a stroke? "I... I..." Why did he need to see him? He couldn't remember...

He put his hand back up to his neck and rubbed it. "I'm not... Could you help me? I don't feel..." The room was now roaring in his ears, but it was going grey, fading...

The other person did not move.

Aboud staggered forward as his sight left him. Now the roaring seemed faraway.

As his legs buckled and his senses died, the last thing he was aware of was a smell.

Jasmine.

Sixty minutes later an old white Transit van pulled up downstairs and three men got out. From the back of the van they pulled three large suitcases.

The front door of the apartment building was on the latch and they went inside.

Ninety minutes later they came back out again with the suitcases which, by the way they were carrying them, seemed decidedly heavier than when they had gone in.

The front door clicked shut behind them.

They loaded the suitcases into the back of the van and drove off.

22 October 2004
17 Ramadan 1425

Ras en Nabaa, Beirut 08:30

Maroun Khoury and Zahia Zalloum sat together in front of the computer in Khoury's office in the DGS building, an unnecessary closeness as they were not looking at anything, just listening to the memory stick, but they had a history which both of them remembered with fondness. Their knees were touching but they pretended not to notice.

It was the same voice as before on the memory stick: male, but this time quite calm, conversational. "I need to trust. If I cannot trust them then they are no good to me."

Another voice asked, "Can you trust them?"

"Not the last one. The first three are good but the last one was bad."

"So what did you do?"

"They cannot linger."

"They?"

"He brought a friend. They both had to be disappeared."

Silence. Khoury asked, "Is that it?"

Zahia nodded. "Yes."

Khoury sat back, the action taking his knee away from hers, which he regretted. "Still no bodies?"

"We haven't heard of any."

"But potentially there are three."

"If we're interpreting it right."

Khoury nodded. "Okay. You are right to let me hear these,

something is going on. Put a marker up with The Listeners just in case they hear anything that could be connected."

She stood up. "Eyes and ears, Chief."

Khoury gave a small laugh. "Eyes and ears, ZiZi."

As he watched her walk from the room it wasn't only her eyes and ears he was thinking of.

30 October 2004
16 Ramadan 1425

Bourj el-Barajneh, Beirut 13:00

Captain Fadi Lattouf of the Palestinian Security Force was in his blue police uniform, epauletted shirt open at the neck. His grey-black bush of chest hair poked upwards out of the shirt and joined the not so bushy neck hairs of his beard. He did not wear his Captain's hat when he was on business about the camp, too showy, too much of a target, too bloody hot. So his comb-over was stuck to his head with sweat.

He was sweating not through heat but because it was Ramadan. He had not had a thing to eat or drink since *Sahur* and would not do so until *Iftar* – unless his will, resolve and religious conviction wavered, as it often did in mid-afternoon. And the smell of raw meat in this butcher's shop made him want to retch.

He nodded in appreciation of the wrapped and bloody package that had been given to him as he entered. Nada would get two good meals out of it for the family.

Normally he would be accompanied by a sergeant when he ventured out into the camp, but when he had been told of the report that had been received he had decided that he needed to handle this personally, and alone.

"Where are they?" he asked.

Karim The Butcher nodded to his left. "Out the back."

"Show me." Lattouf put his package on the counter and followed.

Karim spoke as he led the way. "I thought somebody had left me a delivery, I couldn't tell at first."

"So they appeared today?"

"I don't know. I don't really use the back. My deliveries when I get them come through the front. And I am closed a lot during the Holy Month."

"So when was the last time you were out the back, before today?"

Karim shrugged. "Don't know. Ten days, maybe two weeks."

A small, dark corridor led to a back door padlocked on the inside. As soon as Karim removed the lock and opened the door, the stench hit Lattouf with such force that he staggered backwards. Quickly he put his right hand over his nose and mouth. "My God!"

Outside was a small yard only about ten metres square. Cables of various thicknesses hung between the surrounding buildings and liquid dripped from more than one cracked pipe. A small passageway hardly the width of a man (and certainly smaller than the width of Fadi Lattouf) led off from the right into another warren. There were a lot of flies.

On the ground to the left of the door was an object about the size of a large goat. A muslin sheet was draped over it, the sheet covered in pink, red, maroon and brown splotches which Lattouf realised must be old and new bloodstains.

"Did you cover it?" he mumbled from between his fingers.

"I thought it best," admitted Karim.

With an inward groan at his aching knees, Lattouf crouched down on his haunches.

"Okay..." he said quietly. This he did not want to do. He swapped his hands so that his left covered his nose and mouth. Reaching out with his right hand, his fingers touched the cloth. He baulked and withdrew his hand and then brought it forward again.

With a snap of his wrist he pulled off the cloth and threw it aside.

In the name of Allah the most merciful!

Lattouf fell backwards onto his arse, his booted heels kicking the ground, instinctively trying to move himself away. He could not believe what he was seeing.

There were indeed two of them, entwined like spoons – probably for ease of carrying. Their clothes were bloodied, ripped and gnawed. Some skin was left, but not all of it. One of them at least was male, a small half-eaten penis was poking out of what had once been the poor soul's undergarments.

And they had no faces, no front of skulls. Their heads looked like the husks of opened coconuts, crawling with maggots. They had probably been bloody, pulpy messes at one time, but the rodents must have thought *Eid* had come early. But at least the hair was partly intact, the shortness of it on each skull confirming that the other victim was probably male also.

And there was something else. Lodged between the two heads, slightly flattened. Lattouf leant his head forward without moving his body – yes, it was an eye. A solitary eye.

His hand covering his face had instinctively moved down and backwards as Lattouf had fallen. Now the stench entered him unhindered, up his nose, down his throat, into his very soul. He could taste rotting human.

Shakily, he stood up. He was a professional policeman, an investigator, a keeper of the peace. He knew that crime scenes should not be contaminated, even in the squalor of the Bourj el-Barajneh Palestinian Refugee Camp. But sometimes it just could not be helped.

He leant forward, both hands against the wall above him, and with an almighty roar vomited with the force of an elephant pissing after a night on the beer. Not once, not twice, but three times, the last one being just a dry retch. His spew splashed over his shoes and across the lower legs of his trousers.

He remained in that position for a minute, getting back his breath. Then he straightened, little flecks of vomit in his beard. He glared at Karim as if he was the murderer. "Inside."

They went in.

"Lock the door."

Karim did as ordered.

"In the name of Allah, the smell!" Lattouf muttered as they went back into the main room of the shop. Several flies had taken the opportunity to come in with them.

"In my trade you get used to it, Captain," said Karim.

"I'm talking about in here. Do you ever clean this place out?"

"I - "

"No, I am sorry, Karim," Lattouf held up an apologetic hand. "That was uncalled for. It's the shock. Just the shock." He supported himself against the counter. "You do not go back out there, you understand?"

"Yes, Captain."

"And say nothing to anybody. Have you spoken to anyone already?"

"No, Captain, I just waited here as I was told, after I went to the police. The shop has not been open."

"Good. And you did not touch the bodies?" Bizarre thoughts of Karim making pies flashed through his mind.

"I only covered them."

"Good. Some of my men will come by later. Let them do what they have to do. They will tell you when you can go back outside."

"What do I do until then?"

"You wait. Skin a sheep or something." He thought that that might not have been the most appropriate thing to say. "Don't let me down, Karim."

"I won't, Captain."

Lattouf turned to leave.

"Captain?"

Lattouf stopped in the doorway and looked back. Karim had his package in his hand. "Your meat."

Hesitantly Lattouf took it. "Thank you. Peace be upon you."

"And you, Captain."

Some hope, thought Lattouf as he made his way back out onto the Champs Elysée. His stomach was empty and he was ravenous. And he needed water, litres of it and quickly. He would have to break his fast. He would increase his *fitra* at *Eid* in recompense.

There was an *hadith* he had heard many years ago:

When Ramadan arrives,
Heaven's gates are opened,
hell's gates are closed,
and the demons are chained up.

So what had gone wrong in Ramadan 1425? Hell's gates were open and the demons were loose. What he had seen with the previous body and now these two was inhuman. Not of man.

Only, of course, it was.

What was going on?

Looking back to make sure he could not been seen from Karim's shop, for he did not want to cause offence, he drew his right arm back and threw his parcel of meat far into a dingy alley.

He was hungry, but perhaps the Lattouf family would become vegetarians for a while.

1 November 2004
18 Ramadan 1425

Jonblat, Beirut 09:30

Captain Jihad Merhi of the Lebanese Internal Security Force was reaching out for his cup of coffee when the telephone on his desk rang. With irritation he changed the trajectory of his hand.

He could do without interruptions. He was halfway through a report on the resurgence of the al-Murabitoun faction in Akkar in the north, a reappearance probably prompted by the shameful treatment of their fellow-Sunni Rafic Hariri whose act of resignation was a thrown-down gauntlet to his political enemies. Also three other thick files had appeared on his desk over the weekend, each of them demanding his immediate attention.

"Yes?"

"I've got Captain Lattouf of the PSF on the line, sir," said Sergeant Deeb el-Gharib from out in the General Office. "Asking for you."

Shit.

"Did he say what he wanted?"

"No, sir."

"Okay." There was a pause, a click, then Merhi said "Merhi."

"Morning of joy, dear Captain."

Merhi sighed inwardly. "Morning of light, my friend."

"How are you?"

"Busy." Hint. "But well. And you?"

"Allah still takes care of me. But I am troubled."

"You wish to meet?"

"That would be nice."

"Where and when?"

"Um, er... Tomorrow at sixteen hundred?" Lattouf was speaking loudly, distinctly, slowly, for the audience he knew was listening. "You chose the place."

Merhi nodded. That was good, Fadi. The Listeners would know he should be fasting, so it would be suspicious to name a restaurant. He had left it up to him. He thought for a moment. "Tomorrow I have to be in Saifi. Debbas Square, you know it?"

"I can find it."

"I'll see you then."

"Debbas Square at sixteen hundred. I'll be there. *Bukra*."

"*A demain*."

Merhi put down the phone, stood up and stretched. He came out from behind his desk and walked over to the window, looking out onto Bank of Lebanon Street.

Not all official telephones in Lebanon were monitored or bugged, but it was safe to assume that the important ones were. A Captain of the Internal Security Force was important enough to be on the radar of The Listeners, especially when he was talking to his Palestinian counterpart.

Their meeting would always be one day and two hours earlier than they agreed. So sixteen hundred tomorrow meant fourteen hundred today. It did not matter what location was named, they would always meet at the food court in the Dunes Shopping Mall.

Merhi stared down at the busy street below, wondering what the Palestinian wanted now. It had only been a month since their last meeting. Usually they might see each other maybe once or twice a year. He hoped Fadi wasn't going to invite him and Gisele to the Lattouf family's *Eid* celebrations, like he had done before. It was very kind of him, but for a Maronite Christian it was, well, uncomfortable.

But Lattouf had said he was troubled, so it must mean

something had happened or was happening. Something that would need resolving, but without official Lebanese involvement. The camps were Palestinian territory.

He really didn't need this, he had enough on his plate already.

Merhi went back to his desk and re-found his place in the al-Murabitoun report. Would the Sunnis really cause unrest because Hariri had resigned?

He continued reading for a few minutes and then stretched out his hand and picked up his coffee.

It was stone cold.

Verdun, Beirut 14:00

The food court on the second floor of the Dunes Shopping Centre was less busy because it was Ramadan and because it was Monday, but the outlets were still open. The huge fat man had a quarter of the seating area to himself, dwarfing the table and chairs like an adult in a school first grade classroom – and dwarfing the small cup of coffee and solitary cup cake in front of him.

Walking towards him, Merhi could tell immediately that there was something wrong. Lattouf looked distinctly uncomfortable, almost nervous. He was dressed in the same ridiculous jeans and shirt as he had been the last time they met. Merhi was in his uniform shirt and pants, no jacket, the insignia on his shoulders ensuring that he would be given a wide berth wherever he went in the mall.

Lattouf stood up as he saw the Lebanese approaching. "Captain."

"Fadi." No traditional greeting from the Palestinian. No morning of light or evening of peace? They shook hands.

"Thank you for seeing me." Lattouf's grip was clammy.

Merhi pulled out a chair and sat down. "Are you okay, Fadi? You don't look well."

Lattouf looked around. "I hope I am not seen."

Merhi shrugged. "Who would see you? I'm going to get a coffee, do you want another? A cake?" He looked down at the uneaten cup cake on the table and then the penny dropped. "Ah."

"It is Ramadan," explained Lattouf. "I should not be..." He nodded at the coffee and cake. "That's why I hope I'm not seen."

Merhi had never realised that he was so devout. "Okay, I won't tempt you." He stood up.

"But..." Lattouf grabbed his forearm. "I want to. I have not eaten since *Sahur*." Suddenly all resolve, as well as the tension, left him. "I will have a large coffee and another cup cake – make it fruit. *Shukran*."

The old familiar Fadi Lattouf was sitting there when Merhi returned with the coffees and a box of six cakes. He noticed that there was no trace of the original cake on the table, not a crumb. Or its case? "Assorted," he said as he sat down. "Help yourself, I only want one."

"Bless your hands."

Merhi let him devour two cakes – which took no time at all – before he asked, "You wanted to see me?"

Half of the third cake was in Lattouf's mouth. He nodded as he chewed and swallowed. Half the large cup of coffee was slurped down, even though it was scalding. He stifled a burp.

"My *fitra* will be a month's wages at this rate," he said, referring to the charitable donation given at the end of Ramadan to feed the poor.

"Which makes those very expensive cup cakes," commented Merhi. "What's up?"

Lattouf put down his polystyrene cup. He rubbed his right hand over his mouth and down his beard. "We have two more bodies."

"What? You are kidding me."

"I wish I was, my friend."

"Same as before?"

"Yes. Found together. Both male. Faces gone, probably done by the perpetrator. Brains gone – probably the rats. Or the maggots."

Merhi looked down at his one cake. "Same MO, same perp?"

"Must be."

"Enquiries?"

"All day yesterday. Nobody saw anything, nobody heard anything. No one reported missing – as yet. But you will understand that in the camp we cannot do house-to-house. We don't even know how many people live there."

"Too many."

"There you are right."

Merhi pushed his cake over to the Palestinian. "So what's going on?"

"I don't know. Two male adults, probably young but we cannot be sure. Plus the previous one, maybe male but we cannot be sure."

"Some sort of feud? Inter-gang rivalry?"

"Quite possibly. Except for one thing."

"The manner of death."

"Yes. It is unusual, no? The gangs, they stab, they shoot, they might even beat. But not like this. The victims must be dead long before he has finished with them. It is like he doesn't know when to stop. Or doesn't want to stop." The case was taken off the cake and thrown over his shoulder. The cake went the way of its brothers.

"You want to report it to me?" asked Merhi.

Lattouf shook his head and swallowed. "No, no. They were accidents."

"Of course they were."

"Already, we have disposed of them."

"Still okay for the quicklime?"

"Yes, thank you. This time they were disposed of *in situ*. It was an interesting place they were found. Plenty of drains."

Merhi did not want to know. He stood up. "Thank you for the information, Fadi."

Lattouf stood up to shake hands. "I will stay just for a moment. It would be a sin to waste that last cake."

"Of course. *A bientôt, mon ami.*"

"Peace be upon you, Abu Samer."

Merhi walked away, noticing the look of animal lust that Lattouf was giving to the *McDonald's* outlet.

He stepped onto the down escalator. He did not need this, not at this time. Lebanon was in a state of upheaval, with the resigned Prime Minister, the political uncertainty and next year's elections. He had much more important things to concern him than the Palestinians. But he was duty-bound to record and report this – *if* Lattouf had reported it to him, which thankfully he had not. Yet.

Hopefully this was the end of it. Just some inter-gang rivalry or vendetta within the camp, which would not spill out onto the streets of Beirut. Deaths of a people who were already nobody. Because if it was not internecine killing, there was only one realistic alternative.

He reached the bottom of the escalator and stepped off.

Was there a serial killer at work in the Bourj el-Barajneh Palestinian Refugee Camp?

6 November 2004
23 Ramadan 1425

Bourj el-Barajneh, Beirut 20:00

Laylat al-Qadr. The holiest night of the holiest month. The night during which God first began revealing the Qu'ran to the Prophet Mohammed through the angel Jibril.

One of God's mysteries is that no one knows exactly which night it is. It is believed to have occurred on one of the last odd-numbered nights of Ramadan. Sunni and Shi'a views differ on the range of dates, but there is one date which both denominations agree is a strong possibility: 23 Ramadan.

Al-Rajul had no faith but he was prepared to use others' beliefs to his own benefit. For *Laylat al-Qadr* is the Night of Power or Night of Destiny.

For the five young men he had chosen, it would be just that.

None of them were friends, he had made sure of that. For friendship between the young bred bravado, rivalry, cockiness and showmanship – four natures that were not required on what they had been told was a mission for their President. Each of them had passed the trustworthy test, unlike Mohammed and the unfortunate Chadi.

Al-Rajul sat in the grey Mitsubishi Express van just off Annan Street. The van was old and battered and fitted in with the area perfectly. No one would pay it any heed, nor notice the newer-looking number plates. Al-Rajul was wearing the Palestinian *keffiyeh*, thrown across the lower half of his face.

People would think he was obviously a local. No one would pay him any heed just sitting there in the van – but if they did, one look from the hard, cold eyes would ensure they went on their way quickly.

He had a clear view of the entrance to the refugee camp. Night had fallen, *iftars* were well under way, some had even finished. He looked at his watch on his right wrist. He had told them to come to the camp entrance at ten minute intervals, where he would be waiting for them. Tonight they would be meeting each other for the first time, although they did not know it yet. Each one thought he was the sole selection for the mission for the President.

Which in a way he was.

The first one was two minutes early. Better to be prompt than to be tardy, but timing would be paramount for the mission.

Al-Rajul climbed out of the van and waved to the young man named Salin Namroud.

Salin saw him, smiled and waved back. He crossed the street.

"Evening of peace, *ustaz*."

"Evening of destiny, Salin," greeted Al-Rajul. "Thank you for coming. Would you mind sitting in my van? Others are coming."

"Others?"

"Yes. I will explain the President's instructions when you are all here. Come, come."

Salin went to get into the passenger seat.

"No, no," said Al-Rajul. "There is room in the back." He opened the back doors of the van. "Please."

Salin scrambled up. There was a bench down either side of the vehicle. He sat down as the man he knew as Mohammed closed the door behind him. There were no windows in the side of the van, but as it was a walk-thru design he could see out the front.

A similar scenario repeated itself four more times. Kabalan

Elb, Elias Massoud, Ahmad Adass and Yazbek Nader. As each one was shown into the back of the van, they looked with surprise and a little suspicion at the others who were already in there, but no one said a word.

When they were all gathered – and the back door of the van was closed – Al-Rajul climbed into the front and turned to face them.

"The President already knows your names," he said without preamble, "and once this mission is completed he will take care of you and your families. He gives you his thanks. Now, I must tell you that I now have to take you all away from here. You will not return until the mission is completed." There were a turning of heads, frowns and quizzical looks. "Do any of you have a problem with that?"

No one spoke, although the general feeling of unease was tangible.

"Because if you do, say so now."

Still nothing was said, although there was a general fidgeting. Then Yazbek, the third one on the left, leant forward. "We are going away, *ustaz*? But where? Can we not inform our families, even if we don't tell them we are on a glorious mission for the President?"

"And what about our clothes, our things?" Elias Massoud, centre on the right.

"My mother will be worried," said Salin, nearest to the empty passenger seat.

"Relax," said Al-Rajul. "Your families will be informed. In the morning." He looked at Elias. "Do not worry about clothes. The Facility will have everything you need."

"The Facility?" frowned Kabalan.

"All in good time."

"We will miss *Eid*," Salin.

"Yes, you will."

"How long will we be gone?" Elias.

"Three months."

There was a collective gasp.

Al-Rajul gave them a frown. "You have been told of the rewards. They will be great. You are in a win-win situation. You are doing this for your future, for that of your families, for your President. Indeed probably for almighty Allah also. Do you think the rewards are just going to come to you, without you doing anything to earn them?"

They looked abashed. "No, *ustaz*," Yazbek spoke for them all.

"So, I'll say it again. If any of you have a problem or have changed your mind, say so now. Once I start the engine of this van, you will be under military discipline and under my command." He stared at each one of them individually. Heads were down but nothing was said.

Then a hand was half-raised. Al-Rajul's eyes stopped on the subject.

"I – I don't think... I don't think I can, *ustaz*," Salin's voice was almost a whisper. He was letting down his family, his President, even Allah. "My mother, she will be on her own."

"Didn't you tell me you have brothers?"

"Yes, but they are too young. I am the eldest. She needs me."

"You are sure? A little inconvenience now will bring untold rewards in the future. Can your brothers not manage for a few weeks?"

"I... I don't think so, *ustaz*. I... I am sorry."

Silence in the van. The other four young men did not look at Salin.

Then Al-Rajul said in a surprisingly gentle voice, "Okay. I understand. Do not worry." He opened the driver's door and climbed out, shutting the door behind him.

A moment later the back of the van opened. "*Yalla*, Salin. I will come with you. I will explain things to your mother."

Salin climbed out. "There really is no need, *ustaz*."

Al-Rajul closed the door. "Yes, there is." He put his hand in his pocket and pulled out a rolled-up wad of Lebanese pounds, letting Salin see it. "The President would like to thank her anyway. You are a very loyal son."

Salin was on the verge of tears. "Bless you, *ustaz*. Thank you, thank you."

The four young men left inside the vehicle watched through the front window in silence as the man they knew as Mohammed walked across the road with his arm around the other guy's shoulders and disappeared into the camp.

They were all loyal Palestinians and, although nervous, were keen to serve their President. And to reap the rewards. They would not have thought of moving from the vehicle. Which was just as well, because none of them realised that with no handle on the inside of the back door and the front doors double-locked they were, in fact, captive inside the van.

Mohammed was back in half an hour. The nights were now getting cooler, so naturally he had worn his leather jacket. The darker, shinier patches on his jacket – almost splashes – went unnoticed.

He unlocked the door and climbed into the driver's seat. "Are you all okay?" He looked over his shoulder.

There was a nodding consensus.

"Good. Right, you are now under the orders of the President of Palestine. *Your* President. And I am his representative and your commander. You will address me as such." He reached down onto the floor and brought up a six-pack of bottled water, passing it backwards. Ahmad grabbed it. It was followed by another bag of dates and other fruit.

"You are travelling," said Al-Rajul. "You are now exempt from fasting for the remainder of this Ramadan. You will need to retain your strength and your wits."

"Where are we going, *ustaz*? Sir? Commander?" asked Kabalan.

Al-Rajul started the engine and pulled out. Traffic was sparse.

"Paradise," he muttered under his breath. Out loud he said,

"You will find out."

Kahale, Lebanon 23:30

The Maronite village of Kahale is in the mountains thirteen kilometres from Beirut, just a turning and a climb off the main Damascus road – an ease of access to the capital which made it ideal for Al-Rajul.

The sprawling two-storey homestead was in a wooded area to the south-east of the village, towards Aley. Set in a few cleared acres amongst the trees, it had at one time been an agricultural farm but had been abandoned during the events and left to fall into disrepair. It had been taken over (perhaps even bought, rural land titles post-events were fluid) in the mid-nineties by someone who had restored and renovated the place as a mountain retreat for himself and his family. It was quiet, it was secluded. The road to it was nothing more than a good quality track which did not go anywhere else.

But Fate had decided that the owner would never be able to use it. So the place in the mountains had been adapted once again, this time more for group or communal use rather than family living. It was hired to whoever could pay the not unsubstantial letting fees: businesses for training or conferences, governmental departments and agencies for whatever governmental departments and agencies did, even to individuals such as Lebanon's latest pop star who wanted a mountain retreat to write their next mega-selling album. It was flexible, it could be adapted to facilitate the hirer – hence its name: The Facility.

Al-Rajul had it on a three-month letting. He had not had to pay.

He was working for the owner.

They arrived in darkness. The building was just a hulking shadow in front of them. Before they were allowed out of the van, the man they knew as Mohammed and were now to call the Commander asked if any of them were carrying mobile phones. Kabalan and Yazbek were. The phones were taken off of them, with promises of state-of-the-art hi-tech models for all once the assignment was completed.

Leading them inside, the Commander showed them to their communal, but well-appointed, sleeping quarters on the ground floor. He indicated the table in the corner on which was water, juices, fruit and snacks, and pointed out the connected washroom facilities.

Then he locked them in for nine hours.

Each of the young men slept exceptionally well that night. The beds were the most comfortable things they had slept on in their lives, the mountain air was the crispest and cleanest they had ever breathed – and their drinks had been dosed with a mild soporific.

7 November 2004
24 Ramadan 1425

Kahale, Lebanon 08:00

When the Commander came back into the room at 08:00 the next morning, the recruits were waking naturally. They were told to pray if they wished, undertake their ablutions and be ready for a tour of the facilities in thirty minutes.

Al-Rajul was pleased that each one of them was ready when he returned. A promising start. He had chosen well. He was wearing the Palestinian *keffiyeh* but it was around his neck, not across his face. He also wore boots and military-style combat pants and shirt.

The recruits were impressed already by The Facility. Elias could not get over the fact that not only did the plumbing work but you could put your toilet paper down the *hammaemaet* and flush it away, you did not have to keep it in a separate bin for later disposal.

They were shown the ground floor. As well as their own sleeping quarters and washing facilities, there was a catering and dining area, a prayer room, a coffee and smoking lounge, a small gymnasium, a meeting room and further toilet facilities. The fridges and cupboards in the catering area were well-stocked. Meal times were 08:00, 13:00 and 19:00. Each would take turns cooking on a rota basis.

Upstairs was the Commander's quarters. They were forbidden to go there.

Outside was a small recreation area and a small swimming

pool, which they could use when they wished.

"Now go and eat," instructed the Commander. "And be in the meeting room at ten. There are clocks on the walls. Be punctual."

The recruits were seated in comfortable chairs in a line. The Commander was in a similar chair in front of them.

"While you were still in bed this morning," he began with a smile, "your families were contacted. They have been told that you are working for the President and that you will be away for three months. Already they have been given a small token of the President's thanks."

The recruits looked at one another, pleased.

"Naturally they have not been told exactly what you will be doing – that is none of their business. It is between the President, yourselves and me."

Tentatively, Kabalan half-raised his hand. "What is it we will be doing? Sir."

"You will be told all in good time. It is of the utmost secrecy, that is why you have been taken into isolation. It would be dangerous for you and your families if anyone found out. The President has many enemies, even within our own society. For now, you will stay here. Regard this as a retreat. Pray, exercise, contemplate, swim, relax, then pray some more. I have pinned an exercise regime on the notice board. I expect you to do them daily. I will know if you have not. Look." He pointed behind them.

The young men turned and after a moment turned back again, their faces puzzled.

"You do not see it, do you? There is a camera in the wall – do not turn round! You will be observed." Hints of consternation rippled across the faces. "The President needs you fit. The President needs you healthy – the kitchen is stocked with only the finest food." The Commander stood up and slowly walked behind the four chairs, touching each man on the shoulder. "I will be asking you to perform little errands. When I do, you will perform them quickly, accurately and without question." He reached the end of the line. "Is that understood?"

The faces turned towards him. Heads nodded. There were some mumbled *Yes, sirs*.

"What? I cannot hear you!"

"Yes, sir!" said the four voices together.

"Good. That is good. You will exercise, you will pray, you will keep yourselves in readiness." He sat back down in his chair. "You will not go upstairs, as I have told you. I will know if you do and you will be removed from the team. Your families will get not one *sou* reward. Also, you will not leave the grounds of The Facility unless you are on an errand for me. It would be dangerous for you even to attempt to do so." His face was hard, unyielding. No one was going to argue with him. "I shall not be here all the time. Can I trust you, Ahmad?"

The young man looked shocked at being singled out. He frowned, confused, and blurted "Of – of course. Of course, sir."

"Elias?"

"Yes, sir."

"Yazbek?"

"Of course."

"Kabalan?"

"Yes, sir."

The Commander nodded. "Don't make me regret choosing you. Once our task is complete, each one of you will be a hero of the Palestinian people. Your pictures will be hung across streets, on the sides of buildings. People will revere your names for years to come."

He looked from one face to the next. Young Palestinians, olive-skinned, wispy-bearded, aged before their time because of their plight. Hard – and yet with the naïveté of youth to believe every word of the bullshit he was expounding.

"My four recruits," he said.

Of which I need only one.

10 November 2004
27 Ramadan 1425

Mount Lebanon 08:00

The text that morning was not the usual terse statement of Hariri's locations. This time there was an actual message.

The Damascene stood on the balcony of the apartment, looking out over Beirut. There were clouds in the sky and the temperature was decreasing in preparation for the two-month winter ahead, but it was still warm enough for him to be naked, drying after his morning shower.

NEED TO MEET URGENT

Not unexpected after the political turmoil of these last three weeks following Hariri's resignation. Instead of slipping away into history as his opponents and enemies had hoped (but had known would never happen), Hariri was planning his comeback. He was determined that his Future Movement would win a landslide victory in the parliamentary elections in six months and he would again, naturally, be Prime Minister.

The Damascene's left thumb moved quickly.

Suggest

While waiting for the response, he began stretching: a pectoralis stretch against the side wall followed by a standing calf stretch, and then a severe standing hamstring stretch with his leg up on top of the glass balustrade. Then he went horizontal and face-down for ten full press-ups, ten diamond press-ups and, walking his feet backwards up the balustrade, ten planche press-ups.

His muscles were taut and hard. He had just returned to his feet and was performing an upper trapezius stretch (left hand over his head and touching his right ear rather than his right hand poking into the hole on the left side of his head) when the four-note text tone played.

He picked up the phone.

KOREITEM 1230

He slid the phone back down without replying, went back through the patio windows and walked upstairs for his second shower.

Koreitem, Beirut 12:40

Rafic Hariri's Head of Security, Abu Tarek, was seated behind his desk when The Damascene was shown into his office. Abu Tarek was dressed in grey suit pants, white shirt and subdued tie, his jacket hanging up nearby. In contrast, The Damascene was wearing trainers, jeans and a loose, collarless white shirt which hung down below his leather jacket. As always, his long black hair was tied back by a single rubber band, covering the sides of his face.

Abu Tarek's glance was disdainful. "You look like *mukhabarat*."

"Maybe I am."

Inwardly Abu Tarek winced. This man always got the better of him in verbal sparring. Really he shouldn't take him on. "Sit down, sit down. Coffee?"

The Damascene shook his head as he sat on the wooden chair in front of the desk. *"Merci."*

"So, how is my firewall working? You have been busy

protecting Mr Hariri?" There was more than a hint of sarcasm in his voice.

"Is he dead?"

Their eyes locked. The Damascene could see Abu Tarek trying, and failing, to find a cutting response.

"And you are still supposedly protecting him, even though he is no longer in office?"

"I have been instructed to continue."

Abu Tarek nodded. He said, "Something else has happened. Do you know Ali Hajj?"

The Damascene nodded. It was his job to know everything about his clients. "The Major General. Head of Mr Hariri's official government security during his first term as Prime Minister during the nineties. Came back with him when he resumed office in 2000, but was soon sacked. Used to be police chief in the north-east Bekaa."

"Interior Minister Franjieh is promoting Ali Hajj to Director-General of the Internal Security Force. We have been informed that one his first tasks will be to reduce Mr Hariri's state close protection unit from its current forty officers down to eight."

The Damascene said nothing while he assimilated the news and considered the ramifications. After a moment, he said "A move calculated to leave Hariri more exposed?"

"What else? They are pretending that it is just normal procedure. President Lahoud has said that as he is now an *ex*-Prime Minister he is entitled only to eight official protection officers under Lebanese law."

"And is he?"

"Hariri is not an ex-Prime Minister. He is *the* Prime Minister of this country. Karami is just a fill-in until Hariri comes again. It is an insult."

"But perhaps not as dangerous as it may seem, or as they may want it," reflected The Damascene.

"What do you mean?"

"Hariri still has – what? How many men do you have? Over

fifty?"

"Yes."

"Fifty men employed by you, by Hariri. Not by the state. Now you have one dedicated, loyal unit. Not two units with different employers and perhaps... different loyalties?"

Abu Tarek nodded, an eyebrow lifting in appreciation of the point.

"Replace them if you need to," advised The Damascene. "I know it will take a while, but there are literally hundreds of highly-trained private armies in the world from which you can recruit. Look at the western 'security firms' in Iraq."

Abu Tarek stroked his moustache. "I acknowledge what you say. Sound advice. And that is what I shall do. I shall recruit." He put both his hands flat in the desk top. "Starting right now. Join us."

"What?"

"Rather than this clandestine role. Come in. Join us. Help us from the inside."

"What are you saying? That I work for Hariri?"

"He will pay you magnificently."

"I already have an employer. And I have a job."

"It will be the same job. Who says you cannot work for two people doing the same job? Kanaan need never know."

"You want me to be the bitch of two masters?"

Abu Tarek grinned. "Or a whore, depending on which job title you prefer."

The Damascene raised his left hand and touched the side of his head.

"Think about it," continued Abu Tarek. "No need to respond right now. But can you take your jacket off?"

The Damascene frowned, pausing in the process of pulling his hair over his ear hole. "I'm sorry?"

"Your jacket. Can you take it off?"

"Why?"

Abu Tarek stood up. "Because it looks scruffy. Without it you will look much more presentable."

"Presentable?"

Abu Tarek looked at his watch as he slipped on his own suit jacket. "It is one o'clock. The Prime Minister is expecting us for lunch."

Rafic Hariri was famous for his Koreitem lunches, sometimes entertaining thirty or more people with whom he was wheeling, dealing, negotiating or compromising. So The Damascene was particularly impressed when that lunch turned out to be just the three of them: Hariri, Abu Tarek and himself.

The repast had been spectacular, an array of Lebanese dishes which more resembled one of the Gulf area's Friday brunches than a simple lunch meeting of three men.

Hariri had greeted him as if he already knew him and, in Hariri style, got straight down to business as they ate. The offer was one hundred thousand US dollars a month to be Assistant Head of Security to Abu Tarek.

The offer was refused, with grace. The Damascene acknowledged that he was a mercenary, but mercenaries abided by contracts, they did not change allegiances for the highest bidder. He explained that Hariri and Abu Tarek both knew that he worked for Ghazi Kanaan, the Syrian Interior Minister. He pointed out that if Kanaan's orders had been different, had Hariri been more useful to Kanaan dead, they would be facing an alternative scenario right now. Indeed, Hariri might not be facing anything at all.

Hariri had tried to keep his reaction in check, but The Damascene knew that the last remark had hit home. Hariri shrugged. "You only die when you die. Nobody dare kill me."

"We hope not," agreed The Damascene. "That is why I have been sent to add to your protection. But if I come in, if I work for you from the inside, that negates my effectiveness. I become just another security man – with all respect," he inclined his head at Abu Tarek. "I am not a security man, I am an assassin. I need to be on the outside, so I can see what an assassin sees, so I can think how your assassin thinks."

"My assassin," mumbled Hariri sadly.

"I cannot see what he sees if I am inside. I must be out there." The Damascene knew that some conciliation was required after the refusal. "But things can change now. You seem to accept the job that I am here to do. And the necessity for it?" He looked from Hariri to Abu Tarek, who both nodded. "There is no need for stealth, for me to be covert. My presence is acknowledged. Abu Tarek and I can contact more openly. Still by cell phone because that is the most secure – and use only the SIM I gave you. Just let me know your calendar as far in advance as possible, and notify me of any changes as soon as they occur, day or night. *Any* changes. Including meetings with Nasrallah."

Hariri sat back in his chair, lips pursed. He raised one bushy eyebrow and turned towards Abu Tarek. The Head of Security looked awkward, shrugging without comment.

"I see," said Hariri. "So you have indeed been doing your job."

"Of course."

Hariri wiped his mouth on his napkin. "As you wish." He put the napkin on the table. "Then I will let you two liaise." He smiled. "Perhaps it will be different when I win the election, eh?"

"Perhaps," said The Damascene.

Hariri stood up, closely followed by the other two. "May I have the pleasure to know to whom I have been talking?"

The Damascene wanted to say "Kanaan's bitch" but instead he replied, "Nobody, sir. You have been talking to nobody."

Hariri held out his hand. The Damascene shook it. "There is something I would like you to have," said Hariri. "Abu Tarek?"

Abu Tarek went over to a side table and took a small, bulky envelope from a drawer. He handed it to The Damascene. It felt like a three centimetre thick bundle of paper.

"Thank you for what you are doing," said Hariri. "Peace be

upon you."

And he walked out of the room.

Ras en Nabaa, Beirut 14:00

In the offices of the Department of General Security, a Listener finished transcribing the lunch conversation from the already-burned disc onto a *Word* document, printed it off and took it down the corridor to his boss. Ten minutes later, his boss sent an e-mail to Captain Maroun Khoury of the External Security Unit.

11 November 2004
28 Ramadan 1425

Bourj el-Barajneh, Beirut 11:00

The slam against the wall was so fierce that the eyes of Karim The Butcher nearly popped out of his head. Yellow, phlegmy gob flew out from his open mouth and landed on his whiskery chin.

"But Captain!" he gasped to his assailant in a nasally whine. "I know nothing about it!"

"Do you take me for a fool?" Captain Fadi Lattouf had his huge left hand around the throat of the butcher. The middle and index fingers of his right hand were up the butcher's nostrils and were pulling outwards.

"It is a co-incidence. Somebody must have it in for me. I – I – I - " Karim tried to shake his head. "I know nothing about it!"

"Another body turns up outside your back door and you know nothing about it? What, is somebody leaving you extra supplies for the *Eid* celebrations?"

"I – I did report it to you."

Lattouf held the butcher against the wall and stared into his terrified eyes. He felt something warm and wet run from Karim's nose, down the backs of his fingers and settle on the back of his right hand. Then he said, "Yes, you did." He removed his fingers and wiped them on Karim's already stained and filthy shirt. A nostril hair and unpleasant attachment was lodged down one of Lattouf's fingernails. He flicked it off and wiped his fingers again. "But are you trying to bluff me?"

"No, Captain, no, no." Karim shook his head vigourously.

"So three bodies turn up in your back yard - "

"The yard is not mine, I don't own it."

Lattouf tapped him lightly on the face. "Three bodies turn up in your back yard and you profess to know nothing about them. The first two, happenstance maybe. But now the third, also with his head caved in? What are you doing, pushing brains as a special holiday delicacy?"

"Captain, please!"

"Take him," Lattouf nodded to the Lieutenant and Sergeant standing near the doorway. "Perhaps a night in the cells will jog his memory."

"No, please!" Feebly protesting, Karim was carted off. The Lieutenant and Sergeant, both of whom had seen the mess out back, looked only too pleased to be away from the place.

"Ibrahim!" called Lattouf. The Lieutenant turned back in the doorway.

"Sir?"

"Go easy on him."

"Sir."

Left on his own, Lattouf walked back down the corridor and stood in the open back doorway, surveying the mess. This one had been a splasher. And it had been recent, not many maggots yet or signs of rodent feasts. By the standards of the killer, this had been a quick job. The face had been obliterated, but everything else was very much intact. There had been no papers or any other identification on the body. Fingers were intact for printing but they would probably reveal nothing – they did not have the prints of all forty-thousand people in the camp!

Four bodies now. All of them would be recorded as accidents, but none of them were. Perhaps none of them should be recorded at all – maybe a little filing cabinet fire was called for.

He sighed. Was this what Palestinian life was worth nowadays?

He would get his officers to bring the saws, hosepipes, quicklime and sulphuric acid along. Again. Or should he show this one to the Lebanese? That would mean he would have to report it officially. The case would not be handed over to them – the camps were no-go areas for the Lubnans – but they would want to interfere.

If he washed another body – another human being – down the sewage channels, how many more would follow? This one might be the end of it.

Or four might only be the beginning.

What to do, what to do...?

There was an English word that Westerners often used. A noun, a verb, a pronoun, an adjective, a curse, a suggestion, a request, all encapsulated in one tiny word. What was it? Oh yes...

Fuck.

His scrotum itched. He put his right hand into his trouser pocket to have a discreet tug – and touched something hard.

Landline telephones were not permitted in the Palestinian refugee camps, but technology had outwitted this sanction. He pulled out his Samsung mobile telephone.

Lattouf nodded. He was being guided.

Allahu Akhbar.

He flipped up the phone and accessed his Contacts folder, the itching of his balls forgotten.

Jonblat, Beirut 11:30

Captain Jihad Merhi of the Lebanese Internal Security Force had just returned to his office after his morning meeting with his boss, Major Ghanem, when the telephone on his desk rang.

Let it ring or pick it up? The boss had been in a pig of a mood (when wasn't he?), lambasting him about his investigations into the re-emergence of al-Murabitoun, and Merhi was not in the mood for anything other than several cigarettes and at least a half bottle of whisky.

But he picked it up.

"Merhi."

"Lattouf."

Oh for God's sake.

"I need to see you tomorrow. At 12:30."

"But that is only... twenty-five hours away."

"Yes. I would see you today if I could." Which meant yesterday.

Oh shit.

"Okay. Er... the pigeon shooting range at Furn Ech Chebbak." It was the first thing that came into his head. It was immaterial, anyway.

"I'll be there." The line went dead.

Verdun, Beirut 12:30

Both policemen arrived in the food court of the Dunes Shopping Centre at the same time. Lattouf was not dressed in his ridiculous casual clothes like he had been before, but he had a black overcoat covering his uniform. Merhi was in uniform, this time with his jacket on.

They nodded and shook hands.

"You still...?" asked Merhi nodding at the food outlets.

"In some parts of the world, Ramadan is over," said Lattouf. "It is in mine."

"Cup cakes?"

"McDonald's. Big Mac meal. Three of them."

After a short delay, Merhi was back with a tray piled high. He put three Big Macs, three large fries and three large Cokes in front of the Palestinian. For himself he had a simple cheeseburger and an orange juice.

"Bless your hands," said Lattouf, ripping the top off the first box and commencing the demolition.

Merhi cracked the lid off his orange juice. "Another one, I

take it?"

"Yes."

"Same as before?"

"Almost. Face gone, contents of skull pulverised. The rest reasonably intact. He was found early." Recollection of the graphic sight did not put Lattouf off his food.

"Another male then?"

"And dumped in the same place as the previous two."

"Interesting."

"Maybe. Or maybe it's just convenient. A small, unused area with just a narrow access. At the back of a butcher's shop."

"A butcher's?"

"We've taken him in for questioning."

"So it's solved then?"

The first Mac and fries were finished. The second lid was flipped up. "I don't think so. That would be too easy. And it doesn't explain the first one, which was found on the other side of the camp."

Merhi slowly ate his own burger. "So what are you going to do?"

Lattouf sighed. "Four bodies. With who knows how many more to come. What can I do?"

"You want to report it formally?"

"What happens if I do?"

Merhi made a face. "It's an unusual situation. You report it to me, I file a report. There'll be a shit-load of paperwork. Formally, we offer you whatever assistance we can – which will be very little if the bodies stay in the camp. We're not allowed in there, as you know."

"But I want you there."

Merhi stopped with the last piece of his burger halfway to his mouth. "Sorry?"

"Abu Samer, I trust you. I want you to come and have a look round. We are conducting our enquiries, but we get inured to the camp. People fear us but that does not mean they help us."

"You want me to conduct your enquiries for you?"

"No, no, not at all. That would be in breach of the rules."

"What you are asking is also in breach of the rules."

Lattouf stifled a burp (two and a half Big Macs down, half to go). "You don't know the camp. I just want you to have a little look over the crime scene. A fresh face. Assess it with your policeman's mind. See if there's anything we can consider."

"Fadi, it has been years since I was in the *Sûreté*."

"But your training never leaves you, my friend."

Merhi was quiet as he finished his orange juice. He watched as the last of Lattouf's fries ended their very, very short existence. He said, "Report it to me formally."

Lattouf sat back in the small chair and shook his head. "No." He wiped his hand down his stubbly beard. "It becomes formal and you cannot enter the camp. But while it is not reported, there is nothing to stop my friend Abu Samer coming to visit me. I tell you what - " He leant forward again, eyes sparkling. "How about you and Gisele coming to celebrate *Eid* with me, Nada and the children? You enjoyed it last time. You and I can just disappear for an hour or two. Leave the women to it."

Merhi wanted to scream. He did not need this. He really did not need this. But if it meant the Palestinian not formally reporting the matter...

It could be a small price to pay.

13 November 2004
30 Ramadan 1425

Kahale, Lebanon 10:00

Elias and Kabalan were outside exercising in the crisp autumn sunshine when they saw the grey Mitsubishi Express van pulling in off the track. "He's back," said Elias.

"Thank Allah," said Kabalan. "I was beginning to think he had abandoned us."

"You have no faith," Elias grinned. "He is our Commander. And we are his men, capable of looking after ourselves."

"Maybe he was testing us."

"Maybe. But so what?"

The van pulled up and the man they knew as the Commander climbed out. He was frowning, his face grim.

The two young men picked up his aura instantly. Four days he had been gone, and something had obviously happened in that time. "Morning of joy, Commander," said Elias but without his smile.

"Morning, sir," Kabalan was a little nervous now that their leader had returned.

The Commander stopped in front of them and sighed. "I wish that it was, Elias. But thank you anyway."

"Sir? Has something happened?"

"Where are the others?"

"Inside in the gym, sir."

"Get them will you? All of you be in the meeting room in five minutes, and bring some coffee."

They were all there in four minutes, sitting in a row in the order that had become rote: Kabalan, Elias, Ahmad, Yazbek, the last two still in their work-out clothes. The Commander was in front of them with his coffee.

He said nothing at first, just looked from one young man to the next, holding their eyes with his. Already they knew better than to say anything. At the end on the left, Kabalan's leg shook a little, an unconscious nervousness which made him look as if he needed the toilet.

Then the Commander sighed. "I have some dreadful, dreadful news for you, my brave Palestinians."

There was general frowning and concerned looks.

"It is my unpleasant duty – my sad duty – to tell you that two days ago our President, Abu Ammar, passed into the hands of Allah."

There were gasps of shock, of disbelief. *What?*

"President Arafat is dead?" asked Elias hoarsely. Next to him, tears were welling in Ahmad's eyes.

"He died in hospital in Paris. May peace be upon him."

"How – how -?" Yazbek was shaking his head.

Al-Rajul knew the rumours that were now circulating about Arafat's death, the suggestions of poisoning or even AIDS that were being put out by his enemies, but he said, "You know he had been ill for a few weeks. They did everything for him they could, but Allah had decided he had served his purpose on earth."

The mood in the room was heavy. Ahmad was now openly crying. "We must pray for him. We must pray," he sobbed.

"And we will," said the Commander gently. "But first after that piece of dark news I must give you some good news. This does not alter our assignment. You are still working for the Palestinian National Authority, for the office of the late President - "

"Do we have a new President, sir?"

The Commander looked at Ahmad. "Not yet. There will be

an election. Rawhi Fattuh is taking over on an interim basis, may Allah bless him. And he has said that all the President's ideals, his opinions, his strategies will live on, a fitting epitaph for a great man, a great Palestinian. And that includes us. We are needed, perhaps now more so than ever."

"Tell us what we are required to do, sir," sniffed Ahmad. "And we will do it. With pride. With honour." He looked at his colleagues who were each nodding earnestly.

Al-Rajul looked at them. You poor, misguided fools. He said, "Nothing has changed. You will be told in good time. But now we pray. Have you all performed *wudu*, your ablutions, today?" Heads nodded. "Then that will suffice for now."

The four recruits stood up and turned towards the window in an approximation of the *qibla*, facing the Kaaba in Mecca. Al-Rajul joined them, standing next to Yazbek. They raised their hands level to their ears and said the first *Takbeer*, "*Allahu Akbar.*" Then Al-Rajul began the *salat al-Janazah*, the funeral prayer. "*Bismillah ir-Rahmaan ir-Raheem...*"

Al-Rajul's voice carried conviction even though he did not believe. But whether the President was with Allah or Shaitan, Al-Rajul was grateful to Mohammed Abdel Rahman Abdel Raouf Arafat al-Qudwa al-Husseini. He had served Al-Rajul's purpose well. Just the mention of his name and lies about his intentions had been enough to snare the recruits.

Now all he had to do was whittle them down.

14 November 2004
1 Shawwal 1425

Koreitem, Beirut 10:30

It was the first day of *Eid al-Fitr*, the Festival of Fast Breaking, the three day holiday marking the end of Ramadan. A time of prayer then celebration, of festive meals and occasional gift-giving. The time when good Muslims give their *fitra*, alms to feed the local poor, and some also pay their *zakat*, annual alms for the poor and needy based on a percentage of the giver's assets.

Rafic Hariri was at home in Koreitem with as many members of his family as could make it at this joyous time. It made The Damascene's job easy, but he also knew that he must not rest or assume. Complacency was the number one killer of important men throughout history. Denial of danger was the second. While Hariri lived, he was in danger – a statement as perverse as it was accurate.

Since his meeting with Hariri and Abu Tarek four days ago, The Damascene had received full and constant text information regarding Hariri's calendar, meetings, appointments, whereabouts – even details of another clandestine trip to see Hassan Nasrallah and Hizbullah a couple of days ago. It was not The Damascene's job to speculate on what they might be discussing.

Now as he approached Koreitem down Madame Curie Street on the appropriated Suzuki, he saw a small crowd of people outside the palace. As he got nearer he could hear shouts and chanting. Favourable chanting.

The Damascene pulled over just after Abd el Rahim Diab Street. In a way this was good. Hariri was effectively imprisoned in Koreitem by his supporters. On the other hand, anyone in this crowd could be an assassin with evil intent, using *Taqiyya* – concealing his true self, a concept which The Damascene had practised himself on many occasions.

Hariri was unlikely to make an appearance to the crowd, as he would know that to do so might whip-up emotions which could get out of hand. Even if he did attempt to do so, Abu Tarek and his men would stop him. But nevertheless a warning had to be given.

The Damascene pulled out his mobile phone. His left thumb moved fast.

Do not let abu bahaa appear outside not even at the window

It was two minutes before the reply came.

MATTERS ALREADY IN HAND. THANK YOU

Good. Not for nothing was Abu Tarek one of the world's top security men.

Now The Damascene would park up and return to mingle with the crowd, practising his own form of *Taqiyya*. While joining in with the chanting and the cheering, he would be looking at faces and bodies, watching for anything suspicious, seeing if anybody was already in his vast mental archive. If there was an assassin in the crowd, he would find him.

An assassin other than himself, of course.

Bourj el-Barajneh, Beirut 16:30

"*Eid Mubarak*, Fadi," smiled Jihad Merhi as he entered *chez Lattouf*. "And to you, Nada." He bowed graciously to Lattouf's wife who was dressed in a black *jilbaab* with no head covering and was almost as fat as her husband.

"*Eid Mubarak*, Jihad," replied Fadi. "And to you, Gisele."

"Welcome to our home," said Nada as the two women embraced.

By the standards of the camp he policed, Lattouf's place was indeed a home. On the edge of the camp so as technically not to be part of it, it was a small two-storey house, part of a terrace of shops and service providers.

Fadi was dressed in his *Eid* finery of a lightly striped white shirt and grey slacks. No shoes worn in the house, of course. "Please, come in, come in."

Children appeared from everywhere as the Merhi's began to hand out small presents, then at a bark from their father they disappeared with their loot as quickly as they had come. Through the thin walls of the building, music could be heard from other celebrations taking place nearby.

"Bless your hands for the gifts," thanked Nada. "You are too kind."

"A drink?" suggested Fadi. "I have some very fine mango juice."

"That would be excellent, thank you," nodded Gisele. She had been well-briefed by her husband on his return home three nights ago with Lattouf's invitation ringing in his ears. She knew what this was all about and she understood: she herself had been a member of the Department of General Security some years ago. She always had to cover up the horrible-looking bullet scar on the left side of her neck, a souvenir from Paris in 1997. "Would you like some help in the kitchen, Nada?" she asked.

"Thank you, Gisele, you are most gracious."

"How long for dinner?" asked Lattouf as the women went off.

"One hour," his wife called over her shoulder.

"In the name of the Prophet, peace be upon him, I could have starved to death in that time! And poor Jihad here could have lost the use of his legs through hunger!"

Nada blew a raspberry and then the two women could be heard giggling and chatting in the kitchen.

Lattouf turned to Merhi. "You are well, my friend?"

"I am good, thank you Fadi." Underneath his North Face Galaxy parka jacket, Jihad was also dressed smart-casual in deference to the festivities: light blue shirt and black slacks with white socks. "No more, I take it?"

"No, thanks to Allah. Finish your juice and let us go, while the women do what women do."

"Will we have enough time?"

"An hour is plenty. The camp is very... compact. *Yalla.*"

Within thirty seconds of entering the camp, Jihad Merhi was lost. So many alleys, so many dead ends, paths that went nowhere, hardly a straight thoroughfare in the place. The ground was hard and dusty, ripe for flooding when the rains came next month. Pipes dripped, cables sagged.

And the smell was... interesting. Much cooking was going on in the small dwellings and the odours were fighting street battles with the underlying sewer smell to provide a general fragrance that was cloying, almost intimate in the way it embraced you, yet not always unpleasant.

He wished he had worn his combat gear, not his fine clothes. But that was something he could not do. On no account could he be identified as a member of the Lebanese Internal Security Force.

Within five minutes they were passing a boarded-up shop front.

"That used to be the butcher's shop," explained Lattouf, his gut wobbling as he walked.

"Used to be?" asked Merhi.

"Sadly he is no longer with us." Lattouf was aware of Merhi looking at him. "My men were a bit too enthusiastic."

"But he was innocent?"

"Oh yes. But we had to take such drastic action to prove it. Allah will look after him."

Merhi shook his head as they turned first one corner then another.

"Down here." Lattouf could only just fit down the narrow alley between the buildings. Indeed, it was so small it didn't deserve the status of alley, it was just a gap. It led on to a small courtyard area.

Only one door led out into the yard, obviously the back of the butcher's shop. The other sides were blank walls with windows above. Even the political daubers did not come in here, but there were some brown splash marks over one wall.

"This was where the three of them were dumped," Lattouf pointed to the left.

"And nobody above saw anything, heard anything?"

"No. Selected use of senses is what keeps people alive in these places. You hear and see nothing if it does not concern you."

"You have cleaned the place up remarkably well."

"Thank you."

"Except the wall. How did you dispose of the bodies?"

"Stand back." Lattouf raised his foot and kicked in the door with one mighty blow. It shot inwards and stood trembling on its single hinge.

Merhi followed him in, and then almost wretched. The place stank like an uncleaned locked-up mortuary. Which, he supposed, it effectively was. Bodies were bodies, be they man or beast. All creatures – living or dead – stank.

"Here," Lattouf indicated a room to his right. In the half-light Merhi could see an old table against one wall. On the other side there was a wide, shallow gulley in the floor with a deep hole at one end leading down and, hopefully, out. A drain for the blood, and probably the butcher's latrine as well. There was a crystal dust residue on the floor along the edge of the gulley.

"The quicklime is not always, er, quick," said Lattouf. "We had to encourage decomposition with knives and hacksaws. Thankfully the skulls were already shattered, otherwise they would not have fitted down the hole."

Merhi turned. He had an overwhelming desire to punch the fat Palestinian on the nose, but then he remembered that had Lattouf not done what he had done, the matter would have been reported formally and he would have been knee deep in something much worse than – what *was* that he was standing in? He looked at his shoes.

"The front of the shop is here," Lattouf beckoned him out. "Just a counter, a few hooks in the ceiling for the carcasses, and a small box where the old bastard used to keep his working money. It is empty now."

Merhi gave a cursory look round. "Yes, nothing of interest. How much was in the box?"

"A few thou – er, I don't know. It was empty when we closed the place up."

Well, I just hope you bought your snot-nosed brats an *Eid* present, thought Merhi. Or is it paying for tonight's meal?

They went back down the corridor and outside into the yard. Merhi looked at the brown splashes on the wall. "This was just the last one?"

"Yes, they weren't there for the first two."

"Blood on the ground?"

"A few stains only the first time, quite a lot for the last one."

Merhi went up to the wall and raised his hand horizontally and up, almost touching the top of the stain which was just over two metres high. "So he brought the first two here, killed the last one here. Allowing for an upward trajectory of about half a metre..." Slowly he brought his hand down and back towards himself. "The victim was about my height."

"Significance?"

"Probably none. But it's not like he was a child. Why didn't he fight back? I presume you checked his hands?"

Lattouf's face lit up. "I did! Young, signs of manual labour."

"But any cuts, grazes or bruises, as if he had been in a fight?"

"No."

"So why did he willingly allow himself to be led down this alley to his death? Why? Obviously he did not know he was in peril. Was he surprised? Was he with someone he thought he could trust?"

Lattouf shrugged. "Maybe he was brought here at gun point."

"Good point. Maybe." Merhi looked around. "But he was not shot. So the assailant would have had to put the gun away, or down, before... what? What were they killed with?"

"We don't know. Heads caved in, beaten to a pulp, but we don't know what with."

"Mr Evil, in the courtyard, with the lead piping. It's not gelling."

"Maybe there were two of them. Assailants. One covered him with the gun, while the other did the business."

"A possibility, granted. But somehow I don't think so. If there were two of them, why bother to squeeze down that little alley? Why not just bump and dump somewhere out there? This one wanted seclusion, to make sure he had enough time – or at least enough privacy – to obliterate the victim's identity. Why? Once somebody is dead, they're dead. To obliterate their identity is to stop us – you – from finding out who they were. From making a connection. From what? To whom?"

Merhi looked up at the buildings above. It was beginning to get dark but there were no lights on, which meant they were having a power cut.

"Fadi, I've seen enough. Let's go. What about where the first body was found? Anything for me to see there?"

Lattouf led the way back down the tight alley. "Nothing," he said. "And we've made a discovery. At least about the place, if not the victim."

"What's that?"

They came out of the alley.

"It is a place regularly used by *lootees*. Male prostitutes."

Merhi stopped, frowning. Then he said, "No. No, that's not what this is. No way." He began to walk on. "Someone setting out to kill *lootees* would want them to retain their identity, as a warning to others. These victims have had their very humanity obliterated, to prevent – or at least delay – identification. Let's say the first one was a *lootee* who stumbled across something. Or someone. But what? What, what, what?"

They were quiet as they walked back the way they had come. Suddenly lights popped on in the windows as the power came back on. Merhi didn't know whether it was an improvement, perhaps the place should remain in darkness.

As they turned out of the camp, Merhi said "Disregard the first one, concentrate on the other three. Three young men. They are somebody's sons, somebody's brothers. Maybe even somebody's husband or betrothed. Somebody must be missing them. Find a connection. It is there somewhere. And place a guard on that fucking alleyway."

"Bless your mind," said Fadi Lattouf.

17 November 2004
4 Shawwal 1425

Mount Lebanon 00:15 – 07:00

The three-day celebrations were over. Hariri remained safe.

The crowd outside Koreitem Palace had grown day by day, thousands of people showing their support. It had remained orderly, sometimes chanting, often with singing, sometimes quiet in contemplation, a solid mass in favour of one man and what he stood for. And The Damascene had scrutinised every one of them.

There were plenty of Syrian *mukhabarat* in the crowd, some disguised, some openly in their 'uniform' of leather jacket, light pants and sandals. There were Lebanese security agents too, obvious by their look of slight discomfiture. But none of the security services attempted any agitation or intimidation. They had let the crowd grow from an amorphous to a structured mass without interference.

Importantly, there were no assassins. The Damascene could tell, by looking at faces, by looking at mannerisms, by general demeanours. And with Hariri not even making an appearance, an assassin had been rendered useless anyway. The most someone with evil intent could hope for was a suicide bombing – and what did that ever achieve other than the unnecessary killing of collateral and the pointless loss of a trained killer?

As darkness fell on the third day of *Eid*, the crowd had begun to disperse, happy that their message had been heard not only here but at the Presidential Palace in Baabda and in Damascus too.

The Damascene had driven back to the apartment just after midnight, had eaten fruit, showered and had lain down on his bed upstairs. Sleep had come almost instantly, a recharging for some busy days ahead.

At 03:30 the front door of the apartment opened then closed noiselessly. A shadow glided in silence across the living area and up the stairs. It paused outside the half-open door of the bedroom, listened and then slid inside.

For a moment the shadow stayed in a corner of the room, watching the outline of the naked man on the bed, his breathing heavy and regular. Then it moved across to the foot of the bed, paused, then stepped up onto the mattress, one foot either side of the sleeping figure. Slowly it walked forward until its feet were level with the sleeper's upper stomach.

The sleeping man's breathing did not alter, but he suddenly said "You are not a real Djinn."

She said nothing, but he could feel her smile above him.

"Real Djinns cannot open doors." He opened his eyes. In the shadow of night he could see she was completely naked above him, her small, perfect, hairless body exuding a subtle warmth.

"I do not open doors... Master." Her voice was low, husky, sure in the inevitability of what was to happen. "Keys do. I just pushed it."

"Very clever."

As he raised himself up on his elbows, she knelt forwards, her knees on his shoulders. She weighed nothing, but he fell back onto the bed as was required.

"It has been three weeks," he said.

"I know," she replied.

She moved her hips forward and he kissed her on the lips.

She was gone when he awoke at 07:00, but the damp patches on the sheets and the inevitable mosquito bite, this time on his right hip, confirmed that he had not dreamed her visit, it had not been wishful thinking.

He lay back with his hands behind his head, his long hair splayed roughly over the pillow, a smile on his face. She seemed to have a thing about the hole where his left ear used to be. At one point during the night, she had whispered into it "Can you hear just as well out of this?"

"Yes, I can," he replied. "It is a burnt hole and the external ear is missing, but the drum inside works perfectly. Things are just sometimes faint and echoey on that side because I have nothing to catch the sound with and direct it inside."

"Fascinating." She moved her body. "Can you hear out of it now?"

He reached up and grabbed her left butt cheek. "How can I possibly with that covering it?"

She squealed as he pulled her down and they kissed, facial lips to facial lips, before making love for the third time.

Now The Damascene laughed out loud at the memory. He wondered if he could buy her off Kanaan, to have as his permanent muse? Money was no object.

He found himself hoping that her next visit was not going to be another three weeks away. The woman was bewitching – even if she was Kanaan's official whore.

Meantime, he had a lot of work to do.

Scratching the mosquito bite, he rolled out of bed.

18 November 2004
5 Shawwal 1425

Kahale, Lebanon 08:00 – 10:15

While the four young Palestinians ate breakfast, Al-Rajul examined their sleeping quarters. It was reasonably neat, reasonably tidy, showing that they were not used to such luxury and were treating it with the respect it deserved. Their removal from the camp and transport to Kahale had been quick purposefully, so that they had no chance to bring anything personal with them.

Nothing to identify them.

Each had taken clothing from the central wardrobe and had stored it in their individual unlockable lockers. Each locker had a *Koran* already in it. Two lockers now also had an item of fruit inside. That was it. Nothing else, nothing personal.

With one exception.

The third locker had a drawing tucked into the inside of the door. It was a pencil drawing of Yasser Arafat, a copy of the familiar, smiling sketch that adorned walls and hung from balconies and across streets in the camps.

Kabalan, Elias, Ahmad, Yazbek.

So, Ahmad then. He was a very good drawer. He had a talent. And he had been visibly and openly upset when he had been told of Arafat's death. So he had a soul as well.

Was that good?

Or bad?

After breakfast, the young men congregated in the communal area by the front door, as instructed. The Commander was waiting for them.

"I have been to see your families, again," his voice was friendly but retained the air of authority. "They send you the blessings of Allah."

The men looked pleased.

"Again I have given them money, to help them, to sustain them while you are away. I hope that is acceptable?"

"Of course, Commander," Kabalan.

"Yes, sir," Elias.

"Thank you," Ahmad.

"Bless your hands," Yazbek.

"I have told them what I am telling you now. Very soon I will be able to reveal to you the task that we are required to do, and you will understand why you will be revered as heroes for ever more. Until that time we have further training to undertake, and tasks to perform. Kabalan and Elias. You are fit, yes?"

"Yes, sir." Kabalan.

"Yes, sir," agreed Elias. "We have all been doing the exercise regime as instructed."

"Good. I have noticed. You are indeed fit. But I need strength as well as agility. I need you to concentrate on strength exercises. I have put up a new programme in the gym. Please start it as from today. You as well, Ahmad and Yazbek – but first I need you two to come with me. Kabalan and Elias, to the gym."

"Yes, sir."

Ten minutes later, the Commander, Ahmed and Yazbek were deep in the woods to the north-west, well away from the house. They were closer to the town of Kahale, and looking northwards up the mountain they could see the imposing three towers of Mar Antonios church at the top of the town. But they would not be bothered, the villagers never came down here, respecting the private property (and helped by the subtle, camouflaged but very effective electrified fence that ran round the whole perimeter).

Although it was the tenth hour of the day, it was dull in the woods. The sky formed a canopy held up by the tightly-packed trees, the sun was a single overhead light whose power was diffused as it came through the blue awning.

It was quiet.

"Okay." The Commander stopped in a small triangle formed by three pine trees. It was mossy under foot. He turned to face the two young men. "How is your orienteering?" He looked from one to the other. "Your sense of direction? Is it good?"

Yazbek grinned, knowing his next words would please the Commander. "I always know where I am, sir. I can always find my way to and from anywhere in the camp."

"You must forget about the camp."

The grin dropped from Yazbek's face.

"The next time you return will be simply to pick up your family and leave there for good." The Commander patted him on the shoulder. "When you have served your President and Allah."

Relief swept through Yazbek and the grin returned.

"Okay, your task is simple," said the Commander. "Get back to the house as quick as possible. Whoever gets there first will be rewarded."

The two recruits stood there, expecting more.

"That is it!" snapped their Commander. "What are you waiting for? Go!"

"Yes, sir!" Yazbek turned keenly on his heels and was off, followed by Ahmad.

The Commander took two strides forward and grabbed Ahmad's left arm in a tight grip, halting his run and pulling him backwards. "Wait, wait," he said softly as Yazbek disappeared back into the trees.

Ahmad winced and frowned a query at his Commander. His

arm felt like it was in a vice. Although Yazbek was quickly out of sight, they could hear the twigs and undergrowth snapping under his feet as he ran.

The Commander unclipped the top of the holster on his belt and drew out a Walther P99. He pushed off the safety and pressed the gun into Ahmad's right hand.

"Kill him," ordered Al-Rajul. "If Yazbek makes it back to the house, you will not."

Bourj el-Barajneh, Beirut 10:15

Captain Fadi Lattouf eased the right cheek of his substantial arse off of his chair, braced himself and farted with the savagery, volume and force of an Airbus A380 at the point of take-off.

The walls of the offices of the security police were thin (the place was nothing more than a trailer, really) and his men were used to the Captain's internal propensities. However, knowledge before and after the fact did not help Sergeant Bassem el-Khazem who was halfway along the short corridor to the Captain's office to report as requested.

el-Khazem paused two paces away from the door-less doorway and waited for the inevitable. The aftershock came on cue (only a Cessna 172) and was emitted with a loud, satisfied sigh.

Embracing the inevitable, the Sergeant turned into the doorway and was immediately French-kissed by his boss's odour. Not for the first time in his long career in this hell-hole.

"Sir." He couldn't help but cough slightly.

"Bloody chickpeas," said Lattouf, a statement not an explanation. "Anything?"

el-Khazem shook his head. "People come, people go. And nobody wants to talk to the police, anyway. We have tried approaching gang members, but they just walk away when they see us coming."

"Should we pull some in?"

"Unwise, don't you think? And hardly worth it. If any of them had anything they wanted to say to us or bring to our attention, they would have done so."

"Huh. What about the posters?"

The posters had been Lattouf's idea. In the absence, and physical impossibility, of conducting door-to-door enquiries, he had ordered that posters be printed and put up on all walls and other available spaces in the vicinities of where the bodies were found. They had no pictures of the victims, of course. So the posters had contained a blunt and simple message:

مفقود.

وإذا كان لديك صديق أو قريب مفقود يتصلون بالشرطة فورا.

Missing

If you have a friend or relative missing contact the police immediately

"No response," said el-Khazem. "Some of them have been ripped down already."

"May Satan urinate on their mothers. What is wrong with these people?" Lattouf took a battered cigarette from a drawer of his battered desk and lit up with a battered match from a battered match box. If his wife Nada knew he had taken up smoking again (in fact, he had never quit – just lied), he would be battered too. "Okay," smoke oozed from his nostrils. "Widen the area. Get more copies done and put them up all over the camp."

"You think it will work?"

Lattouf snorted. "Do you want me to say yes and lie? But we have to try. Someone somewhere must care. Four young men are dead and no one is missing them? The camp is small, it is not like we are talking the whole of Beirut - " He stopped, staring at the Sergeant's face but not seeing him, the cigarette dangling out of the corner of his mouth. Something had occurred to him.

Slowly his brow creased. Surely not? It couldn't possibly be. Could it?

Slowly his brow raised again. One thing his many years in policing had taught him: as well as the old investigator's adage of Suspect Everyone, Trust No One, there had to be added another truism: Discard Nothing.

He would have to run this by Jihad Merhi.

"Shall I do it then?" asked el-Khazem.

"What?" Lattouf was still with his thoughts.

"The posters? All over the camp?"

Again the Captain stared at him. Then he said, "That's what I said, didn't I? Shit - !" Two centimetres of ash had fallen off the end of the *seejaere* and onto his lap. He leant back in the chair, brushing down his groin as if it might combust at any moment.

Sergeant Bassem el-Khazem left him to it.

Halfway back down the corridor el-Khazem heard the sound of a Boeing 747 applying reverse thrust as it landed, and he was grateful he had left the room when he did.

Kahale, Lebanon 10:20

Ahmad ran through the trees, gasping, trying to catch breaths which just would not come. He had no time to think, no time to reason. The house was less than five minutes away at running speed. In five minutes he could end up dead, for he had no doubt that the Commander would fulfil his threat.

The moss was spongy under foot, in some places slippery. Twigs were broken where Yazbek had already run past but Ahmad still managed to get caught in the face by a wayward sapling, scratching his right cheek. He hoped he would not bleed, but he had no time to worry about that now.

Yazbek had a head start, therefore Ahmad had to run faster than him to catch him up. Could he do it? And if he did, could he pull the trigger? Kill a fellow human being?

He hopped past a boulder, the downhill trajectory taking him faster and faster. Yazbek did not know what was at stake, so he might not be running to his maximum. But where was he?

It was getting lighter up ahead as the wood thinned out. Two minutes to go – three at the most – until they reached the grounds and then the house.

Then Ahmad saw him. Up ahead, about twenty metres in front, Yazbek's head was bobbing up and down as he ran. Ahmad forced his heavy legs to go faster. Should he take a shot? *Could* he take a shot? He had used a gun before with the *Fatah* group he belonged to, but his experience was confined to firing in the air in celebration. He had never shot anyone or any thing.

He raised his right hand, tried squinting his eye to aim, cannoned into a tree, buckled at the left knee, but kept on running. He must do this. For Allah, for the President. For his life.

Then Yazbek disappeared.

Right on the edge of the wood, he vanished. One moment his head was bobbing, then he was gone. Out of sight.

What the...?

Ahmad kept his pace. He looked far ahead, over the open ground in front of the house, expecting to see Yazbek triumphantly running the last few hundred metres, but there was no one there.

He burst out of the wood – and nearly fell over Yazbek's body.

Ahmad forced himself to stop, his momentum taking him two metres past his prostrate colleague. Yazbek was face-down in the dirt, hardly moving.

"Yazbek?" Ahmad was puzzled. "Yazbek, you okay?"

Yazbek moaned and moved his right leg.

Ahmad looked back the way they had run to see if there was

a rock or something his friend had fallen over. There was nothing. He must have slipped on the moss. Falling face down on the gravel, suddenly and unexpectedly, would knock the wind out of anybody.

Yazbek was still moaning. Ahmad knelt down and reached out with his left hand.

Yazbek began to move, to get up. But his moaning changed. Into a laugh.

As he rose onto his knees, his right hand moved up. He was pointing a Walther P99 at Ahmad.

Jonblat, Beirut 10:30

"Merhi."

"Jihad, my old friend! It's Fadi Lattouf."

Bollocks.

"How are you, Fadi?"

"I am fine, fine. Good in fact. And you and the lovely Gisele?"

"Well, thank you. You have another?"

"Another? No. But I have a thought, an idea. I would like to run it past you."

Merhi hoped his sigh could not be heard down the phone line.

"Are you free on Saturday?" asked the Palestinian. Which meant he wanted to meet tomorrow, Friday.

Not even fighting against the inevitable, Merhi said "Gebran Garden, fourteen hundred?" Which meant the Dunes Shopping Mall at midday.

"I will be there."

Kahale, Lebanon 10:30

Instinctively Ahmad raised his gun. Both young Palestinians were in identical positions, on their knees facing each other three metres apart.

Yazbek's laughter stopped when he saw the Walther in Ahmad's hand, the same as the gun as he had been given by the Commander earlier, before breakfast. He frowned. "But I am to kill you."

There was surprise on Ahmad's face. "And I am to kill you."

One of the guns started to tremble lightly.

A finger tightened on the trigger of the other one.

"I – I do not understand," said Yazbek.

"Neither do I." Tears were welling in Ahmad's eyes.

The sound of the shot echoed through the wood, a sudden loud explosion cutting through nature's tranquillity. Birds flew out from the trees, wings beating hard and fast, taking them up and away from the human danger below.

Up in the house, Elias stopped his weight-lifting abruptly. Kabalan was still thumping on the treadmill at a fair speed.

"Did you hear that?" asked Elias.

"What?" Kabalan did not stop running.

Elias stood up from the bench. "That noise. Sounded like a shot."

Kabalan reached forward and lowered the speed on the treadmill. "A shot? I heard nothing."

"It was a shot, I'm sure of it."

Kabalan reduced the speed in quick stages to zero. He stepped off, sweat on his brow. Elias passed him a towel as he came over.

"Perhaps it was the locals hunting," suggested Kabalan as he wiped his brow.

"Perhaps," agreed Elias, walking over to the window. "But they have never hunted down here before in the two weeks we have been here."

Kabalan came over and put an arm around his colleague's shoulders as they both looked out over the grounds.

"I wonder where the other two and the Commander are?"

mused Elias.

Ahmad's eyes were wide, staring at Yazbek. His hand gripped the gun with such force that his fingers would have had to be prised off of it if he was dead – which he was not.

Yazbek's eyes were equally as wide and staring. The gun and his hand still trembled, only now more strongly.

Both young men knelt there facing each other.

"Very good." The Commander walked out from the wood, nodding in satisfaction. "You have both passed."

Incredulity creased Ahmad's face. Yazbek still stared, unable to believe that he was still alive after Ahmad had shot him.

The Commander leant forward and took Yazbek's gun. Then he tugged at the warm gun in Ahmad's hand. "Ahmad?"

Ahmad looked up at him, in incomprehension.

"Ahmad, the gun."

Ahmad looked down at his own hand. Then his fingers quickly snapped away from the weapon and the Commander took it.

"Well done both of you," said the Commander. "Next time it might be live ammunition."

Snot dribbled down Yazbek's staring face. Ahmad let out a huge sigh and sat back on his haunches, then he immediately came back up again. His face creased.

"Come. Back to the house, both of you," ordered the Commander. "And say nothing of this to the others."

Ahmad began to cry as he stood up. Yazbek fumbled onto his feet like a newborn fawn.

The three of them began to walk.

"It upsets you to kill, Ahmad?" The Commander saw the tears on the young man's cheeks.

For a moment Ahmad did not reply. Then he said, "I – I am ashamed, sir."

"Ashamed? There is no shame in serving your President and your country."

"N – no, sir, it's not that. I – I've soiled myself." There was a dark and growing patch on the back of his trousers.

Al-Rajul tried not to laugh. "It is the sign of a man. It is not easy to kill another human being, not the first time. Defecation is allowed, indeed expected."

"Thank you, sir." Sniff.

"Sir?" said Yazbek who was walking two paces behind.

The Commander looked over his shoulder. "Yazbek?"

"I think I've shit myself too, sir."

Ras en Nabaa, Beirut 11:00

"Four will have to do. He did not want to come. Too scared," said the voice on the memory stick.

"So what did you do?" asked the other voice.

"Relieved him of his duties."

"Did you kill him?"

No response. "Did you kill him?" asked the other voice again.

Nothing, just heavy breathing.

"That's it?" asked Captain Maroun Khoury.

Standing in front of his desk, Zahia Zalloum shrugged. "For this time."

"So, another killing?"

"If our interpretations are correct."

He smiled. "I have every confidence in your interpretations, Zeez. So now we have four. Anything else? Where? Why?"

"Not yet."

"And no reports of bodies found?"

She shook her head.

Khoury reached for a cigarette. "And we don't know what this is all about. Might not be anything that needs our... intervention. You want to drop it?"

She sighed, not a little frustrated. "No. No. Something is happening, Moro. I just cannot figure out what yet. If a body would show up, just one, then we could progress. At the moment we just think there have been four killings."

"So in the meantime?"

"Eyes and ears."

"Listen and gather. L and G. It will break. It's just a matter of patience."

"Never my strongest point, as you know."

Through a mouthful of smoke, he said "You never did like preambles."

"I always believe in getting on with things."

They looked at each other, mischief and memories bouncing between them like pinballs. Out of the blue, she asked "Do you want to come round tonight?"

Khoury sat back in his chair. Oh yes, he would like nothing better. Sucking on a cigarette only gave so much pleasure. But he knew he would regret what he was about to say. "Perhaps not the best idea. Considering."

It was the answer she was expecting, and in some ways she was relieved. It had been her groin talking. You should never go back. "Yes, considering."

"Maybe when all this is over...?"

"Maybe."

She left the room, leaving Maroun Khoury thinking of the times when L and G meant something completely different between them other than listen and gather. Lick and gyrate.

19 November 2004
6 Shawwal 1425

Verdun, Beirut 12:00

Friday at midday is a busy time in the shopping malls of Beirut, and the food court on the second floor of the Dunes Mall was crowded. Nevertheless Fadi Lattouf had managed to secure an empty table for four, by a combination of glares, unfortunate personal habits and his sheer physical bulk.

When the man in uniform approached the fat Palestinian, people around him were glad that they had not sat any nearer. The onlookers expected a scene, anticipating that the Palestinian would at least be turfed out and might even be arrested, but they were surprised when the two men shook hands.

"Jihad, my friend!"

"Fadi, how are you?"

"I'm fine, fine. And you?"

Merhi looked down at the table. An open box from *Cup Cake* had two specimens still inside and a plethora of dead cake cases. One cake – a chocolate one – had been placed neatly in front of the empty seat opposite Lattouf. Next to it was a polystyrene cup of black coffee. Next to Lattouf's detritus were two polystyrene cups, one empty, one half full.

"Busy, but I'm good." Merhi sat down, picked up the cup and sipped the luke warm beverage.

"Thank you for seeing me again – oh, and Nada sends her thanks for the children's clothes. And I do too. It was very thoughtful of you and Gisele."

"It was our pleasure. I hope I got the teams right."

"Hmm! At their age, their allegiance is to colours, they don't care who the team is. Walid likes blue, so I gave him the Chelsea one. Yussef likes red, so he got Arsenal. The girls got the fancy Italian and Spanish ones."

Merhi smiled. Kids, the same the world over. How did they become so different when they grew up?

"So you don't have another victim then?" Merhi unwrapped his cup cake and bit.

"Thanks be to Allah, no. I had a thought, a theory, which I would like to run by you. You've said before you don't like talking detail on the phone because..." He waved his hand in circular motions in the air then pointed to his ear.

"Quite."

"I have put up posters in the camp. Firstly in the vicinity of the murders and now over the whole of the camp."

"Any results?"

"Sweet diddley."

Merhi wiped his mouth on a paper napkin. "Nothing at all?"

"Squat. Absolutely nothing. Zilch. Which set me thinking. Even if we discount the first one, we still have three men dead. And no one is missing them?"

"Or is it that no one wants to talk to the police? You do have, shall we say, a reputation?"

Lattouf wanted to look affronted, but he accepted the truth. "Maybe. Sometimes necessary measures in policing and crime control do not make us popular. You know that yourself."

"Granted."

"And we have spoken to the gangs, and also through official camp *Fatah* and *Hamas* channels. I am sure they will let us know if they hear anything or miss anybody." One of the remaining two cup cakes was unwrapped and popped into his mouth whole in one well-practised movement. It was followed by coffee lubricant.

"And you have a theory?" prompted Merhi.

"Mmm."

"Based on what?"

Lattouf put his huge right hand up to his mouth and stifled the burp down to the level of a minor earthquake rather than the Richter Scale busters he did at home. He received several glances from nearby tables. "Based on exactly that. Nothing. Based on the silence."

"And...?"

"The last murder was obviously done *in situ*. The first one we simply don't know about. But the middle two? We accept they weren't killed in the yard. They were brought there from somewhere else. But nobody in the camp knows anything or misses anyone? Well, supposing they didn't come from the camp?"

The skin on the back of Merhi's neck began to tingle. "What are you saying?"

"Supposing they were killed outside the camp? Somewhere else? Somewhere in Beirut? Or even further? And they were brought to the camp and dumped to put us off the scent. Or to put the blame on the camp when actually there is something else going on? When actually it is nothing to do with the Palestinians at all?"

At that moment Jihad Merhi hated Fadi Lattouf. He wanted to go round to his house, rip the shirts off his children and strangle them with them so that the fat slob's genes would die out and not pass on to future generations. Because, Merhi realised straight away, the bastard was right. It could be that way. It might not be, but it could be.

He spoke slowly. "Which would mean that... if it was nothing to do with the Palestinians... if it was not a Palestinian problem..."

Fadi Lattouf beamed through his beard of cup cake crumbs. "Then it is a Lebanese problem. Your problem."

Jonblat, Beirut 14:00

Damn Lattouf. Damn his wife, damn his children. Damn his parents who had the nerve to bring the bastard into the world in the first place. Damn the camps, damn the Palestinians. Damn the Dunes Shopping Mall, damn *Cup Cake*, damn you, damn me, damn the whole fucking world.

Jihad Merhi was grateful he was in his office alone, with the door closed. He had already snapped six pencils in half, had kicked over his waste bin, picked it up and then launched it with the venom of a pitcher throwing the last ball of a perfect game. He had smoked four cigarettes consecutively and now found himself with two alight at the same time between the fingers of his right hand. What the hell – he put them both in his mouth.

Opening his drawer, he pulled out his bottle of Johnnie Walker whisky and filled his mug to the brim.

He really did not need this. Really, really he did not need this. Major Ghanem, his boss, was already on his back about his interest in the resurgent al-Murabitoun (frankly Ghanem was telling him to leave it alone), the political situation was tense (the sooner next year's elections came round, the better), intermittent and spasmodic bombings were taking place (usually with a victim, either actual or intended) – and now this.

Lattouf might be wrong, of course – and Merhi hoped to God he was. But it was certainly a theory. Lattouf had played it well. Knowing the oaf as he did, Merhi was certain it was by luck rather than design.

Lattouf had never formally reported the murders. Which meant that Merhi could not now announce them without a shit-load of concern being expressed upon him from above. And Merhi could take no direct action on the theory that at least some of the murders had not taken place in the camp unless he had proof that the theory was correct. So he could not put out a formal bulletin or contact the *Police Judiciare* to put them on the alert. Which meant that the only course open to him was the time-honoured Lebanese tradition: contacts. Just as Lebanese business ran on contacts, favours made, favours called in, wheels oiled, with nothing on paper until the deal was already done, so could Lebanese justice. He knew people, people owed him favours. Time to call them in.

Stubbing out the conjoined twins of his cigarettes, he took a large mouthful of the whisky.

Opening another drawer, he took out a leather-bound indexed notebook and threw it on the desk in front of him. He picked up his telephone and then put it back down again. The Listeners.

This would be a cell phone job.

21 November 2004
8 Shawwal 1425

Kahale, Lebanon 23:00

The dormitory was in darkness. Outside, the moonlight was blocked from the earth by a picket line of cloud so any natural illumination was at a minimum. But the man who now silently entered the room had excellent night vision, so the lack of light coming through the open window was not a hindrance.

He stopped just inside the door. Four beds, three shapes. One bed was empty.

Three sets of heavy breathing, one light snore, one moan. The room had the musty, dank smell of humans asleep.

He moved across to the beds...

Elias was asleep and dreaming impure dreams when the hand was placed firmly over his mouth. He awoke with a start, eyes confused and still in a state of rapid movement. His natural instinctive reaction to fight off the predator was restricted by the body pressing on top of him.

"Elias? Elias!" whispered the voice. "Wake up. Wake up. It is me."

Still confusion, then slowly followed by recognition. "Mmm?" he said into the hand.

"Be quiet. Don't speak. Don't wake the others. I need you to do something. Do you understand me?"

Elias nodded.

"Good." The hand was removed from his mouth. "Ssh. Come with me." The Commander stood back as the young man swung his legs out over the side of the bed. Elias still looked a little bewildered, his senses adjusting after returning with such a sudden shock. He wore only his underpants.

"Get your clothes," instructed the Commander. "You can put them on outside. Come."

Elias grabbed his shirt, trousers and trainers from the chair next to his bed and followed the Commander out through the double doors. There were no lights on, the corridor was in dim shadow.

As Elias pulled on his clothes, the Commander asked, "Have you seen Kabalan?"

Elias frowned in the darkness and shook his head. "No, sir. At least, not since we went to bed."

"He did not wake you, tell you where he was going?"

"Where he was going?"

"He is missing. I looked in to check on you all, as I do every night, and his bed was empty. Do you think the others know anything?"

"I – I wouldn't think so, sir." He finished buttoning his shirt and flipped his feet into his trainers.

"Okay. Well, I want your help. I trust you more than the others."

"Yes, sir. Thank you, sir."

"I have searched The Facility, he is not inside. We must look for him outside. He could not have gotten far. The van is still out there so he has not taken it. *Yalla.*" The Commander led the way down the corridor, Elias close behind. They reached the front hall and the Commander let the young man catch him up. "Has he said anything to you, Elias?" He was still speaking softly even though they were well away from the dormitory. "Has he been unhappy here? Does he want to leave?"

"I – I don't know, sir. He has not said anything. I know he has been anxious to find out exactly what it is we will be doing – but so have we all." Too late, he bit off the last remark. It might be unwise to let the Commander know of their concerns.

But he was relieved at the response.

"You all have every right to know. And you will very soon now. You are all good Palestinians. But I must be sure I can trust you. Most of you have proved this to me, but I have been worried about Kabalan."

"Has he done something wrong, sir?"

"No, no, just little things I have noticed. Nothing to worry you. But we must find him, he must be out there somewhere. Here - " The Commander grabbed a backpack from the floor near the main door. He rummaged inside and brought out a WiseLED Tactical flashlight. "Take this. We'll search the woods."

Three minutes walk from the house, they reached the edge of the woods. It was quiet, with eerie noises of unseen nocturnal creatures occasionally punctuating the silence. It was dark, but their flashlights were powerful, and here and there red or green eye reflections bounced back at them.

"Kabalan?" The Commander's voice was pitched, loud but not shouting. "Kabalan, are you out here?"

Nothing.

"It is good tactics to split up." The Commander sounded like he was giving a lesson. "I'll go to the north," he moved his flashlight to the right. "You go to the west."

"What shall I do if I find him, sir?"

"Tell him to come back! It is cold. It is no time to be out in the woods. I will meet you back here in half an hour, no later. If I find him, I will call you. *Yalla.*"

The Commander moved quickly and within two seconds was consumed by the darkness of the woods.

Elias had to admit he was frightened. Shit-scared actually. The noise his feet made as he trod on the twigs and fallen branches below the trees seemed so loud they must have been able to hear him kilometres away, way up in the village. If Kabalan was out here, he would hear him too. Hopefully he would appear, grateful his colleague had come looking for him after he had gotten lost in the woods.

The powerful 1500 lumen of the flashlight helped ward off the monsters that must surely be lurking out here. At least in some ways. In other ways, the light was so strong that it made the areas it did not hit all the darker. Anything could be there. Watching him.

He had been walking for ten minutes when he came to a small clearing between three pine trees. He stopped suddenly.

What was that?

He had heard something. A sound. Not a twig cracking underfoot, not a rustling of night creatures, not even a feral cry. It was not an unfamiliar sound, but not one that you would associate with the woods and at night, and that made it disorientating.

There it was again!

It was... it was... a *creaking* sound. He jerked the flashlight over the ground and over the base of the two trees in front of him. He caught one pair of tiny red eyes, which quickly vanished, but otherwise there was nothing there.

"Kabalan?" he said in a whisper. "Kabalan, is that you?"

Nothing. Then it came again, a low creak, sounding like... like... *rope*?

As the thought entered his mind, something lightly thumped him on the back of his head. He nearly jumped out of his skin, dropping the flashlight. He dived to the ground, grabbing the light and turning, pointing it up into the branches next to him.

Kabalan was hanging from the tree.

Mount Lebanon 23:45

The Djinn sat in the corner of the living area in The Damascene's apartment, silent and still. She was fully clothed in jeans and T-shirt - and, she realised, tonight she would remain so. The Damascene had not come home. Hariri must be on one his night-time sojourns, probably into southern Beirut to see Hizbullah or maybe further south-east to see Druze leader Walid Jumblatt in his palace at Moukhtara. And where Hariri was, The Damascene would be somewhere nearby.

She rose to her feet, lithe and supple, not a sign of stiffness even though she had been in the same position for two hours. When he did eventually return, he would be too tired for her ministrations (although he would be too polite to refuse), but the new trick she had thought of to pleasure the side of his head would need his full attention and support. Pity, but never mind. It would keep until the next time.

Barefooted, she walked across to the front door and opened it with her toe. She clicked down the latch and closed the door behind her as she went out.

She did not have far to go.

Kahale, Lebanon 23:45

Kabalan's body was swinging, its back to the gawping Elias. The rope came up from around the neck and was attached to a branch about a metre above the head. The eerie creaking seemed to be louder now that Elias could pinpoint its cause and location.

Slowly the body swung clockwise. Elias did not want to see what he was about to see. He had heard that hanging made your face go purple, your tongue hang out and sometimes your eyes popped right out of their sockets.

He lowered the flashlight and put his head down as the feet turned towards him. No. No, he was not going to look up. He would not. He could not.

The feet stopped turning and floated in front of his face, swinging, daring him to look up.

Shaking, the flashlight made its way up the body. Elias felt sick, physically sick. He did not want to look up. He would call the Commander.

He tried to shout, but his mouth was dry. Nothing but a croak came out. In the name of Allah, he had to do it.

He looked up.

And at that moment he lost control of every bodily function.

Snot flowed from his nose, spit flew from his previously arid mouth as he gasped, he pissed and shat himself simultaneously.

Kabalan was grinning at him.

And he had a gun in his hand.

"K – K – ?" Elias could not even speak.

Kabalan raised the gun, pointing it at him.

Then there was a shout. The Commander's voice. "Elias, here!"

Something flew at him from his left. Somehow he managed to catch it, but in doing so he dropped the flashlight. He had caught a gun.

"Shoot him, shoot him!" screamed the Commander. "Now, now!"

Blindly, unthinking, Elias raised the gun and fired.

So did Kabalan.

The bangs and flashes lit up the forest like fireworks at a festival. There were ten reports in all, maybe five from each gun, maybe one had fired more than the other.

Then there was silence.

Then after a few moments there was light. The Commander had switched his flashlight back on.

Elias was sitting on the floor in a terrible state, his face creased in terror, his jeans damp, warm and smelly.

Up above, Kabalan also gaped, but he had retained control of his functions. Why was Elias not dead? The Commander's orders had been specific, he was to shoot him. He raised the gun again and pulled the trigger. The hammer came down on an empty barrel. He looked at the Commander, whose face was stone.

"Well done both of you," said the Commander without

emotion. "You have both passed."

Kabalan wriggled. The rope under his arms was beginning to chafe. He did not understand what had happened but he wanted to get down.

"Go back to the house, Elias," ordered the Commander. "I am very pleased and therefore your President is very pleased. You have proven yourself. Clean yourself up and do not mention this to any of the others. Go, *yalla!*"

For a moment Elias was bemused, then he picked up his flashlight and scurried off without a word, leaving a faint odour in the night air.

The Commander looked up at Kabalan then walked around the dangling legs and stepped up onto a large, jutting root of the tree. Level with the young man, he pulled a knife from his waistband.

Kabalan was relieved as he felt the rope being cut. "Th – thank you, sir." The Commander supported his weight, holding his legs in his right arm, cutting with his left hand. "Was – was that a test?"

"Yes," replied the Commander.

But what he didn't mention was that, unlike the test he had set the other two recruits, and unlike the bullets in the gun he had thrown to Elias, the bullets in Kabalan's gun had been live.

And he had missed with every one.

"But," said the Commander. "I lied. You failed."

The rope had been cut from underneath Kabalan's arms but it was still wound tightly around his neck. Holding the young man's legs, the Commander jumped off the root and pulled hard downwards as he landed.

Kabalan's neck broke with a crack like a stepped-on twig.

22 November 2004
9 Shawwal 1425

Kahale, Lebanon 08:00 – 09:00

Elias was quiet at breakfast the next morning. Quiet and just a little bit concerned.

On returning to the house in the early hours, he had stripped off his soiled clothing and showered in the communal washrooms, not the dormitory *en suite*, so as not to wake the other two. He had wrapped his ruined clothes in two plastic bags and had gone back outside to bury them deeply in the rubbish bin.

Then he had returned inside and slipped into his bed. He would get fresh clothes from the wardrobe in the morning.

Overall he felt relief. He was still shaking from what had happened in the woods, but he was grateful it had only been a test – and one that he and Kabalan had passed. The Commander was pleased with them.

But the adrenaline in his body took its own time to assuage, and it had been over an hour before he could get back to sleep. Which meant that he knew Kabalan had not returned.

About forty minutes after getting into bed, he had heard the van start up outside and drive off. The Commander must have a task – a real task – for Kabalan, and they had gone off together.

Which was why his relief had turned to concern. Was Kabalan the Commander's favourite? Was he going to become a sergeant while the rest of them remained foot soldiers? That was so unfair. They had all done whatever was asked of them –

exercised, cooked, cleaned, read, prayed. Why was Kabalan being singled out for preferential treatment? He had noticed the way the Commander sometimes looked at Kabalan. He was handsome, if you liked that sort of thing. Was there an ulterior motive in his preferential treatment...?

On waking up, Yazbek and Ahmad had commented on Kabalan's bed being empty, but Elias had claimed ignorance, telling them he had been asleep all night.

Then Yazbek had beckoned them over to the window, pointing out that the van was gone. What was going on?

With two minutes to spare before their daily gathering in the meeting room, the Mitsubishi Express van pulled in at the gate and drove up to the front of the house. Only the Commander got out, Kabalan was nowhere to be seen.

The Commander said nothing as he walked past them in the hallway. Like little chicks they followed him into the meeting room, taking their usual places. The chair on the end on the left was noticeably empty.

"Morning of light, my brave men," began the Commander.

Mornings of peace were wished back.

"You will notice that Kabalan is no longer with us."

"Where is he, sir? Has something happened?" asked a worried-looking Yazbek.

The Commander smiled. "Not at all. I told you I would tell you of your mission, your tasks, when the time was right. Well, Kabalan has his task and he has left us to fulfil it. Already his family are preparing to move out of the camp."

"Will he be coming back, sir?" Ahmad.

"No."

"And what about our tasks? Will we get them soon, sir?" Elias's concern had turned to enthusiasm. Perhaps he had been wrong. One of them had to be the first to be entrusted, it just happened to be Kabalan.

"Very soon," nodded the Commander. "When the time is right. There will be several tasks, including some where we will be working together."

The three young men looked pleased. Elias shook his fist in satisfaction. Soon they would be serving their President. Soon their families would be moving from the camp.

"One of the tasks will involve strength," continued the Commander. "So I want you to continue with your exercises. I have to go away for a while, but when I come back you will be closer to starting your first part of the mission." He looked keenly from one to the other. "My brave Palestinians."

None of them knew that, as he was saying those words, thirty kilometres away in a secluded part of the swamps at the Aammiq Wetlands in the Bekaa, a greater spotted eagle was pecking an eye from the remnants of the skull of Kabalan Elb.

Mount Lebanon 12:00

The Damascene returned to the apartment around midday. He had not slept in thirty hours and the first thing he did was to strip off his clothes and head for the shower.

As the water cascaded through his long hair and down over his body, he allowed himself a feeling of satisfaction. Hariri had been busy. It was remarkable how a man who had just had his sixtieth birthday could keep going at such a frenetic and constant pace. In the space of twenty-four hours he had not only been to see Hassan Nasrallah and Druze leader Walid Jumblatt, but he was also in liaison with some unlikely bedfellows from across the political spectrum such as the Christian Qornet Shehwan Gathering, the Democratic Forum, the Democratic Leftist Movement, exiled General Michel Aoun's Free Patriotic Front and even the banned Christian Lebanese Forces. There were rumours that they were organising a meeting soon – but this was really of no interest to The Damascene.

He was satisfied because all this coming and going, all the secretive, furtive and sometimes clandestine meetings, the whispered discussions in the bathrooms of Koreitem (with the taps running), the mobile telephone calls out in the gardens, all had proved that Hariri was almost impossible to assassinate.

His movements and whereabouts were too flexible for any snipers; his heavily-armoured motorcade with its state-of-the-art jamming devices would thwart any remote detonation of roadside bombs; a timer-bomb was out of the question as spot-on timed accuracy could never be guaranteed; and a close-range shooting or stabbing would always be prevented by the close-quarter protection of Abu Tarek and his excellent security team.

After ten minutes, The Damascene turned off the shower and stepped out. As the water dripped off his body, he walked downstairs to the open-plan living area, the place brightly lit by the weak November sun coming in through the floor to ceiling windows. He looked out over Beirut.

Hariri could be poisoned, of course (there were rumours that had happened to Arafat, just one of the many wild theories flying around about the Palestinian leader's death), but that just would not happen. Poisoning could be covered up as a natural death – they would call it a heart attack, quite believable for this ebullient, overweight, ageing man. Anyone who wanted Hariri dead would want it done in a spectacular fashion, as a message to the world.

And The Damascene knew how.

Now he needed sleep, to recharge himself. As he turned away from the window and back towards the stairs, something caught his eye. He made a detour towards the kitchen.

A small object was sitting on the otherwise empty breakfast counter that separated the kitchen from the living area. He picked it up, turning it over in his left hand.

It was light, hardly heavier than a circle of tin foil. It was a decorative golden coin – the sort that would adorn a belly dancer's outfit.

He smiled. She had been here and he had missed her – in more ways than one. It had been just five days – her visits were becoming more frequent.

He sniffed the coin. There was no odour. Pity.

He hoped she would visit again soon. He would welcome the relief of her body.

23 November 2004
10 Shawwal 1425

Damascus, Syria 19:00

Ghazi Kanaan, the recently-appointed Minister of the Interior of Syria, sat at his desk in his office overlooking the Barada River and absentmindedly tappy-tapped a pencil on the papers in front of him. It was a report on the interrogation of Kurdish detainees still in custody eight months after the football riots up in Al Qamishli. But his mind had wandered from the file, distracted by the fact that Kurds were majority Sunni – and there was another Sunni that was at the back of his mind.

Rafic Hariri. The thorn in his side was more popular than ever since his 'resignation', and his Future Movement was beginning to roll. Even at this stage, with six months to go until the Lebanese elections, the force was building for a political landslide. And that was not popular with some people, either in Damascus or Beirut.

Over a month ago, Kanaan had sent one of his foot soldiers to Beirut in response to his man's telephone call. The foot soldier had never returned. It was worrying but not surprising – anything could have happened. He could have been captured by one of the myriad Lebanese factions and either killed or held prisoner somewhere for future leverage. He could have simply deserted. Or Captain Mebarak might have done for him – Mebarak was, after all, first and foremost a killer.

Mebarak was faring well. Hariri was still alive. Kanaan now wondered whether he should call him off. He liked Hariri, had gotten along with him as well as he could have over the years, had even done some clandestine business deals with him, but the juggernaut of the Future Movement was not something Kanaan could now be associated with. His plans were slowly, slowly coming to fruition in Syria. His anonymous efforts at subtle destabilisation from within were beginning to crack the eggshell facade of the hierarchy. And soon, if everything went well, Syria might have a new leader.

And if everything did not go well...

Well, history would decide.

Should he call Mebarak in? He might very well need his pet mercenary for other internal elimination projects very soon. Or simply for protection.

Any outside source wanting to kill Hariri would have done so by now. Hariri was going to become Prime Minister again next May, a Prime Minister of a new, vibrant, independent Lebanon, no longer under Syria's protection.

Kanaan, on the other hand, would be under severe threat once those hierarchical cracks turned into fissures. It would be a matter of life or death.

Literally.

So what should he do about his man in Beirut?

1 December 2004
18 Shawwal 1425

Kahale, Lebanon 16:00 – 18:00

"Very good," Al-Rajul nodded his approval at the three young men prone on the ground in front of him. Each was face down, each holding a Russian SKS rifle with a bipod attached to the front of the stock. They had been firing empty at a target on the edge of the woods, about a hundred and fifty metres away. The target was a man's jacket, spread open and draped over a tree branch at about average head height. "Do you feel confident?"

There were mumbled agreements from the ground.

"Then next time you will use ammunition. Now, come on up. That is it for today. It is time for *Maghrib salat*. Go wash then pray. Then join me in the meeting room. I will pray on my own."

The three young men handed their rifles to their Commander one by one and headed off towards the house, chattering. Al-Rajul followed, rifles under his arm.

He knew that shooting Hariri was not what his employer had in mind, but sniper training was of benefit as a contingency. His employer had specified the date of Hariri's death. The manner, although important, was secondary. The date was unchangeable.

He could already hear the showers being run when he entered the house. He would not, of course, be praying (for what? To whom?), but he would shower and change in his own quarters upstairs.

Twenty minutes later, he was in the meeting room ahead of the recruits. He did not believe in God, he did not believe in Chance, but he did believe in Fate. The order of their entry into the room would determine the next selection – as natural a selection as there could be. Decided by Fate.

Ahmad was the first in, closely followed by the other two. They took their usual seats.

Al-Rajul was half-sitting against the edge of a table in front of them. He nodded. "How did it feel with the rifles this afternoon?"

"Good, sir. Good," said Ahmad.

"A little heavy, I have only used a pistol before," Elias hoped his conspiratorial glance at the Commander would be returned, but he was disappointed. "But I can get used to it."

"It was okay," said Yazbek. "I look forward to using ammunition next time."

"As you will, as you will," confirmed Al-Rajul. "Right," he pushed himself up off the desk. "The next stage of our mission is upon us. I will require one of you - "

"Me, sir!" Elias's hand shot up.

"I will decide." The look he gave Elias was hard. The hand went down quickly. "I will require one of you to assist me in a task. Ahmad, can you drive?"

"Yes, sir." Ahmad smiled.

"Yazbek?"

"Yes, sir!"

"Then Yazbek it is you."

Ahmad looked as sullen as Yazbek looked elated. Elias looked like he might cry.

"Your time will come," Al-Rajul reassured the unchosen. "Soon now. For now, it is Yazbek. The three of you, go eat. Then Yazbek, join me out at the van an hour."

Mount Lebanon 19:00

It was dark by the time the van pulled away from The Facility. Its full beams pierced the blackness as it made its way up to the Beirut – Damascus road and turned right. The Commander was driving, an excited Yazbek was next to him.

As soon as they hit the main road, Yazbek asked "Where are we going, sir? What am I to do?"

"All in good time, Yazbek. All in good time," replied the Commander calmly. "Just relax and enjoy the ride."

Yazbek knew it would be pointless to push the matter, so he did as he was told – at least the enjoying the ride bit.

They drove past the town of Bhamdoun and upwards into the mountain. The main road was in good condition so the climb was not arduous. It was busy, as this road always was, no matter the time of day or time of year.

Up past Mdairej, the road peaked as it passed between the Barouk and Knisse mountains where they could already see snow. Then they began their descent into the Bekaa Valley. At Chtaura they turned left, into the foothills of Mount Sannine.

Towards Zahlé.

Zahlé, Lebanon 21:00

At night the red roofs of the town could not be seen, hidden beneath a hazy patina of diffused light. The lights became stronger and more distinct as they came closer to the town until the van's full beams were no longer necessary.

"Ever been here before?" asked the Commander as they turned left into the town.

"Me, sir? No," replied Yazbek, adding "I have never been further than Beirut."

The Commander's eyebrows rose but he made no comment. Then he said, "The city of wine and poetry."

"Really?"

"So they say. Personally I do not like poetry and of course I do not drink."

"Of course."

They drove north and found a place to park alongside the Berdaouni River at the bottom of the Wadi el-Aarayesh (Grape Vine Valley). Here innumerable restaurants stretched alongside the river, tree-shaded during the day, lit up by multicoloured lights stretched between the branches and across the road at night. Here the place was busy, each restaurant (known as casinos) vying for trade. An old woman was making bread outside one of the cafés. In a nearby casino a man dressed in traditional baggy trousers, shirt and waistcoat, fez on his head, poured thick and dark local coffee from an urn which he actually seemed to be wearing on his hip. Music played, voices were loud.

Nobody gave the parked van a second glance.

"Right," the Commander turned towards Yazbek. "Your job is to drive this van. You can do that?"

Yazbek's face shone brighter than all the lights in the Wadi. "Oh yes, sir! Where are we going?"

"*We* are not going anywhere. You are. I've got something to do."

"Sir?"

"Drive back the way we came. You remember it?"

"Y-yes. Just the main road. Am I to go back to The Facility? I don't understand. Have I disappointed you?"

"You will be doing exactly what I want you to do. You know el-Mdairej, up at the top? Near the snow. We passed by on the way."

"I – I think so."

"The bridge. The big bridge we came across."

Yazbek nodded. "Yes, yes of course."

"There is a rest area this side of the bridge. Meet me there in one hour."

"But how will you - ?"

"Do not question me! Do as I say." The Commander opened the van door and got out. "Come." He beckoned with his hand and the frowning Yazbek slid across into the driver's seat. "This is your task," the Commander's voice was more conciliatory. "Tomorrow you go and collect your family from the camp."

Yazbek nodded, conflicting emotions playing across his face.

"Do as I say," pressed the Commander. "Do not worry about me, I will be there in an hour. Now go. *Yalla!*"

He slammed the door as Yazbek started the engine, and stood back as the van jumpily pulled away from the kerb. He watched the van go as he began walking south.

Then he turned west and quickly disappeared into the back streets of the town.

It took just five minutes for him to find what he was looking for.

Yazbek was both excited and nervous. Nervous because he had never driven a manual vehicle before (he stalled three times on his way out of Zahlé and then drove the next five minutes just in second gear) and excited because he was at last serving his President and his country. He was one of the chosen ones. Tomorrow he and his family would be out of that wretched camp forever. He was, he thought, fulfilling his destiny.

And in that he was right. Every human being fulfils their destiny. It is only a pity that most of them never know what their destiny is...

Mount Lebanon 22:45

Yazbek needed the full hour the Commander had given him to get to the bridge at Mdairej. He lost count of the times he stalled the van on its climb up the mountain, even though he was on a main road. And it was an unfriendly darkness out there, up here at night in the cold. There was still some traffic coming towards him, but it was thin now, the oncoming full beams slicing through the windscreen like lasers. The van's own lights cast a dim jaundice into the darkness in reply.

Sixty minutes out of Zahlé he thought he recognised the rest area coming up. He leant forward, squinting into the night. Yes, this was it, he was sure. Although the bridge was the highest in the Middle East, he couldn't see it from road level, it was just black ahead. He turned in to his right and pulled up, leaving the engine running so that he could keep the heater on.

He turned off the headlights and then turned them back on again quickly. Too dark, *merci ktir*, he didn't want the monsters coming out! Just to be on the safe side, he flicked down the door lock.

Only one car came along in the next ten minutes, going down towards Chtaura, its headlights glaring at him, piercing into the van, and then going out instantly as the car passed.

Five minutes later he noticed some lights in his left wing mirror, coming up the mountain. They seemed to be approaching quickly, probably somebody in a rush to get back to Beirut before midnight. He averted his eyes as the lights filled the mirror, but then he was aware that there was light on the right side of the van as well. The vehicle had pulled in behind him.

Then the lights behind went out, and he was grateful but momentarily disorientated. There was a knock on the window and he jumped out of his skin. *Shit!* The Commander's face was staring through the glass, frowning as he tried the handle. Hastily, Yazbek opened the door.

"You are okay?" asked the Commander as Yazbek climbed out.

"Yes, sir, yes. I didn't know it was you."

"Why would you?"

Yazbek looked at the vehicle behind. It just seemed like a large shadow in the darkness, bigger than the van but with the word MITSUBISHI emblazoned across the grill.

"Our new van," explained the Commander. "It will suit our

mission just fine. Now we must ditch this one. Here," his hand went into his jacket pocket and produced a screwdriver. "You take the number plates off the Express. I'll do the Canter. We'll swap them over."

It was done within five minutes – a perfect job on the Canter van, a not so perfect job on the Express because it didn't really matter.

"Are we leaving the van here, sir?" asked Yazbek as he handed back the screwdriver.

"What do you think?" the Commander's reply was scornful. "Of course not. We must get rid of it." He looked at the watch on his right wrist. "Has it been busy along here?"

"Only one car going down in the last twenty minutes. Just you coming up."

The Commander looked behind him into the blackness. Then he said, "Right. We move and we move now. The van goes off the bridge. Get in."

"What!"

"Get in. Do as you are ordered. Crash it into the barrier, then get out and we'll push it over. Hurry."

"But I don't think - "

"In the name of Allah the Almighty! I will do it. Get out of the way. You follow to help me push it." The Commander climbed in and slammed the door. Immediately there was a crunching of gears and the Express van moved back out onto the road and onto the bridge. Yazbek ran after it. The Commander was angry with him, and rightly so. He would have to make it up to him. He did not want to fail in his mission at the last minute.

Halfway across the bridge, the van veered to the right and with a squeal of brakes rammed into the crash barrier. Both the barrier and the front of the van buckled. The van reversed back over the other side and shot forwards again, hitting the same part of the barrier, the Commander applying the brakes right at the last moment.

Again. And again.

At the fourth impact the barrier broke. There was still a metre of bridge left on the other side, and the van's wheels stopped with a few centimetres to spare before the edge.

Carefully, the Commander got out and stepped back over the barrier. "Come, Yazbek. Help me."

Yazbek had been staring open-mouthed from the other side of the road. "Sh – should we turn the lights off, sir?" He came over.

"Don't be stupid!" The Commander's left hand went into his jacket hip pocket. "Do you think someone who crashes pauses to turn off his lights before the fatal moment? Sometimes you Palestinians can be idiots."

Yazbek winced. That was uncalled for. And wasn't the Commander Palestinian also?

"Come, help me," ordered the Commander. "I can't do this on my own."

Looking sullen, Yazbek went to the back of the van, ready to push. Suddenly he did not like the Commander.

"Not there. Push from the front, by the door."

With a sniff of disrespect, Yazbek went round to the open driver's door.

"There is one more thing we need," said the Commander matter-of-factly, taking his hand out of his pocket. In his palm he held the hard chunk of olive wood, the Holding Cross. "The driver."

"The what - ?"

The cross slammed into Yazbek's forehead above his left eye. At the same time, Al-Rajul pushed him backwards into the van so that the blood would not splash out onto the road.

He hit him again and again, the hard wood hitting hard bone, hit, hit, hit, just like the van breaking the crash barrier, with the same cracking noises.

Yazbek died in silence and shock and in a state of hatred for his murderer, the man he had trusted. He was on his back across the front seats of the van.

Al-Rajul leant in and kept on hitting until his fist stopped hitting bone and moved into pulp and then liquid. Then he stopped, breathing heavily through his flared nostrils. He withdrew his dripping hand from inside Yazbek's head and wiped it first on the cadaver's shirt and then on its trousers, carefully cleaning the cross as well. The smell of brains was filling the cabin.

Al-Rajul pushed himself up off the body and out of the van. With two swift movements of his head, he looked around. There were still no lights in the distance. No one was close. He leant back in and released the parking break. The gears were in neutral.

He kicked Yazbek's protruding feet into the van and slammed the driver's door. Then quickly he went round to the back. Bracing his feet, he leant against the van and pushed. One... two... three...

The van rolled forward.

And the front wheels tipped over the edge.

The van rocked, it beams nodding up and down in the darkness like searchlights.

Al-Rajul bent at the knees and grabbed the base of the van. Using its own rocking momentum and his own malevolent strength, he heaved. One – down... two – down... three – down... four – down... five – heave...! He let out a roar.

The van slid on its undercarriage off the edge of the bridge. The force of the wheels hitting the edge made it spin on the vertical as it went over.

Four seconds later a deep, loud *whump* shook the night as it hit the floor of the valley below. The lights were obliterated. Running to the edge and looking over, Al-Rajul could see nothing. There was no fire, no explosion. Good. Such things rarely happened in real accidents.

And this was a real accident.

He hastened back to the Mitsubishi Canter van, switched on

the engine, turned on his beams and pulled back out onto the road. As he drove across the bridge, his lights illuminated the break in the crash barrier.

Wonder what had happened there? Bad workmanship? Or had somebody crashed? There was no sign of any vehicle. Maybe the accident had happened a long time ago and they had just not been bothered to repair it. Still, what did he care? It was nothing to do with him. He was just one of the farmers of the Bekaa Valley, taking his produce into the capital for sale...

2 December 2004
19 Shawwal 1425

Kahale, Lebanon 07:30

When Elias and Ahmad woke the next morning, they were surprised to see a white Mitsubishi Canter van parked outside. It had a separate cabin at the front and a large, half soft-sided cargo area at the back. It was the sort of van that the richer farmers would use for carrying produce to shops and markets (the poorer farmers would use smaller and more clapped-out vehicles). Was this a food delivery? The Express van was not out there, so the Commander must not be back.

But as they entered the dining room to get breakfast, the Commander was there waiting for them. As usual he wore his Palestinian *keffiyeh*, but tied around his neck as he had taken to wearing it recently, not on his head. For some reason it looked very bulky today.

"Morning of light, my brave Palestinians." He was in a good mood.

"Morning of peace, sir," smiled Elias.

"Morning of joy, Commander," nodded Ahmad.

"Before you eat I have something for you. Have you prayed?" They had. "Good. Do you like our new van?"

"It is ours, sir?" Elias.

"For our mission, yes. Yazbek helped me to get it last night. He has now fulfilled his task successfully and has left us. As promised, he will not be setting foot in the camp again."

Elias and Ahmad exchanged pleased glances, but they were

also envious. They wished their turn would hurry up and come.

"I have also been in touch with the new President. He extends his congratulations to us, and especially thanks you two for your patience. As we are the only ones here, I can tell you now that you two have been singled out for more glorious, more trustworthy tasks than the other two. And your rewards, and the rewards for your families, will be that much larger."

"Indeed a morning of joy," nodded Ahmad. Elias was beaming.

"And he has sent you each a token of his appreciation." The Commander's hands moved to his neck and he took off one then two black-on-white *keffiyehs*, his own remaining underneath. He held them out. "For you. From the President. Wear them with honour and pride."

Elias and Ahmad accepted their gifts in subdued awe, not knowing what to say. For them? *From the President?* Smiling, glowing like little boys with their *Eid* presents, they put them on, giving each other approving looks.

"Today we will undertake more firearms training," announced the Commander. "And then more weight training. Soon the three of us will have a mission together, and I need you fit and strong. Now, go eat." He smiled dismissively.

Elias and Ahmad were pleased to the point of euphoria, and Al-Rajul knew that at that moment, and from then on, they would do anything for him.

He watched them filling their plates. He needed them physically fit and physically strong, but also mentally subservient. He did not want them thinking too much for themselves.

And apparently they hadn't.

Because neither of them had noticed that the cabin of the new van outside only sat two persons...

6 December 2004
23 Shawwal 1425

Jonblat, Beirut 10:00

"*Marhaba.* Captain Merhi?"

"*Naam.*"

"Jihad, *kifak?* It's Selim Himo, Bekaa Inquiry Brigade."

"Selim! *Mnih! Kifak?* It's been a long time."

"*Mnih, mnih.* That training course was too long ago now."

"How are you doing out there in the wilds?"

"It has its own problems, but it's a darn sight more peaceful than Beirut. And the *Gendarmerie* doesn't have the same problems as the ISF."

"Tell me about it. You made a good move."

"Jihad, I heard on the wire that you wanted to be informed if anything, er, unusual turned up."

"Ah."

"Well, I think I have something."

"Say no more."

"I understand."

"I'll call you back. You have a mobile?"

Himo read out a number.

"Okay, Selim. Ten minutes.""

Fifteen minutes later, Jihad Merhi was walking along Hamra Street with the Monday morning shoppers, smoking his third consecutive Cedars King Size and with a polycup of triple espresso in his left hand. His right hand held his mobile phone to his ear.

"Selim? Sorry about that, you know how it is."

"Only too well. Jihad, I have something that might interest you. Turned up on Friday, report was waiting on my desk when I came in this morning. Injuries consistent with your description."

Damn. "Where is it?"

"Still in place. Hasn't been moved."

"Can you leave it there for another day, so I can come see it?"

"Bien sûr, pas de problème."

"I'll be bringing somebody with me. Just a... consultant."

"Fine, I'll ask no questions. And Jihad?"

"Oui?"

"Bring your *caoutchouc*."

Verdun, Beirut 14:00

"What?! No way, no chance." Sesame seeds from either the quarter pounder with cheese or the Big Mac fell into the beard of Captain Fadi Lattouf of the Palestinian Security Force as he exclaimed, ate and shook his head at the same time. Special sauce lined his lips.

"Why not?" Jihad Merhi's intolerance was barely concealed. He knew this would be the big man's reaction, and he knew the game would have to be played out to its inevitable conclusion.

"It is not my case anymore."

"Says who? Yes it is, my friend."

"Now you have another body that proves it. My theory was correct," reasoned Lattouf.

Merhi sighed and pursed his lips. He looked at the plainly wrapped simple cheeseburger in front of him which had been waiting for him when he arrived. "You want this too?"

"You don't want it?"

"I am going home straight after this. Gisele is cooking one of her fish dishes. Don't want to spoil my appetite."

"You are a lucky, lucky man." Lattouf pulled the burger into his personal space (which was most of the table).

"We seem to have our first body outside of the camp, I grant you," agreed Merhi. "But how can we be certain unless you verify it? I haven't seen any of them, remember?"

"Send me a photo."

"That's not a chain of evidence or identification and you know it, not even in Palestinian law."

Lattouf shrugged.

"I am asking you as a colleague in law enforcement," persisted Merhi. "As a friend."

The last one hit home and a look of anguish briefly flashed across Lattouf's face. "Jihad, I have no jurisdiction outside of the camp, you know that. How would it look if a Palestinian policeman was involved in a Lebanese investigation?"

"The same way it looked when a Lebanese policeman was involved in a Palestinian investigation. I should not have been there, but I did it for you. As a friend."

"Yes, but that was - "

"Different? You were going to say that was different, weren't you?"

"I - "

"There's no difference. I'm not asking you to come in full uniform with sirens blazing. Just accompany me."

Lattouf slurped half of a supersize cup of coffee. "I could get in serious trouble. With the groups, you know."

"Let me run another theory by you, Fadi."

"Mm?"

"You contend that the murders are occurring outside the camp and the bodies are being brought to the camp and dumped - " Merhi stopped and watched the spectacle of Fadi Lattouf putting the entire cheeseburger into his mouth whole, folding it neatly at either side as it went into the cavern. Then he continued. "What if the murders are occurring inside the camp and your serial killer has now started to dump them outside?

Have you thought of that? That puts the problem right back in your lap, my friend. And it also means that we would then have the right to liaise with you in whatever way we see fit, having been dragged into Palestinian affairs. And the groups certainly will not like that, will they?"

Lattouf stopped chewing, a small piece of bun poking from the left corner of his mouth.

"That," continued Merhi, "would be serious trouble with a capital S."

A puzzled frown creased Lattouf's brow as he started chewing again. He swallowed and said quietly, "How has it come to this?"

It was Merhi's turn to shrug. "Not your fault, not my fault. And we can possibly still keep a lid on this. Work it between us. Our masters would want that. No boat rocking. No," he made bunny ears with his fingers, "upsetting the delicate balance of Lebanese and Palestinian relations regarding the camps. Just come with me, Fadi."

Lattouf sighed. "When?"

"Tomorrow. Be downstairs here outside the car park at eight. The shops won't yet be open so it'll be quiet. I'll pick you up. And Fadi?"

"Yes?"

"Bring your *caoutchouc*."

7 December 2004
24 Shawwal 1425

Aammiq Wetlands, West Bekaa, Lebanon 11:00

The body was lying face down entangled in the reeds at the edge of the swamp, the water about twenty centimetres deep. It had been discovered by a Jordanian conservationist engaged in winter ecosystem studies, who had spotted what he thought was dumped rubbish and had gone to remove it, quickly stepping away and contacting the police when he realised it was – or had been – human.

"It has not been moved?" asked Jihad Merhi.

"Just turned over then quickly turned back again," replied Lieutenant Selim Himo of the Bekaa Inquiry Brigade. Himo was taller and younger than Merhi, having risen quickly through the ranks, a future star as yet uncorrupted by the pressures of future higher rank.

"Fadi - ?" Merhi turned. "Where the hell is he?" Lattouf was about ten metres back, still ploughing laboriously through the reeds. He had not brought any *caoutchouc* (there was not much call for waders in a Palestinian refugee camp in the Middle East) so had to borrow a pair – which of course were a few sizes too small, making him walk like an inexperienced cross-dresser in high heels. He wore an old black padded jacket, denim shirt frayed at the collar, and jeans. It was cool and damp down here in the wetlands, but up behind them the mountains were covered in snow. Merhi and Himo were in their uniforms, their waders of correctly-fitting sizes.

"I'm coming, I'm coming," mumbled Lattouf. "The things I do! These accursed rubbers are killing me. And I don't know what I'm doing here anyway."

"You are my expert witness," said Merhi sternly. "Come, witness."

Himo had asked no questions about the huge fat giant that accompanied Jihad Merhi, but obviously he knew he was Palestinian. Were they allowing them into the Lebanese police nowadays? Or was something else going on?

"Can we turn him?" asked Merhi as Lattouf reached them.

Himo nodded. "If you'll give me a hand. Best take off your jacket in case of accidents."

"Good idea."

Both men removed their jackets and gave them to Lattouf to hold. There were some mumblings about coming all this way to be a cloakroom attendant, but they ignored them. Rolling up their shirtsleeves, they crouched down. Merhi put his hands into the water this side of the body.

"No, no, reach across and pull him over towards us," advised Himo. "The swamp does not give up her possessions easily. It will be better if we tug rather than push. And there might be some other effect also."

They reached across and grabbed the body by its far side. The first tug achieved nothing, the second raised the body just a little before it fell back down again, making ripples. The damn cadaver seemed heavier than Fadi Lattouf. Merhi had a sudden empathy with the Palestinian's wife Nada. Five children conceived with that on top of you!

They put all their power and effort behind the third heave, both groaning to give themselves strength, and, with a sucking sound, the body rose and rolled with its back towards them.

Suddenly a shot of swamp water sprayed out from the head about a third of a metre into the air.

"Did that before," explained Himo breathlessly. "Suction where the hole is."

The body's own weight brought it over and it flopped onto the policemen's feet. Both stepped back rapidly.

"In the name of Jesus Christ!" Merhi stood up quickly. Oh my good God.

Himo was grimacing.

Lattouf leant forward and looked. There was no face, the swamp life had seen to that. It was just the shell of a human head filled with murky water. The clothes on the body, still intact, were straight young person's wear: cargo pants and light shirt.

For the first time in his career, Merhi thought he was going to be sick. Thank God the swamp water was taming the smell, but he expected it to hit his nostrils any minute.

Lattouf nodded and calmly straightened up. He seemed unaffected by the sight. "The others were worse," he said. "The waters have looked after this one."

"But it's the same?" Merhi swallowed back bile.

"Oh yes."

"There have been others?" queried Himo.

Lattouf's eyes shot to Merhi.

"We think we have a serial killer," explained Merhi. "Operating in... Beirut. This is the first outside."

"You want jurisdiction?"

"No, no. Do whatever checks and searches you think you need to do, but I doubt you'll find anything. This is the fourth young Pal... person... that we know of. None of them have had records, none reported missing. The murder would not have been committed here, this is just a dumping ground." He looked around, wondering: but why here? Probably thought the marsh would consume it, that it would never been found. But where was it brought from? He said, "If you could just give me a report, Selim, how long dead *et cetera*, that will be fine. We will eventually subsume it within the general enquiry."

"As you wish."

"Do you, er... want any help?" Merhi waved a hand at the

body.

"No, no. I'll send some men for it."

"Perhaps you should just leave it here," suggested Lattouf. "A decomposing tourist attraction come the spring. Nobody will claim it, you'll only take it out to dispose of it later." He saw the look both men were giving him and closed his mouth. Suddenly there was a severe tickling in his nose at the same time as his stomach rumbled. He tried to breathe in, but the tickling only got worse with each small inhale. His face screwed up as if he was in excruciating agony, his mouth opened in a grimace. He threw his head back, making a growling *ahh* sound, rising in volume.

Then his head shot forward and he emitted a stentorian sneeze at the same time as a loud fart blasted from his rear. Birds flew into the air nearby.

"Bloody damp," mumbled Lattouf, still bent from the waist. Two more smaller farts popped out as he straightened up. "Sorry about that, gentlemen." The two policemen were staring into the swamp at his feet. He looked down and saw their two jackets resting on the water. Quickly he bent down and grabbed them, water running off them as he lifted them up. "They'll be fine," he said cheerfully. "Fine. It's just a little water." He held them out.

Slowly Merhi and Himo reached out and took back their jackets, nonplussed.

"Talking of this being a dumping ground, I think I need to," announced Lattouf. "Can we stop by your office on the way back? Or actually, I could do it here, couldn't I? It wouldn't make any difference. It is a bog, after all."

That, thought Merhi, would be something the swamp would never tame. In years to come, future ecologists would analyse Lattouf's dump and conclude that yes, earth had been colonised by creatures from another planet in the past. The poisoned marshes of Aammiq, where all life was extinct. "Not near the body," he said. "Go over there somewhere."

"You might want to give me a good clearance," advised the Palestinian. "I can sometimes be, er... vociferous."

"Too much information," Merhi held up his hand as he walked away with the bemused Salim Himo. "And don't cause a tsunami."

"My arse is always considerate of others," proclaimed its owner.

Merhi and Himo kept on walking. Twenty seconds after, they heard the three-tone trumpet blast, and while they were still walking and were at least fifty metres away, the swamp water around their feet actually rippled violently.

Chtaura, Lebanon 12:30

Back in his regional office, and with Captain Jihad Merhi and his idiot sidekick back on their way to Beirut, Lieutenant Salim Himo picked up the telephone. A future star as yet uncorrupted by the pressures of future higher rank he may be, but he also had the self-centred interest of all high-flyers.

He dialled a number.

Ras en Nabaa, Beirut 12:31

In his office in the Department of General Security, Captain Maroun Khoury answered his ringing telephone.

Five minutes later, with the call ended, he picked up the phone again and keyed a number. It took a few rings for the person to answer, then Khoury said "ZiZi. Some good news. We have a body..."

11 December 2004
28 Shawwal 1425

Jonblat, Beirut 11:45

Four days later and Jihad Merhi was a happy man.

He realised as he thought it that 'happy' was too strong a description. How could you be happy when you were a Captain of the Internal Security Force? That was not part of the job description, not one of the required competencies. Mildly contented, perhaps? Still too strong. *Pleased.* Yes, that would do.

Four days later and Jihad Merhi was pleased. Lieutenant Selim Himo of the Bekaa Inquiry Brigade had been good. Merhi was impressed. Himo would go far.

The report had been awaiting Merhi when he came in this morning. Copied to him 'as per ISF request', it reported the discovery of a body in the Aammiq Wetlands. Cause of death: unknown. No reason to suspect foul play. Probably an accident, it sometimes happens in the marshes. An unwary visitor gets stuck. No one else around. Dies of hypothermia, or possibly even a heart attack brought on by desperation to free himself from the cloying, sucking mud. Time of death: hard to say, probably no longer than two weeks. Identification: hindered by faunal digestion of face; local male, between 18 and 25. No fingerprints on file. Body to be disposed of in accordance with internal guidance.

So the case could be buried (Merhi winced at his own graveyard humour), which meant that the other deaths could still be kept quiet. Lattouf was off the hook.

And Merhi was off the hook too.

He looked at his watch. He best hurry. It was 11:45. Gisele was doing some shopping down on Hamra Street, and he had arranged to meet her at midday. She wanted his advice on some shoes she was thinking of buying (the advice being the one word: yes), then they were driving home together. It was Saturday and they had guests coming round for dinner, Gisele's brother Joe and his wife Jacqui, whose wedding they had been to two months ago. Gisele would prepare several of her sumptuous dishes, and as always Jihad would be the ebullient, perfect host.

As he waited for his computer to shut down he again gave mental thanks to Selim Himo for a job well done.

He did not realise that Himo was only doing as he had been told. The Lieutenant was, after all, a future star.

Jounieh, Lebanon 14:00

The shoes were, in fact, very nice. Red Jimmy Choo copies. They suited the elegant Gisele perfectly and, importantly from a male perspective, they had heels.

Gisele had also bought him a new shirt, which he would wear this evening, so it was a contented *Merhi à deux* that drove back along the coastal highway towards their apartment in Jounieh, twenty kilometres north of Beirut.

Gisele was driving the Toyota Land Cruiser (not in her new shoes) to give Jihad a chance to relax. This was the first day he had left work early in a long time (and a full day off for him was a thing of distant memory). Gisele knew he liked his brother-in-law immensely and he was looking forward to seeing him and his wife.

Over the south-bound carriageway to the left, the gently-waving Mediterranean formed a tranquil and timeless backdrop, a contrasting sedative to the frantic traffic on the highway. Lebanon's coastal road is always very busy, but on a

Saturday even more so. Buses, coaches, lorries, vans, cars, old and new, gleaming and rusted, you name it.

So it was not until they had reached Kaslik and were close to the turnoff for home that Jihad realised they were being followed.

If Gisele noticed the sudden tension that filled her husband, she did not say anything. Merhi did not turn round, but his attention was now fully on the wing mirror. The tail was three cars back. He had been aware of the black Ford Explorer for some time, but it had not registered that it was any different to the rest of the Saturday traffic heading out from the capital – not until Gisele had pulled out to overtake a slow-moving Datsun. The two cars behind plus the Explorer had pulled out too, but then the Explorer had stayed out but had not overtaken the other two cars as would have been expected with its obvious extra power. After a few seconds it had pulled back in, so keeping the same formation, two cars in between the Explorer and the Merhis. A classic solo tail.

Merhi's subconscious had noticed the movement and swiftly brought it to the attention of his awareness, at the same time ordering a shot of adrenaline to kick him out of his reverie. His fist tightened on the end of his armrest, his eyes locked on the wing mirror.

They passed the statue of the Virgin Mary, *Notre Dame du Liban*, at Harissa, high up on the cliffs to their right, and then turned off the coastal highway towards Haret Sakhr.

Merhi watched. Car One continued on the highway. So did Car Two.

The Ford Explorer turned off.

Now there was nothing between them. The Explorer was three hundred metres back, but it was not hurrying to catch them. It was just following.

Calmly, he said "We have a tail."

Gisele looked in her rear-view mirror. There was neither

shock nor surprise in her voice as she asked, "Want me to lose them?" She was well-experienced in surveillance and counter-surveillance techniques from her days in the field for the Department of General Security.

"No. Let's play it out, see what happens."

They drove on up into the coastal mountain, slowly because of the hairpin bends. The Explorer drove equally carefully.

"Obviously they want me to know," Jihad turned and looked back. "They're in plain sight."

"You want observation?"

"Yes please."

They continued up the mountain for two more minutes and then turned onto the track that led to their apartment block. Immediately they turned, Gisele pulled up sharply, wheels kicking up dust. Jihad turned around, kneeling on his seat.

A few moments later, the Ford Explorer carried on past. But Jihad observed the driver, their eyes meeting for a second as the driver looked towards them.

It was a woman.

He turned back round. Gisele had watched the Explorer pass in her rear-view mirror. "Well," she said, "we haven't had anything like that in a long time."

"No..." Jihad was thoughtful.

"Why would they be following you?"

"Don't know. Intriguing. Our address is not a secret, so it's not like they wanted to know where we live. They could have looked that up in records."

"So the only other reason for following, especially in plain sight - "

"Is to let us see them. A warning. To let us know they know."

"Know what?"

"Don't know."

Gisele put the car back into Drive and they moved the few hundred metres downhill to their cliffside apartment block. As she put on the parking brake, she asked "Jihad, what have you got yourself involved in now?"

16 December 2004
4 Dhu'l-Qa'dah 1425

Mount Lebanon 07:30

The Damascene looked at the still sleeping woman beside him. The Djinn. He reached out and lightly stroked the cashmere skin of her naked left buttock. Instinctively her bottom moved towards him, inviting or reminiscing. Maybe both.

He swung his legs around and got up off the bed. He always slept well after he had been with her, the natural physical release of his climaxes had a morphean quality giving him deep and dreamless rest, and he awoke refreshed and recharged.

Naked, and with his long hair falling either side of his face, he went downstairs to the living area and switched on the television, keeping the volume low.

It was on every channel, the slant given to it depending on the bias of the broadcaster.

Two days ago, the Bristol Declaration had been issued. It was the result of an extraordinary recent meeting at the Bristol Hotel, the first time since Lebanon's independence in 1943 that Maronites, Druze, Sunnis and many other sects and organisations (but not the Shi'ites) had formed a cross-communal political bloc. The Declaration was as direct as it was inflammatory, denouncing the amendment of the constitution and the extension of President Lahoud's term in office and demanding a fair and just law for an honest and free election and calling for the resignation of the Karami government and the installation of a new impartial government to supervise the upcoming elections in May.

Although Rafic Hariri had not attended the meeting (he had asked a friend to attend 'in a personal capacity'), he was immediately denounced as the instigator and ringleader, the government accusing him of whipping up sectarian dissent.

The Damascene flicked from channel to channel. The familiar faces kept popping onto the screen: Jumblatt, Nasrallah, Lahoud, Karami, Berri, Geagea, Aoun, Assad. And always, always Rafic Hariri.

As the Declaration had stated, Lebanon was indeed entering 'a very dangerous phase'.

But dangerous phase or placid phase, The Damascene was satisfied that Hariri was protected by Abu Tarek's excellent security team, augmented by his own risk analysis and presence if Hariri made an unfamiliar trip outside.

As he had figured out before, there was only one way Hariri could be killed. Today Hariri was ensconced in Koreitem, unless The Damascene received a text message to the contrary, and it would not happen there.

He walked over to the window. It was 07:30 but it was still dull and grey out there. He saw some lights still twinkling in downtown in the distance. The two-month winter had started on cue, and the last few days had been cold, wet and windy with more inclement weather predicted.

He was staring out the window, lost in his thoughts, when he saw a naked woman floating in the sky above Beirut.

At first he was perplexed. Was this an angel? Was he having a religious experience (the apartment was, after all, on the road to Damascus, so it would not be the first time it had happened on the highway)?

The woman was standing still and smiling at him, her long black hair pushed back over her shoulders not falling down her front, so she was fully exposed. He smiled back and she began to walk across the sky towards him.

He appreciated the hallucinatory effect of her reflection in the glass and his desire reacted as she came up behind him and ran her fingers down his spine so lightly that he wondered if she had in fact done it at all.

"*Bonjour.*" Her voice was morning-husky.

Without turning, he raised his right arm and she slipped underneath it, her arms trying to reach round his body but not connecting. She put her head against his hard right breast. She could smell his sweat and the natural scent from lower down. "Did you sleep well?" she asked.

"Of course."

"And I don't suppose you made any coffee?"

"Of course not."

She squeezed him. "Then I suppose if a Djinn wants some, she will have to make it herself."

"Of course."

She wriggled out from under his arm, and he admired the movement of her firm cheeks reflected in the glass as she walked back across Beirut to the kitchen area. "Is that all there is on TV?" she said, a comment rather than a question.

"Every channel," he said over his shoulder. "These are interesting times."

As rain started to pit-pat on the glass, he turned back to the window. There was a flash of lightning out at sea, heading towards land.

Storm clouds were gathering over Beirut.

PART THREE
الجزء الثالث

COMPLETION
الانتهاء

18 December 2004
6 Dhu'l-Qa'dah 1425

Hamra, Beirut 13:30

"Has anything unusual happened? You been followed or anything?" Although he wanted to keep his voice low, Jihad Merhi had to talk loudly into his mobile phone to be heard above the cries of the stallholders selling their wares and the honking horns of the cars. It was a cool day but that had not stopped the Saturday shoppers. Hamra Street was buzzing.

"Followed?" boomed the voice on the other end, tinny as it came out of the Samsung. "Nobody would dare follow Fadi Lattouf! My presence usually makes people flee. I repel, I do not attract."

"Could your phones be bugged?"

"Bugged! First they've got to work before they can be bugged! Thank Allah for mobiles. Why are you asking, my friend? Has something happened?"

"This day last week, Gisele and I were followed on our way home."

"Not nice."

"No."

"Did anything happen?"

"No, they followed us to the entrance to our block and then drove on. A woman."

"A woman! You haven't been...?"

"No, I certainly haven't. I think it was a warning."

"About what?"

"A good question. I have many ongoing cases, but it happened just four days after we went to Aammiq. I think it's connected."

"How? You have not reported the bodies, have you? Made it official?"

"No. Your four are still yours and the one in Aammiq has been reported as an accidental death. But the morning Lieutenant Himo's report lands on my desk, I get followed. Coincidence?"

"There are no such things."

"Exactly. Hey - !" Merhi slammed his hand down on the bonnet of a car which missed him by a centimetre as he stepped off the kerb. The driver's face glared but then changed into a raised palm of apology when he saw Merhi's uniform under his leather coat. He drove away quickly.

"Jihad, you okay?"

"Just some stupid driver."

"Where are you?"

"Hamra."

"Hamra! You couldn't pick me up some pickles from that stall on the square, could you?"

"No."

"Just two jars? I'll give you the money."

"Fadi, I'm serious. Be extra vigilant. If anything should happen or even seem just out of the ordinary, let me know straight away."

"If anyone dares to follow me in the camp, I will arrest them. See how they like a taste of Palestinian remand. You Lebanese are too soft."

Too soft! This coming from a man whose girth was the original template for bouncy-castles, thought Merhi.

"But yes, thank you Abu Samer," continued Lattouf. "I appreciate your warning. But why is this happening, if no one knows about our little... discoveries?"

"A very good question. One I don't yet know the answer to."

"And your phones are bugged?"

"Fadi, I am a Captain of the Internal Security Force. Of course my phones are bugged, as are everyone else's."

"I have one piece of advice for you, my friend."

"What's that?"

There was silence. For a moment, Merhi thought he had lost his signal but a quick look at the screen showed he was still connected. "Fadi?"

"Buy me three jars of pickles and I'll tell you."

"Fadi!"

"A small price to pay for advice which could save your life."

"Oh, you really are..." Merhi shook his head and stopped walking. As chance would have it he was on Hamra Square. "You're a blackmailer, do you know that? An extortionist."

"I've been called worse."

"Okay, okay. Two jars of pickles it is."

"Four."

"Three."

"Done."

"So what is this advice that I'm paying so dearly for?"

After a moment, Fadi Lattouf said "Always check under your car."

25 December 2004
13 Dhu'l-Qa'dah 1425

Kahale, Lebanon 09:30

Elias and Ahmad both felt proud and resolute as they walked outside. It was a grey, cold and damp day but they both had on new Timberland padded and waterproof jackets – the most expensive present either of them had ever been given in their lives. They tried to keep their faces serious, but their eyes gleamed – like children on Christmas morning.

"Right," the Commander came out two minutes later, carrying some bright red textile items in his hand. "Put these on so we will blend in." He threw one to Elias, one to Ahmad and kept one for himself.

Both young men caught the items and turned them over in their hands quizzically. Elias looked up and then burst into laughter. "A Santa Claus hat?" The Commander put his on, long and pointed with white fringing and a white bobble on the end. He adjusted it so that the long pointed bit fell down over his left shoulder.

Ahmad was giggling too. "But we are not Christian!"

"Since when has Christmas been a Christian festival?" asked the Commander. "Not for a long time. It marks the birth of the Prophet Jesus. You are perfectly entitled to celebrate. And anyway, as I said, we will fit in. Come." He nodded towards the van. "Elias, you will ride with me in the front. Ahmad, you go in the back."

Ahmad knew better than to query or argue. The back of the

van was dirty and smelled of the fruit that used to be transported in it. But, he supposed, it could be worse. Imagine the putrid smell if this had been a butcher's van instead of a fruiterer's! "Where are we going, sir?" he asked as he undid the soft flap on the side.

"We're going to pick up some sugar," said Al-Rajul.

Mount Lebanon 09:45 – 11:00

The white Mitsubishi Canter van drove up to the Beirut to Damascus road and turned left for the downhill journey into the capital. Elias sat proudly in the passenger seat next to the Commander. Obviously he was the favourite, he thought. The taciturn Ahmad had been put into the back like livestock.

The road was less busy but by no means quiet. Shops and entertainment venues still opened in Beirut on Christmas Day and people would be out and about, having enjoyed their Christmas dinner yesterday evening. They passed through Jamhour and hung right, avoiding the Presidential Palace area at Baabda.

Christmas lights were in many shop windows, and in some areas downtown they would even be strung across the streets. Santa Claus hats just like the ones they were wearing were stretched across the headrests in many cars, and more than once they experienced the Lebanese phenomenon of a car going past blaring out Christmas songs to be followed under two minutes later by another car blaring out Muslim prayers. A friendly rivalry, in the spirit of peace...

They stayed on Damascus Street all the way into the city and up to the coast. They turned right at Trieste Street.

Into the port.

Marfa'a, Beirut 11:00

They drove quite a way in, along roads bordered by stored

containers stacked on top of each other, past warehouses and sheds, and so many cranes. Elias was confused by the time they reached the warehouse they wanted, one of twelve in the general cargo area.

As the Commander stepped from the van, a fat bald-headed greasy man emerged from a wicket door in the warehouse and grunted. They exchanged nods.

The Commander banged on the side of the van as Elias got out. The flap moved and Ahmad climbed out, stepping straight into a puddle, looking a little dishevelled. Both young men came round to stand by their Commander. With their hats on the three of them looked like Santa Claus and his helpers.

Producing papers from an inside pocket, the Commander handed them to the greasy man who looked at them, looked up at the Commander, raised his eyebrows and then nodded, handing the papers back. The greasy man turned and, with another grunt, slid open the main doors to the warehouse. The Commander did not move to help him; everyone had their job, even in the port of Beirut.

The greasy man clicked on several light switches and the warehouse lit up like the Camille Chamoun Sports City stadium when the floodlights are turned on. Inside, the place was stacked almost to the ceiling with pallets of sugar imports from India.

"Yours are over here." The greasy man led the way in and to the left. He nodded at a block of fifty-kilogramme jute sacks, which looked no different from any of the others in the area. "You can back the van in if you want."

"*Shukran*. Ahmad."

Ahmad looked at the Commander and then quickly understood. Ignoring Elias's sulky frown, he dashed back outside and climbed into the front of the van. In no time, the van was reversing skilfully into the warehouse. It stopped exactly in the right position and Ahmad climbed back out.

"Those twenty sacks at the front are ours," said the

Commander. He paused, waiting, and then said, "Well, go on then you two. Load them up."

Now they knew what the exercises had been for. It took the strength of the two of them to carry each of the sacks to the van and throw them in. Elias, as always confident and cock-sure, attempted one on his own, managing it but looking very pale afterwards.

It took them nearly half an hour to load the twenty sacks, and they both looked physically drained. Elias was ordered into the back – yes, he could rest on the sacks if he wanted to – and Ahmad was allowed to climb up into the front. The Commander shook hands with the greasy man, an envelope changed hands, and shortly they were making their way back along the wet quayside.

They stopped at the Customs office down near the Charles Helou Transport Station. The Commander climbed out, papers were handed over, examined, the side of the van was opened, the load visually inspected, the side of the van was closed, papers were stamped, and they were on their way back out of the port.

Kahale, Lebanon 13:15

Ahmad slept on the fifty minute drive back into the mountains, waking as they turned off the main road. They passed through the town and headed back downhill again towards The Facility.

They pulled up at the side of the main building, near the garages and outhouses. Getting out, the Commander pulled the Santa Claus hat from his head and threw it back onto his seat. "Dispose of that, Ahmad." He banged on the side of the van and lifted the flap.

Having slept on the sugar, Elias seemed more refreshed than Ahmad, and he jumped out, looking at the Commander for orders.

"Store the sacks in the garage," instructed the Commander.

"And try to stack them neatly. After that, you can both rest. You have done well. Your families will deserve their extra reward."

"Thank you, sir," Ahmad came round.

As they both reached back inside the van, dragging the first sack over, Elias said chattily "I'm glad it's stopped raining, sir. We wouldn't want the sugar to get wet."

"No. We wouldn't," agreed Al-Rajul.

29 December 2004
17 Dhu'l-Qa'dah 1425

Mount Lebanon 10:00

The Damascene tied back his long hair with a rubber band into the simple ponytail, pulling the left side down to ensure it covered the hole of his left ear. He slipped into his leather jacket and grabbed the motorcycle keys from the breakfast bar. He had a 'touching base' meeting with Abu Tarek at Koreitem.

Yesterday the second meeting of what was being called the Bristol Gathering had taken place at the Bristol Hotel. Again, Hariri had not attended. His friend, Dr Ghattas Khoury, had gone in a personal capacity along with Basil Fleihan, Hariri's close advisor and former economy minister.

The only confession not on board this movement for change were the Shi'ites, and Hariri had continued his clandestine late night meetings with Sayyed Hassan Nasrallah whom he viewed as a potential Shi'te partner in the Arab cause.

Koreitem Palace was now campaign headquarters for the wave of change that would sweep through Lebanon once Hariri was re-elected next May. Today The Damascene would be refreshing his risk analysis with Abu Tarek and confirming his need for details of Hariri's itinerary whenever he left the palace.

He closed and locked the apartment front door behind him, his preconscious mind pleased that it was not raining today. Nothing worse than riding a bike in the rain – especially with the drivers of Beirut trying to kill first and ask questions later!

As he walked down the stairs he saw the door of the

apartment directly beneath his closing quickly. Such was the strong and insulated construction of the building that he did not even know that there was anybody living down there.

As he passed by the door and continued on down, he smelt something. What was that? Seemed familiar.

Jasmine.

The smell of The Djinn.

He laughed. Now *that* was wishful thinking! Imagine him knocking on the door and ravaging the housewife because she was wearing jasmine perfume!

It had been nearly two weeks and his body wanted The Djinn again. He hoped she would visit again soon. He wondered what she did in the weeks between her visits? Probably some other jobs for Kanaan, on a similar line. Well, so be it, he was not a man of jealousy.

And, he rebuked himself, he must not let his desire get in the way of his task. The mission would be over soon and, although Kanaan did not know it, he would not be returning to Damascus. He wondered if he could persuade The Djinn to come with him on his future adventures...

He reached the front door and went out. Moments later the Suzuki was roaring up towards the main road.

30 December 2004
18 Dhu'l-Qa'dah 1425

Ras en Nabaa, Beirut 13:30

Captain Maroun Khoury ate falafel and bread for his lunch as he sat at the side of the desk of Zahia Zalloum. There were ten people in his team, but at that moment Zahia was the only one in the open-plan Listening Suite. But Khoury knew that others would be returning with their food soon, so he pushed to the back of his mind the thoughts he was having about ZiZi, the desktop and the pot of yoghurt in front of her.

"Why they keep the Watchers separate from us Listeners and Gatherers, I don't know," he was saying. "It would be so much better if we were one team. Bureaucracy and Lebanon are like inoperable conjoined twins."

"But still, they've paid off," Zahia tipped a spoonful of yoghurt into her mouth, fully aware that Khoury's powers of concentration were waning every second he sat next to her.

"Only because you had the bright idea to ask the question. Bravo you."

"Well, it didn't take us long to figure out who the fat guy shitting in the Aammiq Wetlands was. Palestinian... Merhi is the liaison for the camps... And let's face it, there are not many people who match the description given by Lieutenant Himo. Monsieur Lattouf. The Watchers had seen him and Merhi meeting quite frequently at the Dunes. Did you know they try to sidetrack them by arranging to meet twenty-six hours later than they actually meet and always name some stupid place?

The Watchers worked it out long ago. But of course, they watch. We listen – and act. So they had no microphones. But they did have video. And," she reached into her drawer and pulled out a disc, "here it is."

Khoury nodded, impressed. "Have you viewed it yet?"

"No, I thought we might watch it together."

Khoury wanted to suggest "Tonight?" but instead he said "Come to my office."

They sat side by side, legs touching, looking at the computer screen. The picture clarity was pretty good for an indoor shot. It showed a public eating area, people moving about, carrying trays. Quite close to the camera was a massive back, obviously Lattouf. Merhi was facing him, his face clearly visible. There was an Americanised date on the top right corner of the screen: 12/06/2004.

There was sound but it was just general noise. Merhi was talking but they couldn't hear what was being said. "See what I mean?" said Zahia. "They watch. We listen and act. It's just as well I'm... good with lips." Khoury was aware of the glance she gave him. "Could you turn the sound off, Moro, so I can concentrate?"

He did as asked. Zahia leant forward, staring hard at the screen, one hand absentmindedly steadying herself on Khoury's thigh, the other on the mouse, clicking, starting and stopping the disc. "He's... he's giving him his own food for some reason. Something about not wanting to spoil his appetite. Okay... Ah, hold on, hold on... Yes! 'Our first body outside of the camp'." She stopped the disc. "So, the bodies have been in the camp, that's why nothing's been reported. Of course. Makes sense now." She clicked the mouse. "He's asking – arguing – saying he shouldn't have been there. The camp, presumably."

"No, he certainly shouldn't," said Khoury. "If Merhi was in the camp, that's grounds for castration in itself."

"He's asking... he's asking Lattouf to come with him. To

Aammiq presumably. Oh! Hold on, hold on. Let's run that again." She stared at the screen, nodding. "'You... something... that the murders are occurring outside the camp... something... what – what if the murders are occurring inside the camp and your... something... killer has now started to...' Hump? Can't be... Dump? Dump them outside!" She leant back, still looking at the screen. "Blah, blah... They're talking about the groups, in the camp presumably... Looks like he's persuaded Lattouf to come with him... tells him to bring his *caoutchouc*. That's it." She pushed the mouse back to Khoury.

He stopped the disc, noting with disappointment that she had taken her hand from his leg. "So, our friend has been killing them like he said. Do you think he has been deliberately dumping them in the camp?"

She shook her head. "No. That doesn't fit. That's probably where he got them."

"But why? For pleasure? Is he just a serial killer after all?"

"Can't be. If he is, we're wasting our time. We can give it to the police. But that's not what this is about."

Khoury nodded. "I agree. It doesn't fit with what we know."

Zahia stood up. "I'm going to have to delve deeper. But I don't want Merhi and the idiot Lattouf stomping around all over this."

"What are you going to do?"

"Leave it to me."

"Okay."

"But, Moro," she leant forward on his desk, "we also have to figure out what's going on. Knowing what we know, why we started this in the first place."

"Why are young Palestinians being killed?"

"It's not for pleasure, there's a purpose." She pushed herself up. "And I'll find out what it is."

31 December 2004
19 Dhu'l-Qa'dah 1425

Kaslik, Lebanon 14:30

Gisele Merhi was preoccupied. She was getting a few last minute things in her favourite supermarket down in Kaslik and then had to dash home to prepare the food for their party tonight. They had about thirty family and friends coming round, as they did every new year, and Gisele was thankful that their apartment was big. The New Year's Eve weather was clement enough for any overspill out onto their double balcony with its views over the town below and the Mediterranean beyond. There might even be some fireworks from boats out at sea come midnight.

They had two extra guests this year: Captain Fadi Lattouf of the Palestinian Internal Security Force and his wife Nada. Gisele had baulked momentarily when Jihad had said he had invited them, but her husband had made a two-fold case: one, it was only right to invite them after she and Jihad had been to their *Eid* celebrations, and two, she could now get rid of the eyesore of the three large jars of pickles that had been glaring at her from her kitchen work surface for nearly two weeks. She only hoped the Lattoufs didn't bring their five fat kids with them.

She put the last item in her trolley (a tin of duck pâté, which was for her and Jihad, not for the party), and queued up at the till. She was thinking of her recipe for *sayoudeiah* as she unloaded her stuff onto the conveyor belt, and she took no notice of the person in front of her, a young woman dressed in jeans and brown leather coat with a brown *hijab* covering her head.

The woman in front paid for her two items, and Gisele's stuff had just started to move along the belt when the woman looked back at her and smiled. Gisele nodded back courteously. The woman said, "Tell your husband that they were accidents. Only accidents. He should leave them alone." Then she turned around and walked away.

What?

"Hey!" Gisele made to run after the woman, but her stuff was being beeped through and her trolley was in the way. She looked at the woman's departing back and then at the cashier. Quickly she threw her goods into the open bag in the trolley as they came through, threw notes at the startled cashier, and ran outside, pushing the trolley in front of her.

She came to a halt, looking right then left. This was a predominantly Maronite Christian location, but there were still enough *hijabs* about to stop her singling out anybody. She looked back and forth, frowning, angry, sighing.

Then from the side of the petrol station further along she saw a car pull out and ease its way onto the six-lane main road, driving off north.

It was a black Ford Explorer.

Jounieh, Lebanon 23:30

"So, we were right," said Fadi Lattouf. "They were accidents. There never was any need to report them."

Jihad Merhi's speech had the mellow timbre of an evening spent in the company of Johnnie Walker. "If they were accidents then your arse looks like the Mona Lisa."

"It has been said," agreed Lattouf.

They were on the balcony of the Merhi's apartment looking out over the blackness that was the Mediterranean, a diamante carapace of stars glinting overhead. In thirty minutes it would be 2005.

Lattouf cupped a cigarette in his hand, smoking surreptitiously in case Nada looked out. He had last seen her in the kitchen giving Gisele unwanted advice on how to prepare her fish correctly, but the cooking lesson might be over by now.

Merhi smoked his Cedars King Size openly. "Another warning," he mused.

"No, not a warning. Advice. It is better than a bomb under your car. And anyway," Lattouf reached out and picked up his pint glass of orange juice from its position balanced perilously on the guard rail. "It lets us off the hook." Half the pint disappeared.

Reluctantly, Merhi nodded. "But it's not right. It's not... justice, if you like."

Lattouf put his glass back on the rail. "Since when have you Lebanese let justice get in the way of convenience?"

Ouch.

"Us Lebanese?" Merhi prickled, but he knew Lattouf was right. He just didn't want to hear it, not from him. "What about you Palestinians? You never wanted to report the deaths formally."

"That is true. Perhaps, under the skin, we are not so different, the Lebanese and Palestinians."

"We are all human beings."

"Brothers."

Merhi took a pull on the cigarette. "Cousins. Maybe."

"If you cut me, do I not bleed? If you give me beans, do I not fart - ?" Lattouf's hand swung out – and knocked his glass over the edge.

Both men looked down over the rail into the darkness. They heard the glass smash three storeys below.

After a moment, Lattouf asked "What are you going to do?"

Merhi shrugged. "Clean it up in the morning."

"No, I mean about the bodies."

The music coming from inside emphasised the silence

outside.

Merhi stared off into space. Then he said, "I don't know."

"We wanted to keep it quiet, now we can."

"We could keep it quiet when only the two of us knew. But now others know."

"And they want it kept quiet too."

"Yes, but why? If it's a serial killer at work, why would they want it covered up? It would not concern them. There's normally a word that goes before 'cover up'."

"What's that?"

"'Political'." Merhi took one final drag on his cigarette and launched the butt over the side to join the smashed glass of orange juice below. He turned to his friend. "What have we stumbled into, Fadi?"

"And what happens," posed Lattouf, answering a question with a question, "if we find another one?"

4 January 2005
23 Dhu'l-Qa'dah 1425

Jbail (Byblos), Lebanon 08:30

Ahmad awoke with a start at the banging on the side of the van. Seconds later the flap was pulled up, flooding the cargo area with light and momentarily blinding him. It had still been dark when they had set off earlier.

"Ahmad, out," ordered the Commander. Elias was standing next to him. "Elias, in." Ahmad rolled out groggily, Elias climbed in reluctantly. The flap was secured back down.

"Come on Ahmad, get your wits about you, boy," urged the Commander. "Hurry, hurry. We're not supposed to stop on the highway unless it's an emergency." Seizing a lull in the traffic, the Commander hastened back round and climbed in behind the wheel. Ahmad climbed in and the driver's door and the passenger door closed almost in unison. "I told you we would stop halfway and let you swap over. Two hours in the back is enough for anyone." Checking his mirror, the Commander pulled back out into the traffic.

"Thank you, sir."

The Commander smiled and cast a glance at the young Palestinian. His attitude softened. "You are growing your beard like I told you to. It looks good."

Ahmad ran a hand down his whiskers. "Elias's is thicker than mine."

"That doesn't matter. You are obeying orders, that is the important thing. I am very pleased with both of you."

"You haven't told us why you don't want us to shave, sir."

"All in good time. Very soon now. Just concentrate on one task at a time."

Ahmad looked out of the window. He did not know where he was but he knew it was a long way from The Facility and a long way north of the familiarity of Beirut. The Commander seemed to be in a good mood, so he would ask. "What *are* we doing today, sir?"

"Today? I have just told Elias and I can tell you. Today we are going shopping in Tripoli."

Tripoli, Lebanon 10:00 – 16:00

The traffic was heavy and it took another ninety minutes for them to reach Lebanon's second largest city. The coastal highway came to a natural end at the north of the city, but they turned off at el-Bahsass and made their way along the beach front and up into el-Mina, the port area.

They parked in an unrestricted side street, all three of them flexing their legs as they got out. It was 10:00 and the shops would just be opening.

"What are we buying, sir?" asked Elias keenly, rubbing his butt.

"Well first," said the Commander, "we're buying *ftoor* – our breakfast. I fancy *mankoushe* if they have it – and some very strong coffee. Then we will hit the shops, just like the women do!" He slapped Elias on the back. "I want you to buy certain things. I will be there with you, but you will do the buying. You will like it. Today is a day for enjoying ourselves. But first, let us eat. Shopping is an arduous business, we will need our strength. *Yalla.*"

They ate in *Brunch* coffee shop and then hit the City Complex, the American-style mall.

Two hours later they made their way back to the van, secured their purchases underneath the seats in the driver's cab and then drove up into the Old Town.

It took another three hours to complete their shopping, and then the Commander took them to the *Hallab* family patisserie on Riad el-Solh Street where he introduced Elias and Ahmad to the delights of *znoud el-sitt* (ladies' upper arms – in fact the house specialty, a cream-filled pastry looking like a large spring roll).

They left Tripoli at 16:00, heading south on the coastal highway. It had been a successful day, and they had purchased everything the Commander wanted, ten items in all: eight working mobile phones, one mid-range camcorder and a packet of blank videotapes.

Antelias, north of Beirut 18:00

They swapped places again at Byblos and then continued on south, but the Commander had warned them that they would be stopping again soon. Thirty kilometres later he turned left off the highway into Antelias.

He pulled in at the *Bourj al-Hamam* restaurant, its lights welcoming in the darkness.

"Get Ahmad out of the back," he instructed Elias, whose eyes were popping at the sight of the oasis in front of him. "It is dinner time."

When both young men were standing next to him, he said "This is a good restaurant. We have had a long and sticky day, but we are still presentable. They will serve us. We can bathe and pray when we get back."

They ate *kastaleta* (lamb chops with fries) plus *chich taouk* (grilled chicken skewers – with more fries), drank Coke, and finished with a dessert of fresh fruit and *achta bi assal* (cream with honey).

Three contented stomachs sat back and relaxed with their coffees. As the two young men chatted to each other about football, Al-Rajul looked from one to the other. He was very pleased with them. They had both suited his needs perfectly, he had chosen well. Had he had a gram of humanity, he would have regretted all the lies he had told them, the fact that he was using them purely for his own ends. But he hadn't and he didn't.

He stared at their faces as they exchanged friendly banter about a Portuguese football manager who was having great success in England. So young, so dedicated, so full of life.

It was almost a pity that, very soon, one of them would have to die.

9 January 2005
28 Dhu'l-Qa'dah 1425

Mount Lebanon 22:00 – 23:59

The Suzuki VL1500 Intruder roared up the Damascus road through Hazmieh. The cold wind pressed into The Damascene's face and blew his hair straight out behind him. It was a damp day.

It had been a boring day too, and The Damascene did not like boredom. Hariri had met with the head of Syrian intelligence in Lebanon, Rustom Ghazaleh, for lunch in Koreitem, but the meeting had ended in discord with Ghazaleh storming out. Ghazaleh had put forward proposals about the election law being drawn up by Interior Minister Suleiman Frangieh (grandson of the former President and an opponent of Hariri), but Hariri had refused them point blank – he did not want to include six pro-Syrians on his list of electoral candidates and he was not going to stop waging a nationwide electoral campaign and concentrate solely on Beirut.

Hariri now openly agreed to what he had known all along: the electoral odds were going to be stacked against him. There were people who did not want him winning and returning as Prime Minister. He decided it was time to declare openly his support of the Bristol Gathering.

The Damascene had watched and listened to all this from another room in Koreitem, at the invitation of Abu Tarek. All well and good, and he was flattered by the invitation, but this was nothing to do with him. He was completely disinterested in politics. The Damascene's job was the protection of Hariri, and whilst the events of the day heightened the danger to Hariri in this arena where death was the first, not the last, recourse of political disagreement, Hariri's claim that he would 'barricade himself inside Koreitem to fight the electoral battle' meant that The Damascene's job was easy to the point of superfluousness.

He needed to talk to Kanaan. But he supposed The Djinn was reporting back to her boss. He would ask her to give Kanaan a message next time she came.

He turned off the main road onto the track that led to the apartment block. His face was wet from the dull, constant dampness in the air, and water actually dripped from the end of his nose as he parked the bike by the main entrance.

It had been over three weeks now since The Djinn had last visited, so she would be with him again soon, any day now. And that pleased him.

It was not only his boredom that needed relieving.

Halfway up the stairs to the third floor, the lights went out. *Damned power cuts.* It was pitch black in the stairwell as he reached for his mobile, flipped it up and lit his way up to his front door.

As soon as he entered, he knew she was there. He could smell jasmine. Not just the wishful-thinking olfactory reminiscence he had had previously when he had walked past the apartment downstairs, but the distinct aroma mixed with just a hint of cardamom from her breath.

As he closed the front door, a hand touched his shoulder in the darkness. Nothing was said. The fingers reached up to his face, feeling the wetness from his journey.

He reached out – and touched skin. He moved his hand up and down - bare flesh, no cloth.

Her hand went round the back of his neck and tugged downwards. He obeyed and their lips touched, softly, tentatively, then strongly with obvious desire.

"You are wet," she said as they pulled apart, his left hand caressing her chest.

"Beirut. Winter." He shrugged.

"Let me dry you." She took his hand. There was enough moonlight coming in through the windows to give about one lux of illumination in the apartment. She led him up the stairs, but he resisted when she made for the bathroom.

"I have a better idea," he said, moving her hand down so that she touched him, and pulling her towards the bedroom. "Make me wetter still."

It was just before midnight and they both lay naked on top of the bed, crumpled sheets beneath them, little damp patches here and there. The Damascene was on his back, snoring lowly, firmly, constantly, the wonderful oblivion of a man who had been brought to climax three times in the last ninety minutes.

Beside him, The Djinn was awake and smiling, lying sideways on to him so that her legs were across the top of his thighs, a tigress who had captured her mate. She also was satisfied, if a little tender. He was as inventive a lover as she was, and two inventors with one common cause always made for good karma.

But – she had a job to do.

She lifted her legs off of his thighs and moved slowly, lightly, into an upright position, careful not to wake him. She reached up and undid her hair clip, gently shaking out her hair. Holding the hair clip in her left hand, she pushed the metal clasp back so that the small needle underneath was exposed. She flicked the body of the clip three times with the middle finger of her right hand.

Calmly leaning over, she injected one milligram of sodium thiopental into the top of his right thigh.

One minute later, she was shaking him gently and saying, "Captain. Captain Mebarak. Marwan. I need to talk to you..."

10 January 2005
29 Dhu'l-Qa'dah 1425

Mount Lebanon 07:00

He had a dull headache when he awoke the next morning, as he always did when she had been with him, but he would soon shake it off.

She was not there. Nowadays sometimes she stayed, sometimes she did not. But he was disappointed that he would have to shower on his own.

He let the hot water scald him everywhere except the left side of his head which he kept away from the spray until he had turned it fully to cold. Absentmindedly he scratched the top of his right thigh where he had been bitten by an insect – a small price to pay for the pleasure she gave him.

In between their second and third bout last night he had asked her to give a message to Kanaan, asking for further instructions regarding the continuance of his mission (he was careful not to tell her what it was, official Pleasure Givers did not have the required Need To Know level – and the last thing he wanted to do was to have to eliminate her!). Naturally she had agreed that his words would be passed on.

Downstairs, he watched the morning news in the nude while he drank his usual breakfast of two strong cups of coffee. Then he dressed and went out.

He had some shopping to do.

18 January 2005
7 Dhu'l-Hijja 1425

Kahale, Lebanon 12:00 – 15:00

By now, ten weeks into their 'training', the remaining two recruits were used to their Commander's comings and goings. Often he would be away days at a time, leaving them with a list of training to be undertaken or tasks to be performed. This time the list had been brief, the task simple: charge up the mobile phones and the camcorder.

Their task completed, Elias and Ahmad had spent the first hour of that morning playing football (one was Atletico Bethlehem, the other Real Gaza), then they had gone for a walk in the woods. They returned to The Facility in time for *dhuhr*, midday prayer. As they came out of the woods they saw the van parked around the side by the garages. The Commander had returned.

He was sitting on one of the sofas in the reception area, eating fruit. Today the *keffiyeh* was worn fully on his head, not just around his neck like a scarf. They had not seen him like that in quite a while. As they came in, he stood up, smiling. "Day of glory, my brave men. Who won?" He nodded at the football in Ahmad's hand.

"Bethlehem, sir," replied Elias with a mock-frown. "But I think he should have been sent off."

"Hah! Gaza are the filthiest players in the league!" countered Ahmad. "You well deserved to lose."

"Twenty – eighteen is almost a draw."

"Losers always say such things."

"Losers! Gaza are not losers. Just you wait till the second leg!"

"When you will be thrashed again."

The Commander let the banter continue until it almost came to fisticuffs, then he stopped them with a curt *"Khallas!* You are worse than the English. Go, wash and pray. Then eat. Join me in the meeting room at fourteen hundred." He looked them both long and hard in the face. Then he said intriguingly, "Gentlemen, our task begins."

Elias and Ahmad could not believe their eyes when they entered the meeting room on the stroke of 14:00. It looked like a movie studio! All but three of the chairs had been pushed back into one corner and on the opposite side of the room a piece of black fabric had been attached to the wall. About three metres in front of it, the camcorder stood on a tripod. The Commander stood next to it.

"Your training is over," he announced without preamble. "Our mission has been confirmed and we must enact it. We have the green light."

The faces of the young Palestinians lit up. "What is it, sir?" Elias looked like he was going to explode with pride. "Can you tell us now?"

The Commander looked at them thoughtfully. Then he nodded. "Yes, I can. Sit, sit." They sat on the three available chairs, Ahmad removing some black and white textiles from his seat and placing them on the floor.

"It was a discovery made by one of our intelligence operatives," lied Al-Rajul. "An undercover Israeli agent has been found in the Lebanese government. He has been there for a long time, influencing decisions, sowing poison against Palestine and Syria. He has probably been the cause of all the unrest in this country since the war. We have only recently found him because he has been so good, so deep under cover."

"Do the Lebanese know, sir?"

"No, Ahmad. If we told them they would probably not believe us. Or at the very least our man would be tipped the wink and he would high-tail it back to the occupied lands. It was reported to our late President, who recruited me to solve the problem. I, in turn, recruited you. Only those in the upper echelons of the Palestinian Authority who needed to know have been told about this traitor, and they have now sanctioned the solution. He is to be removed, publicly, as a warning to others."

Elias leant forward. "And we are to...?"

"We are to kill him."

Elias and Ahmad looked at each other.

"What did you think the training was for?" questioned the Commander. "Firearms, combat. Did you think we were going to rob a bank?"

"No, sir, no," Elias shook his head. "Of course not. It – it has just come as a bit of a shock, that is all. But don't get me wrong. I am pleased. At last we can serve our country."

"Did the others know?" asked Ahmad.

"No. Their tasks were minor. Their rewards have been minor. They are now back in Palestine, but they will not be living as you and your families will be living. You will be heroes. Your actions will influence they very future of Lebanon, freeing this country from the pernicious Israeli influence that they haven't even known has been there."

Elias's eyes had filled. "You honour us, sir. Truly."

"You honour yourselves. You are two strong, brave Palestinians. Your actions will go down in history."

"Thank you, sir, thank you." Elias looked at Ahmad, who nodded his agreement.

The Commander slapped his hands on his thighs and stood up. "Now, our first task. As I said, this is to be a public removal – so we must prepare the background. Ahmad, here."

Ahmad walked over with the Commander to a nearby table.

The Commander picked up a thick white marker and gave it to him, then he picked up the card that was underneath it. "I know that you are good at drawing. Write this on the fabric." He nodded to the wall, passing the card over. "Big enough to fill it, as if it is a flag. Can you do it?"

Ahmad read what was on the card. He looked up. "You want me to write this?" He saw the look in the Commander's eyes and hastily said, "Of course, of course."

As Ahmad began to write, the Commander went over to Elias, bending down to pick up the textiles from the floor. "Put these on, Elias. You will do it first, then Ahmad will do it after. I will decide which is the best.

Elias took the proffered textiles, opening them out and holding them up. A plain black robe and a white turban. He frowned, then said "Shall I undress?"

"No, put them on over your clothes. They should fit, and you are both about the same size."

Elias did as he was told, the Commander helping him with the pre-formed turban.

Ahmad had finished writing on the fabric on the wall and he turned round, only just managing to stop himself laughing at his colleague.

The Commander studied what Ahmad had written, nodding his satisfaction. "Good, good. You truly have artistic talent, Ahmad. That could be your future," he lied again.

All three of them stared at the white writing on the black cloth.

لا إله إلا الله. هو محمد رسول الله. الله أكبر.

There is no God but Allah. Mohammed is the messenger of Allah. God is greatest.

19 January 2005
8 Dhu'l-Hijja 1425

Kahale, Lebanon 01:00 – 13:00

01:00 hours. In his room upstairs, Al-Rajul worked in the dim light given off by the screen of the laptop computer. He had watched the performances given by the two young Palestinians over and over, considering them not only from the point of view of the local news media – who would eventually receive the tape – but also from the international aspect.

He had made up his mind.

He watched his selection once more. The Palestinian sat in front of the flag with the holy words. He was dressed in the black robe and white turban, his bearded face serious as he read from the paper in his hand.

"To support our brother mujahidin in the land of the two holy mosques and to avenge their righteous martyrs who were killed by security forces of the Saudi regime in the land of the two holy mosques, we resolved, after relying on Almighty God, to carry out fair punishment against the agent of this regime and its cheap tool in Greater Syria, the sinner and maker of illegal money, the Israeli, through implementation of a resounding martyrdom operation. This confirms our promise to support and wage jihad, and will be the beginning of many martyrdom operations against the infidels, renegades and tyrants in Greater Syria."

Now Al-Rajul had to make a subtle amendment and then

transfer the finished product back to tape. It was so tempting simply to burn it onto disc, but the fictitious *al-Nasr wa al-Jihad fi bilad al-Sham* group (Victory and Jihad in Greater Syria) – from whom the message would purport to come – would not be that sophisticated.

He picked up the microphone attached to the laptop and said two words into it. Then he selected the edit function on the program. Over and over, the two words he had recorded came out of the speakers, so he could tweak them into the slightly higher tone of the person on the screen, and time and match them precisely to the moving lips.

It took him twenty minutes.

Twenty minutes to exactly find and replace *the Israeli* with *Rafic Hariri.*

At 05:00 The Facility was still in darkness. It was fifteen minutes before *Fajr* prayer, which they usually missed anyway, and over a hundred minutes to sunrise prayer. The only sound that could be heard was muted snoring.

In the corridor, a figure walked quietly. His night vision was good and he did not need a torch. He certainly would not put the lights on.

He stopped at the closed door to the meeting room and looked cautiously behind him. Noiselessly he opened the door and went in.

They had tidied up the room before retiring last night. The flag had been taken down and would be disposed of later, the camcorder box was in a far corner next to the eight mobile phone boxes and the loose tripod.

He went over to them, bent down and selected what he wanted.

He had done what he wanted to do. He should not have, but he was pleased that he had. Nobody would know and he would have put some minds at rest.

At 05:15 he left the meeting room, softly closing the door behind him. He walked carefully back down the corridor. Suddenly there was a flash of lightning. Then another, and another.

He gasped, looking up at the overhead fluorescent light as if he had never seen it coming on before. There was no clap of thunder, but the shock as he looked back down sent a jolt through his system greater than any lightning strike.

The Commander was standing at the end of the corridor.

"What were you doing in there?" His voice was flat, emotionless.

Nervousness made Elias giggle. "N-nothing, sir. I – I couldn't sleep. I thought I would pray."

The Commander nodded as he came towards him. "That is good. That is good." Suddenly his right hand shot out and grabbed Elias around the throat. Spit flew from the young Palestinian's mouth as he was pushed back into the meeting room.

"I'll ask you one more time," growled the Commander. "What were you doing?"

"I was just praying - "

The Commander's left fist rammed into Elias's stomach. The young Palestinian doubled over and the force knocked him onto his knees and into the chairs.

"What were you doing?"

"I – I - "

The Commander's left foot swung back, but Elias's hands raised in defence and supplication. "No, sir, no, sir, please! I am sorry, I am sorry. I was just..." He sat up, sliding backwards out of reach. "I... I wanted to contact my family. Just to tell them I was okay. It has been a few weeks."

The Commander's eyes shot over to the pile of boxes in the corner then back to Elias. "Which one did you use?"

"Sir?"

"Which phone did you use? Show me."

Elias scurried over on his knees, pulling out a box from the middle of the pile. "Nokia," he laughed nervously. "My favourite."

"Give it to me."

Quickly Elias opened the box and held out the handset. The Commander moved forward and slapped it out of his hand onto the floor.

"Don't you realise," he said angrily, "our location can be detected if we turn these things on?" He raised his booted left foot and slammed it down, again and again, the phone splitting and breaking.

Elias stared at the phone, terrified of the fury on the Commander's face. He shook his head. "I'm sorry, sir, I'm sorry. I didn't think."

The Commander stood there, looking down at him, his anger palpable. There should have been scorn in his eyes, but there was nothing. They were blank. After a minute, he sighed. "Okay, get up. No harm done. We all make mistakes, that's why we're human."

Elias stood up, humble. The Commander put his arm around his shoulders, leading him out of the room. "Let's go eat."

As they were walking back down the corridor, the Commander said "Actually, you are right. It was wrong of me to keep you out of contact with your family for so long. They will indeed be worried, even though their rewards will be great. I think we should pop back to see them. Just for a quick visit, so that they know you are all right..."

When Ahmad awoke sixty minutes later, he was surprised that Elias was not in his bed. He was even more surprised when he realised he was on his own in The Facility and the van had gone.

During the morning, Ahmad bathed, prayed, ate, read the Koran, undertook a gentle exercise regime and bathed again.

It was just after midday, as he was on the verge of letting his concern upgrade to worry, when the van returned. He watched out of the window as it pulled up in front of the building. He expected the Commander and Elias to get out, probably triumphant after some morning task that he had not been privy to, but nothing happened. The van had stopped, he could see just one person inside it, but no one got out.

Ahmad frowned. Did they need help? Had they gone to pick up something?

Then there were three loud peremptory blasts of the van's horn.

Quickly, Ahmad ran outside. The Commander was looking out of the open driver's window. He did not look happy. "Ahmad, I need you to do something for me, immediately."

"Sir?"

A key flew through the air and landed on the gravel. "Go and check on the sugar. Count the number of sacks. Then join me in the meeting room in half an hour."

Ahmad bent down and picked up the key. "Now, sir?" He straightened up.

"Yes!" barked the Commander. "Now, now. Go!"

Ahmad scurried off towards the garages and outbuildings around the side – allowing Al-Rajul to get out of the van and walk into the main building unseen.

He was covered head to foot in blood.

Half an hour later in the meeting room. The Commander was freshly bathed and he was dressed in a long white *dishdasha*, his head unadorned, hair damp. Ahmad was surprised when he came in – he had never seen the Commander dressed like this before. He looked good. Very noble, very Arabic.

The Commander went straight to the point. "Ahmad, I have made a decision. I broke the news to Elias earlier. He has now left us and is with his family. They have been rewarded. They will never see that accursed camp again."

"That is good, sir."

"It is. So now it is just you. You will be the biggest hero of all my recruits. You have been chosen."

"For what, sir?"

The Commander stood in front of Ahmad and put both his hands on his shoulders. The young Palestinian looked up at his mentor. The Commander smiled. "You will kill the Israeli traitor."

Bourj el-Barajneh, Beirut 13:00 – 16:30

At the same moment that the Commander said the words to Ahmad, Sergeant Bassem el-Khazem of the Palestinian police hurriedly entered the office of his Captain, trying not to recoil. The stench in the room could be cut with a knife.

"Captain, there's some people you should see."

Captain Fadi Lattouf quickly closed his drawer containing his lunch box of *kibbeh*, tomatoes and cucumber, as if he had been caught doing something he shouldn't. "What? Can't it wait? I was going to have my lunch."

"I think you will want to see them."

"After lunch."

"It's about this." el-Khazem waved the crumpled, dirty piece of paper he had in his hand.

Lattouf frowned before recognising it as one of the 'Missing' posters they had put up, but it looked like somebody had been drawing on it in red. His eyebrows rose in interest. "They have some information?"

"Better. Or worse."

Lattouf heaved his massive frame out of the chair. "Shaitan's scrotum, Bassem, must you talk in riddles?"

"You will want to hear this for yourself."

Outside, an elderly man stood nervously against one of the walls. Next to him was a boy of about thirteen, sniffling, sobbing, eyes downcast.

Lattouf's booted feet clumped down the corridor. "Well?" he shouted. "You have something to tell me?" The subtleties of coercive interrogation had never been Lattouf's strong-point.

The old man cowered backwards, his arm protectively around the boy. "Th – they are dead, sir."

"What? Who?"

"All of them. All five of them. Please, I will show you."

"What are you talking about, man? What is your name?"

"M - my name is Mohamed Hassan."

"Where do you live?"

"The camp."

"Of course you live in the camp! I meant where?"

"I am the neighbour. Sir, they are all dead. Please, you must come."

As Mohamed Hassan waived his free hand expressively, Lattouf noticed it was marked with the same red ink that was on the poster el-Khazem was holding. "You an artist?" he asked.

Hassan was thrown. "What?"

"I said..." Lattouf stared at Hassan's hand, then slowly turned and looked back at the paper in el-Khazem's hand. The penny dropped, as did the colour from his face. "Where?"

"I will show you."

There are many specific and stringent requirements for a job with the Palestinian police, but a degree in criminology is not one of them. So Fadi Lattouf was unaware of the history of the world's most heinous murders, but he knew that what he was confronted with now would rank alongside some of the worst excesses ever perpetrated by human kind. He was so glad his stomach was empty, because if it hadn't been it would be now.

The room on the upper floor of the old breeze-block building would have stank normally anyway. Now it reeked of iron, urine and faeces – the unmistakeable perfume of death.

There was blood everywhere. Pooling on the floor and indiscriminately splashed up every wall and across the peeling ceiling, as if somebody had stood in the centre of the room and let fly with a paint spray gun. It was over the sparse furniture and was probably dripping through the floorboards to the dwelling underneath.

There were five of them. Each with their faces caved in. At least two of them had had their necks broken, the angle of their heads was hideous – probably a quick *en bloc* despatch with the facial abuse as a post mortem cosmetic. No other parts of their bodies had been defiled though, so Lattouf could tell there was one middle-aged woman, one middle-aged man, a younger man and two young women, one of them pre-pubescent. An entire family.

And no accident.

He watched transfixed as a piece of grey matter oozed out of the hole in the head of one of the young girls and spread across the floor as if it was trying to escape. He turned quickly.

"When did you find them?" he snapped at the old man standing in the doorway, still with his arm around the sobbing boy. Sergeant el-Khazem was next to them, trying not to look at the bodies.

"I –I didn't," said Mohamed.

"What?"

"He – he did." He nodded downwards at the boy.

"Your son found them?"

"He is not my son, sir."

Lattouf sighed loudly in irritation. "Then, in the name of the Prophet, peace be upon him, who the - ?"

"They are my family." The boy said it so quietly that Lattouf wondered if he had heard him at all.

"What did you say?"

The boy looked up, eyes bloodshot, red-rimmed and wet. "My father and mother. My sisters. My older brother."

"What?"

"My - "

"I heard you, I heard you." Lattouf looked back at the bodies, then at his sergeant, then back to the boy. "You found them? So you had been out?"

"I – I didn't know my brother was coming back. He has been away for a while. He never told me last night he was coming back - "

"Wait a minute, wait a minute. You spoke to your brother last night?"

"He telephoned me." The boy fished into his pocket and pulled out a battered old mobile phone and held it up.

"Where has he been, your brother?"

"I – I don't know."

"You don't know? Did your parents know?"

"No, none of us did. We saw your piece of paper a few weeks ago," he nodded at el-Khazem. "But we went to the groups. They said not to contact you."

Lattouf cursed under his breath. Who ran the camps anyway? Well, he knew the answer to that, and he knew it wasn't the PSF. "What did your brother say to you?" he asked.

The boy replied, and moments later Fadi Lattouf was running back down the stairs shouting into his mobile phone.

This time there was no subtlety, no oblique speaking, no meeting at the Dunes with a twenty-six hour time difference. There couldn't be any flashing blue lights, that would have been suicidal, but ninety minutes later the blue Toyota Land Cruiser sped into Annan Street and pulled to a halt next to the waiting figure of Fadi Lattouf.

Jihad Merhi had not had time to change out of his uniform, but being the middle of winter he did not look incongruous with his North Face Galaxy parka zipped up to the chin. "How many?" he asked without greeting as he got out of the car.

"Five." It was getting colder as night fell, and Lattouf was rubbing his hands together. "Five little accidents."

"Five! Where are they?"

"Some way in. You don't need to see them. Same as before.

Only this time fresh. Done today. The bodies weren't cold."

They spoke as they walked into the camp.

"Five..." Merhi shook his head. "In the name of Jesus..."

"And all the other prophets. It was a family. An entire family. Or so the perpetrator thought."

Merhi looked up at the big Palestinian. "What do you mean?"

"He missed one," grinned Lattouf. "He thought he had taken them all, but one was not there."

"What are you saying, Fadi?"

"We have him. And he's talking. Come."

They had reached the police office. Lattouf led the way inside, past the front area and down the corridor past his own office to the small cell at the back.

Behind the bars, an old man was sitting with glum resignation on the bench against the wall. Next to him was a young teenager with a swathe of padding taped across his nose, eyes black. He wore a grubby white polo shirt and had an even grubbier towel around his waist, original colour indeterminate. He had no trousers on.

"What happened to him?" asked Merhi.

"Clumsy youth. Fell against the table in the interview room."

Merhi gave an 'Oh yeah?' grimace but said nothing.

"But he had some interesting information to report." Louder, Lattouf said "He is an upright citizen. A good Palestinian."

"Will he talk to me?"

"No need. He is a bit nasally at the moment, sounds like a fighter after fifteen rounds. But I've got it all down. Come to my office."

In the office, Lattouf indicated an old wooden cafeteria chair in front of his desk. It wobbled as Merhi sat on it.

"Coffee?" Lattouf held up a huge black flask. "Nada made it this morning, but it should still be warm."

It was the last thing Merhi wanted. "Yes. Thank you."

Lattouf poured some sludge into an old cracked cup which looked like it hadn't been washed since before the war. Merhi took it and hoped his show of gratitude wasn't too insincere.

Lattouf swilled from the flask and then wiped his mouth with the back of his hand. "They are – were – the Massoud family. Father, getting on a bit – well, he isn't anymore, but up until this morning he was. Mother ten years younger. Eldest son in his early twenties, a daughter in her late teens, another son in his early teens and a younger sister. The younger boy was out at school when... the visitor called."

"And he found the bodies?"

"Yes."

"Shit."

"Yes. And he did. That's why he's wearing the towel." Lattouf took another swig from the flask. Out of politeness, and much against his better judgement, Merhi raised the cup to his lips, pleasantly surprised to find that the coffee was not that bad. A knife and fork would have helped, though.

"He has an interesting story," continued Lattouf. "His brother went missing in early November. Went out one night, just did not come home."

"About a month after the bodies started to appear. Connection?"

Lattouf shrugged. "I would have said no. Until today, of course."

"Didn't his family report him as missing?"

Lattouf's look was pitiful. "This is the camp. What do you think? Young Palestinian males often go missing, perhaps lost in fighting, who knows? But yes, once my notices started to go up they decided to report him. But not to me, not to the police."

"Ah, I see."

"They were told to do nothing. Then early this morning, just before *Fajr*, the boy received a telephone call from his brother."

"I thought phones weren't allowed in the camp."

"On his mobile. He had found the phone a few months ago in Beirut."

"Found?"

"Found. He had changed the SIM but kept the handset. His parents didn't know he had it, but his brother did. His brother told him he was safe and had been selected for a mission instigated by our late President. They had been training up in the mountains. Now the mission was starting. He just wanted to let his family know he was safe and soon he would be getting them out of the camp."

Merhi curled his lip at the sick irony. Well, they were certainly now out of the camp. Then he said, "They?"

"What?"

"You said *they* had been training up in the mountains?"

"What of it?"

"Don't you see? *They.* Young Palestinian males, early twenties?"

Slowly Lattouf's mouth opened. "The bodies."

"Exactly. Until today all have been young local males." Merhi paused in thought, tapping his nails against the side of his cup, making a pleasant tinkling sound. The incongruity of the situation was not lost on him: here he was, in the squalor of the Bourj el-Barajneh refugee camp, drinking coffee out of a bone china cup, cracked and dirty though it may be.

Lattouf leant forward, elbows on his desk, chin resting on his hands. After a minute, he said "Baby seals."

Merhi was snapped out of his thoughts. "What?"

"What is it they do to baby seals? You know, when they bash their heads in."

"When they...?" For a moment Merhi didn't understand. Then he said, "Oh my God. Culling. They call it culling."

Lattouf sat back, pleased with himself. "There you have it."

Merhi was aghast. "But..."

"He has been culling young Palestinians," Lattouf was speaking in the tolerant tone of master to apprentice. It was good to get one up on the Lebanese, no matter how much he liked him. "Only the strong survive."

"Or only the chosen. He has been testing. Choosing.

Whittling. One or more young Palestinians. For what? To do what?"

"Oh, that we know."

"We do?"

"Oh yes. The deceased, Elias Massoud, told his brother. There is an Israeli agent at work in Beirut. They are going to kill him."

20 January 2005
9 Dhu'l-Hijja 1425

Jounieh, Lebanon 00:45

Jihad Merhi arrived home after midnight – nothing unusual in that with the job he did – and Gisele was already in bed, tucked up warmly under the quilt. The Levantine winter would soon be ending, but for now it remained cold. She had left a dim bedside light on for him so that he could see and not crack a toe against the bottom of the bed, as he had done in the past (the Merhi's had been in the apartment only six years and, being a man, Jihad was still getting used to the geography of the furniture).

Having had a cigarette out on the balcony accompanied by a nightcap of a small Johnnie Walker, Jihad now slid into the bed. "Unbelievable," he was shaking his head. "Absolutely unbelievable. The idiot Lattouf actually worked it all out. Well, there's a first time for everything, I suppose." He stretched out and turned off the light. "The murders have been nothing more than a recruitment and selection process. Probably by one of the Palestinian groups. Who knows? They are always so damned extreme. Why kill their rejects? Why not just throw them back into the pond? Crazy. And what is it are they going to do? Kill an Israeli agent at work in Beirut. Lattouf presented it as if I would never have known that the Jews had agents working here! The Palestinians can kill them all, for all I care." He lay back, hands behind his head. "But that gets me out of it. The body up in Aammiq has already been recorded as an accident. Lattouf is now fully writing up the murders and reporting them to his superiors as a solved case – the why if not the who. And considering the nature of the operation, I doubt his superiors will even worry about reporting it to us. They'll let us hear it on the news if the killing ever happens!

"Still, that's good. Let Lattouf get the credit. Perhaps he'll leave me alone for a while. God knows, I've got enough to do..."

He looked at the shadow of his wife next to him. She was fast asleep, as she had been all along. His talking had not disturbed her. She had not heard a word he said.

But somebody else had.

21 January 2005
10 Dhu'l-Hijja 1425

Kahale, Lebanon 11:30

The Commander had his hands around Ahmad's throat. The young Palestinian's eyes were popping, staring at the face just centimetres in front of him, a booger wobbling on the end of his nose.

"You know what to do," snarled the Commander, his garlic breath wafting into Ahmad's face.

"But - "

"Do it! Or I will kill you."

For a minute the terror stayed in Ahmad's eyes, because he knew the Commander wasn't going to let go. Then all of a sudden the fear was gone and he relaxed. His mentor was right, he did know what to do.

His right hand shot out and grabbed the Commander by the balls. As the Commander shouted out, Ahmad pulled his own arms down and then thrust them upwards in an inverted V-shape, breaking the hold around his throat.

The Commander staggered backwards, half bent over. "You little bastard. I didn't teach you that!" There was a hint of admiration behind the anger in his eyes.

Ahmad was worried he had gone too far, but he was pleased with what he had done. "I knew a man of your skills would be waiting for the upward V," he said a little breathlessly, wiping his wrist across his nose. "It would not be enough to get you off me."

"So you decided to improvise?" The Commander straightened up.

"Yes."

The Commander stared, cold, and for a moment Ahmad thought he was going to lunge for him again. Then he smiled. "Excellent. You have learnt well. Good. As I explained, we are unlikely to be apprehended. There will be too much confusion. But it is worthwhile to have these skills, just in case." He rubbed his testacles. "Bravo."

Ahmad picked up a towel and wiped his face. "When will it be, sir?"

"Soon. I have an exact date. Problem is, until the day, until the hour, I will not know where the Israeli will be. That is why we must have a rehearsal, a trial run."

"When?"

The Commander undid the *keffiyeh* from around his neck and began to unbutton his shirt. "Today is Friday. We will have our trial run on Monday, so that we have the correct experience of the weekday traffic. I have prepared and tested the electrics but we must try them out in the real theatre. Later today I must leave. I will be back on Sunday. Enjoy yourself this weekend, and now no more exercise. You are at the peak of fitness. I don't want you overdoing it and injuring yourself."

"Thank you, sir." Ahmad was proud.

"Now," said the Commander. "Let us shower before we pray."

22 January 2005
11 Dhu'l-Hijja 1425

Mount Lebanon 23:50

It would have been funny if it was not so serious.

Since the tumultuous, abruptly-ended meeting two weeks ago between Hariri and the head of Syrian intelligence in Lebanon, Rustom Ghazaleh, the verbal attacks on Hariri had increased to the point where they were so incessant as to be ludicrous. The wildly-flying accusations were absurd – but absurdity did not decrease danger.

Abu Tarek had become aware of a plot to have both Hariri and Druze leader Walid Jumblatt arrested on fabricated charges. Jumblatt was to be accused of ordering the assassination of former Lebanese president Rene Mouawad, while Hariri was going to be charged with something equally as ludicrous.

Nothing had come of the plot to remove the two major opposition leaders, due in no small part to Nayla Mouawad[*] warning Jumblatt of the plot after she had been informed by Suleiman Frangieh, the Interior Minister.

But The Damascene had been called in immediately by Abu Tarek. He had considered the situation and concluded that his risk assessment remained the same: it was Hariri's movements that presented the security risk, not the bombastic words and fantasies of his enemies. But the alert status was increased from

---

[*] The widow of Rene Mouawad and a leading member of the Qornet Shehwan group.

Black to Black Special.

The Damascene knew that no matter what they did, no matter how they stacked the electoral law against him, Hariri was going to triumph in May.

And there were those that did not want that.

She was there when The Damascene returned to the apartment just before midnight. They made love tenderly and roughly, slow and fast, with consideration and selfishness, but always with the skill and precision of experts in carnality.

At 02:00, The Damascene was bitten by a mosquito.

24 January 2005
13 Dhu'l-Hijja 1425

Beirut 11:00 – 14:00

The white Mitsubishi Canter van drove down the Beirut to Damascus road towards the Lebanese capital. Al-Rajul, the Commander, was driving, Ahmad next to him. It was an overcast but dry day. They were dressed in normal working men's clothes – jeans, shirts, old winter jackets – to match their cover story if they were stopped. They were farmers from the Bekaa, collecting orders from their customers. On the actual day of operation, when the sacks of sugar would be in the back, they would be wholesalers from Zahlé delivering the sugar to customers.

The journey had been timed so that they hit the Beirut traffic at 11:00, operational conditions for the trial run. They parked in the pay area on Weygand Street, opposite the Grand Café, stopping as near to the exit as space allowed.

"On the day you will be on your own," explained the Commander. "I will be using other transport. Park as near to this exit as you possibly can. It is imperative that when I tell you to move, you move. You understand?"

"Yes, sir." Ahmad's thoughts flashed back to the briefing last night when the Commander had explained exactly what would happen on The Day. Now they were having the practice run, and he had to admit to being nervous.

The Commander could sense it, and he put a reassuring hand

on Ahmad's knee. "It will be all right, my brave man. That is why we are having this trial run, so that you will be prepared on the day. You just do what you have to do and leave the rest to me. Okay?"

"Yes, sir. Thank you, sir."

"And I promise you the camp will be a thing of the past." He removed his hand. "Now then, you have the three phones?"

Ahmad tapped his jacket pocket.

"Right. When I get out, move over into this seat and put them on the seat here beside you. You remember the meanings?"

Ahmad took the phones out of his pocket one by one. "Nokia – the northern route. N for north. Samsung – the southern route. S for south. LG – the western route. LG – *la gauche*, going left."

"Good. And the three places?"

"North – the St. George Hotel. South – the Four Points Sheraton Hotel. West – the Future TV building. At the precise moment the subject passes by, I press the red button." He nodded to a button which the Commander had installed near the parking brake, but not too near as to be accidentally touched. It looked like a domestic doorbell.

"Press it now."

"Now?"

"Yes, just to test it."

Ahmad reached forward and pressed the button. Immediately a buzzing sound came from inside the Commander's jacket. He reached in and turned it off.

"Excellent. Right, we'll try it out. When you get the signal from me, move and move fast. You must get to the location before the subject. When he passes by, you press the button. I will be waiting further along the route. Ten seconds later, he reaches me, I fire, he's dead. You are already driving away, I will vanish into the back streets. We meet back at The Facility. How will you know the subject?"

"He will be in a convoy, a Toyota, four black Mercedes plus a Chevrolet ambulance behind."

The Commander unlocked the door. "Today, of course, we have no subject. So just pretend. Stay where you are after you've pressed the button. I will be working in real time, so between thirty and forty seconds after you've pressed it, I will be with you." He stepped out then looked back as Ahmad shuffled over into the driver's seat.

Then the Commander did something unusual – he smiled. Then he said, "Go with God, my hero." He slammed the van door and walked off towards the Omari Grand Mosque.

Al-Rajul walked straight down Omari Grand Mosque Street and into Nejmeh Square (Star Square, Place de l'Etoile). A symbol of the destruction of the city during the war, it had been rebuilt by Rafic Hariri and Solidère into a crisp and impressive modern version of how it used to be, many of the streets pedestrianised and lined with up-market shops and restaurants. In the centre was the renovated clock tower, originally erected during the French mandate. To his right was the Parliament building.

He walked on, down Parliament Street. The pedestrianisation of the area did not worry him. On The Day, he would have his own means of transport.

Stopping at the end of the street by Kuwait Airways, he scanned the junction. Riad es Solh Square at eleven o'clock, Federal Express at one o'clock. Away back at four o'clock, the Grand Serail and the Prime Minister's offices. If the northern route wasn't chosen, on The Day this was where the southern and western routes would split.

He made up his mind which route to use for this rehearsal and walked on.

Ahmad wanted to pee. He sat in the driver's seat of the van, his right leg bouncing up and down. A copy of that day's *Al-Mustaqbal* newspaper was open across the steering wheel, something the Commander had told him to do so that he wouldn't look suspicious simply waiting in the van. The face of

Rafic Hariri stared up at him from the paper.

It had been forty minutes, and he was wondering whether he should just nip into the back of the van and piss into a corner when one of the phones buzzed. He jumped, and just a little bit of pee-pee shot out into his underpants. He looked at the phones on the seat next to him.

It was the LG. The western route.

Ahmad pulled out into Weygand Street, turning left. They had gone over and over the routes last night, and a point the Commander had hammered home was that he was not to take the same route as the convoy would take. He did not want to be seen near them or following them. He just needed to *be* there at the right time. And he must not speed or draw any attention to himself.

He entered the Bab Idriss area, heading west and south. He hit Soleiman Franjieh Avenue, where the traffic was heavier but the street wider, and then took a right into Michel Chiha Street. A left, taking him past the Sierra Leone Consulate, then he stopped at the junction with Spears Street. He waited for a few cars to pass, then pulled out right. He parked where he could, just opposite the Future TV building, the Beirut Chamber of Commerce ahead on the right.

It would never have occurred to Ahmad that the paper the Commander had given him, *Al-Mustaqbal*, was owned by the former Lebanese Prime Minister Rafic Hariri, as was Future TV where he was parked. Why would it? He had no interest in Lebanese politics – he was on a mission to kill an Israeli agent, for the sake of Allah! And the Commander would be pleased with him, he was parked exactly where he should be.

Reaching forward, he pressed the red button.

And waited.

Half a minute later, he saw the Commander walking quickly from the direction of the Sanayeh Gardens. He was intent, not looking at the van. Had he seen him? Should Ahmad beep? No, no, don't be so foolish.

The Commander reached the van and it looked like he was going past, then his hand shot out, opened the door, and he climbed in. "Good. Go."

Ahmad pulled out and took the first left down Medhat Bacha Street, heading south.

Mount Lebanon 14:30 – 16:30

The Djinn opened the front door to The Damascene's apartment and let herself in. Real *djinni* could not open closed doors, but a door was never closed if you had a key.

She was dressed in a plain pink T-shirt, split-at-the-knee jeans which looked old and worn but cost a fortune in Ashrafieh, and Nike trainers. Her long black hair was down but, as always, the hair clip was in place at the back. She wore no make-up – there was no need, she knew he wouldn't be there. In her hands she carried a large cardboard box.

Her prey was spending more and more time away from the apartment now, spending more and more time concentrating on Hariri as the elections approached, which meant that she had to time her visits more and more carefully – both when he was there and when he was not.

She put the cardboard box down on the breakfast counter and then began her thrice-weekly search of the apartment – every drawer, every cupboard, inside and under every piece of furniture, every nook, every cranny. She never found anything, but she knew it had to be done – one day he might slip up.

She then checked on the eight strategically placed bugging devices inside the electricity sockets. All in order, not touched or tampered with. Unlike herself! She smiled naughtily as she went back to the kitchen and, after a struggle with the packaging, took out the contents of the cardboard box: a Krups filter coffee machine. A present for the best lover she had ever had (and, in her job, she had had many). It was just a pity his coffee making skills did not match his bedroom skills. She always enjoyed a stiff coffee after a stiff... interrogation session.

She primed the machine and then filled it with water for its first coffee-less drip-through. She wanted it ready so that, after their next joining, she would have to wait only the few filtering minutes for her caffeine fix while he slept after she had questioned him.

As the water dripped through, she went over to the window and looked out over cloudy Beirut. She was glad to be back here after her many months of foreign assignments. The place had changed while she had been away: so much building, so much reconstruction, new projects starting everywhere. She hoped there were never any more wars or attacks from foreign enemies to harm this beautiful city – and her love of Beirut was why she was so pleased when she had been given her current mission, so she could come home. The mission would be coming to a head soon because these were dangerous times to be a public figure in Lebanon.

She turned as a louder-than-the-rest gurgle indicated that the water had run through the machine. Back into the kitchen, she poured the steaming water down the sink, dried the pot and put it back in place, leaving the machine sitting squarely on the breakfast bar so he would see it as soon as he came in and he would know she had been there. A little tease, a little promise.

As she walked towards the front door, she heard a tap-tapping at the window. She turned. It was starting to rain, one of the heavy Beirut winter showers. And she had only her T-shirt on, no coat.

It was just as well she didn't have to go outside.

She only lived in the apartment below.

Her apartment on the second floor was geographically identical to the one above it but naturally the furniture was different (it did not, for example, have the boy-toy of the massive wall-mounted widescreen television). It was more homey than the functional apartment above, but it still had that not-really-cared-for look of a rental. She was here only temporarily, for as long as the current job took.

Dressed in a white towelling robe, she was in the open-plan kitchen preparing her favourite pasta dish when she heard a single, solitary bump from the speaker sitting on the coffee table in the living area. She stopped stirring her sauce, straining to hear over the hum of the hob. There was nothing else, but she was professional enough to know that she hadn't imagined what she'd heard.

She moved the saucepan off the ring and stepped lightly across to the coffee table. The speaker was attached to a VHF audio receiver, the base hub for the listening devices hidden in the apartment upstairs. She knelt down next to the table, listening.

Nothing. No sound. Nobody moving about, not even the sound of a coffee machine being put on. But she had heard something, that lone bump. She fingered the clip in her hair. The sound of the apartment door opening would be too subtle for her to have heard above the cooker. If he had arrived home, she would be hearing other sounds like she usually did. Unless someone had come in and then immediately gone out again.

Quickly she rose to her feet and ran over to her front door, opening it cautiously. Nobody there, she went out into the stairwell – just in time to hear the front door of the block closing downstairs.

She took the stairs two at a time in her bare feet, her robe flapping open, reaching the bottom in no time. It was getting dark as she went outside into the rain.

But it was still light enough for her to see a van pulling up onto the main road and heading east.

27 January 2005
16 Dhu'l-Hijja 1425

Jounieh, Lebanon 06:15

Jihad Merhi climbed into his Toyota Land Cruiser, turned on the ignition and quickly put the heater on max. It was still cold, especially at this godforsaken hour of the morning. He needed to be in early, he had his bi-annual appraisal meeting with Major Ghanem later and he wanted to be prepared – the old bastard would take the opportunity to quiz him on the finer details of each and every case he had on hand, as he always did.

At least the traffic on the coastal highway would be lighter at this hour, and he should be in the office by 07:00. He turned on the Toyota's full beams and moved slowly up the track towards the mountainside road.

As he reached the road, a large shadow shot in front of him, blocking his way. Had he been going fast, he would have crashed right into it. He pulled up sharply, wheels crunching on the gravel of the track. *What the hell?* Quickly he reached for his gun.

The driver's door of the Ford Explorer opened at the same moment as Merhi leapt out of the Toyota, aiming the gun over the open door. "Hold it! Hold it right there!" he shouted.

The figure in the darkness stopped, arms raising into the air. "I am unarmed," said a female voice.

"Walk into the light," ordered Merhi.

Squinting against the full beams, she moved sideways. She

was a local woman, probably late twenties, dressed in jeans and thick woollen jumper. There were no visible weapons.

Keeping her covered with the gun, Merhi stretched in and dimmed the beams. Then he stepped around his door and came towards her, gun still raised. "What do you want?"

Tentatively she lowered her arms a few centimetres. He said nothing to stop her so she put them down. "Captain Merhi," she said. "I'm Zahia Zalloum of the Department of General Security. Your wife was a trainer on an unarmed combat course I did a few years ago."

"Really? Wow. Impressed."

"Captain, we need to talk."

29 January 2005
18 Dhu'l-Hijja 1425

Mount Lebanon 01:00

It was an interesting situation.

Politically, it was an intense time for Rafic Hariri. The electoral law had been unveiled a few days earlier and, as expected, it was hedged against him. National constituencies were smaller. Beirut had been split into three electoral districts, which strengthened the Christian, Shi'ite and Armenian representation while weakening the Sunni. On the other hand, it was widely accepted that even this would not stop an overall opposition victory in May.

But from a security point of view – which was all The Damascene was interested in – things were locked-down tight. Hariri lived and worked in Koreitem. Any official trips outside (for example, to and from Parliament) were undertaken in the convoy of armour-plated vehicles with the electronic jamming devices to prevent roadside bomb detonation. Unofficial trips (for example, the trips into the south of the city to visit Hassan Nasrallah) were only ever arranged at the last minute and were now done in a single armour-plated vehicle – and usually had a man with long hair and a missing left ear riding on a motorbike a little way behind.

That day, Hariri had met with his two main political allies – his Protestant economic advisor Basil Fleihan and Dr Ghattas Koury, a Maronite Christian surgeon – and had reaffirmed his alliance with the Bristol Gathering. With gallows humour, he had asked Walid Jumblatt, the Druze leader, "Who will be assassinated first? You or me?"

Well, The Damascene knew who it wasn't going to be. He had a job to do, and he was on top of the situation. But he must never, ever, become complacent.

Now he turned in his bed – and kissed The Djinn full on the lips. It was something they actually rarely did.

When they broke after thirty seconds, she smiled. "That was nice."

"Of course it was. For me too."

Laughing, she punched his shoulder. "You arrogant male!"

He sniffed. "Just male. The arrogance comes with the territory, it's a given."

"Okay then, you male. Well, I'm a tiger and I'm going to claw you!" She threw her leg over him and rolled up onto his stomach. She meowed as her hands moved backwards up his glistening body, her nails giving him kitten scratches.

"Oh really?" He reached up and grabbed her face in his hands. "Tigers have to be tamed. And I know just how to do that." His left thumb was in her mouth and he tugged lightly sideways as he kicked upwards with his right leg.

Growling, her teeth closed over his thumb as she fell, her mouth sucking. He rolled over her. She feigned defiance, trying to push him off, her nails scratching down his back, one nail sharper than the rest. She let him push his hips between her legs, and she felt him pressing upwards.

"Tigers on top," she hissed into the hole in his head as she shoved back against him and deftly slipped out from underneath.

He flopped face down on the bed. And did not move.

He was fast asleep.

She had fallen off of the bed and was kneeling on the floor, breathless. A few moments later, she was shaking his shoulder, saying "Marwan? Captain Mebarak? I need to talk to you..."

30 January 2005
19 Dhu'l-Hijja 1425

Hamra, Beirut 10:45

The lid of the jar opened with a satisfying pop.

"You're not going to eat those walking along the road?" queried Jihad Merhi.

"Why not?" shrugged Fadi Lattouf. "It has been a long time since breakfast." He saw Merhi look at his watch. "I was up early. And anyway, that woman makes the finest *mekhallel* this side of Gaza. I'm glad you said to meet here so I could get these. Those jars you gave me at new year didn't last long." Juice trickled into his beard as he shoved two pickled cucumbers and something long, pink and shiny into his mouth.

They were walking along busy Hamra Street, Merhi with his leather coat open revealing his uniform, Lattouf with his old padded windcheater done up to the neck, concealing his uniform. Merhi carried a jar of pickles in each hand, looking after them while Lattouf gorged from a third jar.

"So ten bodies that we know of," salivated the Palestinian. "And your Department of General Security wants us to do nothing about it. Did this woman say anything about my culling theory?"

"She really didn't say anything. Said they were in the dark as much as we were – but they've been getting information from somewhere, they've been following leads of their own. They've only recently realised our, er, interest."

"How?" A large piece of pepper flopped over Lattouf's lips like a deformed tongue and then disappeared with a sucking slither.

"Don't know. They've been listening, of course, but I thought we'd been careful."

"Perhaps not careful enough."

"Perhaps. But it's worked out okay, as you say. We don't have the threat of an official murder investigation hanging over us."

Juice dripping through his fingers, Lattouf crunched down on a piece of cauliflower. "Do we have any threats hanging over us?"

They paused to cross over Omar Ben Abd el-Aziz Street. "No threats, just two requests," said Merhi. "One, back off. Two, let them know if any more turn up."

"They are expecting more?"

"Didn't say." There was a break in the traffic and they crossed the road.

"Well, at least we now know who we're dealing with on the official side. Why you Lebanese have to skulk around with your mysterious car-followings and secret warnings, I don't know." Lattouf took the last items from the jar, two more pieces of cauliflower and a gherkin.

Merhi gave an ironic nod, acknowledging the truth. "In Lebanon the balance is always... delicate. Right hands never want left hands to know what they are doing."

Lattouf huffed. "I think thumbs don't want index fingers to know what they are doing! I will never understand you, I have given up trying." Still walking, Lattouf swilled the remaining juice around the jar, raised the jar to his mouth and drank it down. Merhi looked on aghast.

Putting his hands out for his other two jars and giving Merhi the empty one, Lattouf said "But we should still keep looking under our cars, my friend. Sometimes thumbs can turn nasty."

1 February 2005
21 Dhu'l-Hijja 1425

Kahale, Lebanon 15:00

"You are in good shape." The Commander stood with a towel around his waist watching Ahmad finishing his shower.

The young Palestinian wiped his hands down his wet face as he came out. "Thank you, sir." He was unashamed of his nakedness. Everything that had happened in the last three months, especially the successful trial run into Beirut a week ago, had instilled confidence in him. He began to dry himself.

"But, as I said, don't overdo it," cautioned the Commander. "You are at your peak. The day of action is fast approaching. Everything is coming together well."

"When is it, sir? The day?"

"Two weeks. Just two more weeks." The Commander announced it matter-of-factly, no great fanfare.

Ahmad's face lit up. It was news he had been waiting to hear. "Two weeks," he repeated.

The Commander dropped his towel and walked naked out into the changing area where they had left their clean clothes. "You are happy about driving the van?" he asked over his shoulder.

Ahmad picked up the Commander's towel, feeling its wetness and warmth as he draped it over the towel rail. "Yes, sir," he called. "It was a good experience for me, in the city. I am confident."

"Good. Because on the day you will be driving it on your own."

There were a few seconds before Ahmad said from the doorway, "Sir?"

The Commander pulled his white *dishdasha* over his head and flicked his hair out at the back. He looked up at Ahmad standing there naked. He shrugged as if it had been obvious. "I cannot be with you, Ahmad. I will be watching for the Israeli and then getting myself into position. I was there on the rehearsal only to tell you what to do. I will have my own transport."

"That... that is logical, sir."

"You are confident in driving the van?"

"Yes... yes, of course I am, sir. I just didn't think."

"Nothing to worry about. We will go in together but we'll have two vehicles. We will split up. You will go and park. I will do what I have to do, and you will be waiting for me when I have killed the Jew."

"I – I am honoured, sir."

The Commander nodded. "You are the chosen one, Ahmad. Out of the four. It is an honour, but you have gained this by your own merits. You will be revered by our people. The new President will probably wish to meet you."

"I don't know what to say."

"There is nothing to say."

Ahmad was still absentmindedly drying his body.

"Just one thing," continued the Commander. Ahmad looked up. "Take off those few body hairs you have. We need to be clean for combat."

Ahmad looked down at himself. Yes, this was combat, wasn't it? He was serving his people. He was a soldier killing a Jew. He nodded. "Whatever you wish, sir."

11 February 2005
2 Muharram 1426

Mount Lebanon 20:30

Rafic Hariri's schedule was hectic. Too hectic for a sixty year old man, no matter what his status or ambitions. In the last twenty-four hours he had been in a constant process of liaison with various people and entities, including dinner at Koreitem with UN envoy Terje Roed Larsen (who was attempting a smooth implementation of UN Resolution 1559 whereby Syrian troops in Lebanon would withdraw to the Bekaa), meeting again with Hezbollah leader Sayyed Hassan Nasrallah (who successfully persuaded Hariri to include two pro-Syrian candidates on his electoral list), meeting with Maronite patriarch Cardinal Sfeir (to reassure him that he was not opposed to the government's plan for the smaller constituencies), and asking to meet the Christian opposition Qornet Shehwan gathering at Koreitem (to discuss a mutual position on the electoral law).

It was the response of the Qornet Shehwan that had given The Damascene the evening off. They did not want to meet at Koreitem as they were uncomfortable at showing too much of a united stance with Hariri at this time, so they had suggested that the MPs of Qornet Shehwan meet with Hariri in Parliament on Monday morning instead. So Hariri was 'relaxing' at Koreitem this evening – which meant that The Damascene could relax at home.

He stretched out on the leather sofa, watching a news programme on the TV. On the coffee table were a glass of apple juice and a box with a selection of baklava and ma'amoul. He wasn't really that interested in news or politics (which were the same thing on local television), he was a worker who obeyed the instructions of his masters – his masters being those who paid him. A true mercenary, created by circumstance, created by the murder of Captain Marwan Mebarak of the Lebanese Army. Created from hell.

There was a knock at his front door. He smiled. Perfect timing. How did she know he would be home tonight? Or was she taking a gamble? Muting the volume on the television, he rolled off the sofa and stood up. Why didn't she use her key? Perhaps she was knocking first, keeping up the *djinni*-can't-open-closed-doors legend.

He was dressed in just a black pouch. Should he put something on, or just surprise her?

Deciding on the surprise, he went over to the front door and opened it.

Ghazi Kanaan was standing there.

"You have been doing well," Kanaan sipped from his freshly-filtered coffee, sitting on the sofa.

"You have been keeping an eye on me?" The Damascene stood with his back to the window. The question was rhetorical, he knew the answer, of course. The Djinn.

He was now dressed in a white *dishdasha*, his hair tied back tightly. He liked to expose his lack of left ear to Kanaan, just to remind the bastard.

"No need. The fact that Hariri is alive is evidence."

The Damascene inclined his head.

"But I need you back," continued Kanaan. "That is why I am here."

"But these are dangerous times for Hariri. You don't want me to stay until the election?"

"These are even more dangerous times for Ghazi Kanaan. I believe I am under even greater threat. There are plots against me in Damascus."

"But surely the Interior Minister has his own security personnel? Talking of which...?"

"They are downstairs. They are being discreet, don't worry. We came in the one car. And yes, the *Interior Minister* has his own security personnel. But what if I was no longer Interior Minister?"

"You are being replaced?"

"Only a matter of time, I suspect."

The Damascene did not ask why. It was none of his business. "When do you want me back?"

"Now."

"Now?"

"You can come in the car."

"No." The Damascene shook his head. "I cannot simply disappear and abandon Hariri. His man Abu Tarek has been very co-operative. They know I come from Syria. How would it look if the man sent from Syria to protect Hariri was summarily withdrawn at this crucial time?"

"I am giving you an order."

"You do not give me orders. You give me instructions."

"I have paid you." The Damascene said nothing, so Kanaan went on. "I have rebuilt you. I have saved your life."

"After you took it from me in the first place." The Damascene's left hand clenched and unclenched, anxious to be let loose on Kanaan's throat.

There was silence while the two men stared at each other.

Kanaan was the first to look away. Sighing, he asked "When then?" When he received no reply, he said one word which The Damascene had never heard him use before nor would he ever hear again. He said, "Please."

The Damascene raised his eyebrows, nothing less than shocked. "It is that serious?"

Kanaan nodded. "Yes, it is. I will either be President in the next few months – or I will be dead."

The Damascene finished the glass of apple juice he had been holding in his hand. "Give me a few days. A few days to round things off with Abu Tarek. Then I'll return."

"A deal. Thank you."

The Damascene walked over and took a ma'amoul from the box. A piece of walnut fell out as he bit into it. He said casually, "I'm surprised you came here yourself."

Kanaan put the empty coffee cup down on he table. "If you want a job doing properly, you have to do it yourself. The last person I sent - "

At that precise moment the lights went out. Power cut.

"Wait." In the darkness, The Damascene went over to the kitchen area and opened a drawer. "There." The beam from a torch pierced the room.

The Damascene lit Kanaan's way to the front door, reaching in front of him to open it. "Will The Djinn be coming back to Damascus?" he asked as he stood back to let Kanaan pass, shining the torch out onto the stairwell.

"Who?"

"The Djinn. The girl."

Kanaan sounded perplexed. "What girl? A Djinn?"

"The one you sent. The one that has been visiting me for a while now. In Damascus."

"What are you talking about? I have never sent a girl to visit you. Why should I do that? The one man I did send never returned." Kanaan walked towards the stairs, his tone saying that he did not wish to be bothered with this trivia.

"The girl. In Damascus. Followed me here. I sent you messages with her." The Damascene stiffened, his mind flying backwards over the months, thinking of her visits.

Then there was a sound. From below. Someone running rapidly down the stairwell. As if they had been listening and knew they were found out. And there was an upward breeze, carrying a faint scent of jasmine.

Kanaan was shaking his head. "I really don't know what the hell you are talking about - " He was cut off as The Damascene pushed him out of the way.

The Damascene took the stairs two, three at a time, the torchlight bouncing, but he was hampered by the flowing *dishdasha* and his bare feet. Reaching the bottom, he slammed through the outside doors.

It was dark outside. He looked from right to left, swinging the torch. Two men were standing smoking by a limousine, obviously Kanaan's retinue. No one else was about. He went towards them. "Did you see - ?"

Suddenly the area was bathed in light. There was a screeching of wheels as headlights came blazing up from the car park under the block, dazzling, blinding. The Damascene put his right arm up to shield his eyes, turning and pushing one of the men against the car, his left hand going under the man's jacket and pulling out his gun.

He turned, fumbling with the safety as the vehicle sped up the slope, kicking up dust and gravel. He fired off one shot and missed as the vehicle turned right towards Beirut.

Instinctively he wanted to leap onto his Suzuki and follow, but he knew that would be impossible wearing the *dishdasha*. And if he took it off he wouldn't get far riding the bike nude, not even in Beirut!

Passing the gun back, he looked towards the doorway as Kanaan came out. "What the hell was that all about?" demanded the Syrian.

For a moment, The Damascene said nothing. Then he said, "Nothing."

One of the men opened the car door. "A few days," said Kanaan, climbing in. "I will expect you back in Damascus."

"I'll be there," he lied.

The Damascene watched as the car drew away, up the slope, turning left for Syria.

A few days and he would be out of this forever, he thought. It would give him plenty of time to do what he had to do.

And maybe also to find a Djinn driving a black Ford Explorer.

The lights went back on ten minutes later, by which time The Damascene was back standing by the window, staring out over Beirut.

What was she? Who was she? She had been with him for months and he had always assumed she was Kanaan's gift. Obviously not. Had she been spying on him? If so, for whom? Kanaan's enemies? Syria's enemies?

It did not really matter as the sum total of their time together had been based on sex. And, latterly, coffee machines. And, of course, damned mosquito bites.

Still, The Damascene did not like not knowing. He would complete the mission he had been paid for, then he would find out.

Al-Rajul also did not like not knowing. But now he knew a lot. From the outset his employer had decreed the date on which Rafic Hariri should die. And now, thanks to the Qornet Shehwan baulking at meeting Hariri in Koreitem, he knew the exact time Hariri would be at Parliament on the chosen day. He would not have to hang around. And, more importantly, he would not have to keep Ahmad hanging around either.

The young Palestinian had his destiny to fulfil.

12 February 2005
3 Muharram 1426

Koreitem 11:30

The Damascene was at Koreitem to tell Abu Tarek of his departure back to Syria when news of the arrests came through. At first he did not know what was going on. A secretary burst into Abu Tarek's office without apology and said something about the Beirut Society for Social Development and, after a curt "Excuse me", Abu Tarek dashed out, leaving The Damascene sitting there.

Not respectful, thought The Damascene. What was happening? Was Hariri under attack? If so, he should be involved.

He did not find out for thirty minutes, when Abu Tarek came back, by which time The Damascene was fuming. It was just as well his involvement was finishing.

"My profuse apologies for keeping you waiting," Abu Tarek sounded sincere. "Yet another attack."

"An attack?"

"Not that sort, not physical. It is one of Mr Hariri's charities. It supplies food packages to the needy during the Holy Month, including olive oil. As Ramadan was before the olive season, this year we left notes in the packages saying that the olive oil would be delivered as soon as the olives were picked, pressed and bottled, which we did recently. Now four workers from the charity have been arrested."

"Arrested? Why?"

"They are accused of giving the olive oil as a bribe in advance of the election."

The Damascene shook his head. Lebanese politics!

"It is nonsense, of course," continued Abu Tarek. "Foolishness. Mr Hariri is taking charge of the situation personally. So I regret, my dear sir, that I have to go."

The Damascene stood up. "Is he going anywhere?"

"No, he is overseeing things from here. It is likely to take some time to get the workers released."

"Then you do not need me."

"No. And thank you for everything you have done, all your advice. It has been appreciated."

The two men shook hands, looking into each other's eyes.

"*Afwan.* You are welcome," said The Damascene. Then he added, "*Fi aman Allah.*"

13 February 2005
4 Muharram 1426

Kahale, Lebanon 15:30

With a grunt, the Commander and Ahmad lifted the last fifty kilo sack of sugar into the back of the van in the garage. Both were slightly out of breath. "Well done, Ahmad. Thank you," said the Commander. "Now, you go and pray and rest. Ask for Allah's blessings for tomorrow."

"Yes, sir." A little sulkily, Ahmad went out. A few moments before he had been snappily reprimanded when he had asked the Commander if they really needed all this sugar as their cover as merchants. Wouldn't just a few sacks do?

The response had been sharp and terse. Twenty sacks were required to create the right image of successful tradesmen, and it was not his place to question the Commander's decisions.

Al-Rajul was pleased the little *contretemps* had arisen, otherwise he would have had to contrive another way of getting the young Palestinian to leave him alone in the garage. Now he went over to the door and bolted it from the inside.

From a cupboard at the back of the garage, he pulled out a taped cardboard box. Cutting the tape with a cardboard-cutter knife, he took out a reel of wire. Attached to the end of the wire was a button that looked like a domestic doorbell, identical to the one installed in the cab of the van.

It took him forty minutes to replace the one in the van with the new model, drilling holes so that the wire went underneath the van and came back in again in the back. When he had finished, there was no way of telling that the button had even been changed. Ahmad would never know.

Then he went back to the box and took out a smaller box from inside: a selection of detonators and initiators.

He chose what he needed and set to work.

Bourj el-Barajneh, Beirut 20:30

Captain Fadi Lattouf was the last to leave the police station that evening. A rare occurrence, but he'd had meetings with camp representatives of both *Fatah* and the resurgent *Hamas* that afternoon and he needed to make a record of both. Only in note form, nobody would ever read it, but it needed to be done. Also there was an unfinished pack of *khobz 'arabi* (Arabic bread) in his drawer that needed his attention.

It was 20:30 when he padlocked the door of the police station from the outside and began the ten minute walk back to *chez Lattouf*. The streets were quiet this Sunday evening, only a few people populating the nearby café. He was tempted to stop for a shisha, but Nada was bound to smell it on him and that might spoil his chances for other activities this fine Sunday evening – for Nada had given him that look this morning, the one he received only about four times a year.

He waved at the café proprietor, shook his head at the come-inside hand signal, and helped himself to a newspaper somebody had left on the solitary table outside. That day's *Al-Mustaqbal*.

Soon he was home. The children were in bed, which was a good sign that he hadn't imagined this morning's promise, and a plate of rice and lamb was awaiting him. The plate stretched into three plates, then he sat back contented, his trousers undone to let his mammoth gut expand even more.

"Nada," he called sweetly, swallowing a burp. "How would you like to make a little Lattouf...?"

Mount Lebanon 22:30

She entered The Damascene's apartment with her gun in her hand, a Herstal 9mm. Careful, cautious. The place was in darkness, and she moved around in silence, like a ghost.

He was not there, she hadn't expected him to be.

Up in the bedroom, she noticed his large holdall on the floor. Some of his clothes were inside. He was getting ready to leave. She had heard the conversation with Ghazi Kanaan. He was to return to Syria.

She was angry because, now he knew she did not work for Kanaan, she could not go back with him and continue their regular... therapy sessions. Pity, but so be it.

But she was also angry at something else. Cold and emotionless he may be. Assassin he may be. The best lover she had ever had he may be. But none of that was an excuse for ignoring simple human decency. Politeness.

The bastard had never thanked her for the coffee machine!

Koreitem 23:59

Rafic Hariri's time was dominated that weekend by the olive oil arrests, then that evening he held counsel with friends and allies including Walid Jumblatt and Ghazi Aridi[*].

It was close to midnight before Hariri went up to his private quarters on the seventh floor of the Palace. He was on his own. Nazek, his wife, was in Paris with their daughter Hind, and he was going to join them there on Friday to celebrate Hind's birthday. His three surviving sons, Bahaa, Saad and Fahd were grown men with their own businesses and families.

He made a telephone call to Saad in Saudi Arabia, but as

---

[*] *The Minister of Culture until he had resigned the previous September in protest at the extension of the term of President Lahoud.*

usual it was constrained and stilted due to The Listeners. But it did not stop him telling his son that he loved him.

He was alone as it became Monday 14 February.

14 February 2005
5 Muharram 1426

Mount Lebanon 06:00

The Damascene was up early. He showered, exercised, showered again, drank his usual breakfast of two strong coffees (he liked the new machine), and dressed in jeans, black T-shirt and his leather jacket.

He wanted to wear his long hair down, but he knew today he must look nondescript, he must blend in, so he tied it back with an elastic band, making sure that the hair was tightly against the side of his head to cover the hole of the missing ear. Kanaan's legacy.

He filled his jacket pockets with what he had to take with him and left the apartment. Outside it was still dark, but it was dry and a fine day had been predicted.

The Suzuki started smoothly, and in a few moments he was up the slope and turning left onto the main road.

Kahale, Lebanon 07:00

"Morning of joy, my dear Ahmad." The Commander was already in the dining area when the young Palestinian came in.

Ahmad was dressed as he had been told: sandals, old jeans, shirt and old jacket, all provided for him by the Commander. He felt good, he felt confident. He had slept well, not knowing that his rest had been assisted by a small draft the Commander had slipped into his tea yesterday evening. "Morning of peace, sir."

"You are ready?"

"Oh, yes."

"These are your last hours here. Later you will be with your family and you will be out of the camp forever. Tomorrow afternoon I have arranged for you to meet with the President, at his request."

Ahmad's face shone. "Really, sir? I am honoured. My family will be proud."

"Your nation will be proud. You will be a hero, Ahmad." After a pause, Al-Rajul added "This is your day of destiny."

Koreitem, Beirut 07:10

Rafic Hariri was called by his personal secretary Adnan Baba at 07:10, though truth be told he was already awake. It had not been a good night. He was missing his wife, Nazek, and he looked forward to seeing her at the end of the week. Today was the start of the parliamentary discussion on the electoral law, which was expected to last three days. That and the fall-out from the olive oil arrests would take up his week until he flew to Paris on Friday. But firstly today was his meeting at Parliament with the Qornet Shehwan, after which he had twenty people coming for lunch at Koreitem.

While Hariri ate his usual breakfast of *labneh,* cucumbers, tomatoes and toast, Abu Tarek and his team began their first security sweep of the day.

Bourj el-Barajneh, Beirut 08:30

Fadi Lattouf decided to have a lie-in that morning. After his exertions with Nada last night (which in fact had lasted little over a minute), he was feeling benign, content and at peace with the world. Sergeant el-Khazem could open up the shop today.

Fadi would have a leisurely breakfast and then stroll in about 11:00.

As he lay staring at the ceiling, his stomach rumbled. Five seconds later his fart shook the walls of the buildings within a ten block radius, like the sonic boom of the Israeli aircraft when they performed one of their regular intimidating flyovers of Beirut.

The mattress increased in height three-fold as he rolled out of the bed. His stomach was right. He needed to get rid of some of the rice and lamb before starting on his morning eggs with sumac (and probably some *zaatar* as well, he was feeling peckish – regular sex did that to a man).

He hoped one of the kids wasn't in the toilet. If they were, he would have to throw them out. His need was greater, not to mention the additional hole in the ozone layer that would be created if he didn't go and go now.

Kahale, Lebanon 09:00

"One final time," ordered the Commander. He was sitting in the driving seat of the Canter van, Ahmad next to him. The van was in front of The Facility, which they had now locked up. Al-Rajul would return later for the final cleaning of the place.

Patiently, Ahmad said "I wait in the car park until you ring. The phone determines the route."

"Say them."

"Nokia, north. Samsung, south. LG, west."

"Good. And the three places?"

"North, the St. George Hotel. South, the Four Points Sheraton. West, Future TV."

"The target?"

"The target will be in the third car of the convoy. I press the button to alert you at the exact moment the target's car passes by me. Not before, not after."

"Good." The Commander sat there for a while, saying

nothing. Then he said, "It is time. I will be right behind you until we reach the city." He held out his hand. Ahmad was stunned for a few moments, and then he reached out and shook it. "Allah is with you," said the Commander.

Ahmad smiled. "May He be with you too, sir."

The Commander got out as Ahmad moved over into the driver's seat. The Commander slammed the door and banged on the side of the van. Ahmad raised his hand and then moved off.

Al-Rajul watched as the Mitsubishi Canter Van reached the end of the driveway, paused and then turned right. The van with the earnest but naïve young Palestinian aboard.

And one thousand kilos of TNT.

Bourj el-Barajneh, Beirut 09:10

The lamb took longer to shift than Lattouf expected. It must have been mutton, not lamb (he would have a word with Nada – his wonderful, sweet, sexy girl Nada – later), and his delicate gut had had difficulty digesting it. Some of it his gut had tried to push through as was, coming out the same as it went in, and that had caused a painful rectal breach birth which had stung his rectum like the tongue of a sand viper. It had taken him fifteen minutes on the toilet, and the neighbours certainly knew about it. Soon the sewage systems of Beirut, if not the whole of the Middle East, would know about it too.

Then he had washed and dressed, so it was gone 09:00 before he sat down for his breakfast. He was ravenous. His stomach was empty.

He began his first plate of eggs, casually reading yesterday's *Al-Mustaqbal* newspaper which he had picked up last night. It was an Hariri-owned publication and the front page was screaming about the arrest of four charity workers.

He was chewing *zaatar* and he had just taken a mouthful of coffee when his eyes reached the bottom of the page. What he read made him shoot forward in his chair, the contents of his mouth spilling out into his beard and down his shirt.

In the name of Allah!

"N – Nada!" he coughed, spluttered, shouted, his voice hoarse. "Nada! Where are you, woman? Nada, quickly! Pass me my phone!"

Jonblat, Beirut 09:20

Jihad Merhi was heading towards the office of his boss, Major Ghanem, when his mobile telephone buzzed in his trouser pocket. He kept walking down the corridor, wedging the pile of folders under his left arm, retrieving his mobile with his right hand. It was probably Gisele checking on the menu for next Saturday's visit of sister-in-law Violette and her husband Toni, she said she was going shopping down in Kaslik today. It was a bit early though.

He looked at his phone and his shoulders sank. Oh for God's sake! Why had he ever given him his mobile number?

He pressed the reject button. He would have to wait.

He reached the boss's door and knocked, making a mental note to add Fadi Lattouf to his blocked numbers list later.

Furn el Chebback, Beirut 10:15

Ahmad had driven carefully, as instructed, and the Monday morning traffic was heavy as always. The Commander had been behind him on the journey down from the mountains, occasionally coming up beside him to exchange okay signs and then dropping back again. They had entered the city through Hazmieh. Now the Canter van turned in to the parking area of City Furniture just beyond the Chevrolet Roundabout and the Commander pulled in behind it.

Neither Ahmad nor the Commander left their vehicles. This stop was planned, this was where they would split. The

Commander stared at Ahmad's face in the wing mirror of the van. Ahmad smiled and nodded.

The Commander returned the nod, then he pulled away, out of the parking area and back into the traffic. Ahmad watched him go past the Abraj Centre and then disappear from view. The Commander would be heading west through Ain el Rommaneh, picking up the main Corniche el Mazraa and then heading north into town on Selim Salam Street. Ahmad would be staying on Damascus Street all the way in to Martyrs' Square.

He gave it five minutes and then pulled back out into the traffic. He was on his own now. Serving his President, serving his country.

Killing a Jew.

Jonblat, Beirut 10:20

The meeting with Major Ghanem had taken longer than expected (why couldn't he just leave this al-Murabitoun investigation to him and not interfere?), so it was a full hour before Jihad Merhi left his boss's office. The phone in his pocket had vibrated regularly throughout the meeting, sending at-any-other-time-not-unwelcome tremors through his groin, to the extent that his movements to get himself comfortable attracted curious looks from the Major. At one point, the Major had asked "Are you all right? Do you need to relieve yourself?", after which it was all Merhi could do to keep a straight face. Perhaps he did need to relieve himself, but not in the way the Major thought!

Now back in his own office, he took the phone from his pocket. Twenty missed calls. Oh Lattouf, you were going down big time for this!

Knowing that the fat slob would not leave him alone, he pressed the Call button. Might as well get it over with, see what he wanted. Three super size Big Macs and fries?

Connection made, the line rang.

And rang.

And rang.

Koreitem, Beirut 10:35

"I will be back at one," Rafic Hariri, seated behind the wheel of his Mercedes S-600, took his reading glasses from his secretary. He had left them on his desk and he would have been lost without them. Thank you, Adnan. Next to him sat his friend and former Economy Minister Basil Fleihan who had returned from Geneva the night before to attend the parliamentary session.

The secretary stepped back from the car. *"Maa Salameh."*

There was a bip of a car horn and the convoy moved off.

It was a bright, sunny Beirut day.

South Beirut 10:40

You do not see Palestinian police cars speeding through the streets of Beirut with their blue lights flashing, horns blaring. It would cause untold political and protocol repercussions. It is simply not done. It does not happen.

Except that day.

Lattouf's vehicle was a dented, rusting light blue police Ford Transit van donated by the British to the Palestinian Authority ten years before, still with the pompous small metal plaque affixed above the Ford sign on the back door proclaiming *Provided under British aid*. It carried the distinctive red number plate of the Palestinian military.

He headed north up Hamid Franjieh Avenue at a speed that would have frightened Formula One drivers, cursing, gesticulating, eyes wild, leaning on his horn. Damned Lebanese drivers! Get out of the way, get out of the way!

This really could be a matter of life or death.

Nejmeh, Beirut 10:50

The convoy arrived in Nejmeh Square, the lead vehicle pulling up in the exact position so that the third car would stop right outside the entrance to Parliament. Rafic Hariri and Basil Fleihan got out and entered the building.

On the southern side of the square by Maarad Street, a man with long tied-back hair sat astride a Suzuki motorbike, watching. Abu Tarek gave him a small nod then followed Hariri into the building.

Jonblat, Beirut 11:15

Merhi had just opened *Word* on his computer when he heard the shouting from out in the General Office. Then scuffling. Not another football discussion that had got out of hand!

But no, the voices were getting louder. One was shouting, booming, the other authoritative but trying to placate. Only when they neared his door could he make out Sergeant Deeb el-Gharib saying "I don't care who you are, you can't just come barging in here!"

"Get your hands off me!" responded the booming voice. "Jihad! Abu Samer! Merhi! Are you - " The door to Merhi's office slammed open as it was given a mighty kick from outside, the frosted glass cracking with the force. " – in here?"

The mountain that was Fadi Lattouf was standing in the doorway, the arms of Deeb el-Gharib on his shoulders in a failed headlock, the hands of a Lieutenant around one of his thighs, the Lieutenant himself horizontal having been dragged along the corridor.

"What the hell?" Merhi joined in the shouting as he stood up. "Cease, all of you. In God's name what is going on? Let him go, let him go."

Reluctantly, el-Gharib took his arms away, bending down to support the Lieutenant who would have a nasty face-down one metre fall to the floor unless he was assisted. "I told him he couldn't just come barging in here," he mumbled.

Giving them an I-told-you-so look, Lattouf shook his shoulder and leg even though the Lebanese were already off. "You haven't been answering your phone," he explained reasonably.

Merhi closed the door as the Palestinian came in, giving a rueful look at the crack across the glass. "What is it now, Fadi?"

"Have you - ?"

He was interrupted by another commotion, this time from out in the street. Shouting, car horns blaring. Merhi went over and looked out. A Palestinian police van, blue lights still flashing, was blocking one half of the road and the other drivers were playing chicken trying to get round it. "You never came here in that!" Merhi growled angrily as he turned – to find Lattouf holding up a copy of *Al-Mustaqbal* newspaper.

"Have you seen this?" asked Lattouf.

Merhi frowned, shaking his head. "I have work to do, I haven't read today's papers."

"Not today's. Yesterday's."

Merhi shrugged.

"Look." Lattouf put the paper flat on the desk, pointing at the main story.

Merhi leant over. "The olive oil arrests. It is nothing. It will blow over."

"Yes, but look." Lattouf's thick index finger jabbed the bottom of the page.

Merhi read.

And tensed.

He read it again.

Slowly he straightened up. "Oh... my God... Oh my God. So that's what it's been about. And we haven't known."

"How could we? It could have been anything."

Merhi shook out a Cedars King Size cigarette from the pack on his desk, Lattouf's hand stretching out and taking one before it was even offered. They lit up and dragged.

"It was a recruitment exercise all right." Merhi bent back over and read the piece for the third time. Just twenty-five words.

> These unjustified arrests come just one month after the foiled attempt to have Mr Hariri arrested on the false charge of being an Israeli agent.

"An Israeli agent at work in Beirut is what the last victim's brother said he said," Lattouf swallowed smoke. He looked Merhi in the eyes. "They are going to kill Hariri."

Nejmeh, Beirut 11:25

Ahmad sat in the van in the parking area on Weygand Street, that day's *An Nahar* newspaper open across the steering wheel in front of him. Today he did not want to pee. He was not nervous, he had done this before – only this time it was for real. He was confident, he was proud.

He wondered how the Commander was feeling. It was the Commander that would be doing the actual killing, of course, Ahmad was just the point man, but it still felt good to be serving his country. And to be getting his family forever out of that accursed camp.

He was not wearing a watch, that was an order from the Commander. At first he had wondered why, but the Commander had explained that, consciously or not, he would keep looking at it and that would attract curiosity from anyone looking at him: a man sitting in a van constantly looking at his watch. Whereas a man sitting in a van reading a newspaper would attract no attention. There was a clock on the dashboard, and Ahmad found himself casting regular glances at it – so proving the Commander's caution.

He smiled to himself. Allah had blessed him the day he had been chosen by the Commander. The Commander had not let him down, ever. He was a true soldier, a true comrade.

He looked at the three muted phones on the seat next to him and wondered which one would buzz.

Horch, Beirut 11:45

The black Ford Explorer was stuck in traffic on Hamid Franjieh Avenue in the Horch district when her mobile rang. The traffic was going nowhere, so Zahia Zalloum had time to rummage in her bag and retrieve the Sony Ericsson. She looked at the screen. It was a number she had put into her Contacts only recently.

"Captain Merhi," she answered.

"Zahia!" Merhi was speaking loudly, a hint of triumph in his voice. "We've worked it out." There was a raised voice-off, then Merhi said "Okay, okay. Actually Fadi Lattouf worked it out."

"He has, has he?"

"The bodies. The Massoud boy. Remember he said his brother was going to kill an Israeli agent?"

"Yes."

"Have you seen the papers?" More mumbling off. "Yesterday's paper. *Al-Mustaqbal*."

"Captain, get to the point, please." The traffic had begun to move slowly.

"I never knew about it, you probably didn't too. Apparently last month there was a plot to arrest Hariri and charge him with being an Israeli agent – Hello? Hello? Zahia, are you still there?" He could hear car horns blaring and wheels screeching.

Then she was back on, screaming "We have to get to Hariri!"

"I'll get back-up."

"No, no! You never know who's in on it." She wrenched the steering wheel, bumping over the central reservation, going up the avenue on the wrong side, horn blasting. "He's at Parliament today, it was on the news. The electoral debate. Meet me at Nejmeh. Now!" She threw the phone onto the seat next to her.

Merde, thought Zahia. *Merde, merde, merde.* What she had seen, what she knew, made her certain.

It was going to be today.

Jonblat, Beirut 12:00

Merhi and Lattouf dashed from the State Security building – and stopped dead. Traffic was at a standstill, both ways. Caused not least by a Palestinian police van, blue lights still flashing, that was blocking half the road. Lattouf looked sheepish, but he shouted "Get in!"

"No, no!" Merhi grabbed hold of his arm. "Where the hell can we go?" He looked right, then left. Then he said, "We'll have to walk. *Yalla.* The exercise will do you good."

Nejmeh Square, Beirut 12:25

From his position at the south side of Nejmeh Square, The Damascene saw Rafic Hariri come out of the parliament building, walking down the steps with Ghattas Khoury. The two men stopped, discussing something for a few minutes. Then they shook hands and went separate ways.

Hariri and a bodyguard walked across the square, and just for a moment The Damascene thought he was coming towards him, but they detoured into the Café de l'Etoile, where some journalists had been waiting for an hour. But was there a recognition, an acknowledgement, in the eye contact Hariri had made with him?

A few minutes later Hariri came back outside and sat at a table with Nejib Friji, the Tunisian head of the UN Information Office. They had a deep discussion for five minutes and then both men returned inside the café. Moments later they were joined by Basil Fleihan and a Sunni MP called Samir Jisr.

Then The Damascene saw movement down a side street next to the parliament building. The convoy was getting ready to leave.

The Damascene stood up from his leaning position on the Suzuki, putting his hands in his jacket pockets.

The convoy rolled slowly out of the side street, across the cobble-stoned square to wait in front of the café.

The Damascene watched.

Serail, Beirut 12:50

As they passed the United Kingdom embassy on Army Street, Fadi Lattouf thought he was going to die. By the time they passed the Grand Serail building, he knew he was. He was a man of strength and intensely intellectual powers – his legs weren't meant for walking!

He got no sympathy from Jihad Merhi who, although he had started off at a pace to rival an Olympic walking champion, had now slowed to a normal, middle-aged walk, trying hard to hide the stitch in his side.

They turned left into Parliament Street. They could see the clock tower in the middle of the Etoile down at the bottom.

Nejmeh Square, Beirut 12:53

Rafic Hariri and Basil Fleihan walked out of the café, Fleihan getting into the front passenger seat of the third car, the Mercedes S-600. The security man who had driven the car over held the driver's door open for Hariri. The big man paused, looking back at the café. He smiled, waving at Nejib Friji and the reporters. Cameras clicked.

This time there was a distinct look towards The Damascene. Hariri nodded. The Damascene inclined his head.

Then the convoy was moving off, around the clock tower, past the Italian embassy and down Hussein el-Ahdab Street.

The northern route.

The Damascene took the three mobile telephones from his

pocket and chose the Nokia.

Nejmeh, Beirut 12:53

Ahmad was waiting in the van round on Weygand Street, thinking of the Commander and how he adored and respected him. In Ahmad's opinion, the Commander was the one who was the true hero, not him. He wondered if they would ever get to be friends after this? Perhaps they could be a team, undertake other assignments together? It would be good to know more about the man. The story of how his left ear had been blown off to leave him with a hole in the side of his head must be fascinating. And those scars on his body -

One of the phones buzzed.

The adrenaline shot through Ahmad, jolting him like a slap round the face. It was the Nokia. N for north. The northern route.

He moved quickly without thought or fear. Sweeping the newspaper onto the floor, he started the engine, manoeuvred, and pulled out into Weygand Street.

There was a gap in the traffic, caused by several black limousines coming out of Hussein el-Ahdab Street to his right and performing a small dogleg by the municipality building and going down Foch Street, which gave him space to turn left for the straight run down to Fakhr ed-Dine Street.

Then north to the corniche and the St George Hotel.

Nejmeh, Beirut 12:54

Zahia had left the Ford Explorer down on Emir Bechir Street because of the traffic. She ran down Maarad Street, not caring that her running was attracting looks from the diners in the restaurants which lined either side of the road. She could see the clock tower in the middle of the Etoile down at the bottom.

She reached Nejmeh Square – just in time to see a Suzuki

motorbike, ridden by a man with long hair tied in a ponytail, zooming off up Abd el-Hamid Karame Street on the other side of the *ronde place*.

"Hey!" she shouted, but she knew it was futile.

Two men standing next to the clock tower in the middle of the square turned, thinking she was shouting to them. Jihad Merhi and the giant Lattouf. Merhi raised his hand in greeting.

Lattouf frowned. "This is she?" he asked. "A mere girl?"

Ain el-Mreisseh, Beirut 12:56

Ahmad slowed to a crawl as he reached Minet el-Hosn Street, driving close to the kerb, allowing others to overtake him. He frowned as he saw a line of cars by the entrance to the St George Beach Club opposite the still war-gutted ruins of the St George Hotel. There was nowhere for him to park!

But the Commander had been most specific. He needed to be exact. The Commander would be a little way along the road with his sniper's rifle ready. So Ahmad did the only thing he could do – he double-parked.

Under two minutes later he saw the convoy approaching in his wing mirror, headed by a Toyota Land Cruiser. They were going very fast, the Commander would need to be a very good shot to get this right. He wondered what sort of a Jew warranted such an opulent cortege. Must be a rich man.

He watched the mirror as the convoy reached him. He leaned forward, finger hovering over the button. This would be like a computer game, shooting down the enemy! The Land Cruiser whooshed past, then the first Mercedes, then the second –

Ahmad pressed the button.

And changed Lebanese history.

Nejmeh, Beirut 12:56

The blast of the explosion was heard all over Beirut and up into the mountains. Kilometres away from the epicentre, buildings shook, windows rattled, glass fell out onto the streets, building and car alarms were set off. A pall of dense yellow and black smoke rose from the seafront like the eruption column of a volcano. Instantly it began rolling its evil shroud over the city.

Standing by the clock tower in the middle of Nejmeh Square, Jihad Merhi and Fadi Lattouf looked at each other, faces blank with shock.

Next to them Zahia Zalloum, The Djinn, began to cry.

Minet el-Hosn, Beirut 12:56

From his vantage point outside the Monroe Hotel at the top of Fakhr ed-Dine Street, the man known as The Damascene or the Commander – or simply as Al-Rajul, The Man – felt the rush from the blast and even a wave of heat. The cloud down at the site was so black as to be impenetrable. One thousand kilos of trinitrotoluene will do that.

He felt neither sadness nor elation. He had a job to do and he had completed it. In a matter of hours, when the already-obvious success of the assassination had been confirmed, another five million dollars would be added to his bank account on top of the five million deposit already there.

Now he must carry out the final cosmetics. Crossing the Ts, dotting the Is.

He gunned the Suzuki and roared off back towards downtown.

Downtown, Beirut 13:30 – 14:10

At 13:30, al-Jazeera news received a phone call at their offices near the United Nations building. Made from a mobile telephone, the caller said that the *al-Nasr wa al-Jihad fi Bilad al-Sham* group had carried out the bombing. The statement was broadcast at 14:00.

At 14:10 another phone call was made to al-Jazeera from a different mobile phone. It said that a tape could be found in a tree by the United Nations building.

The tape was retrieved and was broadcast three hours later. It showed a man in a plain black robe and a white turban sitting in front of a black flag on which were the words *There is no God but Allah. Mohammed is the messenger of Allah. God is greatest.*

The man read from a paper in his hand. "To support our brother mujahidin in the land of the two holy mosques..."

The cosmetics had been applied.

Damascus Street, Beirut 15:30

Now that it was over Al-Rajul, The Damascene, could properly relax for the first time in six months. After hiding the tape in the tree, he was enjoying a pasta meal at *La Piazza* restaurant, in the Sodeco area. Not only was it one of his favourite restaurants in Beirut, but it was on Damascus Street, the city end of the main road which led back up to his apartment.

Damascus Street. The Green Line of Beirut during the events of 1975 to 1990, the division between the Muslims to the west and the Christians to the east. Called the Green Line because of the foliage that grew in the uninhabited space. It was a fitting analogy for his two jobs: one to kill Hariri for ten million dollars, the other to protect Hariri for Kanaan. To protect Hariri from himself! It felt good to have deceived and ultimately thwarted Kanaan, far better than putting a gun into the bastard's mouth (although he still gave himself the option of doing that one day soon).

Now he would not be returning to Damascus. He had many options. Perhaps he would follow many of his fellow-Lebanese and head south-east to the UAE. Become The Emirati rather than The Damascene!

And what would be the consequences of his actions today? There might now be a sizeable shift in Lebanon and Lebanese politics – he did not really care. But he knew it would be ironic. Everyone would assume it was a political assassination, they would never guess it was personal.

He thought back to his meeting nearly six months ago with The Owner on board the yacht. The *Heliopolis* – the City of The Sun, the Roman name for Baalbeck. Once Al-Rajul had made the decision, agreeing to carry out the assassination, The Owner had explained his requirements. He did not mind how it was done, but it had to be spectacular. But he was adamant on the date. He wanted to give his dead wife a fiftieth birthday present. She had died at forty-two, but she would have been fifty on 14 February 2005, Valentine's Day. The man The Owner considered responsible for her death was to die on this day.

And he had.

Al-Rajul signalled to the waiter for his check. He would leave a sizeable tip. He could afford it.

Mount Lebanon 16:30

Al-Rajul parked the Suzuki by the front door of the apartment block. There were no official limousines around, he had no visitors. Kanaan was probably too worried about what had happened in Beirut today, too busy with his colleagues in the Syrian government, to worry about his man in Beirut – his man who ultimately had failed in his mission to keep Hariri alive. But even if he did spare a thought for his puppet, the last place the Syrian Interior Minister was going to appear was in Beirut on the evening of 14 February 2005!

The stairwell lights were out – another power cut! – but the daylight had only just started to fade so he could see his way easily up the stairs. In the apartment, he retrieved his large holdall from the bedroom and began to pack his things into it. The only possessions of The Damascene, who would be no more. He had a Syrian passport in another name, and that would see him out of Lebanon and into wherever he decided to go.

By the time he had finished, the night had fallen quickly, as it does in the eastern Mediterranean. He flicked switches up and down but the power was still off.

Looking out the window over Beirut, he saw lights twinkling on in the areas that were still connected to the grid. It was a beautiful city, restored to its former splendour due in no small part to the efforts of Rafic Hariri and Solidère. But as from today it would be a changed city. Whatever the future held for it, Beirut – The Wells – would be forever etched in human history.

But not in his. He needed to leave.

He zipped up the holdall and threaded his right arm through the handles, hoisting it up onto his shoulder. Over at the door, he managed to get the keys in the lock at the third attempt in the dark. He had an amusing thought: what should he do with the keys? Put them back through the letter box? This was still a Syrian-owned property.

He pushed down the handle then suddenly stopped as he experienced two unexpected sensations at once.

One was a smell: jasmine. The other was the feel of cold steel pressed hard into the back of his neck.

He did not move, but his left hand fell away from the door handle to rest near the trouser pocket which contained the piece of solid olive wood, the Holding Cross.

"Turn," ordered the voice from behind.

Slowly he obeyed, his hand going into his pocket, his fingers circling the cross. He could see the small shadow in front of him, within striking distance.

As his hand came back out of his pocket, the lights went on. The gun was pointed straight into his face. Behind it, the black eyes of The Djinn were as cold as a she-wolf's.

They stared at each other.

Then she smiled. "Fancy a cup of coffee?"

In memory of
Rafic Bahaa el deen al-Hariri
1 November 1944 – 14 February 2005
15 Dhu'l-Q'adah 1363 – 5 Muharram 1426

I trust revered Lebanon and its good people to God Almighty
- Rafic Hariri
20 October 2004
6 Ramadan 1425

Also in memory of

Yehya al-Arab (Abu Tarek)
Basil Fleihan
Samir Kassir
George Hawi
Gebran Tueni
Walid Eido

and all the others

POSTSCRIPT
حاشية

The Syrian military presence in Lebanon – ended on 26 April 2005 after thirty years.

Ghazi Kanaan. On 12 October 2005, Ghazi Kanaan, still Syria's Interior Minister, telephoned *Voix du Liban* radio in Beirut to refute allegations made on New TV the previous evening that he had received bribes from Rafic Hariri during his time as head of Syrian intelligence in Lebanon. His phone call was a rambling monologue, a valediction in which he justified Syria's role in Lebanon. He ended it by saying "I believe this is the last statement I might make."

Just after 10:00, Kanaan was found dead in his office in the Interior Ministry in Damascus. He had been shot through the mouth by a .38 Smith & Wesson. The official verdict was suicide.

There was no regime change in Syria.

The Owner of the *Heliopolis* was last seen by his crew on the upper deck of his yacht just before midnight on 14 February 2005. His wheelchair was still there the next morning. The Owner was not. No trace of him has ever been found.

The Damascene disappeared without trace on the evening of 14 February 2005. His existence is not formally acknowledged.

The Djinn also disappeared without trace on the evening of 14 February 2005. DGS agent Zahia Zalloum is recorded as 'missing during operations' on or around the same date.

Jihad Merhi and **Fadi Lattouf** – will return in *The Byblos Discovery*.

DAVID CULLEN

THE EYE OF MAKARIOS

IN A WORLD OF TERROR THE ONLY TRUTH IS BETRAYAL

THE EYE OF MAKARIOS

David Cullen

1974. A world in turmoil. Terrorism is rife.

In the Middle East, *El Fateh* plan their first nuclear strike. The Irishman, their hardware supplier, wants a very special item in payment.

In the Mediterranean, Cyprus is an island about to be divided. Resistance leader Grivas is dying. He wants to hit his enemy from beyond the grave.

In Israel, the security services want to finish off their enemies once and for all.

In Europe, Sally wants to find her missing lover.

In a world about to implode, they all have one common link:

THE EYE OF MAKARIOS

ISBN: 978-0-9559911-0-3

Available from *amazon, Lulu* and other online booksellers and thru all good bookshops.

DAVID CULLEN

THE MESRINE CONCLUSION

ONLY ONE MAN CAN RETRIEVE THE SECRET - IF HE CAN STAY ALIVE

THE MESRINE CONCLUSION

David Cullen

1978. Only two people still alive know the explosive dark secret of the British Royal House of Windsor.

One lies in her dotage in France, the other continues to rule the royal household in Britain as she has done for 40 years.

A robbery in Paris. The secret is stolen. It must be found at all costs. Police enquiries draw a blank. They need help. There is only one man with the skills to locate the secret – Jacques Mesrine, France's Public Enemy Number One.

But there are those that want the secret for themselves and others who will stop at nothing to ensure the secret remains hidden.

Can Mesrine find the secret before the hunters find him? Death, treachery and double-cross all lead to

THE MESRINE CONCLUSION

ISBN: 978-0-9559911-1-0

Available from *amazon, Lulu* and other online booksellers and thru all good bookshops.

DAVID CULLEN

THE WINDSOR SECRET

ANYONE WHO KNOWS THE SECRET, DIES - ANYONE

THE WINDSOR SECRET

David Cullen

1997. Three women are out for revenge.

In Greece, a lover discovers that justice has not been done.
In England, a princess seeks to humiliate her ex-husband.
In France, a daughter vows retribution after eighteen years.

A secret which they thought was buried forever comes back to
haunt the British Royal House of Windsor. And the deaths must
start again.

And this time to preserve the secret they will even kill the
mother of the future King of England…

Exactly what happened in Paris on August 30 1997?
Who really killed Princess Diana?
And what is

THE WINDSOR SECRET

ISBN: 978-0-9559911-2-7

Available from *amazon, Lulu* and other online booksellers and
thru all good bookshops.